THE NAME OF THE G...

He calls himself Earl Drake. That's not his real name, but it'll do. Hell, he's changed his identity so many times, it hardly matters anymore. Right now he's calling himself Chet Arnold. After the last bank robbery, after they made their escape and Bunny ended up taking most of the money with him to Florida, he figured it was time to collect. But something's happened to Bunny. So here he is in Hudson, Florida, trying to find Bunny and the money. First he finds Hazel, six feet tall, red hair, all woman. Then he meets Lucille, the local man-hungry postmaster. Finally he meets Blaze Franklin, a cop who's just about ready to kill somebody. It's one helluva situation. And that's the kind that Drake likes best.

ONE ENDLESS HOUR

Sheriff Blaze's double cross is a good one. But Drake finds Bunny and he finds the loot. Trouble is, it all blows up in his face this time. Literally. And now they've got him behind bars and covered in bandages—and under the thumb of a particular sadist named Spider Kern. The authorities think they've got a monosyllabic basket case named Chet Arnold locked up in a ward for the criminally insane. But thanks to the experimental plastic surgery treatment of Dr. Afzul, they soon have an Earl Drake who is not only armed with a new face, but a plan as well. All he needs is a gun, and it's payback time. Sweet payback time.

DAN J. MARLOWE BIBLIOGRAPHY

Fiction
Doorway to Death (1959)*
Killer With a Key (1959)*
Doom Service (1960)*
The Fatal Frails (1960)*
Shake a Crooked Town (1960)*
Backfire (1961)
The Name of the Game is Death
  (1962) [pub in UK as Operation
  Overkill, 1973]**
Strongarm (1963)
Never Live Twice (1964)
Death Deep Down (1965)
Four for the Money (1966)
The Vengeance Man (1966)
The Raven is a Blood Red Bird
  [w/William Odell] (1967)
Route of the Red Gold (1967)
One Endless Hour (1969)
  [pub in UK as Operation
  Endless Hour, 1975]**
Operation Fireball (1969)**
Flashpoint (1970) [pub in UK as
  Operation Flashpoint, 1972]**
Operation Breakthrough (1971)**
Operation Drumfire (1972)**

Operation Checkmate (1972)**
Operation Stranglehold (1973)**
Operation Whiplash (1973)**
Operation Hammerlock (1974)**
Operation Deathmaker (1975)**
Operation Counterpunch (1976)**
* Johnny Killain series
** Earl Drake series

As by Major D. Lawn
The Orphan Girls (1971)

As by Rod Waleman
The Young Librarian (1971)
The Stepdaughters (1971)
The Innocent Schoolteacher (1971)

As by Alma Werdon
The Unwilling Mistress (1971)

As by Gar Wilson
Guerilla Games (1982)

As by Mande Woljar
The Reluctant Wives (1971)

THE NAME OF THE GAME IS DEATH
ONE ENDLESS HOUR

Two novels by Dan J. Marlowe

STARK
HOUSE

Stark House Press • Eureka California

THE NAME OF THE GAME IS DEATH / ONE ENDLESS HOUR

Published by Stark House Press
1315 H Street
Eureka, CA 95501, USA
griffinskye3@sbcglobal.net
www.starkhousepress.com

THE NAME OF THE GAME IS DEATH
Originally published by Gold Medal Books and copyright © 1962 by Fawcett
Publications, Inc. Revised edition copyright © 1972. Copyright renewed 1989 by
Bob W. Ragan, Executor of the Dan Marlowe Estate.
Text for this edition is taken from the original 1962 edition.

ONE ENDLESS HOUR
Originally published by Gold Medal Books and copyright © 1969 by Fawcett
Publications, Inc. Copyright renewed 1996 by Bob W. Ragan, Executor of the Dan
Marlowe Estate.

Reprinted by permission of the Estate of Dan J. Marlowe.

"Dan J. Marlowe: Hardest of the Hardboiled" copyright © 2013 by Charles Kelly.
Revised from "Mystery Man: Dan J. Marlowe" copyright © 2007 by Charles Kelly and
published by Allan Guthrie's *Noir Originals*.

"Dan Marlowe Remembered" copyright © 2013 by Gary Brandner.

ISBN: 1-933586-44-3
ISBN-13: 978-1-933586-44-1

Cover design and layout by Mark Shepard, www.SHEPGRAPHICS.COM
Proofreading by Rick Ollerman

PUBLISHER'S NOTE

First Stark House Press Edition: March 2013

0 9 8 7 6 5 4 3 2 1

Contents

Dan J. Marlowe: "Hardest of the Hardboiled"

by Charles Kelly

Dan J. Marlowe, who spent much of his writing life pounding away at a typewriter in a picturesque but isolated small town on Lake Huron in northern Michigan, was a master at depicting criminal sociopaths who lived and died in the fast lane of life. Author Stephen King alluded to that in the dedication of his novel *The Colorado Kid*: "With admiration, for DAN J. MARLOWE, author of *The Name of the Game is Death*: Hardest of the hardboiled." In the 1960s and 1970s, Marlowe was recognized as an ace suspense writer in the paperback market. Several of his works, such as *The Name of the Game is Death*, *One Endless Hour* and *The Vengeance Man*, are classics.

Marlowe was a study in contrasts—a businessman who had been a professional gambler, a Rotarian whose novels captured criminal personalities, a sedentary sports fan who wrote from the viewpoint of the athletic he-man. He also was a crossword-puzzle aficionado, an enthusiastic drinker, a lover of the theater who disliked movies, a womanizer despite his ordinary looks, and late in life, an amnesiac.

Born in 1915 in Lowell, Mass., Marlowe received an accounting certificate from Bentley School of Accounting and Finance in Boston in 1934. From then until 1941, he was the assistant manager of two country clubs in Connecticut. For the next four years, he worked as a night timekeeper at United Aircraft Corp. in Stratford, Conn. In 1945, Marlowe took a job as an office manager and credit manager for Washington Tobacco Co. in Washington, D.C., and worked there for the next 12 years.

At one stage in his life (probably in the late 1930s and early 1940s), Marlowe spent seven years as a professional gambler, betting on the horses and playing poker. Marlowe also worked as an insurance agent, a bartender, a public relations man, an advertising agent, a bookkeeper, an accountant, and a traveling salesman for a pharmaceutical firm. His career as an author was triggered by the sudden death of his wife, a secretary, from acute hemorrhagic pancreatitis in 1956.

Her death stunned Marlowe, but it also freed him to change the direction of his life. He walked out of his home in suburban Washington, D.C., and never went back. At that point, he was not a heavy drinker, but over the next couple of years, he became one. His life did not go to pieces, however. He was too practical for that. He moved to New York to run the office of a jewelry importer and, in April 1957, started his first mystery novel. His dedication to learning the craft of writing served him well. He became a fulltime writer in February 1958 and sold his first two novels ten months later.

Marlowe's first published novel was *Doorway to Death*, issued by Avon Publications, Inc., in New York and Digit Books in London in 1959. His murder-solving hero, Johnny Killain, is a bell captain in a New York hotel. Four more Killain books and a novel called *Backfire* were to follow before Marlowe's masterpiece, *The Name of the Game is Death*, was published by Fawcett in New York in 1962. While writing the novel, Marlowe was living with a friend in Woburn, Mass. But in late 1961 or early 1962, he moved to Harbor Beach, a small town two hours north of Detroit. There, Marlowe joined the Rotary Club, was elected to the city council, and patronized Smalley's Bar and Grill, where he drank, played pool, and talked sports and politics.

During his 15 years in Harbor Beach, Marlowe continued to churn out fine hard-boiled novels. *Strongarm* was published in 1963, *Never Live Twice* in 1964, *The Vengeance Man* in 1966, *One Endless Hour* in 1969. During this period, Marlowe's sociopathic bank robber character, who uses the false names Roy Martin and Chet Arnold in *The Name of the Game is Death*, took the name Earl Drake in that book's sequel, *One Endless Hour*, and—under the influence of Marlowe's editors—became a series character as an international spy and adventurer in a series of "Operation" novels (*Operation Fireball, Operation Checkmate, Operation Whiplash*, etc.).

Starting in 1962, Marlowe's books benefited from the criminal expertise of Al Nussbaum, a bank robber, gunrunner, locksmith and pilot who worked with a violent partner—Bobby "One-Eye" Wilcoxson (sometimes called Bobby "Bad-Eye" Wilcoxson: the news writers couldn't agree on a nickname). While running from the law in July 1962, Nussbaum—probably without revealing his true name or occupation—called Marlowe in Harbor Beach to praise *The Name of the Game is Death* and to get advice on writing that would help Nussbaum launch his own writing career. After Nussbaum was caught, Marlowe befriended him, helped him become a writer and—more than a decade later—helped him get paroled.

In the nonfiction collection, *I, Witness*, published in 1978, Marlowe said of Nussbaum, "I haven't written a word for years about weapons and ballistics that he hasn't vetted for me. Ditto with locks and bolts and their manipulation. Ditto with safes, vaults and alarm systems. It's not every writer who is fortunate enough to get his technical information from the horse's mouth."

Though Marlowe acknowledged Nussbaum's help, the author was more circumspect about a more significant collaborator—retired Air Force Col. William C. Odell. Marlowe and Odell shared credit on the 1967 novel *The Raven is a Blood Red Bird*. Thereafter, they decided only Marlowe's name would appear on the books they produced together: Marlowe's name was more marketable. They partnered on more than a dozen novels, with Odell contributing much of the research, plotting and writing.

Marlowe traveled a great deal, including trips to Mexico, where he wound up living off and on. During his trips, he frequently attracted girlfriends, though he didn't look like a matinee idol. The author stood a little over 5-foot-9, weighed 165 pounds, and was rotund, with chubby cheeks and thinning dark hair often swept straight back. Though not prepossessing, he had lively eyes, a ready smile, boundless energy, and a knack for humorous self-deprecation. Marlowe readily bedded women, and some of them visited him in Harbor Beach. His sensual experiences found their way into his books, which, for their time, contain plenty of sex flavored with kinkiness.

One of Marlowe's girlfriends phoned him on June 6, 1977, at his apartment in Harbor Beach. He was speaking gibberish, and she became concerned. She ended the call and phoned for help. Marlowe was taken to the local hospital, where he was diagnosed with memory loss. He then was taken to hospitals in Saginaw and Detroit. One physician decided the source of Marlowe's amnesia was "neurosis" that was possibly "psychosis-depressive."

Marlowe also was suffering from aphasia (partial or total inability to write and understand words). His ability to communicate and write letters returned quickly, but—except for general information about recent presidents of the United States—his knowledge about past events had been erased from his mind. Later, Marlowe would say he suffered a stroke, but doctors at the time were uncertain. Shortly before his release from the Detroit hospital, some members of the medical staff speculated that his memory loss was psychological, and that his writing might have triggered the problem.

Some people who knew him suspected he was faking, possibly to evade personal obligations. Marlowe had been under financial pressure, had taken out several loans, and knew enough about amnesia to feature it as a plot element in *Never Live Twice*. However, many were convinced his amnesia was real, and his letters appear to show it was.

Once Marlowe left the Detroit hospital, he took a job as a bookkeeper in Detroit. By this time Nussbaum was out of prison, living in Los Angeles and making his living as a writer for a scholastic publisher, mystery magazines and television. He invited Marlowe to come and live with him, and Marlowe did so. They collaborated on stories, and Marlowe continued to try to recapture his memories and his writing ability. He wrote a number of "easy-reading" novels meant for young people or adults trying to learn to read. And he completed one more commercial novel, a generic action-adventure called *Guerilla Games*, written under the name Gar Wilson as part of the Phoenix Force series published by Gold Eagle.

In 1982, the year the novel came out, Marlowe moved to his own apartment, dissolving the living arrangement with Nussbaum, who eventually moved out of L.A. and back to upstate New York. Marlowe, who had begun to regain his memory in 1985, died of heart failure in August 1986.

Over the years, writers and film makers have shown interest in basing movies on some of Marlowe's books. In 1969, so Marlowe told an acquaintance, *The Name of the Game is Death* was optioned by MGM. However, that option never led to a movie. *Never Live Twice* was optioned in 1995 by Niki Marvin, producer of the 1994 film *The Shawshank Redemption*, but financing fell through and the option was not renewed.

For many years, Marlowe's novels fell into obscurity. However, the year 2012 saw a reawakening of interest in Marlowe, with the publication in the online *Los Angeles Review of Books* of "The Wrong Marlowe," about the years Marlowe spent in Los Angeles, and the appearance of the story "Dan J. Marlowe: Echoes of a Hard-Boiled Past" in the graphic novel *Fatale*. Most of Marlowe's novels are now available once again as ebooks. I'm sure that this edition of *The Name of the Game is Death* by Stark House Press, which issued Marlowe's novel *The Vengeance Man* in 2007 in *A Trio of Gold Medals*, will help reinvigorate Marlowe's reputation among a new generation of readers. Enjoy.

Charles Kelly is the author of *Gunshots in Another Room: The Forgotten Life of Dan J. Marlowe*, available as a trade paperback on Amazon and as an ebook on Amazon and other digital platforms. Kelly is also author of the novels *Pay Here*, issued by Point Blank Press, and *Grace Humiston and the Vanishing*, a finalist in the 2012 Amazon Breakthrough Novel Award contest. Kelly's website is hardboiledjournalist.com and his e-mail address is pulpnoir22@aol.com.

The Name of the Game is Death

By Dan J. Marlowe

I

From the back seat of the Olds I could see the kid's cotton gloves flash white on the steering wheel as he swung off Van Buren onto Central Avenue. On the right up ahead the strong late September Phoenix sunshine blazed off the bank's white stone front till it hurt the eyes. The damn building looked as big as the purple buttes on the rim of the desert.

Beside me Bunny chewed gum rhythmically, his hands relaxed in his lap. Up front, in three-quarter profile the kid's face was like chalk, but he teamed the car perfectly into a tight-fitting space right in front of the bank.

Nobody said a word. I climbed out on the sidewalk side, and Bunny got out opposite and walked around the rear to join me. His dark glasses and bright yellow hair glinted in the sun. The thick, livid scar across his throat was nearly hidden in his week-old beard. Across the street the big clock said five minutes to three. Under it on another dial a long thermometer needle rested on ninety-four. A shirt-sleeved man stood idly beneath the clock.

We crossed the sidewalk and passed through the bank's outer glass doors. I'm five ten, but Bunny towered over me six inches. I could see the rolled-up canvas sack under his arm. In the vestibule the air conditioning bit hard at the sweat on my face and arms. Bunny led the way through into the main floor lobby. He went left. I went right. Two guards on the main floor.

I found my guard showing an old man how to fill out a deposit slip. I moved in behind the guard, and when I saw Bunny's arm go up across the way I slammed the red-creased neck in front of me with a solid chunk of Smith & Wesson. He went down without a sound. The old man kept right on writing. I heard a choked gurgle from Bunny's guard. That was all.

I took my first good look around while I switched to the Colt Woodsman. If we hadn't gotten those two, we were nowhere. A dozen to fifteen customers, scattered. I fired the Woodsman three times, taking out glass high in the tellers' cages each time. Shattering glass is an impressive sound. In the echoing lobby the glass and the little Woodsman sounded like a turret of six-teen-inchers in a china closet.

"All right, everybody," I said, loud and clear. "Everybody stand still and nobody gets hurt."

Nobody moved. Nobody breathed. Bunny vaulted the low gate up in front. I jammed the Woodsman back in my pants, and balanced the Smith & Wesson again in my palm. If somebody fast-pitched us, I might need the three heavier caliber bullets I'd saved by directing traffic with the Woodsman.

Inside the railing with Bunny, two big-assed women huddled together against the door leading into the cages, empty trays in their hands. Right where they should have been at two minutes to three. Bunny motioned with his gun at the cage door. They stared at him, cow-eyed. Inside the cages there wasn't a sound. Bunny whipped the flat of his automatic up against the jaw-line of the nearer woman. She fell over sideways, mewling. Someone inside opened the door. Bunny stepped in quickly, herding everyone to the rear. He began yanking out cash drawers. Bundles of hundreds and twenties went into the sack. Everything else went to the floor.

The only thing I could hear was the whimpering of the woman on the floor and the clatter and bang as Bunny emptied and dumped drawers. On my left something moved. I turned, and the movement stopped. Dead ahead on the balcony overhead I caught a rapid blur of gray. I belted the guard over back-ward with the first shot I banged up there. Bunny never even turned his head.

Two minutes, I'd figured, after we took out the first guards. Two and a half, tops. All over town now bells would be ringing, but in sixty seconds we'd be gone. I did a slow turn, eyes skimming the balcony and the main floor. Nothing.

Bunny burst out the cage door, hugging the sack to his big chest. He jumped the railing, landing on his toes. I fell in six feet behind him, and we went out through the vestibule at a fast walk. Bunny had just reached out to open the right hand outer glass door when there was a sharp crack-crack-crack from behind us. The best part of the door blew right out onto the sidewalk. Heat rolled in through the splintered glass in an arid wave.

Bunny unhunched his neck and started again for the Olds. Out on the side-walk I whirled and took down the remaining half of the door. One high and one low. It made a hell of a noise. Anyone coming through that vestibule in a hurry should have thought again about his hurry with a square yard of glass in his hair.

When I turned I caught a flash of the shirt-sleeved man under the clock across the street running into a store. I headed for the car. I nearly yelled out loud when I saw the kid had panicked. All the way to St. Louis we'd gone for a driver, and now he'd panicked. Instead of staying under the wheel and drawing no attention to the car, he'd jumped out and run around and opened the doors on our side. His face was like wet cottage cheese.

Bunny went through the front door in a sliding skid. The kid took one look at my face and started to run back around the front of the Olds. Across the street something went ker-blam! The kid whinnied like a horse with the colic. He ran in a circle for three seconds and then fell down in front of the Olds, his white cotton gloves in the dirty street and his legs still on the sidewalk. The left side of his head was gone.

Bunny dropped the sack and scrambled for the wheel. I was halfway into the back seat when I heard the car stall out as he tried to give it gas too fast. It was quite a feeling. I backed out again and faced the bank, tried to have eyes in the back of my head for the unseen shot-gunner across the street, and lis-tened to Bunny mash down on the starter. The motor caught, finally. I breathed again, but a fat guard galloped out the bank's front doors, his gun hand high over his head. He got it down in a hurry.

I swear both his feet were off the ground when he fired at me. The odds must have been sixty thousand to one, but he took me in the left upper arm. It smashed me back against the car. I steadied myself with a hand on the roof and put two a yard behind each other right through his belt buckle. If they had their windows open they could have heard him across town.

I stumbled into the back seat and Bunny took it out of there. The Olds bumped hard twice as it went over the kid. Across the street I could see the shirt-sleeved man pumping frantically at his jammed shotgun. I raised the Smith & Wesson, and lowered it again. I still needed every bullet. I couldn't afford any luxuries. I got the car doors closed within half a block.

"Handkerchiefs!" I yelled at Bunny as we flew up Central and spun east on Roosevelt on the red. "Ditch those glasses. Slow it down. Stay in traffic." Without looking back he tossed two handkerchiefs over his shoulder, snatched off the dark glasses, and grabbed up a blue beret from the seat beside him. He crammed it down on his yellow head. With the glasses off and his hair hidden he looked like a different person.

I wadded up his handkerchiefs with my own and tried to staunch the double-ended leak in my left arm just below the short sleeve of the sport shirt. I accomplished exactly nothing. All that stuff about a bullet's initial impact being shock with no pain; that's horse manure. I felt it going in and I felt it coming out. Like a red-hot saw-tooth file.

I reloaded the Smith & Wesson. I ignored the warm molasses running down my arm, except to keep it from dripping on my pants. I watched the lights. The kid had had the lights timed all the way back to Yavapai Terrace, but we didn't have the kid. I couldn't sit still. I wanted to get back south of Van Buren again so bad I could taste it.

They had to figure us for a main highway. Highway 80 East, to Tucson and Nogales, if they'd seen the right turn on Roosevelt. North to Prescott or Wickenburg, if they hadn't. Even west, to Yuma and the coast. There'd be road blocks up by now on every main artery out of town. We weren't going out of town. Not yet.

We'd passed Seventh Street while I was fooling with the useless handkerchiefs, Twelfth while I was reloading. The first red light caught us at Sixteenth. We sat in tense silence with people in cars all around us. My guts shriveled down to pebble size. I opened my mouth to holler at Bunny to make a run for it, and closed my teeth down hard. So far we hadn't even heard a siren.

In motion again we sailed up to Twentieth and turned south. We were back across Van Buren before I even had time to begin holding my breath. Past Adams and Washington, over the tracks to East Henshaw, and back toward town at the light. Up to Twelfth in the double-back, a left, and then a right. Shimmering in the sun under a eucalyptus tree, the black Ford sat ahead of us on Yavapai Terrace, close enough to a Chinese grocery to assure that kids wouldn't bother it. Bunny pulled in behind it. We might have been three miles from the bank, but I knew we weren't four.

"Get something out of your bag for this arm," I told Bunny. He was out of the Olds before I had the words all the way out of my mouth, over to the Ford, and back again. He had the jacket to my lightweight suit, and a shirt. "Shred it and fold it and tie it around this thing. Tight." Heat and dust and nausea filled my throat as he complied. I choked it down, whacked some of the dried blood crust from my arm, and slung the jacket loosely over my left shoulder to hide the crude bandage.

After glancing up and down the deserted street, I slid out and followed Bunny back to the Ford. I watched the two-handed carry he made with the sack, and for the first time I wondered how much was in it. In a fifty-pound sack with twenty-five per cent hundreds and the rest twenties, a man can walk away with two hundred thousand dollars. If he walks away.

The Olds we'd leave right here. Bunny pulled ahead to get clear, then backed out onto Twelfth again. He headed south, slowly. The street names were Indian—Papago, Pima, Cocopa, Mohave, Apache—but the area was Mexican. The bushy shade trees were stunted and gnarled. The houses were small, sun-blistered, shacky and close together. The front yards were overgrown tangles. Bunny nosed the Ford into Durango Street, and parked across the street from the dark blue Dodge sedan in the middle of the block.

I drew a long breath as he pulled up the brake. "Okay," I said. "New script. Listen close. I'm grounded. We're not going to the cabin in the canyon." With the kid gone and me with a torn-up arm we had to throw away the book. I rummaged in the sack at my feet. The first three bundles I picked up were hundreds. Fifteen thousand dollars right in my hand. I dropped two of them back, found two packages of twenties, and shoved the three into a jacket pocket.

"We split up here, big man. You take the Dodge. Duck into a cheap motel. Don't forget to wash the yellow dye out of your hair. Day after tomorrow after dark pull out and head east. Stay off Highways 80 and 66. Go back on 70. Roswell, Plainview... that way."

I tried to think of it all. "Take the sack. At Memphis head south, for Florida. The gulf coast. Pick a small town. When you make it, once a week mail me a thousand in hundreds, not new bills, registered mail. To Roy Martin, General Delivery, Main Post Office, Phoenix, Arizona. Got it? Take off. I'll join you the minute I can travel."

Bunny got out of the Ford and walked around it and opened the door on my side. His big, hard face was solemn. We shook hands, and he picked up the sack and crossed the drowsy street to the Dodge, his shoes making little puffs in the inch-thick dust. There was a layer of it on the Dodge from passing cars. Bunny opened the back deck, rolled in the sack, and slammed down the lid. With his hand on the door handle he looked over at me and waved before he

got in and drove off. Just before he reached the corner I remembered the rest
of my clothes were in the Dodge. I reached for the horn, and pulled my hand
back. I had more immediate problems than clothes.

I sat there with kind of an all-gone feeling. All the adrenalin-charged-up excitement had drained away. My mind chugged busily, but the rest of me was
numb.

Letting the sack go with Bunny hadn't been in the blueprint, but it was
the best place for it now. I had some scrambling to do, and the first rule of
the game is don't get caught with it on you. If they have to sweet-talk you
to try to find out where it is, twenty-to-life has a way of coming out seven-
to-ten. If only so they can follow you when you hit the street again. Although
on this little frolic, plank-walking the guards could have made everything else
academic, if they'd done the big somersault. That one on the sidewalk—

Clean away, except for the hole in my arm. And except for the silly bastard
kid. If he'd stayed with the car, I wouldn't be sitting here improvising on an
iron-clad plan. Yeah, and if wishes were horses, beggars would ride.

I roused myself, with an effort. I had a lot to do. I had a doctor to find. A
doctor would be trouble, but I'd cross that bridge when I came to it. I slid
over under the wheel and started up the Ford, and then I had a real bad moment. Bunny's strength pulling up the hand-brake was almost too much for
my weakened left arm. Salt perspiration stung my eyes fiercely before I finally
succeeded in backing it off. The shirt-bandage was sopping.

Turning the first corner, the sun through the windshield nearly seared my
eyeballs. The first two signs I slowed down for in front yards were a realtor
and a plumber. The third one drew down the money. Santiago E. Sanfilippo,
M.D. I drove by slowly. A garage connected with the house. There was no
car in the garage, none in front of the house.

I had no time for anything fancy. I drove up the driveway and into the
garage. I draped the jacket over my left shoulder again and walked up the enclosed passageway that led into the house. Through a glass panel in the door
I could see an office inside. I had to knock twice before a man in white ducks
and a white jacket with a stethoscope sticking out of a pocket opened the door.

Dr. Sanfilippo was a tall, thin, young-looking job, coffee-colored, black-eyed,
and good looking. He had a misplaced-eyebrow type of mustache. From the
look he gave me I wasn't exactly what he'd been expecting to see. "Yes?" he
demanded impatiently when I out-waited him. I couldn't see or hear anyone
in the office behind him. "This is a private entrance." He looked over my shoulder at the Ford. "Is that your car? What do you mean by driving it into my
garage?"

"I'm a patient, Doc," I told him.

"Then go around to the patients' entrance," he snapped. "And get that automobile out of there before you do."

"Let's arbitrate it, Doc." I showed him the Smith & Wesson about ten inches from his belly. He backed up in a straight line until he ran into a desk behind him. I stepped inside and closed the door. "You alone?"

"I'm alone," he admitted. He looked unhappy about it. "I keep no drugs on the premises," he added. His English was better than mine.

"Inside, Doc." I motioned with the gun and followed him from the cluttered office into a small examination room with whitewashed walls and a wash basin in one corner. Both room and basin looked fairly clean. There was a phone in the office, but none in the examination room. There was only one door, and I was between him and it. A framed diploma hung on the near wall, and I stepped up and read it. It looked legitimate, and I sat down on a white stool beside the elevated examination table. I wanted no self-appointed abortionist whittling on my arm.

Dr. Sanfilippo had been watching me warily. I removed the jacket from my shoulder, and his mustachioed upper lip tightened when he saw the shredded, sodden shirt around my arm. "Madre de Dios!" he breathed. His black eyes flicked from a battered radio on a green cabinet back to my arm. "You know I'll have to report this," he said huskily.

"Sure you will," I soothed him. "But you're a doctor. First you'll dress it." I held out the arm. "Like right now."

His smooth, trim features still expressed shock. "Those bank guards—" he began, and stopped. He swallowed, hard. His face was suddenly damp.

"The arm, Doc," I reminded him. So the guards had died. Without ever knowing it, Santiago E. Sanfilippo, M.D., had just passed over an invisible line.

He washed his hands in the basin, and after drying them, unwrapped the arm and examined it, front and back. "Large caliber," he said professionally.

"Large," I agreed.

He turned to the green cabinet. "A half an ampule—"

"No anesthetic," I cut him off.

He shrugged. It was my funeral, and for him it couldn't happen soon enough. He was getting his confidence back. He felt superior to the sweaty, gun-holding type sitting in his office with a ragged bloody hole in his arm. Next he'd be planning my capture. I had a feeling this boy was going to make it easy for me.

He laid out a tray of sharp-looking things on the table, and I spread a towel in my lap. He bathed, swabbed, probed, disinfected, and bandaged. He was rougher than he needed to be. "Don't move until I put a sling on it," he said brusquely when he finished.

"No sling," I said. I picked up the dry end of the towel and mopped off my face. I reached in my jacket pocket where it was slung over my knees, and took out the wrapped package of fifty one-hundred-dollar bills. I broke the seal and put it in my pocket, counted out fifteen bills in three little piles of five each on the examination table, and pushed them toward him. "Nice job, Doc."

That changed his expression *tout de suite*. His tongue ran over his lips, his black eyes never leaving the money. He reached out almost tentatively and picked it up, riffled it nervously, then stuffed it into a wallet and the wallet into his pocket again.

I stood up and kicked the stool I'd been sitting on in his direction. "Sit, Doc. Real still." At the basin where he'd washed up I looked in the small mirror at my short black hair and tanned hard face. I laid the gun on the edge of the basin. I ran the water, and found a clean towel. Stooped over, I could watch his feet. If he could get to me before I got to the gun, he was a better man than I thought. One-handed I washed the oil and lampblack from my hair, and the suntan lotion from my face and neck. When I emerged from behind the towel, Sanfilippo stared in rank disbelief at skin a nationality lighter and iron-gray hair a generation older. "You—you're an old man!" he blurted, incredulously.

"Forty-four, Doc." I patted my crewcut. "The snow on the mountain? Just all the years of taking in washing." His mouth hung open. I looked him over. Thin as he was, I knew I couldn't carry him out of the office. "Walk out to the car ahead of me," I told him. "I'm going to tie you and leave you in the garage."

He didn't like it. He thought it over. I could have predicted the instant he brightened. Would I have paid him if I were going to kill him? Certainly not. The stupid bastard never stopped to realize that if I'd been going to leave him around to do any broadcasting, he'd never have seen me out of the war paint. Following him from the examination room, I picked up something from his surgical tray with a bone handle and six inches of steel. I stuck it in my belt.

In the passageway I got out the Woodsman and put it under my armpit, where I could get to it in a hurry. At the car Sanfilippo turned and looked at me expectantly. I kept a careful ten feet away from him. "Think—something's wrong—" I mumbled, weaving on my feet. I did a long, slow pinwheel to the ground, staying off the bad side. From beneath nearly closed lids I could see Sanfilippo's startled look as he stared down at me. My right hand was close enough to the Woodsman's grip to stop his clock if he came after me, or if he tried to run out of the garage. I didn't expect him to do either. I'd tabbed this guy as a weisenheimer, and I was just egotistical enough to want to make him prove himself out.

He took a final look at me, and spun around to the Ford. He flung open the rear door, and I could hear him pawing through the back seat. He left that in a hurry and tried the front. He ripped out something in Spanish, and darted around to the rear. I'd paid him in hundreds. The swag had to be in the car.

He wasn't bad, the doc. I couldn't see what he used—all I could see were his legs under the Ford—but he popped that back deck lid in no time. I heard the whaaang of broken metal as he snapped the locks on my tool chests in the trunk and went through my stuff like an Indian husking an ear of corn. He sounded off again under his breath, and came around the car on the trot. He dived into the back seat again, only his legs outside.

I eased myself to my feet and got over there. Sanfilippo had a knife out, and was slashing away at the seat cushion. He was right down to the springs in a couple of places. I pulled the surgical tool from my belt. He whacked away at the cushion, cursing like a madman, and then all of a sudden my presence got through to him. He started to turn, and I gave him four and a half inches between the second and third ribs. He was looking over his shoulder at me, and the black eyes didn't believe it. I pulled it out and gave it to him again, then grabbed his belt and steered him down outside the car. He went down like a deflated balloon, slowly at first and then with a rush.

His own knife was still in his hand. I left the steel in him after wiping the handle. I reached down again and yanked his wallet from his hip pocket, stripped it, wiped it, and threw it down beside the body. It would be open and shut to any investigator: killed while pursuing a thief from his office. And, for a bonus, no bullets in him to be matched up with what they took out of the bank guards.

I backed the Ford out of there and drove up to Nineteenth and Van Buren to a big motel, The Tropics. I went in and registered, my jacket again over the bandaged arm. "I'll try your Western hospitality till my office gets me out a new sample line," I told the middle-aged desk clerk. "They busted into my car down in Nogales last night and cleaned me. Clothes, samples, camera— the works. I'll pay you for a week."

The clerk clucked sympathetically as he handed me my change. "Excellent shops within a block or two, sir. Sorry to hear of your misfortune. Hope you enjoy your stay with us."

I took the number 24 key he gave me and ran the car down in front of that unit number. I went inside and locked the door. I washed my face, eased down carefully into an inclined chair with a footrest, and closed my eyes. I had a lot of unwinding to do.

The last conscious thought I had before I drifted off was that those people at the bank were sure going to have one hell of a glass bill.

I lived in that chair for a week, outside of short trips to the on-premises restaurant. Without a sling on the arm I didn't dare get into the big double bed. The first incautious movement would have broken the bullet hole wide open again. With a sling on, I might as well wear a sign "Here I Am." I stayed in the chair.

After the first day I didn't sleep much but I dozed all the time. The next morning I caught a bright-looking busboy in the restaurant, gave him a list of sizes, and sent him out for clothes, specifying long-sleeved sport shirts. He came back with stuff that would have turned a bird of paradise pale with envy. I started to heat up until I happened to think it might be a good switch to have people looking at the clothes instead of at me.

The papers that first morning had a ball. TWO GUARDS SLAIN IN BOLD DAYLIGHT ROBBERY. KILLERS ESCAPE WITH BANK'S $178,000. ONE BANDIT, TWO GUARDS DEAD IN DOWNTOWN SHOOTEMUP.

I looked at that figure of $178,000 a couple of times. Even allowing for the bank's president adding in his personal loan account—which isn't exactly unknown—it was still a nice touch.

The newspapers speculated that one of the escapees might have been wounded. The descriptions were interesting, not to say varied. One eye-witness insisted there'd been five of us. The consensus, though, settled for a husky Swede and a little Mexican. Like I said, I'm five ten. I go one seventy, but I've noticed before that a really big man doesn't always seem so big himself. He just makes anyone with him look small.

FBI IN CHARGE, the papers blared. The dear old FBI. I hadn't talked to them in sixteen years, and I wasn't planning to in the next sixteen. They'd trace the kid's prints to St. Louis, and between here and there they'd tear everything up, down, and sideways. And a hell of a lot of good it would do them; when he left St. Louis, the kid didn't know where he was going, and either Bunny or I was with him all the time to make sure he didn't talk about who he was going with. It should make for less heat on the west coast of Florida.

Way on an inside page there was a short paragraph. Area Physician Stabbed In Garage, the small-type headline said. The story continued: The body of Santiago E. Sanfilippo, M.D., 31, of—. I read it three times before I put the paper down. The police would be out rounding up all known arm blasters and goofball users. It plugged the last hole the kid had kicked in the blueprint by not staying with the car.

I wasn't afraid of Bunny's getting picked up. He had the best natural protective coloration I'd ever seen. It was one of the reasons I'd picked him, that and his nerve and his confidence in me. I've been in this business a while. Two guys with guts and a go-to-hell-with-you-Jack regard for consequences have about three chances in ten of pulling off a big, well-planned smash-and-grab. If one of them can shoot like me and the other one is Bunny, the odds are a damn sight better.

The first week I had a fever nearly all the time. The arm needed treatment, but I couldn't get treatment. I swallowed aspirin by the gross. When the thing wasn't throbbing it was itching. I let it throb and I let it itch. The second week my temperature was gone, but my legs felt like two pieces of spaghetti. I'd wake from a nap dripping with sweat, and have to change from the skin out.

It was lonely in that motel room. Around the country when I hide out I always have a dog and usually a couple of cats with me. Animals I like. People I can do without.

For the first five days the headlines had us as having been sighted in half the towns between Guantanamo, Cuba, and Nome, Alaska. After that we dropped back onto the ninth page, and then right on out of the news. The third week I began to take an interest in a menu again, instead of just shoveling something down. The arm was going to be all right. A couple of times when it had been real bad I'd debated slipping down into Nogales and trying for a doctor. I decided I couldn't risk it. If they didn't watch anyplace else in the world, they'd watch that Mexican border.

About the middle of the third week I drove uptown to the main post office. From its front steps I could have thrown a stone kitty-cornered across the street to the bank we'd taken. I could see they had new glass doors up.

I had a wallet full of crap identifying the non-existent Roy Martin. There were two envelopes at the window, and I signed for them. In the car I slit the first one and unwrapped ten hundred-dollar bills neatly sealed in oil-skinned paper. The second was a duplicate. There was no message in either. The return address said Dick Pierce, General Delivery, Hudson, Florida. Bunny had made it big.

Five days later there was another envelope.

Seven days later there wasn't.

The mail clerk handed me a telegram addressed to Roy Martin. I got away from him fast and opened it. IN TROUBLE STAY PUT DO NOTHING WILL CALL YOU. DICK.

I stared blankly at the recruiting posters on the post office walls. Bunny was in trouble, all right, but not the kind I was supposed to think. The telegram was a clinker. When we'd first teamed up, I'd arranged with Bunny that a message from either of us calling for a change in plans had to be signed "Abie."

But that was nothing compared to the other thing the matter with the telegram. If he lived to be a hundred and four, Bunny would never call me about anything. The knife slash that had left him with the livid throat scar had reached his vocal cords. Bunny was a mute.

Bunny hadn't sent the telegram.

The only person who could have was someone who had intercepted a thousand-dollar envelope for Roy Martin. I looked at the telegram again. It had originated in Hudson, Florida.

I drove back to The Tropics and found Hudson on an atlas. It was a crossroads town south of Perry on U.S. 19 on the way down to Tampa.

I checked out.

The soreness was gone from the shoulder, but it was still stiff. It would have to do. Three-fifty, four hundred miles a day, I figured, without killing myself. Five days.

Knowing Bunny, I was sure of the only way he could have been dealt out of the game.

I had business in Hudson, Florida.

I settled down behind the wheel.

2

The only time I was ever in the pen, the boss head-shrinker gave me up as a bad job. "You're amoral," the prison psychiatrist told me. "You have no respect for authority. Your values are not civilized values." That was after he'd flipped his psychiatric lid at his inability to pierce my defense mechanism, as he called it. I had him tapped from the first sixty seconds. He didn't care what I was; he just wanted to know how I got that way. It was none of his damn business. I gave him nothing but a hard way to go.

Oh, I could have told him things. I could have told him about the kitten. I was maybe eleven or twelve. Fifth or sixth grade. I saw this kitten in the window of a pet shop. A blue Persian, although right then I couldn't have told the difference from a spotted Manx. I ran my finger across the glass and watched her little pink nose and big bronze eyes follow it, and I knew she was for me.

I went back to the house to make my case. I wasn't from any underprivileged home. The kitten's price might have jolted them, but I wasn't in the habit of asking for much. I was the youngest in the family and I had a bushel of sisters and aunts. Getting me the kitten became a family project. The family had also had for some time a project to get me to play more with the neighborhood kids. I'd given up trying to explain to them that the other kids gave me a pain, king-sized.

The sisters and aunts did a lot of yatating before I got the kitten. They always did a lot of yatating. Once—I was fifteen, maybe—eight or nine of them were going it forty to the dozen in the living room. I stuck my head in the door and gave them my very best rebel yell. When they climbed down off the tables and chairs, I told them: "The male of the species gives voice." They didn't think it was funny.

But that was later.

I named the kitten Fatima. First syllable accented, all short vowel sounds. It seemed to suit her coppery eyes and smoky coloring. I played with her by the hour. I taught her tricks. No one teaches a kitten anything it doesn't want to learn, but Fatima humored me. We had a wonderful time together.

I still got a load of guff frequently from the family about not participating more with my age group. That's probably not the way they put it then; it's not the day before yesterday I'm talking about. I paid no attention to them, I had Fatima, and she was all the company I needed. In some moods she was a natural-born clown, but in others she had an aloof dignity. I'd never have believed that anything so tiny could be so fearless. Fatima would have tackled a lion if one had got in her way.

Some organization in the town gave a pet show. YWCA, Junior League,

Woman's Club, American Legion Auxiliary, B.P.O. Does—I don't remember which, but I remember women were running it. I bought a little red leash for Fatima out of my paper route money, and entered her in the show. I liked having a paper route. It was something I could do myself, not some group project I was always being pushed to get into with a bunch of moronic kids.

Fatima and her red leash knocked their eyes out at the pet show. She was a real ham. She sat up in the center of the outdoor ring and went through her whole bag of tricks, better than she'd do them for me in private. She went through the kitten and cat classes like a streak of blue lightning, and we were brought back for best-in-show. In the ring for the final judging there was Fatima, a big boxer dog, a black rabbit, a hamster, a goat, and a bowl of tropical fish shaded from the sunlight.

The boxer belonged to a kid who went to the same school I did, a fat tub of lard a grade or so ahead of me. I knew him by sight. If I ever knew his name, I've forgotten it. When I saw the boxer, I steered Fatima around to the other side of the ring. She just plain didn't like dogs. The fat boy saw what I was doing, and he followed me in a smart-alecky way. Fatima swelled her throat ruff and hissed at the boxer in a Persian's surprisingly loud hiss. The fat boy laughed. I asked him to move his dog away. Deliberately he gave him more leash. The boxer leaned down for a closer look, and quicker than I can say it, Fatima raked his nose. The boxer snarled, and snapped. Just once.

Fatima lay in the grass, one tiny little dot of blood on her ruff. Her neck had been broken. The big dog nosed at the inanimate bit of blue-gray fur, then looked up at me as though half-ashamed. I didn't blame the boxer. He'd done the natural thing for any dog. I picked up Fatima's body, and turned blindly away. All I wanted was to get out of there. The fat boy—who first looked scared, and then defiant—grabbed my arm and spun me around. "Look!" he crowed. "Lookit him! Cryin' like a baby!"

I beat the stuffing out of him.

The women got me off him, finally. I was scuffed up and so were they. There was a hell of a lot of gabble-gabble. I walked out on it. I took Fatima home and buried her in the back yard.

That was Saturday. Sunday I hung around the house most of the day. Monday afternoon I waited in the schoolyard for the fat boy to come out, and I beat the stuffing out of him all over again.

That night his father came over to my house. There was a big pow-wow. My family was surprised to learn about Fatima's having been killed. They hadn't even missed her. Finally they settled everything to their satisfaction.

The fat boy's father would get me another kitten, and I would apologize to the fat boy.

I told them no. I was nice and polite, but I told them no. When they jumped me for reasons, I told them I didn't want anything from anyone. My father took me upstairs for a talk. I listened, and said nothing. When he saw he was getting nowhere, he went back downstairs.

The meeting broke up with them all making baffled noises at each other.

The next afternoon at school I had to chase the fat boy from the schoolyard clear over to within a couple blocks from his house before I caught him. It didn't help him when I did.

There was a lot of telephoning around that night. My father was mad. He took me upstairs again and gave me a licking. He said we were going over to the fat boy's house, and I was going to apologize. I was still crying from the licking, but I told him I wouldn't say it after he got me over there. He made a lot of spluttering sounds and walked out of the bedroom. We didn't go anywhere.

Later that night the minister came to our house. He talked to me for a long time. All about the unexplainable things that happen in life, and the necessity for understanding. I understood, all right. What was all the talk about? I understood. I listened to him, though. I was polite. I wasn't going to give them a chance to call me surly or bad-mannered. When he was tired talking, the minister went away. I don't think even he thought he'd accomplished much.

The fat boy wasn't in school the next day. I was disappointed. When I got home there was something for me. The fat boy's father had left a carrying case with a blue Persian kitten. I didn't say anything to my mother or my sisters. I took the case out in the back yard, and when they stopped watching to see what I was doing I walked crosslots downtown to the pet shop and gave the case and the kitten back to the pet shop man. I told him to give the fat boy's father his money back. The pet shop man looked funny, but he took the kitten. He didn't say a word.

When he got home that night my father blew his stack. I didn't answer him back when he started in on me. All I wanted was to be let alone, and no one would leave me alone. My father said I was damn well going to do what I was told to do, and that if the kitten wasn't back in the house by the next night the consequences would be mine. I knew it just wasn't going to be that way.

So when I got a licking the next night it was partly for having caught the fat boy again on his way home from school, and partly for not having gone back to the pet shop for the kitten.

The next day in school I was called down to the principal's office. He talked a long time, too. The gist of it was that one more go-round with the fat boy and I would be expelled from school. I asked him politely what it had to do with school. I can still see his face tightening up, muscle by muscle. He said sharply that I was persevering in an attitude I would regret to the last day I lived, but he never did answer my question.

The fat boy wasn't in school that day, but I got a licking anyway that night for not having brought the kitten home. I got another the next night, and another the next. By then they were ritualistic, without a word being said on either side. I overheard my mother arguing with my father about his handling of me. I was sorry to hear it. I didn't want sympathy. I didn't want anything. I was stronger than they were, and I knew it. I had undivided purpose. I did-n't feel like a martyr. I felt like someone doing what he had to do.

At school I was having trouble finding the fat boy. He was leaving by dif-ferent doors, at different times. It was three more days before I caught him again. The next morning I was back in the principal's office. He wasn't there, but his secretary told me I was expelled. She looked kind of funny at me all the time she was telling me. I just kind of hung around during the day and went home at the usual time.

My mother and sisters were all waiting for me. At first I thought it was about being expelled, but they hadn't heard. They'd bought me a different Persian kitten. I thanked them. I wasn't mad at them about anything. I was-n't mad at my father about anything. Because the new kitten was a poor dumb animal that needed my help, I fed it. I didn't play with it.

My father came home early, in a tearing rage. The principal had called him. When he saw the new kitten and learned where it had come from, he clouded up and thundered at the women about going behind his back. They turned on him *en masse*. It astonished him. They didn't back him up, exactly, but for the first time in better than a week I got to bed that night without a lick-ing. Even to myself I had to admit I was glad of it. My right shoulder had been hurting worse each of the past three days. I made a bed for the new kitten, and went to bed early myself.

By noon the next day I had caught up on lickings. Before breakfast I slipped out of the house and waited for the fat boy on his way to school. By now he screamed just like a girl at the sight of me. I was in the house at ten thirty when my father came home and marched me upstairs. He really laid it into me. These days they might send a twelve year old to a home, or to reform school. Then they didn't. My father didn't know anything to do but lick me. About an hour afterward I was sick to my stomach.

I didn't go downstairs for lunch. My stomach still felt bad and my shoul-der was really giving me a hard time. I tried lying down, but that made the shoulder worse. Around two o'clock my mother came into my room. She looked at my eyes, put her hand on my forehead, and called the doctor. When he came he said I had a broken collarbone. He strapped me up like a mummy. He asked a lot of questions about the marks on me. I didn't answer him. It was none of his business. Afterward I could hear him talking to my mother out in the hall.

I took it easy that afternoon. Mostly I wondered how I was going to keep after the fat boy with an arm strapped down. I knew I'd find a way. As it turned out, I didn't need to. I was sitting downstairs leafing through an en-cyclopedia when my next oldest sister came flying into the house. She ran past into the kitchen without seeing me, and I could hear her breathlessly telling my mother that there was a big moving van in front of the fat boy's house.

The fat boy's family was moving away.

I don't know why I was so sure they were moving out of town. Maybe because I knew they were sure I'd find him if it was anywhere in the same town. I sat there looking at a picture of a Roman legion in full battle-dress, and I felt a deep sense of peace.

And just like that, it ended.

The shoulder healed in five weeks. In eight they let me back into school. Around the house the subject was never mentioned.

In a year I think everyone had honestly forgotten.

Except me.

I made El Paso the first night.

Highway 70 through Mesa, Safford, and Duncan in Arizona brought me into Lordsburg, New Mexico. Between Safford and Duncan the desert is for real. The stark, multicolored rock and sand of buttes and coulees grimly over-shadow the sparse greenery of saguaro, mesquite, and palos verde.

Highways 70 and 80 join up at Lordsburg and run together through Dem-ing to Las Cruces. I turned south there on 80 to El Paso. The temperature when I left Phoenix had been eighty-five. Rolling past the railroad marshal-ing yards in El Paso there was a flurry of snow in the headlights. Altitude makes a difference. The speedometer on the Ford said 409 miles when I pulled into a motel on the east side of town.

I'd pushed it a bit to make El Paso. I had a reason. I had to get my arm at-tended to before the bandage became a part of the tissue. Across the Inter-national Bridge in Juarez I knew where I could get it attended to, and no ques-tions asked.

The motel office had signs on the desk advertising fabulous guided tours of the fabulous city of Ciudad Juarez in fabulous Old Mexico. I had them call their agency, and in thirty minutes a pot-bellied little Mex in a business suit showed up to guide me. He was about thirty-five, and had the eyes of a well-fed weasel. Four dollars changed hands, and we took off in his car.

He was a cheerful talker. Compulsive, rather. He had been baptized Jaime Carlos Torreon Garcia, he told me, but his friends called him Jimmy. He worked for PanAm in El Paso, but lived in Juarez. He guided nights and week-ends. Would I care to see the most excellent Mexican filigreed silver, hand-worked? I regretted that on Mexican filigreed handworked silver I was loaded. Jimmy was too old a hand at the game even to look disappointed.

It was a twenty minute ride from the motel to the bridge. On the way across Jimmy had a sparkling salute for everyone at the check-in stations, English for the U.S. guards, Spanish for the Mexican soldiers. Unanimously profane in their replies to him, none of them bothered to look at me. The number of trips he made over that bridge, he was better known than the president of the country. Either country.

The fabulous city of Ciudad Juarez was—as always—dirty, dusty, and squalid. Except when it rained, and then it was muddy beyond belief. Mexican authorities show a reluctance to put drains in their streets. God sends the rain and the mud. God will take it away.

My mentor headed unerringly for a bar. "My friend," he told me, with an encompassing wave of his hand at the swarthy, shock-headed proprietor. "He has the finest *cantina* in the old town."

I looked around at the empty booths and fly-specked walls. "He's not a relative?" I asked Jimmy.

"My cousin," he admitted blandly. Since I so obviously knew the rules of the road, he sat down and ordered Canadian Club for us both without consulting my taste.

"Have a couple," I told him. "Take your time. I'm going to walk around to the Street of the Girls."

He slid from his stool immediately. "I must go with you," he protested. "They will cheat you, amigo."

"I'm the bashful type, Jaime Carlos," I said. "I'll go it alone. I'll pay you your commission just as you'd get it from the house." He eyed me doubtfully but returned to his Canadian Club.

Out on the street I side-doored it a couple of times to make sure he wasn't following me. I couldn't see any sign of him, although probably at least half the Mexican male population resembled him in outline. I turned up the third street on the left. I hadn't been in Juarez in years, but I knew where I wanted to go. The side street macadam ended ten yards in from the intersection, and the sidewalk vanished and dropped down eight inches to an earthen footpath.

I found the old woman's place with no trouble at all. I recognized the half-rusted-away iron fence around the scruffy, postage-stamp-sized front yard the minute I saw it. The last time I'd been here Ed Morris had been with me. Ed had been pushing up daisies quite a while now.

The old woman looked me over through a hole in the door panel when I knocked. I don't know what she thought she saw, but she unbolted the door. There was no conversation. She tested the bill I gave her under three different lights while I took off my shirt. Her fat hand made a swooping movement somewhere into her clothes, and emerged without the bill.

She went to work on the arm, humming to herself in a tuneless monotone. I'd been afraid she might have to steam the old bandage free, but she cut it carefully in several places and with little dabs of ether worked it loose. She knew her business. It wasn't a painless operation but considering the length of time it had gone unattended it went a damn sight easier than I'd expected.

I looked at the scar while she prepared a new bandage. A beauty contest queen might have hollered foul, but it was healing. The new bandage was smaller and more compact, easier to hide. The old woman never opened her mouth while she put it on. The last time I'd been there she'd looked three years older than the Archangel Michael, and she sure as hell hadn't found the Fountain of Youth in the meantime.

Outside again I headed back up to the corner. As I stepped back up on the sidewalk, I turned automatically for a look behind me. A street light away I could see a figure of Jimmy's general dimensions. It bothered me. I stepped into a doorway and gave the half-seen figure a chance to catch up. I waited five minutes, but nobody passed my doorway. I wasn't satisfied, but I had to be satisfied. I used my handerkerchief to wipe the red dust of the earthen footpath from my shoes, and walked back to the *cantina*.

Jaime Carlos Torreon Garcia wasn't there.

His cousin, the bushy-haired proprietor, looked surprised to see me. "No sport?" he inquired with a raised eyebrow.

"No sportsman," I said. "Too old."

"It comes to all of us," he philosophized, but crossed himself against the approach of the evil day.

Jimmy bustled in the front door. He, too, seemed surprised to see me. His well-managed expressions of first astonishment and then sympathy would have gone down better with me if it hadn't been for the thick coating of red dust on his shoes.

The second I saw it I was in motion. I tossed a bill down on the bar and hustled him out of there before he could speak. Whatever he knew, it was going to stay with him. Let the cousin think my sudden exit the frustrated petulance of a sexual loser. Cousin Jimmy had acquired some dangerous knowledge.

I sat in Jimmy's car and thought it over. Beside me he kept shooting nervous little glances at me. If he had information, I was sure he didn't know what to do with it. He needed to put his head together with someone and plan a financial coup based on his knowledge of the gringo's movements. Jaime Carlos Torreon Garcia had the proper piratical instincts but a deficiency in a method of operation. And he wasn't going to live long enough to acquire one.

"I think I've had enough sightseeing," I told him, turning toward him. Under cover of the movement I got the Woodsman into my hand. "I think you have, too." I showed him the gun. His eyes popped like a frog's on a hot rock. "Drive up to the checkout zone. Tell them 'no purchases' in Spanish. Just that. Nothing more. Let's hear you say it."

"No compra," he said huskily.

"That's all you'll say," I warned him. "Let's go."

At the barrier he had trouble getting that much out, let alone anything else. We went through in a breeze. I repeated my warning before we reached the U.S. inspection station. Two minutes later we were back across the bridge. I felt better. Trouble in Mexico I didn't want. Authorities there have a habit of tossing a gringo into a flea-infested calaboose and conveniently losing the key. Sometimes a man can buy his way out. Sometimes he can't.

That left Jimmy.

"Drive up one of these side streets," I told him.

He nearly let go of the wheel. "S-señor, don't do this theeng, I beg of you! Don't do—"

"Left, Jimmy. Now." The car lurched around as he yanked convulsively at the wheel. In three hundred yards the street lights spaced out conveniently. We were about half a mile from the motel, comfortable walking distance. "Pull over. Park between the lights." He did so, babbling unintelligibly in a half-English, half-Spanish high-pitched wail. I rapped him on the arm to snap him out of it. "Dump out your pockets on the seat. Be quick."

It was dark, but I could see. About the third item he showered down on the seat cushion was a pocket knife of the type known as Nacional. Heavy-bladed, in a solid casing, it's a lethal weapon. Jimmy was still turning out his pockets. I picked up the knife and opened it.

I don't know if he saw the movement of my arm or heard the snick of the opening blade. He screamed hoarsely and went for the door handle. I grabbed his collar and jerked him back. He collapsed beside me like a blob of melted butter, his high, keening voice yammering at me. I hit him in the belly to shut him up.

In the sudden silence I took his neck in my hand and found the carotid artery with my thumb. I opened the door on my side. A carotid can be messy. I didn't want to get splashed. I braced my heels against the floorboard and reached for him.

And hesitated.

In the quiet I seemed able to think for the first time since I'd seen clinging red dust on this man's shoes. I'd let myself get so upset at my stupidity in letting the fool follow me that I hadn't thought the thing through.

Alive, he'd talk. Later, if not sooner. That I knew.

But dead, his body would talk, and even more to the point. His cousin expected him back with a tale of where he had followed the turista. If he didn't come back, the cousin might get nervous. If he went to the police, they'd have little trouble tracing Jaime Carlos to the motel through the agency. I had had the motel call the agency. The motel would furnish the police with a description of me. And of the Ford.

Dead, this man was an anchor around my neck.

Alive? Not much better, but a little better.

I clicked the knife blade shut. "Sit up and listen to me," I said to him.

He gave a kind of shuddering sigh. "S-señor, I implore—"

"Shut up. Drive back to the motel."

It took him a full minute to get the car started. His coordination was gone. He drove like a sleepwalker. In the street lights his face looked like wax. The car bounced high as he turned into the motel driveway going too fast. For a second I thought we were going to take out a cabin before he hit the brake and we skidded in the gravel.

I got out, and motioned at him. "Take off, man."

He stared out at me suspiciously. Was it a trick? It didn't take him long to decide if it was—he still liked it better than where he'd been. He tramped on the accelerator. His car hit the street doing forty-five.

He'd been right up to the gates, and he knew it. He might not know why, but he knew it. As a type he should head straight for his bed and stay there with the covers over his head for three days.

But I couldn't count on it.

Five minutes after his tail-lights winked out of the motel driveway, I was headed east in the Ford.

3

It was odd in a way about the fat boy's family leaving town that time. Six years later it was my family who were going to leave.

The way it happened was like getting struck by lightning. I was eighteen, in my senior year in high school. It was late in the spring, and after a succession of chill, rainy days we'd finally caught a hot one. I had my sweater over my arm when I came out the school's back entrance and cut through the parking lot like I did every day on my way home. I saw these four policemen standing in the middle of the lot, and I wondered what they were doing there.

I knew one of them, Harry Coombs, and I nodded as I passed. He said something to the others, and the biggest one, who had been standing with his back to me, turned around to look. "You," he said to me. "Come over here."

I went over to them. I knew who the big one was without really knowing him. His name was Edwards, and he was a sergeant. He was a beefy man with thinning red hair. I didn't like him. No good reason. His voice was too loud. He took up too much of the sidewalk when he swaggered by. Things like that.

He looked me up and down when I stood in front of them. "What d'you know about hubcaps missing from the faculty cars three times a week?" he demanded. He looked hot and uncomfortable, still in his winter uniform.

"I don't know anything about it," I answered him. I didn't, except what I'd been hearing in school assemblies for a month.

The lower lip in his red face swelled pugnaciously. "Harry here says you spend enough time in this parking lot to be able to tell us what's going on," he continued aggressively.

"I said I see him going through here on his way home!" Coombs cut in.

Edwards paid him no attention. "Well?" he said to me.

"You think whoever's doing it waits for me to come by so I can see them?" I was mad. "Or maybe you think I'm doing it?"

"I'll ask the questions," he snapped, scowling. "What's your name?" I told him. I was liking him less and less by the second. "Now you know you must've seen what's been going on out here. Who you covering up for?"

I looked at Harry Coombs, to see if Edwards was kidding. Harry looked away. "Look, you can't mean it," I said finally. "I don't—"

"Answer the question!" Edwards roared at me.

I turned and started to walk away. He grabbed me by the arm. I've always hated having people put their hands on me. I jerked my arm out of his hand. He must have outweighed me three to one, but I caught him on the wrong foot. He staggered sideways two or three paces. His red face looked bloated.

My sweater fell off my arm, and I stooped automatically to pick it up. Edwards kicked me, hard. I went over and down, flat, skinning my palms on the parking lot cinders.

I scrambled up and went after him, the hate of the world in my heart. Be-fore I could reach him Harry Coombs had me clamped in a bear hug. He was muttering in my ear but I was struggling so hard I didn't hear him. I had my head twisted around yelling at him to let me go. I never even saw Edwards when he stepped up and slapped me heavily in the face.

"Goddamnit, sarge!" Coombs said angrily. His arms relaxed, then tightened as I lunged.

"Shut up, you!" Edwards barked at him. "This is a wise one. We'll take him down to the station and talk to him."

"Then take him down yourself," Coombs said. Deliberately he released me. "I'm on duty right here."

"You're on duty where I tell you you're on duty, Coombs," Edwards warned him. "Get him in the patrol car, and get in yourself." The sergeant clumped heavily back to the other two who had been silently standing by.

It was only by an effort of will I kept a hand away from my smarting face. Don't fight it, I told myself. Not here. I walked toward the cruiser parked in a corner of the lot. Harry Coombs tramped along beside me, muttering un-der his breath.

The five of us rode downtown. I never said a word. In the police station one of the ones who had taken no part previously took me by the arm and led me to a door beyond which were two steel cells with cement floors. He motioned me inside. I went in and looked around. There was a steel cot without even a blanket on it. Nothing else. The policeman didn't close the cell door, but he closed the outside door. I got a good look at his face before he went out.

I sat down on the cot and tried to get myself organized. I knew they'd be coming in. I didn't feel worried, just mad. I knew I was going to get that Ed-wards some day if it was the last thing I ever did. And if it could be today, so much the better.

I stood up quickly when the outside door opened. It was only Harry Coombs. He closed it and stood with his back to it. "Listen, kid," he said to me hurriedly. "I got through to him at last that you're no juvenile delinquent. He don't think so much of himself right now, but when he comes in here he'll make a little noise to justify himself. Get smart. Do what he says, y'hear?" I looked at him. "Ahhhh, you're as thick as he is," Coombs growled, and walked out.

I took off my shoes and put them on the steel cot beside me, and stretched out on my back. I stared up at the ceiling covered with misty cracks. Do what Edwards told me? Not a chance. Not a bloody chance. If he was on a hook because of me, he'd stay there till his liver and lungs rotted for all the help he'd get from me.

I sat up when the outer door opened again. Three of them filed in, Edwards in the lead. I didn't know the names of the other two, but by now I knew their faces. Harry Coombs wasn't with them. I sat there and watched them come in.

"Let's hear the answers to a few questions, now," Edwards began. His voice was rough. He looked the same, his red face shiny, but even without what Coombs had said I knew he didn't sound the same. His voice said he didn't like where he was. "I want a statement from you as to what you were doing in that parking lot," he blustered. "A signed, witnessed statement."

I didn't say anything. His face grew dark. He walked toward me, slowly. I sat still. "I said I want a statement from you!" he bellowed.

I sat there. Any statement I gave him he could probably twist around for his own purposes. He'd get no statement from me. When I said nothing, Edwards made a slight movement with his left hand. Just a gesture. Testing my nerve. I sat there. "God, how I love you boy scout tough guys!" he said between his teeth. He loomed up over me as I sat on the cot. He jabbed me in the ribs with a stiffened thumb. "Stand up when I talk to you!"

I sat there. He slapped me. My head hit the wall behind me. One of the men with him made some sort of sound, whether assent or protest I don't know. I couldn't see them. All I could see was Edwards' bulk, his red face and his hot-looking little eyes. My own were squeezed hard trying to keep the tears behind them. "Stand up, damn you!" Edwards barked. He stiffened the thumb and advanced it slowly toward my ribs, waiting for me to flinch. I didn't flinch. He jabbed me in the ribs. He jabbed me again. And again. Each time it felt like a red-hot poker.

When I saw he meant to keep it up, I reached around in back of me and picked up one of my shoes by the toe. When Sergeant Edwards' arm moved again, I came up out of there, fast. I smashed him right across the bridge of the nose with the heel of the shoe. I hit him with every ounce I had in me. He went reeling backward, blood spurting like a gusher. Only the men behind him kept him from going down. He rebounded from them and clubbed at me with both fists. He hit me about three more shots on my way down to the floor. On my way up I hit him in the belly with both hands. He knocked me down again.

There was a lot of noise and confusion. People yelling. People hurting me. I couldn't see very well. I went down and got up twice more. I think it was twice. If I could have seen Edwards, I'd have butted him squarely in the middle of his ugly face with the top of my skull.

But I couldn't see him.

And after a while I couldn't get up any more.

It seemed like a long time later I heard my father's voice. I wondered how he'd got there. "—Someone's going to sweat for this," he was saying angrily. "And I don't care if it's you, John!"

I opened my eyes cautiously. I could see from the left one. I was in an iron bed, and my father and John Mullen, the Chief of Police, were nose to nose at its foot.

"Take it easy, Karl," the chief said. John Mullen lived just up the street from us. I'd taken his youngest daughter, Kathy, to one of the school dances. "I'll get to the bottom of it."

"You're damn right you will!" my father said hotly. "And I want him moved out of here to a hospital right this minute!"

"Doc Everhardt says it isn't necessary, Karl."

"Don't try to tell me what's not necessary! I said right now! Don't think you can keep my boy from the treatment he needs just because you've got a stinking situation you'd like to cover—"

"I said I'd get to the bottom of it!" Flint-edged steel ridged Chief Mullen's tone. His voice had risen, too. "The boy could have been at fault, too, Karl."

"Fault? Fault? Good God, John, have you gone out of your mind? If he burned down the orphans' home, should he look like this? I know this Edwards. A thug in a uniform. A disgrace—"

Chief Mullen had seen my opened eye. He walked quickly around the end of the bed. "What happened, son?" he asked quietly. My father pushed in beside him where he stood looking down at me.

I had to make three starts before I could get out anything. "I—fell down," I said finally. My voice was a breathy rasp.

"Fell!" my father echoed incredulously. "Fell?" He stared at me, then whirled on the chief. "What kind of intimidation is this, John? I'm going—"

"Take it easy, Karl." There was a warning note in the official voice. The chief's shrewd eyes were studying me. "Don't forget we walked in here together. Don't let me hear you say 'intimidation' again." He was still looking down at me thoughtfully. "We'll talk to him later."

"We'll talk to him right now, damn it!"

But the chief finally got my father out of there.

I never told them any more than that, then or later. I never knew what Edwards told them. I didn't care. I think my father thought at first the beating had affected my mind. Right from the beginning, the chief came closer to the truth. Day after day he came to the house with patient questions. After a while I stopped answering him at all. Eventually he stopped coming.

I was out of school three weeks until my face healed up. When I went back, I still had three broken fingers on my left hand, and from shoulders to knees I was spotted like a leopard. I didn't remember anything about the fingers. They must have got stepped on.

Nobody at school—or anywhere else—knew what happened. The police didn't say anything, and I didn't say anything. I found out without too much trouble that the two men in the cell with Edwards that day had been Glenn Smith and Walt Cummings.

I took to skipping classes at school, even whole days. I spent more time out of the house at night than I ever had. The first three marking periods I'd been on the honor roll, and the school office called me in about my sliding grades. They said I might not even graduate if I didn't straighten up. I didn't give a damn. With such a short way to go I didn't think they could flunk me after the marks I'd carried, but I didn't care if they did. I was busy.

Glenn Smith was easy. He was a heavy drinker. I watched him till I found out he spent a lot of time in the Parokeet Tavern. He had a habit of parking his car on the street in back, and walking up a narrow alley to the Parokeet's back door. Sometimes he was in uniform.

Late one night he came back down the alley, staggering a little. I formed a one-man reception committee. I took him from behind, and I lumped him good. I kicked in a few of his ribs, finally, and left him crawling around on the ground like a wingless beetle. He never even got a look at me. I felt good all the way home.

The next morning Chief Mullen came over to school and took me out of my history class. We went outside and sat in his car. He talked for a long time. He didn't accuse me of anything. I knew he couldn't, because Glenn Smith had never seen me.

The chief went on about the idiocy of people attempting to take the law into their own hands. He talked like a damn fool. I'd taken the law into my own hands, and I liked the feel of it. The chief must have seen the expression on my face. He stopped talking and opened his car door. I went back into school.

Walt Cummings took longer. It was better than a month before I found out he dropped in a couple of nights a week at a married woman's a mile out of town. When I had him clocked so I could depend on him, I caught him at her back door one night. I smothered him in wet-down potato sacking as he came out. I got him down, and when I finished with him they carried him in from there. I went home and went to bed.

Chief Mullen was at our house before breakfast the next morning. He was really warm under the collar. He asked me point blank what I knew about Cummings. My father saved me the trouble of lying. He jumped in and wanted to know if the chief was accusing me of anything. Either make a charge you can support, he told Mullen when the chief hesitated, or get out of my house. The chief left, red in the face. I almost laughed out loud. My father didn't ask my anything afterward. He didn't seem comfortable with me.

Two down and one to go. Every time I passed Sergeant Edwards on the street, I smiled at him. Every time I smiled, he scowled. He knew. I wanted him to know. His scowls said plainly he wasn't letting his nerves get jumped up by any crackpot kid. He watched himself, though. He watched himself so well I couldn't get anywhere near him.

School let out. I graduated, barely. My college entrance credits were all shot. I'd have to pass exams to get in. I didn't take the exams. I hung around all

summer, into the fall. Twice my father, exasperated, demanded that I get a job
if I had no intention of continuing with my schooling. I paid no attention. I
had a job. A job I had to take care of before I could look for a job.

Harry Coombs cornered me late one Saturday night when I was coming out
of a diner on his beat. He herded me into a corner. "I suppose I'm lucky they
sent me out of there before they went into the cell with you that day?" he inquired, prodding me in the chest with his nightstick. I grinned at him.
"They're going to sit you down in a square-looking chair one of these days,
kid," he told me. "They'll turn on the juice, and there'll be a sizzling noise
while they burn your ass up, but you won't hear it. Think it over." He
walked away from me.

By October I knew more about Sergeant Edwards than his wife did, but
he never gave me an opening. I began to get restless. I didn't know what I
was going to do after I got through with him, but I wanted to get it over with
and find out.

Then early in November we had an unexpected sleet-and-ice storm. Edwards came up his porch steps that night with his chin shrunk down into his
coat collar, careful of the slippery footing. His head was lowered against the
stinging blasts. He never saw the piece of pipe I got him with before he
reached his front door. When I finished with the pipe, I rolled him back down
his porch steps, and went home. He was lucky. Someone found him before
he froze to death.

I didn't find that out until morning. Or at least the clock said it was morning but it was still dark outside. A police cruiser came by for my father and
me. They hardly gave us time to dress. My father kept asking them what had
happened. They wouldn't say anything. In the cruiser my father kept sneak-
ing looks at me from the corner of his eye.

At the station Chief Mullen really gave me a going-over. He was trying to
scare answers out of me. He should have known better by that time. For
twenty solid minutes I sat there and smiled at him. I never said a word. My
father horned in finally and asked Mullen what basis he had for his unfounded
accusations. It really flipped the chief. You've got a wild animal running loose
around town, he told my father. You've got a choice. Cage him, or leave town.
Leave town, he repeated with emphasis. Better all around.

I felt like laughing until I saw the stricken look on my father's face. I could-
n't understand it. The chief couldn't do anything. Nobody could do anything.
I didn't give a damn what they thought they knew about me. They could-
n't prove a thing.

On the way home my father said tiredly he hoped I'd realize some day it was
necessary to live with people. He said a lot of other things. I felt sorry for him.
He just couldn't stand up to a situation.

I couldn't believe it when the FOR SALE sign went up on our front lawn.
I was disgusted. My father was letting them bluff him right out of the game.

They couldn't make him do a thing he didn't agree to do. That's why I couldn't understand it. My father was a weakling.

I couldn't let his spinelessness affect my mother and sisters. I left home that night. I knew I could manage. Obviously my father couldn't.

I left.

I never went back.

I had to switch cars.

The minute my pot-bellied Mexican guide's tongue came unlatched, the police would get a description of the Ford—and of me—from the motel. It didn't matter a damn they wouldn't know why they were looking for me. It was up to me to change the appearance of what they'd be looking for.

Highway 80 east out of El Paso is a long, straight, black stretch of road. Not many headlights came at me. Ground fog began to drift in from the fields on either side of the highway. It began to close in over the road. I wanted to make time, and if this kept up I wasn't going to be able to make time.

Most of the gas stations I passed were dark. When I came up on a lighted one, I slowed down, tempted. I hit the gas again and went on by. It wouldn't solve anything. I could grab the attendant's car or anything he happened to be working on, but unless I buried him in his grease pit he'd pass the word on that would tie me to the new car. And even if I buried him, the presence of the Ford when I abandoned it would put the collar around my neck for anyone checking the highway from the motel on up the line.

I needed a setup that would let me run the Ford over a cliff, or the equivalent. Even more I needed to get off Highway 80. The john in a girl's dorm doesn't get any more action than that damn highway.

I went over it in my mind. Van Horn is a hundred twenty odd miles east of El Paso. A dozen miles the other side Highway 80 plows ahead due east, but Highway 90 ducks south. It looked like a better choice. I couldn't count on Jimmy's pulling the covers over his head. They could be out looking for me already.

I made it in an hour and thirty-five minutes, fog and all. I had to fight my eyes closing down all the way, and I hit the shoulder a couple of times, dozing off, but at twenty minutes to midnight I turned onto 90 and headed south. It was a narrower road, much less traveled. I began to watch for a motel. When I saw one with a car parked out close enough to the road, I'd drive a mile beyond, walk back, jump the switch on the car in the motel yard, and take off. There'd be nothing to tie the abandoned Ford to the stolen car, even if the best I could do with the Ford would be to run it off into a field.

I couldn't have been more than twenty miles in on 90 with everything around me as black as the inside of a closet when a pair of headlights came on suddenly in my rear-view mirror. A red flasher started bouncing off the Ford.

He must have come up behind me with his lights off, because I hadn't seen a thing. I took a quick look at the speedometer. Sixty-five. Should be no sweat there. I heard no siren, but there was no doubt he intended me to stop. He pulled out alongside, then burst ahead and cut in.

I had to jam on the brakes and cut the wheel hard to avoid scraping fenders as he herded me to the side of the road. As he went past me I could see he was in an unmarked car. I hadn't known the Rangers used unmarked cars. Live and learn.

I was ready when he walked back and leaned in the window I'd rolled down. I handed him my driver's license made out to Roy Martin. Paper-clipped to it was a twenty dollar bill. I could see a trooper hat silhouetted against the dark, but I couldn't see the face beneath it at all. I could sense rather than see him looking around the Ford's interior before he walked back to the rear and put a flash on the license.

He returned and handed it in to me. The twenty dollar bill was gone. "Drive up the highway a quarter mile," he said. His voice sounded as if he regularly had steel filings for breakfast. "Turn right the first road. A hundred fifty feet in there's a white fence. Turn left and stop. I'll be right behind you." He walked back to the cruiser. I hadn't got to say a word.

I could feel a slow burn coming up. If this sonofabitch thought he was going to take my twenty and then write me up anyway, he was damn well going to find out differently. When I buy someone, I expect him to stay bought.

He pulled ahead to let me out, and I eased back out on the highway. I rolled down the road slowly, watching for the first turn on the right. Even at that I almost missed it. It was hardly more than a dirt drop-off. Halfway into my turn I thought I'd made a mistake, but the headlights behind me turned in, too. I came up to the white fence, and turned left. In twenty-five yards I faced a dead-end, an impenetrable, jungle-like brush tangle dead ahead in the headlights.

I was getting hotter by the minute. I was losing time. I had missed a turn despite his directions, and wound up in this jackpot. The clearing was too small to swing around in. I started to back out. A red glow filled my rear-view mirror. I turned my head. The cruiser was backing into the clearing, sealing me in. Even as I looked he cut his lights.

All of a sudden I had a feeling.

I cut my lights and motor, fumbled a flashlight out of the glove compartment, and went out the door on the passenger's side. The unmarked car, the absence of a siren, this dead-end deserted spot he'd directed me to—

When I heard him walking I put the flash on him. He stopped dead in the beam of light. He was holding a gun, a blued-steel job. He had on a campaign hat that looked like a Ranger's hat. His clothes didn't look anything like a uniform except for the color. The bastard was no more a cop than I was.

He brought his gun up and snapped off a shot at me just as I let go at him with the Woodsman. He turned and started to run. I put one in his ankle that brought him down with a crash. He landed all sprawled out, the gun flying off in the bushes. I got over to him fast in case he had another.

When I got the flash full on him I saw it didn't make any difference. He'd been running on reflex. The hard core of the light shone down on a round, dark hole just a hair to the right of center between his eyes. The little old Woodsman might not have the stopping power of a .38, but it gets there just the same.

It was quiet in the clearing. I walked over and put the flash on the bandido's car. It was a Ford, too. It looked in better shape than mine. I got his car keys out of his pocket and got under the wheel and started it up. The engine vr-r-roomed with power. Something extra under the hood.

It looked like I had won myself an automobile.

I put on the dimmers on both cars and opened the trunks of both. I loaded his gear in mine and mine in his. I took the license plates off both cars and chopped them up with a hammer and cold chisel. With a screwdriver I worked on the red flasher on the roof until I was able to unscrew it. I knocked down the edges of the socket that held the bulb with the chisel, and slapped a square of tape over it. The black friction tape merged with the color of the car. I rummaged around through saws and climbing irons in my tool chest till I found a set of Florida plates. I put them on the new Ford.

I cleaned out my wallet and started from scratch. When I put it back on my hip again I was Chester Arnold of Hollywood, Fla. I had business cards in the wallet identifying Chet Arnold as a tree surgeon. When it pleases me I'm a tree surgeon. A good one.

When I was all set I went back for my unknown benefactor. I dragged him over and stuffed him into the trunk of the new Ford. With the tool chests already in there it was a tight squeeze, but I finally got the back deck lid closed.

I took off out of there.

Out on the highway every five miles I threw a piece of chopped up license plate out the window. It helped to keep awake. Then it started to rain. It doesn't rain often in West Texas, but when it does it doesn't fool around. I hunched down over the wheel, watched the road in the streaming windshield, and pitched license fragments.

Forty miles up the highway I ran into a torn-up section under repair. In those parts they're so sure it's not going to rain they don't bother with the nicety of preserving one lane of macadam. They tear up the road from shoulder to shoulder, roll it, and drive on the dirt till they get the blacktop back on. If it does rain they have a driving rodeo through four to six inches of Texas gumbo. Never let anyone tell you the Texan is not a sporting animal.

It was raining so damn hard that in less than a mile the whole graveled roadbed was solidly under water. The Ford slipped and slithered along. Even at five miles an hour, a couple of times I wasn't sure I was going to make

it. It was like driving across a ten mile lake. I had to watch the highway department right-of-way stakes as they glistened in the headlights alongside the
road to be sure I was still in the channel.

I finally got out on hardtop again, and for the next ten miles I listened to
Texas mud slurp off the undercarriage at every little jounce. From what I
could see of it I could have set up a fair-sized sweepstakes selling chances of
the Ford's original color. I concentrated on driving and staying awake.

When the speedometer said I was two hundred miles from El Paso, I
started looking for a deep culvert. When I saw a likely looking one I pulled
over on the shoulder. I got out and walked around to the back. I never saw
as black a night. It was raining like someone had turned on the petcock and
gone off on vacation. I was soaked in less than a minute.

I got the trunk open, and hauled out my passenger. I hoisted him over to
the bank and rolled him down it. He went in with a satisfying splash. I got
back in under the wheel and started slogging up the highway again. When
they found him, no one would connect my benefactor to me or to much of anything else. Ditto the Ford I'd left behind in the clearing.

I'd passed Marfa and Alpine a long way back, clusters of lights in the dripping night. I was between Marathon and Haymond when I dumped the body.
Twice on the long stretch between Sanderson and Del Rio I nearly went to
sleep. I was driving myself as hard as I was driving the car.

Outside of Brackettville dawn was breaking in a dirty gray sky when I got
a leg cramp so bad it pulled my foot clear off the accelerator. I stopped the car
and got out and limped around it a couple of times, but I couldn't shake it
off. I drove through town with my left foot on the gas pedal and into a motel on the outskirts. I woke up the owner, shut up his grumbling about the
ungodliness of the hour, took the key he gave me and headed for the cabin he
pointed out.

I figured I was about 450 miles from El Paso, and it had been a long, long
day.

I shed clothes all the way from the door of the cabin to the bed, and I was
asleep before I was halfway down to the pillow.

4

A year after I left home I was up in northern Ohio working the midnight-to-eight shift in a gas station on the edge of town. It was colder than a whore's heart up there in December, but it kept me eating. From two to seven I wouldn't average half a dozen cars. I'd sit inside with my feet cocked up on a gasoline heater, and wait for daylight.

Or listen to Olly Barnes.

He was an odd one. I couldn't figure why a good-looking guy with a college degree should spend his time hanging around the station till all hours in the morning, talking to a kid like me. Naturally I thought he was a queer at first. Then I decided he wasn't, but I couldn't make him out. He was slender, with a pale, narrow face dominated by steel-rimmed spectacles, a high forehead, and straw-colored hair. He was about thirty. His hands were small and usually fluttered nervously while he talked. He had a beautiful speaking voice.

Two or three nights a week he'd be around the station till five in the morning. I never could see how he could keep his eyes open on his bookkeeping job. One thing I noticed about him. He talked a lot about the places he'd been and the things he'd seen, but never about the people. He talked travel, books, paintings, opera, ballet; talked with a passionate intensity. In the beginning I tried to tell him he was way over my head with most of what he had to say. When I saw it didn't matter, I shut up and listened. Olly brought me books I didn't read, and tried to hide his disappointment when I admitted it. And then one morning the police came and took him away. It was about three thirty, and he'd been talking, as usual, when the cruiser pulled up outside. Olly's good-looking face crumpled like wet cardboard when he saw the big man in plainclothes walking toward the station door. I thought he was going to run, but if he thought of it he didn't have time.

The big man stood in the open doorway, cold air pouring in all around him. "Let's take a ride, Oliver," he said. He had a broad, flat face with high cheekbones and no more expression than an iron skillet.

"No," Olly whispered. "No!" That time it was a scream. He did start to run then, aiming at the garage area, but the man in the doorway took two steps forward and picked him off by the shirt-front like I'd scoop a fly from the wall. He half-carried, half-dragged Olly outside without saying another word. The door slammed behind them.

I went outside to the cruiser. It was none of my business, but I went out, anyhow. A uniformed man was driving. I rapped on the rolled-up front window. I could see Olly and the big man in the back seat. Olly was crying. The uniformed man lowered the window and looked out at me. "What's it all about?" I asked him.

He sat with his head cocked as if he were listening for something from the back seat. When nothing came he rolled up the window and wheeled the cruiser around the pumps and out on the highway.

I stood and watched the tail-lights diminishing up the road. It was a bitter cold night, without a star or a light of any kind, except for the lights of the station. It wasn't any of my business. And I couldn't walk off and leave the place. I went back inside, out of the cold. Olly's overcoat still lay on a chair where he'd dropped it when he came in.

Between then and seven o'clock I called the police four times. No one had ever heard of Oliver Barnes. I described the big man. They knew him, all right. His name was Lieutenant Winick. No one had seen him, either.

A little after four it started to snow. Between calls to the police I was kept busy clearing the station's driveways. By dawn there was six inches on the ground, and it was blowing hard. After seven I was too busy to call any more. When my relief came on at eight I had to stay over an hour to help with the rush of cars.

When I was able to get away there were no buses running. I put Olly's overcoat over my arm and walked the mile and a half into town. Drifts were already a couple of feet in some places, and the storm was spraying line-drive sheets of snow. Cold as it was I was sweating by the time I reached the police station. That kind of weather made heavy going.

I didn't really know what I was doing there. I guess I'd always known Olly wasn't exactly a hundred cents on the dollar. Still, a deal like that—

What if it had been me? Wouldn't I have wanted someone to at least find out the score?

I might as well have talked to a wooden Indian as the sergeant at the desk. He asked a hell of a lot more questions than he answered. Who I was. Where I lived. Where I worked. What my interest was. He finally made a pretense of checking the blotter, and said that no Oliver Barnes had been booked for anything. I knew he was lying, but for him that ended it.

I hung around. Nobody tried to run me out, but they didn't make it easy for me to stay. I tried my questions on two or three newcomers, with the same results. The heat in the waiting room kept putting me to sleep every time I sat down. At eleven o'clock I gave up. I left Olly's overcoat at the desk—in case he came in looking for it, I told the sergeant—and went home to bed.

When I woke at four it was still snowing. I dressed and walked back up to the station after getting a cup of coffee at the corner. When he saw me come in the same sergeant spoke before I could. "Lieutenant Winick wants to see you, kid," he said to me. "Inside. Second door on the left."

Winick looked up from behind his desk when I knocked and entered his office. His high-cheekboned features were just as expressionless as they'd been before. He leaned back steeply in his chair, folded his arms, and looked me over. "Stanton said you wanted to see me," he said at last. As though he'd just got the word, and I hadn't been trying since eight thirty.

"Where's Olly?" I asked him.

"In a cell. Where he belongs."

"Why? What for?"

Winick's slitted eyes were unwinking. "Your friend has a bad habit. He coaxes little girls behind buildings and takes their panties down." His harsh voice deepened as his eyes bored into mine. "*Little* girls. Seven, eight, nine. And you know what he does then?" He told me. "Like day before yesterday," he concluded. "It wasn't hard to know where to look, even without the kid's description when her mother brought her in."

The roof of my mouth felt dry. "How good—what kind of a description?"

"Oliver Barnes' description." Winick's voice blared at me suddenly. "Did you know he'd served a reformatory sentence and a prison term for the same thing?"

"No, I didn't."

"Then you know now. You're not very choosy of your company. How long've you been in town?"

"Six months. When—what time did it happen?"

The big shoulders rose and fell in an elaborate shrug.

"Five, six o'clock. The kid wasn't sure."

I felt a sense of excitement, "Five or six o'clock in the evening?"

"Five or six o'clock in the evening," Winick agreed with exaggerated patience.

"Then it couldn't have been Olly," I said triumphantly.

Winick smiled. "He confessed."

"Confessed? Look, you said it happened between five and six day before yesterday?"

He was watching me narrowly. "That's what I said."

"Then it couldn't have been Olly. He brought some books over to my place at four in the afternoon day before yesterday, and he stayed talking until I went out to eat at seven. It couldn't have been Olly, you hear me?"

He stood up behind the desk. "You're mixed up on the days. It happens to you night workers. He confessed."

"The hell I'm mixed up on the days! How could he confess to something he didn't do? You—"

"Careful of the territory you're taking in, kid." Winick's voice could have cut wood. "Where do you fit in this? What kind of friend is Barnes to you?"

"Why don't you ask me what kind of friend I am to Barnes? The way I see it, I'm the one he needs. I want to talk to him."

"He's not seeing anyone. He has fits of remorse."

I could feel myself shaking. "Listen, I'll testify Olly couldn't possibly have—"

"You're going off half-cocked, kid," the hard voice cut me off again. "Did you hear me say Barnes had confessed? In detail?"

"You made him confess! He was afraid the minute he saw you. Because he did it before doesn't mean he did it this time. You must have—"

"Listen to me." Winick's voice was quiet again. "He did it. He confessed it. Can you get that through your thick skull?"

"There must be somebody else for me to talk to around here besides you," I said desperately. "You're not even listening. I tell you Olly couldn't—"

"You're not listening to me." Gimlet eyes drilled into mine. "Barnes is a menace to society. He's proved it. He should never have been out on the street. This time I'm tucking him away for a good long stretch."

"But he didn't do it! Not this time, anyway!"

"He did it." Winick's heavy voice was flat with authority. His eyes appeared almost closed as he looked across the desk at me. "Should I ask Barnes if you were with him?"

My hands clenched. "Is that supposed to make me run out of here? By God, I know what I know. I don't care what he did before. This he didn't do, and I'll talk till I get someone to listen."

"You sound to me like someone fixing to get his balls caught in the machinery." Winick leaned down over the desk, resting his weight on his big-knuckled hands. "I know what Barnes is. The people in this town know what he is. When you talk to me, you're talking to all of them."

I got out of there.

I didn't believe Winick, but I found out he was right. Everyone I tried to get to listen to me gave me nothing but a blank stare. Nobody would believe it couldn't have been Olly.

And then I found out the hard way some of them weren't going to believe. The next day I lost both my job and my room. Winick had been to see my boss and my landlady. All of a sudden I was on the street with twenty-three dollars between me and the snow.

I stuck around another day, trying to get someone to listen. I was half out of my mind, crazy-mad at the town and the people in it. And at Winick. Especially at Winick. That night I slept till four A.M. in the railroad station with my head on my bag. Winick's cops found me then and threw me out. I must have ground a quarter inch off my teeth, stumbling around the slippery, frozen streets, lugging my bag. I was half frozen by the time the first one-arm coffee joint opened up.

In the cold gray light of the morning I gave up. I walked out to the edge of town and stopped a highway bus and told the driver to get me eleven dollars worth away from there. I purposely hadn't bought a ticket at the bus station because I figured if Winick wanted to keep a string on me he'd have counted on that.

I wound up across the state, a hundred eighty miles away. I got a job as stock boy in a chain grocery. Three times a week I bought a northern Ohio news-paper and read every word of it, looking for news of Olly.

It wasn't much of a surprise when I finally saw it, three months later. The black headlines said Olly had been sentenced to fifteen years.

That day I quit the human race. I never went back to my job. I've never done a legitimate day's work since. The work I've done since then has always been with an illegitimate purpose in mind. If that was the way it was, they could damn well have it that way.

I bought a gun in a hock shop. I didn't even own a car. The local paper nipped hard at police heels over the series of gas station holdups by a quick-moving pedestrian who always disappeared into the darkness.

I was surprised at how easy it was. I had only two close calls. Once I was scared off before I'd committed myself, and another time I had to stop an at-tendant from chasing me by shooting over his head.

The money piled up. I knew what I was going to do with it. I bought a sec-ond-hand car and learned how to drive it. About ten weeks after Olly started his sentence I drove the hundred eighty miles back across the state. Back to Winick. I rang his doorbell at ten o'clock at night. He came to the door himself. Not that it made any difference; I was all set to go right into the house after him.

I shot him in the face, four times, as he stood at the door looking out at me. He went backward in a kind of shambling trot. "That's for Olly, you bastard," I told him. I don't think he heard me. I think he was dead before his big shoul-ders hit the floor.

Winick was the first.

He wasn't the last.

I woke up at sundown in the Brackettville motel, humped myself across the street to a combination grocery-restaurant, and loaded up on bacon and eggs and black coffee. I re-crossed the highway and went right back into the sack. I woke up the next time at five thirty in the morning, feeling better physically than I had in weeks.

I had breakfast at the same restaurant, and was ready to leave. I climbed into the new Ford, listened appreciatively to the engine sound when I started it up, and tried to back out of my parking place. The car rocked back and forth, but wouldn't budge. I sat there blank for a minute before it dawned on me what must have happened. All that Texas gumbo I'd run through—when half-dried it had frozen the brakes down tight.

Back across the road I went again. I rousted out a barefoot kid at the restau-rant and brought him back with me. He crawled underneath and clawed out a couple of pecks of rich-looking mud. He had trouble freeing the emergency, but finally managed it. I tied a handkerchief on the emergency to remind not to use it. Those brakes wouldn't be fully dry for two or three days. I gave the kid two dollars, and he turned cartwheels all the way back to the restaurant.

It was a beautiful morning when I hit the road. After the storm everything was fresh and clear. The highway was dry and there was no traffic that early in the day. At the first straight stretch I laid down on the accelerator to see what the Ford could do. I chickened out at 105, and it felt like I had an inch left. The thing was a bomb. It held the road well, too.

I drove on through Uvalde, San Antonio, Seguin, and Luling. I had lunch in Weimar. In the afternoon I piled on through Houston, Beaumont, and Orange. I made it into Lake Charles, Louisiana, and spent the night there. The speedometer said 469 miles for the day.

I'd pushed it a little because I wanted to make Mobile the next night. In Mobile I could get guns and other things I needed from Manny Sebastian. I had to ditch the artillery I had. One gun traced back to two bank guards in Phoenix, the other to a body floating in a rain-swollen ditch. If Manny hadn't lost his contacts, I could get a Florida license and registration from him to match what I was driving.

I was out on the highway again by six thirty the next morning. Ten miles east of Lake Charles I turned north on Route 165 at a little place called Iowa. I stayed with the new route for twenty miles to Kinder, then headed east again on 190. This was the New Orleans bypass. I sailed through Eunice, Opelousas, Baton Rouge and Hammond in Louisiana, and crossed into Mississippi at Slidell. A few miles further on 190 hooked back into 90 again, and I rolled along the Old Spanish Trail through Bay St. Louis, Pass Christian, Gulfport, Biloxi, and Pascagoula. Along that sunlit stretch I was seldom out of sight of white sand and blue gulf. When I pulled into a motel in Mobile about five o'clock the speedometer said 343 miles.

I washed up, had dinner, and drove downtown to the Golden Peacock, Manny Sebastian's joint. After midnight the place really swung far out, but at this time of night it was quiet. Manny had a finger in a lot of pies. He hadn't seen me in four or five years, but he recognized me the minute I walked in. He came over and shook hands. He'd put on a lot of weight since I'd seen him last, and his jowls and extra chins transformed the face I remembered as jovially ugly into something sinister-looking.

"The back room?" he asked me with a cocked eyebrow.

I nodded. He walked over behind the bar and engaged in small-talk with two of the half dozen customers. In five minutes I saw him select a key from a huge key ring and let himself out through an unmarked door alongside one marked "Office". The unmarked door was just outside the enclosure of the bar. I gave it another couple of minutes and walked around and tapped. Manny let me in and then closed and barred the door. He had a bottle and glasses already out on the small table that was the room's only furnishing besides an old-fashioned iron safe in one corner.

"Long time, man," Manny said to me. "How's old hit-the-squirrel-in-the-eye-at-a-hundred-yards?" He walked to the table and poured and handed me a drink. "What's your problem?"

"Not the same as yours. You talk too much, Manny." I took a swallow of my drink. "How're you fixed on Florida registrations?"

He nodded. "What're you driving?"

"A Ford all over mud on your parking lot." I handed him one of my Chet Arnold cards. "Have your boy run off a license while he's at it."

Manny went to the door and unbarred it. He called someone over to whom he spoke in a low tone, and closed the door again. "Ready in an hour. Like what else?"

"Hardware. A Smith & Wesson .38 and a Colt Woodsman."

He nodded again. "I'll have to send up to the house for the Woodsman. I've got a .38 right here." He was already whirling the dial on the old safe. "I range-tested it myself. Shoots a fraction high and to the left. The Woodsman's perfect."

"You know where they came from?"

Manny looked hurt. "Right out of the factory." He produced the Smith & Wesson with a flourish, still in the original box. "Never been fired except by me, either of 'em."

"Okay, Manny. What's the damage?"

He squinted up at the ceiling. "Oh, say four hundred for the lot. Paperwork comes high these days."

I paid him. Paperwork wasn't the only thing that came high, but I had to have those guns.

"Grab a seat at the bar. On the house," Manny said, pocketing the cash. "I'll give you the office when I get your stuff together. How're things in general?" The shrewd eyes in the larded-over face studied me.

"Quiet."

He chuckled. "A hundred seventy odd thousand quiet?"

I forced my face into a smile. "I read about that. Nice touch. Sounded like Toby Coates. Or Jim Griglun."

"Toby's in Joliet," Manny said smoothly. "And Jim lost his nerve after that time in Des Moines."

"Sometimes a man gets it back."

Manny shook his head. "Not if he didn't have too much to start with." He grinned at me companionably. "Your pawprints were all over that Phoenix job. You ought to miss a shot once in a while."

Out of the mouths of fools. I made a mental note.

"Sorry to disappoint you," I said as lightly as I could manage. "I've been in hibernation." A growing feeling of irritation mounted within me. This kind of earache I couldn't use.

He seemed to sense my mood. "Who should know better?" he said, cryptically enough, and opened the door. "Order up. It's on the house, remember."

I sat at the bar and ordered a highball I didn't want. Through a window at the right I could see out on the parking lot. A slim redhead with a limp was walking around the Ford. As I watched he raised the hood, leaned in and then out, and wrote something down on a piece of paper. The engine number, I thought.

I nursed the drink for half an hour, and then ordered another. I was two-thirds of the way down to the bottom of it when Manny slid onto the next stool and laid a package down on the bar quite openly. "Eddie says that's a real fireball out on the lot," he said to me softly. "I got a wheel-man would give his front teeth for it. You want to trade? I'll give you something to boot."

"Not right now, Manny. I'll keep you in mind, though." I picked up the package and went out to the car. I pulled over to a corner of the lot and unwrapped the package. I put the new license and registration in my wallet, and switched loads from the old guns to the new. I tried them for balance. They felt all right. As soon as I had a chance I'd check out the Smith & Wesson. If Manny said it was throwing a little high and to the left, it was probably more than a little.

I drove out of the lot. More from force of habit than from any real belief that someone might be following me, I doubled and twisted over a circuitous route back to the motel. The conversation with Manny bothered me. Manny was a gossip. Never to the wrong people, so far as I knew, but a gossip is a gossip. This driving around the country so soon after a job bothered me, too. Before I'd always had a nice, quiet place to hole up in between jobs. This time I wasn't calling the tune, though.

I promised myself that as soon as I got straightened out in Hudson, Florida, I'd go to earth in a hurry. Back at the motel I sacked in and slept solidly.

The next morning was the fifth day since I'd left Phoenix. I got another early start and left Highway 90 about thirty miles beyond Seminole, Florida, at Milton. On 90-A I busted along through Galliver, Crestview, DeFuniak Springs, Marianna, Chatahoochee, Tallahassee, and Monticello. I was on the homestretch now. At Capps I turned south on U.S. 19. Out in the country I picked out two swift-running rivers about fifty miles apart, and I threw the old Smith & Wesson into the first one and the old Woodsman into the second.

At four in the afternoon I saw a sign at the side of the highway: Town Limits, Hudson, Florida. I was forty or fifty miles south of Perry. I drove through the main square and found a motel on the south edge of town called the Lazy Susan. I'd covered 362 miles since morning. I registered, showered, ate at the motel, went into the lobby and worked my way through half a month-old *Time*, and went to bed early. After that stretch on the road I wanted to start out fresh in the morning.

I had breakfast in town at a place called the Log Cabin. It looked like stucco but could have been stucco over logs. It was early, but the place was busy. It looked like a factory crowd. Not much conversation, even with the good-looking young waitress who wore an engagement ring but no wedding band.

After breakfast I walked around the square. Driving through yesterday, I'd estimated the town at six or eight thousand. This morning I upped that a little. The store windows were clean, and the displayed merchandise looked fresh. There were no empty stores. The merchants must at least be making the rent money.

I walked past the still unopened bank. It was an old building, bristling in its external impression of maximum security. Like a two-dollar watch of the type that used to be called a bulldog.

I bought a local paper in the drugstore, carried it under my arm to the little park in the square, and sat down on a bench in the morning sunlight. The park faced the town hall and the post office. I looked at the post office a couple of times. To be diverted, registered mail almost had to be tampered with by post office personnel. Although of course the packaged money didn't need to have been registered yet at the time it was intercepted.

The paper turned out to be a weekly. I read every line of it, including the ads. It's a habit of mine. Tips are where you find them. I've had a subscription for years under one of my names to *Banking, the Journal of the American Banking Association*. There's a column in it called "The Country Banker," and two of the best tips I ever had came right out of that column. Banking used to publish pictures of newly remodeled bank interiors. Lately they've pretty much cut that out. It must have occurred to someone they were being too helpful.

In the Hudson *Chronicle* I read right down to the Help Wanted and the Positions Wanted ads. There's something to be learned about a community from each. I read all the other ads. If there was a tree surgeon in Hudson, he wasn't using the *Chronicle* to attract customers.

I folded the paper up and walked back to where I'd parked the Ford. Main Street in Hudson ran east-west from the traffic light in the square, not north-south on 19. I drove east on Main. When the stores thinned out, I slowed down. The first houses were small, with tiny yards or none at all. No work for a tree surgeon there.

A mile beyond the built-up section of town the whole area south of Main was a swamp. I remembered seeing it on a map as Thirty Mile Swamp. From what I could see of it, it was no kitchen-garden swamp, either, but a fibrous jungle of cypress and mangrove in brackish-looking water, the whole drearily festooned with Spanish moss. At the side of the road beside a shack a hand-painted sign said: AIRBOAT FOR HIRE.

I turned the Ford around and started back. Back at the edge of town again I turned north and began criss-crossing the side streets. Gradually I worked into higher ground and an improved residential area. I turned finally into a block-long street with only three houses on it. Big houses. Estates. I slowed down. This was what I needed. Property that needed to be kept up, and people with the money to pay for it. I drove around, and made notes on the edge of my newspaper.

When I'd accumulated half a dozen I headed back to the square and parked. I found a real estate office above the local five-and-dime and climbed the stairs with my paper under my arm. A young fellow hopped up from behind a desk as I entered. He had on a short-sleeved white shirt with a tie. Below the executive level in this latitude the short-sleeved white shirt is practically a uniform. Nobody wears a jacket, and after lunch the ties come off. Nobody is ever in a hurry.

"Yes, sir?" the boy said briskly. He had a nice smile. "Jed Raymond, sir. May I be of help?"

"Chet Arnold," I said, and handed him one of my business cards. "I just came in to pick your brains." I looked at my newspaper. "There's a big white Georgian house up on Sand Rock Road and Jezebel Drive." I looked at Jed Raymond. "Odd name for a street, that."

"Old Mr. Landscombe named it, Mr. Arnold. They do say he had his reasons." Jed Raymond looked up from his inspection of my card. "You want the tree work?" He shook his head doubtfully. "Mr. Landscombe died six months ago, and there's an unholy dust-up about his will. Three sets of heirs suing each other. The estate'll probably be in probate for years." The boy had a soft drawl and a mournfully humorous smile. He had a bright, heart-shaped face under a ginger-colored crewcut. Any woman over thirty would have taken him to raise and be glad of the chance.

"Who's the estate administrator?" I asked him. "He shouldn't want the estate to run down."

Raymond looked impressed. "I b'lieve it's Judge Carberry." He pronounced it "Cah'bry". "If it's not he'll know who it is. You could have somethin' there."

I wrote the name down. "How about a fieldstone rancher up on University Place and Golden Hill Lane?"

"Belongs to Mr. Craig at the bank. His daddy used to be in the lumber business. So'd Roger Craig until he had a heart attack a while back. He came into the bank then. Guess his family owned most of it, anyway."

I looked at the rest of my list and decided to skip them for the time being. A judge, and a banker. Better still, a banker who had been in the lumber business. These two looked like solid leads. If I could crack either one, I was in business in this town. "You know your real estate, son," I told Jed Raymond. "Anything in the regulations says I can't buy your lunch one of these days?"

"If I find anything I'll get it amended," he grinned. He tucked my business card into his shirt pocket. "I'll keep this, if you don't mind. I might hear of something for you."

"Fine. I'm at the Lazy Susan now. If I change, I'll let you know. You happen to have a detailed map of the area?"

He reached in a counter drawer and handed me a thickly folded-over packet. "This one's even got the projected streets in the new development east of town." He waved me off as I put my hand in my pocket. "Hope you do y'self some good locally, Mr. Arnold."

I went back down the stairs to the street. I always carry two tool kits with me, a large one to work out of and a small one for show. I walked back to the Ford and got the small one out of the trunk. I tucked two double-bitted axes into the loops on either side of the chest. When a man formerly in the lumber business saw such a kit, I shouldn't have too much trouble getting into his office.

I walked back up the street toward the bank.

5

I was twenty-three when I killed my second man. Funny thing: it was in Ohio, too. Massillon. Five of us had flattened the bank on the northeast corner of the main intersection, but one of the boys got trigger-happy inside. In the getaway Nig Rosen and Duke Naylor were burned down in the street before we made it to the getaway car. A mile out of town I got a deputy in a cruiser trying to cut us off. Two days later the rest of us were flushed out of a farmhouse. Clem Powers was killed. Barney Pope and I were bagged.

Barney was an old lag. He knew he'd have long white whiskers before he made it outside again, if ever. Go for yourself, kid, he said to me as we stood in the farmyard with our hands in the air. I'll back your play.

I'd left my gun inside beside Clem's body. That scored the deputy to Clem. I told the mob scene that surrounded us I was a hitchhiker who'd been sleeping in the barn when the bandidos took over, and I stuck to it. True to his word, Barney backed me up. The police didn't believe it, but the jury came close. The identification putting me inside the bank was fuzzy. The guilty verdict was lukewarm.

Even the judge was leaning. I had no rap sheet. They'd checked my prints from Hell to Hoboken, and they couldn't even find a speeding charge. Two things licked me with the judge, finally. I wasn't using my family name, of course, and the probation officer couldn't get a line on me. The judge refused to believe I'd sprung full-blown from the earth age twenty-three without previous documentation of some kind. Also—and fatally—I could produce no visible means of support.

The judge cleared his throat and said three-to-five. I think he'd been considering probation. Barney Pope drew twenty-to-life. We weren't tried for the deputy. They figured they had us cold on the bank job, and on the other there was a question of jurisdiction and identification. The local D.A. didn't want to give up his own headlines by letting us go up on the other charge.

I hadn't graduated overnight to a five man bank detail. Once I'd found out which end of a gun was which, I'd come up the ladder, from filling stations to theater box-offices to liquor stores—the whole bit. I worked alone until I met Nig Rosen. Nig talked me into the Massillon setup. I guess I was flattered. I was far and away the youngest of the five.

We worked four months on that job. I kept my mouth shut, and listened. Parts of it I didn't like; instinctively, it seemed. Afterward I knew I was right. Complicated action with a bunch of hot sparks was no good. Even before we were hit I'd decided that what I wanted in the future was some kind of deal I could control myself.

In the can I had plenty of time to figure how it was going to be the next time. From the middle of my second year on, Doc Essegian was my cellmate. Everyone called him The Doctor. Maybe because he was such a wise old owl. I know he was no medical doctor.

The first three months he never even said good morning to me. Then I had a little trouble with one of the screws. When I came back from solitary, Doc laughed at me. "Don't let it burn a hole in your gut, kid," he advised me. "You're even a better hater than I am, and that's saying something." After that he kind of took me over. "Life is the big machine, kid," he'd growl at me in his after-lights-out rasp. "It chews you up and it spits you out. Don't you ever forget it."

He had the most completely acid outlook on life I'd ever run across. He really knew the score. He was consumptive to his toenails, but over the years he'd given them so much trouble inside they wouldn't certify him for the prison hospital. Each day he systematically coughed up a little bit more of his lungs, and grinned and thumbed his nose. Don't bother telling me it's impossible for our prison authorities to function in any such cold-blooded manner. I was there.

If it hadn't been for Doc I'd have applied for parole when I was eligible at the end of three years. Go ahead, if you can't tough it out, he told me, but remember this: the minute you do it you're the yo-yo on the end of the string. The least little thing they don't like they twitch the line and back you come. Do the five, he urged me. Go out clean. Spit in their eye. Get a decent job, something you can't do with a parole officer checking on you every time you turn around.

You're young, Doc said to me. Develop something you can work at once in a while and show as a means of support when a prosecutor wants to put you over the jumps. Put in time on the job occasionally. Keep a name clean to work under, because when a judge hears no visible means of support, you're gone.

I'd been there already, so I knew he was right. I had an even better reason for listening to him, though. The swag from the bank job had never been recovered. I knew where it was, and Barney Pope knew where it was. Nobody else. They'd about taken that farmhouse to pieces, but they hadn't found it. At least not publicly. A man working alone could have tapped the till. That you never do know till you get back for a look.

The reason I was sure it hadn't been found officially was that every three months I had a visit from the FBI. They always came in pairs, sharp boys, smooth dressers with faces like polished steel. I used to wonder if they came in pairs to eliminate the chance of my splitting with a single man after making a deal.

Not that I ever knocked down to them. I always insisted I was an innocent hitchhiker caught up in the middle of a police-bankrobber gunfight. They knew better, but they couldn't crack me. Each time they came we'd go over the same tired old question-and-answer game about the whereabouts of the boodle. From me they got a big fat nothing.

I found out Doc was right the first time they came back after I was eligible for parole. They turned me upside down as to why I hadn't applied. I told them I liked it where I was. That was the day I moved up to the top of their list. I knew right then that as the first pigeon out of the coop I was due to get a hell of a lot of their attention the second I hit the street. When I did I wanted it to be with as few strings as possible.

I did the bit. The day I walked out of that stinking hole I didn't have to say mister to any man. And I'd made up my mind: I wasn't going back. I didn't care what it took to stay outside. I wasn't going back.

An FBI tail picked me up at the front gate. I rode with it until he got to thinking it was a breeze. The second day I triple-doored him in a hotel lobby, and lost him.

Give the devil his due. With nothing to go on but persistence, they located me at the first two jobs I found. I wasn't on parole, but I lost the jobs. They saw to that. I'll leave it to you whether they didn't want me working so I'd be driven back to the farmhouse and the swag.

I shook them for good finally by hitchhiking up into the Pacific Northwest and hooking on in a lumber camp. I never saw a town for a year and a half. The work damn near killed me at first, but I got to like it. When I came out of there I could handle a crosscut saw and a double-bitted axe with the best of them, and I could do things with a handgun people pay admission to see.

I drifted into tree work later on. It seemed a natural for part-time work, and for getting a close-up look at a few places I was interested in. Like banks. When I worked, I worked hard. If I couldn't promote something for myself, I had no trouble at all catching on anywhere with a crew.

It was eight years before I went back for the Massillon boodle. I didn't need the money—I'd had two good bank popovers almost back to back—but it seemed about time. The farmhouse was gone, the farm cut up into a sub-division. I had to buy a lot to do it, but I got the swag. The deed to that lot is still in a safety deposit box in the Riverman's Trust Company in Cincinnati.

In the can nights I used to read before lights-out. At first it was at Doc's insistence. Learn something, you lazy, illiterate slob, he'd say to me. He had two gods, the dictionary and the encyclopedia. I'd read aloud to him because he had incipient cataracts. He could have had them operated on, but I think he was afraid to let them work on him while he had any light left.

An encyclopedia article would start him talking. He'd been everywhere and seen everything, twice. There were no degrees from the school I attended, but I'd've had to be a complete jerk not to learn.

Doc had been a bank man himself. A blaster, of the old dynamite school. He had a lot of theories, but he wasn't afraid to admit the world had personally passed him by. Forget the gangs, he'd say to me. Forget the big, involved jobs that hang up on the first weak link, because there's always a weak link. Two good men is all it takes, he insisted. Smash them. Never let up on the pressure. Never take a backward step once you're committed.

I listened, and I developed some theories of my own. I worked it out down to a few decimal points while I was up in the lumber camp getting the smell of the FBI blown off me. I divorced myself for all time from the vault-blowing jobs and the armored-truck jobs and the kidnapping-the-bank-manager-and-his-wife jobs. That was the hard way. A fast, clean operation: that's what I wanted. Hit-and-run. Smash-and-grab. They'd get a look for a hundred fifty seconds, average, with the disadvantage of surprise.

When I left the west coast I drove to Atlantic City and looked up Bosco Sheerin. Bosco liked the sound of what I had to say. I was younger than he was, but I insisted on calling the play. Bosco went along with it. He was a happy-go-lucky type, anyway. We had a two year run that was peaches-and-cream. Then one night in Philadelphia the husband of the blonde Bosco had been seeing came home early. Bosco wound up on a morgue slab with foreign matter in his gizzard. I needed a new partner.

All told in eleven years I ran through four partners, but not one of them punched out on the job. They'd have been better off if I'd kept them working steadier, but how much money can you spend? I'm no big liver. I had a shack in Colorado at timberline on the road up to Pike's Peak. In June it would snow half the mornings, and in July there were still six foot drifts in the back yard. I had another place on the Connecticut River near the Vermont-New Hampshire border. If I was there in August, I'd jump over to Saratoga and make the race meeting. I tried to spend part of every winter in New Orleans, but when the notion took me I'd settle down for a month or two almost anywhere.

When Ed Morris was killed in a drunken argument in a bucket-of-blood in Santa Fe, I went a year without turning a trick. Then one night in a tavern in Newark I met Bunny. I watched him for a month, and I liked what I saw. He could handle himself, and he had the big advantage that he could pass as a deaf mute. He even knew the finger-language. He'd been small-time before I picked him up, but he did as he was told. After our first job he had complete confidence in me. He was the best partner I ever had.

Bunny—

I couldn't get away from the feeling that the scorecard was going to read five dead partners in thirteen years.

I entered the latched-back doors of the Suncoast Trust Company and approached a gray-haired woman near the railing enclosing the executive desks. "I'd like to see Mr. Craig," I said to her, handing her my card. "He won't know me. If he's busy, I'll wait."

"Will you have a seat, please, Mr. Arnold?" She rose and walked to the desk of a big man in a dark suit. She placed my card in front of him and said a few words. He looked up at me just as I turned from the railing to sit down. His eyes lingered on the flash I gave him of the double-bitted axe in its straps on the side of the tool kit. I sat down to wait.

The bank exterior might have been old-fashioned, but the interior showed signs of a recent face-lifting. Indirect fluorescent lighting was bright without being harsh. The tellers' cages were behind head-high glass panels. The only bars visible were around the vault that stood in the rear with its huge door gaping open.

A safe prediction nowadays is that a bank resculpting job will result in the appearance of a lot more glass at the expense of a lot less steel. Many tellers are as approachable as librarians. They've made it a little too easy. The pendulum's got to swing the other way. These people shoving notes and paper bags through tellers' windows are beginning to get under the skin of bank personnel. To say nothing of bank architects and the bonding companies.

In the forties, knocking off a bank on a smash-and-grab was tough tissue. It will be again. It goes in cycles. Right now the thinking is positively no violence within the bank. Whatever the bank-robber wants, give it to him. Most likely it will be recovered, and if it isn't, it's insured.

Human nature being what it is, people don't always follow the script. Bank guards suddenly acquire hero complexes. So do bank customers. It's a rare banker who hasn't testified at an inquest or two concerning the last moments of just such a paths-of-glory candidate.

The only edge a pro has is in the way he plans his getaway. The amateur is more likely than not to run into the beat patrolman's arms outside the door. Once outside the door, the pro's three-in-ten chances of getting that far blossom into three-in-four of going the rest of the way.

The amounts of cash carried even by branch banks today make anything over a job or two a year an unnecessary risk. It leaves time to study an operation. Most bankers tend to become rigid in their defensive thinking. A little probing for the soft—

"Mr. Arnold?"

I looked up. The big man in the dark suit was standing at a gate in the low railing, my card in his hand. His eyes were again on the tool chest at my feet. I rose to my feet. "Yes, sir."

"I'll have to ask you to keep it brief," he said, holding the gate open. I picked up the tool chest and followed him to his desk. Up close his color was flat-white, and there were pain-lines at the corners of his mouth. He had a big lion-like head with shaggy gray hair. He was still looking at the axe, so before he could sit down I slipped it from its loops and handed it to him.

He swung it lightly in his left hand, his right unbuttoning his jacket before he remembered where he was. He rebuttoned it. "Nice balance," he said. "Feels a bit light, though."

"You're a big man, Mr. Craig."

His mouth twisted wryly. "I was a big man." He sat down, running a fingertip along the helve. I hadn't made any mistake in coming here; this man had seen an axe or two before. "Make your own handles?"

"Yes, sir."

"I used to, too. Except for boning and polishing them." He handed me back the axe. "What's your business with me, Mr. Arnold?"

"I'd like to clean up the trees on your place up on Golden Hill Lane, Mr. Craig. They need it."

He nodded. "References?"

"Nothing local. I've been working up around Bellingham, Washington. Ducked out ahead of the rainy season. At your convenience I'd be glad to meet you at your place and show you I know my business. You were in lumber. I couldn't kid you three minutes."

He nodded again. "Per diem or flat contract?"

"Write your own ticket, Mr. Craig. I'll do a job for you, because with your recommendation there's work in this area I should be able to get. Like the Landscombe estate."

"Be out at my place at eight in the morning," he said. He rose to his feet. "When did you get into town, Arnold?"

"Yesterday afternoon." His calling me Arnold with no Mr. in front of it was the best sign yet. I was three-quarters of the way inside the door.

"I like your style. You've rounded up your information and boarded ship here this morning before the sun's over the yardarm. We've got a breed around here doesn't move that fast. Eight o'clock," he said again.

"I'll be there, Mr. Craig. And thanks."

"Don't thank me yet." His eyes had already returned to the papers on his desk. "If you can't cut the mustard, you don't get the job. And you're right about one thing: you won't be able to fool me. See you in the morning."

"With bells on," I promised. Walking away from his desk I slipped the axe back into its straps. At the counter I caught a fat lady's eye and opened up a checking account with eighteen hundred dollars in cash.

On the way out I glanced back at Craig's desk. I felt sure he'd know about that deposit by the time I saw him in the morning. I wanted him to know. I wanted to look to him like something more than a fly-by-night county-jumper.

Around Hudson, Florida, Roger Craig's good will could be as sharp a tool as any I had in my kit.

That afternoon I called Jed Raymond's real estate office from the motel. "Chet Arnold, the tree man, Jed," I said when I had his molasses drawl on the line. "Where do you recommend I do my drinking in town?"

"There's a place north of town on 19, Mr. Arnold. Its name is the Dixie Pig, but everyone calls it Hazel's."

"The name is Chet, son. Can I get a meal there?"

"If you're not a vegetarian. Hazel's got a habit of running a side of beef between a candle and a light bulb and calling it well-done steak. You've got to
watch it her steaks don't get up off the platter and bite you back."

"That's for me. See you out there?"

"Not tonight." Regret tinged his voice. "Tonight I'm doin' a little mis-
sionary work with a gal whose daddy's plannin' a development on the edge
of town. Ain't it hell what a man's got to do to make a livin'? Say, how'd
you make out with Roger Craig?"

"I take a test flight in the morning."

"Hurray for our side. Tell Hazel I sent you out there, Chet. Don't let her
bull you around. She's a character."

"Like what kind of a character?"

He laughed. "You'll see." He laughed again, and hung up.

I took a shower, and shaved and dressed. A drink and a good steak sounded
just about right. In the early twilight I drove north from the Lazy Susan. Five
hundred yards beyond the business district I took my foot off the gas as a big
German shepherd burst out of the underbrush and loped along the shoulder
of the road in front of me. I was still trying to decide if he was going to cut
across the road when a blue sedan swung around me. It must have been doing sixty-five in a thirty mile zone. The driver crossed over sharply in front
of me, out on the shoulder, and hit the dog. Deliberately.

At the last second the dog either heard or sensed the car. He jumped sideways, but not far enough. Either the fender or the wheel rolled him down into
the ditch. The blue sedan veered back onto the highway and roared off
down the road.

I stuck my foot into the accelerator and held it there for three seconds. Then
I took it off. I couldn't afford to catch that sonofabitch. If I left him lying in
a ditch I could be in trouble on the project that had brought me to Hudson.
I braked the Ford, went into reverse, and backed up. Maybe I could do something for the dog.

I stood on the edge of the ditch and looked down. The dog was trying to
get up. He had a long scrape on his head and one leg wasn't supporting him.
I reached in the car window and got my jacket off the back rest, wrapped it
tightly around my left hand and forearm, and scrambled down into the
ditch. The shepherd was still trying to get up. "You gonna let me help, fella?"
I asked him, and held out the wrapped arm until it touched him. I had to know
if he was hurting so bad he'd bite anything that came in contact with him.

He didn't bite. I moved closer, stooped down, and picked him up. He
growled a little, but that's all. An animal's got to be in a real bad way to bite
me. They just don't do it. He was a big dog, and it was a steep bank, but I
made it up to the car and put him on the front seat. I turned around and started
back to town. A guy walking on the road told me where I could find a vet.

"Shoulder sprain," the vet said when he'd gone over him on the table. "A few gashes. Nothing serious. He'll be lame for a week. Leave him with me overnight. Your dog? You ought to get tags for him."

As though on cue the shepherd reached up from the table and took my wrist in his mouth, lightly. "I'll get the tags tomorrow," I told the vet. "Give him whatever he needs."

Outside I had to stop and think where I'd been going.

I headed out north for the second time.

6

I had no trouble finding the Dixie Pig. It was a long, low building, encrusted with neon. No cars were parked in front although there were marked-off parking places. I followed a crushed stone driveway around to the rear and found a half-dozen cars. Evidently Hazel's customers didn't care to advertise their drinking habits to the highway.

Inside it was like a thousand others, low-ceilinged, smoke-musty, and dimly lit. The booths were empty. Six or eight customers lolled on the bar stools with their elbows on the bar. Nobody even looked around at me as I sat down.

A curtain rustled in an opening at the center back-bar, and a woman's head poked through. At the sight of a strange face she stepped in to the business side of the horseshoe-shaped bar. My first impression was that she was standing on elevated duckboards. She seemed enormous. I looked again. The back-bar flooring was on the same level as my side of the mahogany. She was enormous. Six feet if she was an inch, and bursting every seam of skin tight levis and a sleeveless fringed buckskin shirt that was no more than a vest. Her upper arms for size looked like John L. Sullivan's, but the skin was like a baby's. She had red hair, and a pleasantly wide mouth. She wasn't young, but she was youthful-looking.

"What'll it be, pardner?" she asked me. Her voice was a ripened contralto, deep and rich.

"You're Hazel?" She nodded.

"I'm Chet Arnold. Jed Raymond sent me by. Make it bourbon and branch."

She smiled, displaying two gold teeth evenly spaced in the center of the attractive mouth. "Jed's a good kid." She turned to the bottled array behind her, and I watched the smooth ripple of muscle in her forearm as she poured my drink. I couldn't see an ounce of fat on the woman, but I'd have bet she outweighed me twenty pounds. She was the best looking big woman I'd ever seen.

She examined me frankly as she set the drink down. "Stayin' with us a while?"

"Depends," I said. "I'm prospecting. I make like Tarzan for a living, only with more equipment. I swing through the trees with an axe and a saw in my belt."

Her head was cocked to one side as she took me in feature by feature, the powerful-looking arms folded over her superb big breasts. "I'm not so damn sure you've got the face for that kind of work," she said finally. I've been in front of X-ray machines that didn't get as close to the bone as that woman's eyes.

I moved onto the offensive. "You off a ranch around Kingman, Hazel?"

The deep voice warmed. "Not bad for a guess. Nevada, not Arizona. I was raised in McGill, north of Ely. Raised? Make it roped. I get so homesick for the rimrock country sometimes I could bawl like a week-old calf."

"The planes are still flying," I suggested.

She shook her good-looking head. "I'm married to this goddam place. I just drink another fifth of my five-star shellac and forget about it. Did you want to eat?"

"Jed said you featured steak."

"Jed said right. Take your drink over to the booth there." She pointed to a corner. "I'll put the steak on the fire."

When she brought it to the booth twenty minutes later with a mound of french fries and a couple pounds of sliced tomatoes, I ate for a quarter hour without coming up for air. I mean that was a piece of meat.

I was divot-digging with a toothpick when Hazel came back to the booth. "Apple pie? Coffee?" she wanted to know.

I tested my straining belt. "Better raincheck me."

She glanced over at the bar. Everything was quiet. Standing beside me, I had my first look at her feet. She had on worked leather cowboy boots studded with silver conches. They went for one-fifty if they went for a quarter. She slid into the booth opposite me and sat down with her chin propped in her hands. Her calm inspection raked me fore and aft. "Maybe it's not the face," she decided. "Maybe it's the eyes. What do you really do for a living, Chet?"

I reached for my cigarettes, offered her one, and got two going when she accepted. "Your pa should have hair-brushed you out of asking questions like that," I told her.

"My pa never hairbrushed me out of anything I wanted to do," she answered. "Well?"

"I've been known to make a bet once in a while," I humored her.

"That's more like it," she said briskly. "A workingman you're not. What's your action? Horses?"

"Horses," I agreed.

"Is that right?" She straightened up as though someone had turned on an electric current in the booth bench. "D'you remember old Northern Star? I saw him one time at Delaware Park run five an' a half furlongs in a tick less—"

So we sat and played Remember When.

It's a damn small world sometimes. Hazel's first husband had been Blueshirt Charlie Andrews, the man who bet 'em higher than a duck can fly. I'd never met him, but he'd been a pal of a friend of mine who unfortunately attracted a small piece of lead a few years back. This I did not tell Hazel.

In five minutes we found out we'd both been in Baltimore for the Pimlico Futurity in which Platter had hung it on By Jimminy, one of the last big bets the Bradley camp blew before the old gentleman checked to his last openers.

We argued whether it had been '43 or '44. I held out for '44.

"I *know* it was '43," Hazel insisted. "It was my first year at the tracks. I was seventeen."

"Which makes you—"

"Never mind the arithmetic, horseman."

"—younger than I am," I finished.

Her inward look turned back down the years. "Charlie Andrews was about the ugliest man I ever knew, I guess. He stopped off for a cup of coffee in a diner in Ely where I was a waitress. He was on his way to the coast, but three weeks later he was still in the diner tryin' to talk me into sharin' it. He was about as subtle as a blowtorch, an' I was green as grass and scared to death. He'd sit across the counter from me, takin' up most of two stools— he was about five five an' weighed two-forty, an' even his ears had muscles— an' he'd say to me, 'Hazel, honey, you got a croup jus' like a thoroughbred mare. I never hope to see a bigger piece of ass.'" She shook her head reminiscently. "He married it to get it. He was a lot of all right, that Blueshirt man. Although it sure was chicken today an' feathers tomorrow livin' with him. That man would bet on anything."

Some people came in the back door, and she stood up to go back to the bar to wait on them. "Don't go away, horseman," she said over her shoulder. "I don't get a chance to talk the language much these days."

I knew what she meant. It's a special language. When Jed Raymond walked in at eleven o'clock we were still at it, re-running races of fifteen years ago. "You must have had the password, Chet," he said to me. "Our hostess doesn't usually unbend like this to the hoi-polloi."

Hazel reached up from the booth and hit him a casual backhander in the chest that nearly collapsed him. "This guy is with it, Jed," she said, leveling a thumb at me. "Where'd you find him?"

"He found me," Jed answered when he could get his breath. "Lay off that strong-arm stuff, woman, or I'll call out the militia on you." He sat down in the booth beside me. "One for the road?"

"One," I agreed. "Then I've got to get out of here. I'm making like a workingman in the morning."

Driving back to the motel twenty minutes later, Hazel's big, handsome face danced in the windshield. With her hearty laugh and golden smile she was the most woman I'd seen in a hell of a while.

For a time I'd nearly forgotten the shape of things.

It wouldn't do.

I pulled into Roger Craig's elliptical gravelled driveway at five minutes to eight. I was wearing my poor-but-honest khakis. Craig was already out in the side yard superintending a young colored boy setting up an eight-foot section of slash pine about a foot and a half in diameter. If this was the test it was going to be a joke. Slash pine is so soft I could have handled it with my teeth. Still, Craig was a native, and this was the wood he knew.

I opened the back deck of the Ford and slid out my big tool chest, and a couple of coils of rope. Craig nodded to me jovially. I could see he knew about the deposit. His manner was a lot easier. Unless I cut a leg off, I had the job. He needed the work done, and I was now a customer of the bank.

I strapped on safety belt and climbers, opened the chest and took out a pair of goggles, and unslung the lighter of the axes. "All set, Mr. Craig?"

"Whenever you're ready, Arnold."

I walked up to the pine log and tested it for balance. It was wedged firmly. I settled myself in front of it, digging in with my heels in the soft turf. With wood like this I had no need for a long, over-the-head axe stroke. Just as well for a still stiff arm. I went at it from shoulder height, placing the cuts more with an eye to accuracy than speed. Still, a deep V narrowed rapidly as the axe rang with the mellow sound of good steel, and the fat white chunk chips flew in a solid shower. Chips were still in the air when I stepped back with the pine log in two sections. The colored boy stood off to one side with wide-rounded eyes.

"I wish I could have tried you a few years back," Craig said. There was a wistful note in his voice.

I almost made the mistake of handing him the axe. That would really have been rubbing it in on a heart attack victim. I pushed back the goggles as I caught myself just in time. "I'd have asked for a handicap," I told him. "You've got a press agent downtown. Bright young fella in the real estate office over Woolworth's. He says you could really go."

Craig smiled with pleasure. "Jed Raymond. Good boy. Knows his way around the woods, too." The smile faded. "I get damn tired of being half a man these days." He turned businesslike. "I didn't want to give you buck fever by telling you beforehand, but you were trying out for two jobs. I ran into Judge Carberry at the club last night. Drop around and see him when you finish up here." He held up a restraining hand when I would have spoken. "What do you propose to do for me?"

"I'll do it all." I waved at the driveway. "I'll shape up that low-bush ficus and wax myrtle when I finish with the trees." I turned to the side of the house. "Just about all of it needs thinning and trimming, especially the live oaks and that shagbark hickory. See the dead limb on that sycamore? On the other side of the house you've got two bad palmettos. The one nearest the house definitely ought to come down. Maybe the other one can be saved." I ran over it in my mind. "All told, two and a half or three day's work."

He nodded. "You're the doctor." He smiled again. "Literally, by God. Jeff here will give you a hand as you go. Just waggle that axe at him when you want him to move." Jeff showed a mouthful of teeth in an expressive grin. "I'll let the Judge know he can expect to see you when you finish here."

"I appreciate it, Mr. Craig."

"Stop in and see me at the bank any time you're ready." He went into the house, and five minutes later his car eased down the opposite loop of the driveway.

I smoked my before-climbing cigarette while I walked around the yard planning the day. One of Roger Craig's forebears had had an eye for trees. There was something for everyone. In the northwest corner he had the biggest magnolia I'd ever seen. It must have gone seventy feet. He had chinquapin, sassafras, sweet gum, red birch, and mimosa. On the other side I'd seen cottonwood and aspen. He even had a chinaberry tree.

It was a bright, sunny morning, and the air felt crisp. It was established in Hudson, Florida, and my sponsorship was the best. With a start like this if I couldn't ease up on the blind side of whoever had sandbagged Bunny, then there was something the matter with me.

I climbed upstairs and went to work. Most of the morning I thinned out tops, occasionally marking a larger limb that had to go. Jeff dogged me from beneath as I moved from tree to tree, raking and burning the scut. At noon I called down to him to grab himself a sandwich. I never stop myself. In the trees food is just so much extra weight. I go right through from eight to four.

In the afternoon I tied three different weight crosscut saws to my belt, and shouldered up a coil of rope. I went to work on the larger stuff. I'd undercut it first, then rope it to the trunk and lower it carefully to Jeff standing beneath when the overcut snapped it off. I wanted no heavy drops tearing up the side of the house or scarring the lawn.

The last half hour I trimmed up stubs and daubed them with paste. I knocked it off at four sharp. I was tired, but not unpleasantly so. The arm had held up well. It was the first real day's work I'd done since I'd cased the bank in Okmulgee, Oklahoma. I'd finally decided against trying, but I'm never too much out of shape.

I packed the gear back into the Ford, told Jeff I'd see him in the morning, and headed for the Lazy Susan and a shower. In the square the traffic light caught me, and I sat there waiting for it to change so I could swing south on 19. I had to hold up for a second after it changed as a slim, redheaded man limped hurriedly across the street in front of me, against the light.

I turned the corner with a teasing tickle in the back of my mind: had I seen him before, or just someone who looked like him? When you move around the way I do, it's hard to fit faces to locations sometimes.

Then it hit me.

The last time I'd seen that limping redhead he'd been out in Manny Sebastian's parking lot in Mobile with the hood up on my car.

I turned into the first vacant parking space.

I got out of the Ford and walked back up the street.

I sat at the wobbly desk in the motel room and spread out under the light the real-estate map of the area I'd bummed from Jed Raymond. On the floor at my feet the German shepherd lay with his muzzle on his paws, his brown eyes watching me steadily. I'd stopped at the vet's and picked him up after I'd spent a fruitless thirty minutes quartering downtown Hudson in a search for the redhead I'd last seen three hundred fifty miles away. I hadn't been able to find a trace of him.

Seeing him meant the honeymoon was over for me. There was only one reason he could be in Hudson. Manny Sebastian had decided to cut himself in on the Phoenix $178,000. It wasn't very bright of Manny. I had to give it a little thought to work out just how I was going to change his mind. Because I was definitely going to change it. First, though, there was the matter of locating the stuff myself.

The shepherd's shoulder was stiff, but he could walk. The scrape on his head had been nothing serious. "How you doin', Kaiser?" I asked him. His big tail thumped the rug. His head came up, and his new tags glistened on his new spiked collar. A twenty dollar bill had straightened me out with the motel proprietor over the added starter in the unit. It wasn't his busy season, so he could afford not to give me an argument.

I turned to the map. Finding the sack with the money in it had suddenly taken on a priority. Since seeing the redhead, I couldn't take this thing in second gear. Slow and easy was out. I had to get moving. I knew Bunny wouldn't have dug himself in too far out of town, but he wouldn't have set up a tent in front of the city hall, either. He liked to batch it alone where he wouldn't attract attention. It was one of the things I'd liked about him.

Looking at the map, I tentatively ruled out the north-south stretch of U.S. 19 above and below the square as the least likely section for Bunny to hole up in. Too much traffic. Too many people. That left Main Street east from the traffic light. And because of Thirty Mile Swamp to the south, it left Main Street to the north. I took a pencil and marked lightly—beginning at the edge of town—two points five miles apart, as close as I could figure it by the map scale. If I drove up every road leading north off Main in that stretch, I might not find Bunny but I might find a blue Dodge sedan with Arizona plates. An automobile is harder to dismaterialize than you'd think. Even the burned-out skeleton of a car would be a starting place.

I looked at my watch. I still had an hour of daylight. "Come on, boy," I said to the shepherd. He was up at once, hobbling but expectant. Out in the yard he was ready to jump up into the front seat when I opened the car door. I picked him up and put him in. "We'll pamper you for a day or two," I told him. He nuzzled my arm and sat down, dignified as a college president.

I went around to the trunk and hauled out knee-high boots, a machete for

underbrush, and a steel-shafted number 3 iron for snakes. I'd seen enough of
the side roads around Hudson to know I'd be doing as much walking as riding. I'd cover every towpath a car or a man could get over in that five-mile
stretch, and if that didn't turn up anything, I'd mark off another five-mile
stretch and do it again. I'd cover it a yard at a time, if I had to. Whatever it
took to do it, I was going to find Bunny.

We drove out Main, out of town, Kaiser sitting up to the window as steady
as a sergeant-major on dress parade. He had a big head and a wicked-looking
mouthful of teeth. His coat was mostly gray, flecked with brown in front. He
looked all business, sitting up there.

The first two roads I turned up weren't bad. The third one I took one look,
pulled the Ford in off the road, and changed to the boots. I didn't have enough
daylight left to do much that night, but I wanted to get the feel of it. In the
first hundred yards I found out I had a bull by the nose. Clouds of gnats and
mosquitoes dive-bombed me. I lunged through knee-deep brush, chopping
steadily, perspiration streaming, only the signs of recent car passage luring me
on to end-of-track. When the ruts petered out by an abandoned tarpaper shack
I turned around and slogged my way back.

I came out on the road again to find a two-tone county cruiser pulled in behind the Ford, and Kaiser showing a handsome set of fangs to a uniformed man
trying to look into the front seat. My brush-crackling progress announced me,
and the man turned to look me up and down.

"Deputy Sheriff Franklin," he said curtly. "You'd better keep that damn
wolf on a leash." I said nothing. Franklin was a stocky man with a red face
of the type much exposed to weather. His gray uniform trousers had red piping on the sides, and his khaki shirt was open at the throat. "What's your business out here?" he asked me.

"I'm a timber cruiser," I said.

"You're a what?"

"I'm scouting the area looking for a stand of second growth black maple I
hear is in here."

He scowled. "We're two hundred miles too far south for black maple. If you
know your business, you know that." He glanced in at the weedy-looking trees
shooting up in an area that had been viciously slash-cut years before.

I shook my head firmly. "I had a drink the other night with an old-timer who
told me they took a million feet of black maple out of here fifty years ago.
Should be a buck in it today for the guy that finds the right spot, if the slash
hasn't been burned over." Franklin was studying me. "I'm doing a job of work
for Mr. Craig and Judge Carberry back in town," I added.

Whatever he'd been going to say, the names stopped him. He wasn't the
type to bow out gracefully, though. He swaggered around to the rear of the
Ford and made a production of taking down the license plate number. "We
keep an eye on these badlands," he said gruffly, and stalked back to the cruiser.

He backed out on the road at fifty miles an hour, punched the shift panel on the dash, and roared down the road, wide open.

I changed back to my cordovans, put boots, machete, and golf club back in the trunk, and patted Kaiser's big head as I got back into the Ford. "Good dog," I told him. He rrrrr'd deep in his throat, and nipped at my arm. I had a feeling Kaiser and I understood one another about uniforms.

It was full twilight when I got back to the motel.

I began to make it a habit to eat my evening meal at Hazel's. Jed frequently joined me, and we'd sit over a drink and talk, and when the bar wasn't busy Hazel would join us.

Like a lot of salesmen I've known, Jed was a complete extrovert. In a roomful of people he'd crawl onto Hazel's lap and talk baby-talk to her. He had a high-pitched, infectious laugh that turned every head in a room. With all that he was a sharp-witted kid who looked in both directions before crossing the street.

Between them Jed and Hazel knew every living soul for fifty miles. I sat and listened while they rattled family skeletons past and present twenty to the dozen. Early in the game I introduced the subject of the post office. They shook a few feathers loose from that bird, but I couldn't see anything meant for me.

Lucille Grimes was the postmistress, widow of a former postmaster deceased five years. Jed said the town couldn't understand why she didn't remarry, since she had suitors and to spare. He also said zestfully that she was a tall, leggy, cool-looking blonde.

Hazel had her own ideas as to why the beauteous Lucille hadn't remarried. She hinted darkly that the favored suitor already had a wife. Since Hazel, minus her usual spade-is-a-shovel outspokenness, failed to name him, I deduced that he was a Dixie Pig customer. From Hazel's attitude, Lucille Grimes was not one of her favorite people. Jed kidded her about it.

In all of it there was nothing for me that I could see, but that post office bothered me.

It took me eight working days to clean up the Craig and Landscombe properties. Evenings I got out and plowed up the side roads on the north side of Main, and discovered nothing. When I finished with the Craig and Landscombe places, nobody remarked on the fact that I didn't seem to be knocking down any stone walls looking for more work. The sun coast of Florida is an easy-going neighborhood.

Jed led an active social life, even for a young fellow his age. The nights he didn't show up for dinner, after a couple or three times of my eating alone, it came to be understood that if I'd postpone my own meal to seven thirty, Hazel would serve us both in the corner booth. Over coffee and cigarettes we'd sit and swap lies about horses and horseplayers we'd known.

The big girl was comfortable to be around. Once in a while she'd have to get up and tend bar, but not too often. She did her real business from nine thirty to midnight. At the tracks she'd seen them all from Ak-Sar-Ben to Woodbine. She didn't go back as far as I did by a dozen years, but as the evenings passed it was odd to see how many times we'd been in the same town at the same time. She'd seen Papa Redbird win the Arlington Classic in '48, and Rough'n Tumble the Santa Anita Derby in '51. So had I. She'd seen Turn-To win the first Garden State, and she'd been in New Orleans the winter old Tenacious first took charge. So had I. It wasn't the biggest club in the world.

Jed warned me Hazel could be moody, and her drinking a problem. I saw no sign of either. With me I think she had a chance to let off steam that had been a long time bottled up. Blueshirt Charlie Andrews had died five years before of a heart attack. Hazel had rushed into and out of a no-good second marriage, the only legacy of which was the Dixie Pig.

I liked her. I could tell she had guts. I knew she'd spit in the eye of the devil himself.

I enjoyed it, sitting around batting the breeze about the old days, but way down deep inside I was getting restless.

It wasn't what I had come for.

We were sitting in the corner booth one night, waiting for Jed. Hazel, as usual, was talking horses. Like all horseplayers, she had strong opinions. Arguing, she'd get excited; her eyes would flash, and she'd pound the table.

She held out for Citation as the best she'd ever seen. I was on the coast the summer Citation couldn't get past Noor in the stretch four straight races. I know he'd been away a year, and I know he wasn't what he had been. Regardless, I've never since been able to make him the best.

I go with Count Fleet. He didn't beat horses, he murdered them. I saw him win the Walden at Pimlico by thirty lengths. Look it up. Thirty lengths. And don't ask me who he beat. He beat the best there was around. No horse can do any more. When he came out of the far turn with his mane and tail streaming and the rest of them nowhere, it was enough to stop your heart.

It's been one of my secret sorrows that he never bred anything approximating himself as a runner. Stake winners, yes, but no Count Fleets. I think now the big horse will come from one of his fillies. If I owned a Count Fleet filly, all the gold in Fort Knox couldn't buy her. Some one of these days a broodmare by him is going to throw a jimdandy.

The forum broke up when Jed came in. He sat down, and Hazel went out back to start the steaks. The bar became busy with before-dinner thirst quenchers and she didn't come back. Everyone came in the back door. As far as I could see Hazel could have nailed up the front door and never lost a nickel's worth of business.

THE NAME OF THE GAME IS DEATH

Jed was in high good humor. "Made a sale today," he informed me. "Drink up, drink up. I'll buy you one. Got to keep the money of the country circu-latin'."

"You can buy me a brandy after dinner," I told him. I could see I'd lost his attention. From his side of the booth he could look out over the back parking lot, and he was leaning forward to look more closely.

"Well, well, well," he said softly. "Here's company for us." He stood up, a bright, artificial smile pasted on his face as a tall blonde walked in the back door. "Here's Miss Lucille now," he said loudly enough to be heard by her. "Maybe she'll have a drink with us." He moved out of the booth.

I could hear his laughing cajolery as he intercepted her in the middle of the floor. In seconds he was leading her to our booth. "—Ol' Chet's been ad-mirin' your post office, especially the fixtures that aren't government issue," he was saying. He winked at me as I rose. "Lucille Grimes, Chet Arnold. Chet's a tree surgeon, Lucille." He grinned at her. "I don't need to introduce you in your official capacity. Chet knew who our beautiful postmistress was fifteen minutes after he'd hit town."

"Won't you sit down, Miss Grimes?" I offered, to cut off the flow of words. She murmured something and slid into the booth opposite me. Her face was cool-looking and composed under the blonde hair. Her face was a bit too long and pointed from brow to chin, but with good features. Her skin was pale, and her eyes surprisingly dark for her low-keyed complexion. Despite the lack of high points, there was nothing washed-out in her appearance.

Jed pushed in beside her and called for drinks. Lucille Grimes folded slim, capable-looking hands on the booth table and looked at me directly. "I hear you're a very capable workman, Mr. Arnold," she said. Her voice was low-keyed, too. No stress or strain.

"Thank you, Miss Gr—"

"Hear, hear," Jed interrupted. "Lucille, meet Chet. Chet, meet Lucille. What's all this Mr. an' Miss business?" He stood up and advanced on the jukebox in the corner. He fed it coins and punched buttons indiscriminately. "Dance?" he offered Lucille, returning to the booth. "Illegal, but the custom of the country," he grinned down at me. He returned his attention to her. "Join us for dinner? Private little celebration of mine."

"Another time, thanks." She sounded genuinely regretful. She danced with Jed. She danced with me. I'm not much of a dancer, but she followed me easily. She wasn't nearly as willowy as I'd thought seeing her come in the back door. She filled a man's arms. I tried to guess her age. Thirty, maybe.

I was on the floor with her when the back door opened again to admit a stocky man in gray uniform trousers with red piping on the side and a khaki shirt open at the throat. My friend from the road the other day, I thought, rec-ognizing the blunt red face. He sat down at the bar and ordered a beer.

After another dance with Jed, Lucille excused herself. "It's been very pleas-

ant," she said to both of us. She smiled at us impartially, gathered up gloves
and bag, and exited through the rear door. Three minutes later the stocky man
left his half-finished beer and followed.

Jed watched me take this in. "They're not usually that obvious, Chet.
That's Bart Franklin, one of our risin' young deputies. Known as Blaze, due
to a well-advertised short temper. I'm a jack-leg deputy around here myself
in emergencies. Blaze isn't one of our better-loved members. He's gone for the
blonde widow."

"Thanks, son. It always helps to know if another dog's after the same bone."

"You go for her?" he asked in a half-protesting tone. "I brought her over because I remembered you asked about her the other night, but—" He shook
his head. "It's all yours, man. Yours and Blaze's. I tell you that gal spooks me.
Somethin' about her just—"

"Nothing another ten years wouldn't help you to handle," I told him as he
sat there wagging his head. The conversation died as Hazel brought the meal.
Jed left at eight thirty to keep a date, and I said so long to Hazel shortly afterward.

I drove back to town, parked in the square, and went into my act. A week
ago I'd marked off four taverns as the type most likely to have attracted
Bunny's trade. Every night I stopped off in two of them for a glass of beer.
I'd sit in each for half an hour, exchanging an occasional word with the bartender. They all knew me now when I came in, and had my beer drawn before I said a word.

Starting with the friendliest, in another few days I'd throw each of them
the same bait. "What's become of that big, dark, quiet fella used to be in here
around this time of night?" I'd ask them. "Haven't seen him lately."

They'd try to remember. A bartender's customers come and go. "Oh, yeah,
the big guy," I hoped one or more of them would say. "That's right, he has-
n't been around, has he?"

If they remembered him, I might get a lead. I needed a lead, badly. I was
on my second five-mile stretch of side roads, and I'd found nothing. If a bartender even remembered the direction Bunny drove off whenever he left the
tavern, it would be more than I had now.

I couldn't racket around this town asking for Dick Pierce. A small town is
wired together so tight it would be sure to get back to the interested party.
Of course if I crapped out all around the green-covered table trying to find
Bunny, a direct inquiry was my ace in the hole.

The day I asked, though, I had to be ready for anything.

I wasn't planning on it.

Not yet.

7

The next night I was making the second of my tavern stops when the limping redhead made a mistake. He didn't know it was a mistake, because he didn't know I'd seen him in Mobile. I'd just climbed out of the Ford, ready to go inside for a beer I didn't want, when he cruised by in a black sedan at about eight miles an hour. I got a good look at him. He didn't turn his head to look at me. He just went on by. The sedan turned the corner above the tavern, and pulled into the curb and stopped. I could tell by the reflection from the headlights. I knew the redhead was tailing me as plainly as if he'd written me a letter.

I went on inside and had the beer, talked a little baseball to the bartender, Bobby Herman, and gave some thought to the redhead. The minute I'd seen him on the street the day before I'd decided he was a luxury I couldn't afford. That left two things to be settled: finding out if he'd already reported back to Manny Sebastian where he'd followed me to, and how I was going to get rid of him.

I said goodnight to Bobby Herman and went back outside to the Ford. I pulled ahead and turned the same corner the black sedan had turned. There wasn't a car in sight, parked or moving. I circled the block twice without seeing a thing. I was just beginning to get a good mad on at myself for having lost him again when car headlights picked me up from about thirty yards behind me. I don't know where he came from. The sonofabitch was good. Tailing a man in a car without calling attention to yourself takes ingenuity. This boy had it.

I took him back uptown and east on Main from the traffic light. Out on the edge of town I settled down to a steady fifty miles an hour. I was in no hurry. Somewhere out in the boondocks I'd find a place to leave him, permanently.

In the first five miles I found out how he'd been able to follow me all the way down from Mobile without my getting wise. He was an artist with an automobile. When he had room to maneuver he didn't just lock himself onto my taillight and leave me to wonder eventually about the lights in the rear-view mirror that remained the same distance behind. There was only a sliver of moon, but he rode some straight stretches with his lights out. For short distances he'd be bumper-to-bumper with me, and then I wouldn't see him at all for miles. Twice he passed me, once doing about eighty, only to pick me up again from behind. The first time he went by I wasted a look at his license plate. It was carefully, unreadably mud-spattered.

Twenty five miles up the line I came out of the woodsy darkness enveloping the road into a sleepy-looking, wide-place-in-the-highway town with a blinking yellow light at an intersection surrounded by darkened storefronts.

The only other illumination was a lighted telephone booth on the main street, just before the blinker. I turned right at the intersection, right again at the next corner, and right again at the next. I was out of the car and sprinting down an alley between two stores before the redhead's headlights turned the last corner and cruised down past the Ford.

The last time I'd parked he'd turned the next corner and pulled in. I was gambling he'd follow a pattern. If he did, I had him in my pocket. I cut left through a bisecting alley, running for the main street.

I was in time to see his headlights arc around as he swung the corner. Sure enough, his car went past me and stopped not fifteen feet from the phone booth. He'd cut his lights before he even stopped rolling. He'd seen I wasn't in the Ford when he went by. In his own mind he could be getting close to the payoff. He was, but not the kind he expected. He climbed out in a rush, took a quick look around the silent town, and started to head back up the street to the corner he'd just turned. He didn't want to lose me.

He didn't.

I stepped out of the alleyway and intercepted him, the Smith & Wesson in my hand. "Hi, Red," I said to him. "How're things in Mobile?"

It would have stopped the average man's heartbeat. This was a different breed of rooster. Even in the poor light I could see him straightening his face out as he went into a deadpan look. "You got me wrong, Jack," he protested.

"Walk up to the phone booth," I told him. I wanted to see his face in the light when I asked him the question that was bothering me. I followed right behind him, shoving the gun under my armpit. "Get inside it," I said when he reached the booth. "Make out you're dialing." He took down the receiver before he turned to look out at me. "Don't make the mistake of putting your hand in your pocket for change."

"You're makin' a big—"

"You must be the wheelman who wanted the Ford," I cut him off. "Manny tell you you could have it if you kept tabs on me for him?"

It must have rocked him, but he didn't lose his nerve. "I don't know any Manny," he said sullenly. "You off your rocker?" He was eyeing me, wondering where the gun had gone. He had a thin, pale face with a scattering of freckles.

"Have you called Manny since you followed me into Hudson, Red?"

He dropped all pretense. "Manny says you're a tough boy," he sneered. "You don't look so tough to me."

"One more time, Red," I told him softly. "Have you called Manny since—"

"Up, with a meathook, buster!" Red snatched the booth door closed with his left hand while he went for the gun in his shoulder holster with his right. His hand was still on its way under his lapel when I put one in his chest and one in his ear. Both of them took chunks of booth glass before they took chunks of Red. He did a slow corkscrew to the booth floor, the freckles stark in his white face. I emptied the Smith & Wesson into the booth, spraying it from top to bottom. I put the last one into the light. Nobody was going to call this one a sharpshooting job.

I went up the alley at a good clip and right-angled back to the Ford. I reversed it up to the next corner without putting my lights on, then retraced the way I'd driven in there. I put my lights on just before I hit the blinker. Lights were popping on in houses here and there as I swung left and headed for the Lazy Susan.

With the booth light out they'd be a while finding Red. When they did, they'd be another while trying to unscramble the jigsaw. I put the Smith & Wesson on the seat beside me in case I had to pitch it if anything came up behind me. I held it down to fifty all the way back. I only passed three cars on the way, and nothing passed me. Kaiser greeted me at the motel-room door. He stretched out at my feet and watched for twenty minutes with only an occasional blink as I cleaned, oiled, and reloaded the Smith & Wesson.

I didn't know whether Manny knew where to find me or not. I knew that if he didn't, he wasn't going to.

I went to bed.

On my next trip out to the Dixie Pig I took Kaiser along with me. There was the usual sprinkling of a dozen cars parked out in back, including Jed Raymond's sports car. I went in with Kaiser padding sedately along beside me, and Jed waved from a booth. I was two-thirds of the way across the floor before I saw Lucille Grimes with her back to me in the booth opposite him.

Jed, with his fey grin, tried to maneuver me into sitting beside Lucille. I pushed him over and sat down beside him. "Good evening, all," I greeted them.

Lucille smiled but didn't speak. Jed reached under the table to pat Kaiser who sat down beside me. I watched closely but Kaiser didn't take any offense. "Hi, there, big boy," Jed said to him. "Who's your gentleman friend, Chet?"

"Kaiser, meet Jed," I introduced them. I noticed that the blonde's long legs were as far withdrawn beneath the booth as she could manage. Evidently Lucille wasn't an animal lover. "Well, folks, what's the chief topic of conversation?" I inquired.

"The star-spangled, unmitigated dullness of life in a small town," Jed answered promptly. "Right, Lucille?"

Her thin smile was noncommittal. "I don't believe I have too many complaints," she said. "And perhaps Chet hasn't always lived in a small town."

Jed got me off that hook. "They're all small," he asserted. "The biggest of them are small, even New York City. How much town can you live in? Outside of a couple of blocks near where you work and a couple of blocks near where you sleep, the rest is as strange as to a visitor from Beluchistan. I'll take little old Hudson."

"Which side of the argument are you on, anyway?" Lucille wanted to know. "You're complaining about dullness, but you'll take little old Hudson. Page the Chamber of Commerce." I thought she looked tired. There were dark circles under her eyes. She kept watching the parking lot through the booth window. So did I, but not as obviously. We hadn't long to wait. A two-tone county sheriff's department cruiser swung slowly through the lot and down the driveway on the other side. The blonde gathered up her gloves and bag. "You'll have to excuse me, gentlemen," she said, rising. "Good night."

"For a guy slaverin' for blonde meat you don't move very fast," Jed accused me when she'd gone.

"You young sprouts just don't understand the logistics of my generation," I told him. "Our theme song is 'But They Get There Just the Same.' Pay attention; you could learn something. Your technique is all wrong."

"Not since I got out of high school it hasn't been," Jed asserted cheerfully. He turned serious. "Listen, don't let me needle you about the widow. She's—well, there's better fish in the creek. Whyn't you let me slip you a number or two from my little black book?"

"Just because a county cruiser circles the parking lot?" I asked him.

He nodded. "So you saw it, too. Blaze Franklin—" Jed hesitated. "Blaze is a little bit primitive. You know? Red-necked all the time. Who needs it to get involved with a thick turd like that?"

"So he's the jealous type."

"In spades, he's the jealous type." Jed pushed his glass around in the wet circles on the table top without looking at me. "I've heard some stories about Blaze." He turned to grin at me. "Some of them might even be true. Hey, Hazel!" he hollered over to the bar in a quick change of subject. "Bring on the fatted calf!"

We ate diligently, with Jed feeding small cuts of his steak to Kaiser, who accepted them with dignity. "You'll spoil him," I told Jed.

"He can stand spoiling. That's a lot of dog. I like his looks." He glanced at his watch. "Say, I got to get going."

When he left I sat around waiting to see if Hazel was going to be able to get away from the bar long enough to sit down. I got a surprise when she did. The first thing I noticed was that she was wearing a dress. She must have changed since she'd served us. It was the first time I'd seen her in anything but the skin-tight levis. Her hair looked different, too. She'd done something to it.

"What's the occasion?" I asked her as she unloaded the tray she'd brought over. I took another look when she set a drink down on her side of the booth table, too. I'd never seen her take a drink before.

"No occasion." Her voice sounded husky. "Every once in a while I take a notion to give the animals something to think about besides my ass." She plunked herself down across from me.

Now that I was looking at her, her eyes indicated that the drink in front of her wouldn't be her first for the day. I remembered Jed's warnings about her drinking. I wondered if the storm signals were up.

She wouldn't have appreciated it, probably, but I decided I liked her better in the levis. They suited her, somehow. In the western ensemble she was the most female-looking mammal I'd seen in a long time. I wasn't the only one to notice it. Every once in a while a half-splashed customer would get carried away by the levis and acquire a sudden biological urge. Hazel fractured the house every time with her rebuttal. "What's with you, fella?" she'd pounce on him in that deep voice, half purr, half growl. "Your insurance paid up? Nobody told you I got my own cemetery out in back for wise guys snatchin' a feel?" Hazel was no shrinking violet. It took a hardy ego to survive that little speech with the speaker looking down on the red-faced snatcher from an average two to four inches superior height.

Hazel tossed off her drink in a swallow and accepted my light for her cigarette. She still had on her cowboy boots, and the heel of one tapped steadily. Kaiser's ears pricked forward as he lay on the floor beside me.

"I need another drink," Hazel announced. She continued right on without waiting for me to reply, if I'd been going to. "I'm not a blonde, but whatever she's got I'll double and throw away the change. I'll be closing up at twelve fifteen tonight. Come back and pick me up."

I opened my mouth, and closed it again. "Twelve fifteen," I said finally.

She nodded, ground out her cigarette in the ashtray, and got up and went back to the bar. She didn't come back.

I had time to kill. On the way into town I thought about Hazel. I liked her. She was easy to talk to. She had a caustic good humor. Despite the gold teeth, when she took the trouble to fix herself up she was a damn handsome woman.

But—

Ahhh, what the hell, I told myself. Play the hand the way the cards are dealt. What did I have to lose?

I backed off in a hurry from that bit of bravado. I knew what I had to lose.

I stopped in at Bobby Herman's tavern. He was the friendliest of the bartenders on my night beat, and I was just about ready to pull the trigger on a few questions to him. As soon as I walked inside I knew it wasn't going to be tonight, though. Blaze Franklin was sitting up at the bar. Must have been a short date. So much for dark circles under the eyes.

He saw me come in, but it took him five minutes to make up his mind to do anything about it. He got up from his stool finally, two-thirds of the way up the bar from mine, swaggered past the half dozen other customers in the place, and pushed himself in on the stool beside mine, his elbows out wider than they needed to be. "Don't b'lieve I've heard your name," he said in a loud voice.

"Arnold," I said. That's all I said.

"Understand you're quite a dancer," he informed me after waiting to see if I was going to continue. I wondered how much of his tomato face was due to weather and how much to alcohol. Around us the little bar-room conversations had died out. He wasn't satisfied to accept my silence. "I see you peart near ev'y day out thumpin' around that bresh out yonder," he said to me. "You keep it up you're gonna put your number 12 down on a still some day an' git your head blowed off."

"I carry a spare."

He didn't get it for a minute. When he did, he clouded over. "You in town for long, Arnold?"

"Depends," I said.

He took a long breath as though holding himself down. "Depends on what?"

I turned around on my stool until I was facing him. "Depends on me," I told him. I looked him up and down for five seconds, and returned to my beer. He put his hand on my arm. I looked down at the hand, and then at him. He removed the hand, his face flushing darkly. I knew the type. He wanted to lean on me just to show he could. I could feel the short hairs stiffening on the back of my neck. It was crazy. This bastard rubbed me completely the wrong way.

Whatever he'd been thinking of doing, he changed his mind. He got up and stalked out the door. Around me the conversation was not immediately renewed. Bobby Herman came sliding down the bar, his long arm going in concentric circles with a dirty bar rag. He was a thin-faced, pimply specimen with lank hair. "That's Blaze Franklin," he said almost apologetically. "He's a little—quick. What was that about dancin'?"

"Haven't the faintest notion," I said. I wasn't supposed to know the blonde was his playmate. Outside we could hear the roar of the cruiser as Franklin petulantly gunned it away. "Quick, huh? Who's he buried?" And as the words hung in the air, I told myself to cut it out. Trouble you can't use. Where are your brains, man?

Herman's laugh was a cackle. "That's a good one. Who's he buried?" He looked up and down the bar to assure himself of a maximum audience. "Well, no one he's stood trial for," he grinned. It was his turn to listen to the sound of his own words in the musty room. His grin faded. "I mean an escaped convict or two—things like that," he amended it hastily. He sloshed the bar rag about with renewed vigor. "Blaze's one of our best young deppities." Having—as he felt—retrieved the situation, he favored me with another smile.

I finished my beer and got out of there. I killed a couple of hours reading at the Lazy Susan, and left Kaiser in the room when I went out again. When I turned into the driveway of the Dixie Pig the lights were out in front except for the night-light. Around in back there was only one car. Hazel's car. She must have been standing just inside the back door waiting for me, because she came out and turned the key in the lock just as I pulled in.

"Let's use my car," she said. She went directly to it and got in on the driver's side. I climbed out of the Ford and walked over and got in beside her. She spun the wheels in the crushed stone backing up.

On the highway she turned south. Past the traffic light in town she leaned on it. She had a heavy foot, but she was a good driver. I watched alternately a full moon off over the gulf and the road unwinding in the headlights. There was no conversation. Sometimes I know ahead of time, but tonight wasn't one of those times.

Fifteen miles down the road she turned left on a dirt road she had to know was there or she couldn't have seen it. About a mile in on it she turned left again, and we bumped along over deep ruts for three hundred yards until a log cabin showed up in the headlights. Hazel switched off the car lights and we sat there and looked at the cabin in the moonlight. "I built most of it myself," she said. "And I mean I drove the nails. Come on."

She was out of the car and up on the little porch and had the door unlocked and open before I had the car door closed on my side. "Well?" she challenged me softly when I came up beside her. "It's a goddam good thing I'm shameless enough for both of us. You weren't going to ask me out. Why?"

"When I think of a good answer, I'll let you know," I told her. She led the way inside and closed the door behind me. I heard the snick of a bolt. In the moonlight that was the room's only light I couldn't make out many details except that the place was furnished.

Hazel came up behind me and dropped her hands down on my shoulders. "Get into something cooler, horseman," she said. She walked into the next room.

I undressed slowly. When I padded in barefoot she was buck naked on the full-sized bed. She could have been the model for all women for all time. Her eyes were closed.

I knelt on the edge of the bed. "Hazel—" I began.

She opened her eyes. Even in the semi-darkened room I could see the golden smile. "Don't you try to tell me I've gone and emasculated you," she said softly. "Come on here to me. You're a man. You'll do all right."

When it became apparent even to her some time later that I wasn't going to do all right, she sat up on the bed. "Get me a cigarette, Chet, will you?" she asked me. She sounded tired. I went back out to my clothes and found my cigarettes. In the glow of the lighter she studied my face. "Is it me, Chet?"

"It's not you."

"You're not a queer." She said it as a statement but with an implied question.

"I don't think I'm a queer," I said.

"But this happens? Often?"

"About half the time."

She blew out a convulsive lungful of smoke. "You shouldn't have done it to me, Chet." Impulsively her big hand closed on mine. "I'm sorry. It was me who did it to you, wasn't it?" The bed creaked under her weight as she changed position. "What do you think it is?"

"Everybody's got his own opium for that sort of thing, I guess." I stubbed out my own cigarette. "Years ago I saw a cartoon in a magazine. A slick-looking battalion is marching along in perfect cadence except for one raggedy-assed, stumble-footed guy out of step with a rock-faced sergeant alongside him giving him hell. The tag line underneath has the out-of-step character telling the sergeant he hears a different drum. The inference being that he can't help it if the rest of them are out of step. That's me. I march to a different band."

"What's the music?" she asked me directly.

"Excitement," I said after I caught myself. I'd nearly blurted out the truth. I'd nearly said "guns." With the air crackling with tension and a gun in my hand I'm nine feet tall and the best damn man you ever saw, right afterward. There's another time, too, but I'm not so proud of that.

"Well, I've read about bullfighters," Hazel said philosophically. "And I've seen gamblers who were on-again off-again with women, particularly when they were losing." She stood up from the bed and walked to the chair where she'd left her clothes. Her superb big body glistened in the moonlight that filtered into the bedroom. She thought of something else and walked over to me and tapped me on the chest with a solid finger. "Forget it, man. Before we take that fence again I'll have my jukebox man wire you up with 'Yes' and 'No' buttons." The attempt at lightness hung in the air between us. Hazel punched me in the ribs. "Let's just scratch tonight from the results, horseman."

But it was a quiet ride back to pick up my car.

In my time I've had a lot of quiet rides.

8

At the Dixie Pig the next night I couldn't see any change in Hazel's attitude. There was no reference to the previous evening. I hadn't gone there expecting to find the details of the disaster soaped in on the back bar mirror, but
I'm old enough to know it makes a difference and that the difference usually
shows. I couldn't see any change in her at all. Hazel wasn't big only in her
physical dimensions.

"I hear you're picking on our poor little deputy sheriffs now," she said to
me, sitting down in the booth.

"Your hearing's pretty damn good, except that you've got the story all
wrong," I told her.

"Not many secrets in this town," she assured me. "Especially not many that
take place in taverns." She studied me as I sat there. "You could be underestimating Blaze Franklin, Chet."

It irritated me. "I'm not over or underestimating him. I don't give a damn
about him."

"Don't get narky. I'm telling you for your own good. He's dangerous."

"So how come a dangerous man is a deputy sheriff?"

"I don't think anyone around here had the whole picture on Blaze until he
had the uniform. It's the badge that makes him dangerous, the leeway it gives
him. A psychiatrist would probably say it gives him an opportunity to safely
work out his aggressiveness."

"And I suppose he's most aggressive where the blonde is concerned?" I
asked sarcastically.

"If you weren't a stranger in town you'd have already heard some stories
about that," Hazel said quietly. "Still, something's happened to that relationship lately." She frowned, a network of fine lines indenting her broad forehead. "I see it in her, not in him. She always had a cocky way of flipping a hip
that had the pigeons crossing the street to bask in the sunlight. It used to be
that when she snapped her fingers, Blaze rolled over. I don't see that now.
She's lost weight. Her eyes look like two burnt holes in a blanket. Something's
gnawing on her. I'll tell you the truth, I've been wondering if she isn't dip-
ping into the till down there at the post office."

I had to hold myself down from sitting right up straight in the booth. "Why
in the hell would she do that?"

Hazel planted both elbows firmly on the table top. "I'll tell you a tale out
of school. When Charlie died, he left me some cash. I invested it. Then I
wound up with this place. In a small town, that kind of thing gets magnified
out of all proportion to the facts."

Her voice took on a brooding quality, as if she were thinking aloud. "Two months ago Blaze Franklin came to me and tried to borrow three thousand dollars. He had a red-hot business opportunity, he said. I'd learned from Charlie years ago how to keep an approach like that from being a problem. Blaze knew that my investments were managed for me by Nate Pepperman, a business consultant with an office up over the bank. I told Blaze to go and see Nate and explain his proposition, and that if Nate gave it his okay I said it was all right for Nate to milk something and finance the deal." Hazel gave me a little-girl grin. "I've seen Charlie send three a week like that to his 'business consultant,' and he'd light up another cigar and tell me that the day the guy okayed such a proposition was the day Charlie got himself a new business consultant. Most propositions when they couldn't lean on friendship turned out to be swiss cheese in texture."

She sobered again, placing her chin firmly in her cupped palms. "It must have been a couple of weeks later that Nate called me about something else, and I asked him about Blaze. I wasn't too much surprised to hear that Blaze had never been near him. A lot of the big-touch boys choke up in a hurry at the idea of trying to explain an if-and-and deal to a gimlet-eye like Nate."

She nudged a cigarette from the pack on the table and leaned forward to accept my proffered light. She blew out a lungful of smoke and licked at a filament of tobacco on her lip. "About the same time I heard from one of my customers that Lucille Grimes had been into his showroom pricing foreign sports cars. That seemed to be two and two adding up to four."

Hazel leveled the cigarette at me. "Then lo and behold, it seemed the very next time I saw Lucille she was burnin' up the rubber on a bright red, brand new MG roadster. I was curious enough about it to make it my business to find out Blaze had paid for it in cash. That's not the way the title reads, but that's what happened. So either old Blaze found himself a golden goose, after all, or Lucille is into the till and waitin' for her pants to be dropped and the paddle to burn her up. She sure looks it."

"Blaze probably saved up for it out of his green stamps," I said.

"For ten days or so Lucille was around everywhere in that car, champagne-bubbly," Hazel continued, unheeding. "Then the blight set in. I don't know what it was, or how he managed it, but the reins are very definitely in Mr. Franklin's hands these days. She looks like a lamp with the flame blown out. It must be that jealous men are hard on the nerves. She really looks like something was grindin' her down. Maybe a man wouldn't notice it, but it's there for a woman to see."

There was a lot that interested me in the story. A hell of a lot. Had I been knocking my brains out on the west coast of Florida's brush-grown back roads and here the two of them had been practically under my thumb all the time? Franklin's persistent interest in my timber-cruising, and then the connection to the post office—

I thought about it when the bar became busy and Hazel went back to it.

I thought about it some more on the way back to the motel.

I was already in bed when something else occurred to me. I got up and slipped into a robe and went outside to the Ford and opened the back deck lid and my big tool chest. I found what I was looking for, a miniature Italian automatic that fired three .17 cartridges. It had a little holster of its own that strapped on a man's shin.

I went back inside and strapped it on mine. I didn't know yet whether Manny Sebastian knew where to find me. When I found out, it could be on goddam short notice. I might need a little extra something like a hidden shin holster going for me.

But right now there was Blaze Franklin.

And Lucille Grimes.

I was in the post office lobby at nine o'clock in the morning. The outer doors were opened earlier to allow boxholders to get their mail, but the windows didn't open until nine. Right on the dot Lucille raised the General Delivery window. I could see two clerks behind her, but they were busy in the back end of the long room. I stepped up to the window, in a hurry to get my piece spoken before we were interrupted by someone walking in off the street. "Morning, Lucille," I said to her.

She looked surprised. "Good morning," she said almost as an afterthought. In the light of what Hazel had said I could see that Lucille was looking something less than her best. The deep, dark circles beneath her eyes were still in evidence, and the blonde hair looked less crisp. A trace of blotchiness marred the velvet pallor of her facial skin.

"May I help you?" she asked me.

"Depends, Lucille," I said with a breeziness I didn't feel. Some things I can do, but exchanging light badinage with a semi-strange female isn't one of them. As a rule I leave that to the extroverts like Jed, but circumstances alter cases. "How about having dinner with me some one of these nights?"

Her original surprise was obviously redoubled. "I don't believe I should," she said. Having said it, she stood there testing the sound of it. "I really don't think—"

"You're not wearing his ring," I interrupted her. "Or his collar, I hope." Her chin lifted. "If you're implying—"

"I'm implying I'd like to have dinner with you. Say Wednesday night?"

"I'll—let me think about it." She appeared confused.

A woman came in the door and walked up to the window. I had to step aside. "Wednesday night?" I pressed her as I did so.

"I'll have to—call me tonight," she said hurriedly, and smiled at the woman. "Yes, Mrs. Newman?"

I backed out tanglefootedly under Mrs. Newman's bright-eyed inspection.

On the street I had to give only a very small plus to the operation. At least the blonde hadn't refused out of hand. For the moment I'd have to settle for that.

I walked across the street to where I'd parked the Ford and drove out east on Main. For six hours I beat my way up and back two dozen monstrously tangled dirt roads, logging trails, and footpaths, some of them no more than ten yards apart. I sweat gallons. I lost my temper. And I found nothing.

I went back to the Lazy Susan and showered and lay down on the bed for a couple of hours. The constant frustration was beginning to do things to the hair-trigger of my temper. I knew myself well enough to know that if it continued much longer some little shove from one direction or another would send me careening off on a course not necessarily the right one, just because action itself would be a release.

I was still in a bad mood when I whistled up Kaiser and headed out to the Dixie Pig for dinner. The first three minutes out there compounded it. I walked in to find Jed Raymond in the corner booth in the khaki shirt and red-piped gray trousers I'd come to associate with Blaze Franklin. It jarred me. "Where the hell's the masquerade?" I asked Jed. He looked up at me curiously. I didn't like the sound of my voice myself.

"I told you I was a jack-leg deputy in an emergency," he said cheerfully enough.

"So where's the emergency?"

His grin was sheepish. "Opening of a new supermarket." He ran a hand down the uniform. "I'm on traffic. I get called out a couple of times a month."

I sat down in the booth. "You must be younger than I thought. I don't see you somehow in this cops-and-robbers bit."

"Cut it out, will you?" Jed pleaded. "Around here a realtor is expected to either do this or go into politics. This takes less time and money."

"Suppose you had to arrest a real estate prospect, Jed?"

"Now you know no prospect of mine could ever be involved in anything requirin' me to arrest him," Jed replied with dignity.

"But suppose?"

"Suppose the moon is made of green cheese. Suppose the end of the world." Jed grinned. "If I hadn't got the deposit, though, he might have a little runnin' room."

Kaiser padded over to Jed's side of the booth and rested his muzzle on Jed's thigh. Jed reached down and scratched him between the ears, and Kaiser reached up and took Jed's arm in his mouth. Jed growled down at him, and Kaiser growled back. I could tell the dog wanted to play. Jed reached the same conclusion. "You want a little roughhouse, boy?" he inquired, and slid out of the booth and got down on his knees. In seconds the big gray-and-brown dog and Jed's ginger-colored crewcut were rolling all over the floor in a ferocious-sounding mock battle. It sounded so real the bar customers scattered like quail.

One of them climbed up on a table.

Jed got to his feet finally, laughing, brushing the floor dirt from his uniform. Kaiser watched him with ears cocked alertly until Jed sat down in the booth again, then came back and sat down beside me. "That's a lot of dog," Jed said to me, and continued on in the same breath. "I heard you're dating Lucille Grimes."

"For chrissake, did she take an ad in the paper? She hasn't even said yes yet, for that matter."

"You broached your invitation in the hearing of a dear lady who can give a large-mouth bass cards and spades," Jed said drily.

I remembered the woman at the post office General Delivery window. "So, she still hasn't said yes."

"But you asked her." Jed held up a hand when I would have bitten off something short and snappy. "Hold it a minute, fire-eater. I feel a little guilt in the matter. Are you trying to prove something to me because I needled your semi-senior citizen status and threw you smack dab up against the shark-toothed widow?"

"Shark-toothed? What the hell are you talking about?"

"I live in this town, Chet. Do you need a blueprint?"

"For God's sake, I asked the woman to dinner. Does that leave me enlisted among her love-slaves?"

"It leaves you on Blaze Franklin's black list," Jed said soberly.

"How come Blaze Franklin's got this town buffaloed, Jed?"

He spread his hands. "You saw him. You sized him up."

"I sized him up," I agreed. "About twenty-five cents on the dollar."

"Goddammit, you're askin' for it with that attitude!" Ted bristled. "Hazel says Blaze came—"

"So Hazel knows about it, too. You sure you haven't taken an ad in the paper?"

Jed stared at me. "Aren't you a little touchy? I don't give a damn if you lay the blonde under the traffic light at high noon. I'm just concerned my big mouth pushed you into something with a stinger attached."

I pulled up on the reins. The kid meant all right. "All right, forget it, Jed. I asked her. She hasn't said yes or no. If she says yes we'll have dinner. If she says no we won't. It's a big deal?"

He folded his hands together on the table in front of him. "A couple of guys who've gone out with our beautiful postmistress have had—accidents. I don't believe she's had an invitation in a year. Until yours."

"How come no accidents happen to Franklin?"

"Maybe because he's got the town buffaloed. These weren't small accidents, Chet."

"I appreciate the concern, but it's premature, Jed. Can I buy you a drink before you go showing off that boy scout uniform?"

"I'll have to ask you to speak with more respect to this minion of th' law, suh. I'll take a raincheck on the drink." Jed rose to his feet, reached down to pat Kaiser on the head in passing, and went out the back door.

For the first time since I'd known the kid, I was glad to see him go. It's strange what the sight of a uniform does to me. On the other hand I was happy to see Kaiser take to him so quickly. If I had to pull stakes in a hurry, it meant I wouldn't be leaving the big dog high and dry.

I got up and walked over to the phone booth and looked up Lucille Grimes' home phone in the directory. There was no one near the booth when I dialed. "Chet Arnold, Lucille," I said when she answered. "How're we fixed for Wednesday night?"

"Oh, ah—" There was a five second pause. She hadn't repeated my name. I wondered if Franklin could possibly be right there with her. Not that I gave a damn. "Would five o'clock be too early? You could pick me up right at the post office."

"Five o'clock will be fine." So she didn't want me picking her up at her home for some reason. "See you then."

"I'm looking forward to it. Good night."

I replaced the receiver. She'd fairly cooed the last words. I felt a tingle at the base of my spine. Something about the way she'd said it—I don't know, I had a feeling. This attractively long-legged female wasn't saying yes only to dinner. Yet there was nothing soft about her. In Dixie Pig conversations I'd surprised an occasional feral gleam under the long-lashed lids. Unless I missed my guess she was a dandy little cutting tool.

Well, so much the better.

For some reason I've never been able to understand, I'm a much better man when I don't like them.

When I got back to the booth Hazel came over and sat down. "Jed coming back tonight after he gets off this deputy routine?" I asked her.

"Accordin' to him, he's goin' courtin'." She checked the bar with a sweeping glance before continuing. "That boy's goin' to make some girl a good husband time he makes up his mind to settle down."

"I wonder what it feels like," I said before I thought.

"You wonder what *what* feels like?"

"Oh, sitting with a girl on her living-room sofa." I tried to pass it off lightly. "Object: matrimony, if you can't get it any other way."

"You never tried it? No, I s'pose not," she answered her own question. She didn't pursue aloud her chain of thought. A silence settled down between us.

"I've been thinking—" I began, finally.

"Do you suppose—" Hazel started in the same breath.

We both laughed, and she waved a hand. "You've got the floor, horseman."

I couldn't seem to find the right words. "Maybe we ought to try it again some night," I said at last.

She didn't reply for a moment. "There's a point to it?" she asked when I'd begun to think she wasn't going to answer at all.

"There could be. You've made a losing bet or two in your day, haven't you?"

"I wish they'd only been cash." She sounded quite sober. "Why do you want to try it again, Chet?"

"Maybe because the next time I came in here after the other night you didn't have 'Chet Arnold is an impotent slob' up on the front in neon lights."

"What the hell do you think I am?" she began indignantly, and then started to laugh. "Can that corn, man. Why do you?"

"It offends my miserly soul to see such a stack of material going to waste."

"I suppose even a left-handed compliment is more than I rate most days around here," she said good-humoredly. "All right, I'll stop fishing." She reached across the table and covered my hand with hers just for a second before removing it again. "And listen, man: the fact you want to is what counts with me. I've been around gamblers long enough to know that a lot of the time they're wired into different sockets." She rose briskly as a glass bottom rapped on the bar. "I'll be back."

I watched her walk away from me back to the bar, and all of a sudden I knew it was going to be all right. I never know how I know, the times I do. I just know.

I waited for her to come back, but the bar stayed busy. I got up finally and walked over to one end of it, away from the customers. "I'll be back at lock-up time," I told Hazel when she came down the bar toward me.

Her eyes widened. I think she started a wisecrack, but choked it off. "I'll be ready," was all she said.

I drove downtown. I had a couple of hours to kill, and I might as well kill them at Bobby Herman's place. I left Kaiser in the car and went on into the tavern. Herman was friendly with me now, mostly because I let him show off his encyclopedic baseball knowledge by asking him trick questions only a buff could know the answers to. Bobby had never seen a major league game in his life, except in spring training, but he read *The Sporting News* religiously, and he remembered what he read. He had the type of mind that could rattle off the batting order lineups for the Yankees and the Pirates in the '28 World Series. I remembered that series myself. That had been the year I'd been expelled from school for stalking the fat boy whose boxer dog had killed Fatima.

Herman's place drew a workingman crowd. He stayed open till midnight, but on week-nights his customers generally packed it in around ten. The last hour he always had time to talk, and over the last three weeks I'd made it my business to see to it that a lot of his talking was done to me.

I was later than usual tonight. There was only one other customer at the bar when I sat down there, and a boy and a girl in the farthest booth. Bobby whisked his bar rag over the mahogany in front of me and slapped down a tight-collared beer. "Big argument in here tonight," he informed me. "You re-member the year Cobb an' Speaker wound up playin' the outfield for the Philadelphia Athletics when they were through in Detroit and Cleveland? Well, the argument was who was the third man in that outfield. I say it was Fothergill. Some of the guys say it was Heilmann. Who do you think it was?"

"If you say Fothergill, I'll settle for Fothergill, Bobby," I told him. He grinned, pleased, and retreated to his wash rack and started rinsing out glasses. The only other customer at the bar finished his beer, grunted good-night, and went out the door. The only sound in the place was the low mur-mur of voices from the corner booth and the clink of glasses as Bobby placed them on the drainboard. When he looked up my way again I was ready for him. I nodded down the bar in a way that took in two thirds of the tavern. "Say, whatever happened to the big dark guy used to stand down there when I first started coming in? Big, rugged-looking guy."

Bobby paused with a sparkling glass in his hand. He frowned, trying to think. "Big, rugged—? Oh, yeah. The one with the scar on his throat. That's right, I haven't seen him lately. Must've found greener pastures. He wasn't a regular, anyway."

I felt a tight sensation in the pit of my stomach. "He work around here? He reminded me of someone, and I finally remembered who it was. I thought I'd ask him if he was related."

Herman had returned to his glasses. "I don't know if he works around here. He's not a native, though. Real quiet fella. Drove a blue sedan with out-of-state plates. Probably a tourist."

A real quiet fella. Even after seeing it so many times it always surprised me the way the mute Bunny could walk into a bar, get his first beer by holding up a finger as the bartender drew one for someone else, and all the refills he wanted by snapping a coin down on the bar. He never joined a group but al-ways stood just in the background, smiling and nodding at the general con-versation. He had a trick of anticipating a direct question and turning his shoul-der so that his attention appeared to be elsewhere and the question flew harmlessly over it. I've seen people lose hard cash betting Bunny could talk after they'd been around him for days.

"Could he be staying up at the Walton House? Seems to me I saw a blue sedan parked up there."

"Don't think so." Bobby dried his hands on his apron front. "Every time I saw him pull out of the lot here he'd swing it around and head out east from the traffic light." He paused as if checking his memory. "I don't think he lived in town."

"Oh, well, it's not that important," I said. I looked at my watch. "Put one more head on this thing, anyway, Bobby. Then maybe your sterling sales-manship can get me to exceed my quota."

I started Herman off on baseball again along with my second beer. He rattled along, happy with the sound of his own voice. I had only to contribute an occasional nod. His confident statistics bounced off me as I sat there thinking about Bunny.

It was a comfort to know I'd been right in my guess that Bunny had hidden out east on Main as I'd originally figured. I'd been beginning to wonder. I might be stubborn, but I had no intention of working my way through to the east coast of Florida a side road at a time. With Herman's memory to strengthen my first guess, though, I'd just have to keep at it. Bunny was out there, somewhere. I had no illusions, of course, that I was going to be able to do him any good.

I was out in the back parking lot when Hazel came out at ten after twelve. She had a dress on again. I walked around the Ford to open the door for her, and she loomed up over me a good four inches. I got a whiff of an exotic perfume as she climbed into the car.

"Relax," I told her as I headed down the driveway. "Everything's going to be all right."

"I just hope you're not building yourself up for a letdown," she said doubtfully.

"It's all right," I repeated.

I drove with my left hand and we held hands, her left in my right. The full moon was past and it was a much darker night. I nearly missed the turn-off road completely. I had to back up for it. We jolted down the final rutted three hundred yards, and sat looking at the cabin that was just a darker blotch in the blackness.

On the porch Hazel gave me her key and I opened the door. It was so quiet it hurt the ears. My pulse must have been doing a hundred and seventy. We didn't bother with any lights. Hand-in-hand we stumbled through the doorway from the living room into the bedroom beyond.

I undressed her myself. With each layer removed she showed up whiter and whiter, until she gleamed in the dark like the phosphorescence in the gulf. I didn't bother with her cowboy boots. She still had them on when we settled down on the bed. She wasn't making a sound. I could hear the click of the boot heels when her legs came together over my back. I went for broke, and made it. Made it so big it was one lumped-up soul-satisfying taste deep in my throat. I could feel the wild pulse in her neck under my lips. When she got excited herself it was a damn good thing for me there were no spurs on the boots.

I don't know how long it was before she spoke. I could still hear her heavy breathing—or was it mine?—and her voice was a deeply muted, husky sound. "Welcome back, horseman. For an off-again, on-again, Finnegan type you cover a spread of ground."

I didn't say anything. I slid my hands beneath her and took a solid double-handful of her powerful buttocks. I pulled her up against me again, tightly.

"Oh, no!" she chuckled. "Honest to Christmas, Chet—" She started to laugh, a full-throated richness of sound that remained in my mind long after it had died out in my ears.

It was the finest sound I'd heard in longer than I liked to think about.

I was on my back, relaxed, smoking a cigarette when Hazel came back into the bedroom and sat down on the edge of the bed. She reached over to punch me on the arm. "You ride a mean rodeo, horseman," she said to me. "An' here you had me thinkin' there was no fire in the boiler at all." I could feel her bending over me, trying to find my face in the dark.

"There's fire enough baby, when the damn engineer's on the job." I threw away the cigarette, remembered too late the wooden cabin, and got up and found a shoe and ground out the cigarette with the heel. I came back to the bed. "Trouble is every so often he takes these two-week lunch hours."

Her big arms reached up and pulled me down beside her. "The hell with it. At the moment I couldn't care less." She stretched beside me, lengthily. A healthy animal. "Although I'll admit I don't understand it."

I understood it. Up to a point, anyway. I was just geared to a different ratio. With me it just wasn't the main line the way it was with most guys. It never had been, and I'd never had any reason to think it ever would be. Although with this big, warm-hearted, two-hundred-percent woman—

She stirred beside me. "Funny how all right it can make things, huh? When it's right?"

"You said a hammered-down mouthful, baby."

Her voice was softer when she spoke again. "Nobody's ever called me 'baby.' It sounds—nice."

I reached for her in the dark. "Turn around here and let me play with the best part of you."

"Oh, well, look, now. Let's not overdo this thing, pardner."

She sounded really worried. I laughed out loud. "You sound like the bride who saw her husband dressing after their wedding night and burst into tears. 'I liked it s-so much,' she sobbed, 'and we've used up s-so much of it!'"

Hazel batted me. I grabbed to find and hold her hard-punching hands. It was remarkable the unanimity with which our intentions changed at the same instant.

I don't know what time it was when we got out of there. The dressing had been interrupted a couple of times. The shower had run, and stopped, and run, and stopped, and run, and stopped. The bathroom looked as if a couple of whales had been turned loose. There was water even on the ceiling.

Hazel came in, dressed, while I was conducting a mopping-up operation with towels. "Leave it," she said. "I'll drive out tomorrow and take care of it."

THE NAME OF THE GAME IS DEATH

We rode back to the Dixie Pig in a comfortable silence. I put her in her car. She ran down her window and waved to me before she drove off.

I set sail for the motel, and bed.

I woke with a start from my first deep sleep. A glance at the luminous dial on the alarm clock beside the bed indicated I'd been asleep thirty minutes. From somewhere my subconscious had put together a neat, tight little package: kick the whole bit in Hudson, and take off with Hazel. For anywhere. Catch up on living for a change.

I looked around the motel room's long, dappled shadows and mottled dark corners. I listened to the thump as someone turned over in bed in the next room, plainly audible through the thin partition.

I didn't even need the cold light of day to squelch that crazy idea.

Don't be a bigger goddam fool than nature intended, I told myself.

I knew what I was.

At my age no leopard changes his spots.

I closed my eyes again.

After awhile I even slept.

9

I picked Lucille up on the dot of five in front of the post office. "Since it's early enough for a drive, I made a reservation at the Black Angus," I said. "Okay?"

"It's a very nice place," she said in reply. She smoothed her skirt out beneath her, palms flat against the pliant thighs. Her eyes were bright, and her nostrils flared. There was something between us from the second she stepped into the Ford.

I headed north on the highway and just rolled it along. It was about a thirty mile drive. Without being obvious about it, I watched the rear-view mirror. I saw no indication of a jealous man in pursuit, but Jed's warning was on my mind.

We didn't exchange fifteen words on the way. She sat beside me in seeming lassitude. I was satisfied to leave it that way for the time being. I thought I'd have a chance over dinner to probe a little bit and see what it was that made this woman tick.

It didn't work out that way. In the huge dining room she had three cocktails in quick succession. She apologized for the third, but downed it quicker than the other two. I ordered a good meal, but she just toyed with her food. Conversation remained at a minimum. She closed out my tentative leads with terse replies, her tone brittle. Her responses featured incomplete sentences, dangling phrases, and half-finished expressions, punctuated by an occasional dazzling, loose-lipped smile. An aura of almost febrile excitement emanated from her. I almost expected to see sparks fly from her fingers and toes. She was the epitome of promise.

I suggested brandy afterward. She settled for a highball. She had two, then another. She took on a high gloss. She pronounced her words carefully. Leaving, she stepped a little bit too high over the threshold.

In the car she lapsed into complete silence. Her eyes were fixed dreamily straight ahead down the road. If she felt the car slow down as I studied the motels we came up to, she gave no sign. When she did speak, she surprised me. "This one," she said huskily, and pointed. I turned down a long driveway that wound between individual cabins set back from the edge of the road. I stopped at the one marked "Office" and got out and went inside. Lucille stayed in the car.

I registered under the bored eye of the bald-headed manager. With practiced ease he read my "Mr. and Mrs. Chet Arnold" upside down. "Anything special, Mr. Arnold?"

"A quiet one."

"Certainly, sir." He turned to the key-rack behind him.

When he faced front again, I was filling in another card. "That one's for my brother-in-law and his wife," I said, pointing to the Arnold card. "I'll pay you for both."

The manager dropped the key in his hand on the Arnold card and turned to get another. Again he performed his upside-down reading stunt on the second card. "This one's every bit as good, Mr. Reynolds. They're together, the last two on the right."

"Fine." I paid him, picked up both keys, and went out to the car. The keys were numbers 10 and 11. Number 10 was the Arnolds' cabin. Number 11 was the Reynolds'. I drove to the end of the wooded lot and stopped in front of number 11. I got out and let Lucille out on her side, opened the cabin door, and stepped aside to let her enter. "Back in a second," I told her.

I went back to the Ford and backed it off the driveway and around on the grass behind the cabin. I parked it between two trees. We'd eaten so early the sky was still bright overhead, but under the trees it was nearly dark.

Lucille displayed no curiosity about my short trip. She had every light in the place on when I got back inside. She was humming to herself, and moving slowly about the room in a way that suggested a dance step. Her eyes were the biggest part of her face. Without saying a word she began to undress, leisurely.

I went into the bathroom and closed the door. I took off my jacket and my shoulder holster. I removed the Smith & Wesson from the holster and a towel from the rack, and I wrapped the gun loosely in the towel. I put the holster in a jacket pocket, put the jacket back on, and went out, carrying the towel.

Lucille was sitting on the edge of the bed in her panties. She smiled up at me lazily. The tip of her tongue flicked over her lips. I put the towel down carefully on the small night table, and sat down on the bed beside her. I stood her up, between my feet, and made a production of removing the panties. Her thighs were tanned, her buttocks milky. She looked like a two-toned animal.

She crawled onto the bed and lay there face down while I stood up and undressed. I left my shoes on. I walked to the door and locked and bolted it. When I turned, she had rolled part-way over, watching me. Her eyes looked almost filmed. Her head was up an inch or two from the pillow, slightly turned, as though she were listening.

I was listening, too.

I walked back to her. I was only a stride from the bed when we both heard it with no trouble at all. There was a splintering crash from next door as the door of number 10 went down. I could hear the thump of heavy boots as Blaze Franklin blundered around in the dark in the next cabin, looking for the light.

Lucille's eyes widened as she realized I'd somehow sucked him into the wrong cabin. Her breasts bobbed as she filled her lungs to scream. I reached down and slapped her squarely in her bare belly. She got out a gargle. That's all.

I knew Franklin couldn't stay to hunt for us. The Smith & Wesson and my shoes were just insurance against his being smarter than I thought he was. Right now he was all done on this caper. He had no business there. He had to get away from the empty cabin he'd broken into. Not seeing the Ford, he had to think we'd come and gone already.

I covered Lucille's mouth with my hand till I heard the whine of the cruiser pulling away. Even in the dirt the tires sang. I took my hand off her face. It was no blacker under the trees outside than in the depths of her eyes. "You get a bang out of watching him beat them up?" I asked her.

Her mouth was wet. "He makes them crawl," she said almost in a whisper. She didn't look particularly afraid. "What are you going to do?"

"I'll show you what I'm going to do." I took hold of her. She may not have been the best I'd ever had in my hands, but she was a useful piece of machinery. She submitted passively until she realized my intention. She fought hard, then. She was strong, but not strong enough. She hissed like a cat all the time I abused her.

It was four in the morning before we left there.

Fifty per cent of us had enjoyed it.

I drove back to Hudson and let Lucille out up the street from her house. False dawn was lightening the sky. I didn't want to drive right up to her door in case Franklin was waiting for her on her front porch.

She hadn't said a word all the way back to town. She looked around when I stopped the car. It took her a moment to recognize where she was. She opened the car door and got out, then leaned back in to spit at me. "Blaze will kill you for this," she rasped.

I appreciate a good hater. "You've got it all wrong, sugar," I told her. "You're going to have a hard time explaining this to your jealous lord and master. You set up the place, and then you weren't there. What does Blaze use on you when he's a little out of sorts? His belt? A jealous man believes what he wants to believe. Blaze is going to figure you as a partner in the disappearance."

I could have counted to ten while she stared in at me. I'd given her something to think about. Without another word she slammed the door and started up the street. She was unsteady on her high heels. I sat and watched her go.

It wasn't hard to see where Jed Raymond had found the adjective "shark-toothed" in connection with the widow Grimes. I owed the kid something for keeping me from making the play with my eyes shut. Franklin and the blonde must have had a Roman holiday with the suitors she'd set up for the deputy to knock over. And of course none of them would talk.

I couldn't show much of a plus on the real purpose of the evening. There hadn't been much of the conversation I'd counted on. On the other hand, it had done me good to vent some poison on a truly poisonous female.

I started the Ford up, and eased through the deserted square in the direction of the Lazy Susan. I parked a block away and came up on it from the rear. I thought I had Franklin figured, but until I knew for sure I had to be ready to see him on short notice. There was no cruiser in the motel yard. I walked completely around it, my feet silent on the grass. Through the office window I could see the night clerk with his head nodding. There was no sign at all of Franklin. Lucille would get lucky if it was tomorrow instead of right now that she was down on her knees trying to explain.

I went into my unit and showered and shaved. It was full dawn when I stretched out on the bed.

I was beginning to get a feeling about Lucille Grimes and Blaze Franklin. I had to figure out a way of getting at them.

I interrupted Hazel in her preoccupied feeding of potato chips to Kaiser in our booth at the Dixie Pig. "That's the third time in ten minutes you've given me the double-O inspection as if you were looking for ringworm. What gives?"

"Just looking for battle wounds. I heard you had a date with the blonde last night."

"This is a small town. You've got her all wrong, though. She's really quite kittenish."

Hazel snorted. "So's a Rocky Mountain panther. I don't get it. Can it be that the light in your baby blues has reformed her?"

"How did she get into the conversation, anyway?" I evaded Hazel. "Let's get to something important, like what's on your schedule after closing tonight."

"I could run out in back and check my social calendar, but I'll take a chance and say I'm free." She smiled, a warm, golden smile. "Did you have a discussion period in mind, horseman?"

"If you can discuss on your back."

"My, my, what a rejuvenation." She knuckled a big hand and pushed gently at mine on the table. The smile on her lips overflowed to her eyes. "Who was the best sprinter you ever saw at four furlongs?"

"I'd have to make it a deadheat among Decathlon, White Skies, and Moolah Bux, I guess."

"Bet you I could give the field a length start an' beat them to the back door tonight." Hazel rose to her feet. "Let me get out of here before I entirely lose my maidenly reserve," she said briskly. She wagged a finger at me. "You watch out for that woman, y'hear? She's tricky."

"And here I thought I'd changed the subject."

Hazel smiled again, and went back to the bar. I took over her job of feeding potato chips to Kaiser. The big dog was gone for potato chips. I'd tested
him with a potato chip versus a piece of steak. He ate the steak, but he ate the
potato chip first. He'd crunch a chip, and then circle his muzzle with his
tongue to get all the salt.

This town had already given me one surprise in the appearance of the redheaded Eddie from Manny Sebastian's parking lot. When I looked up toward
the rear entrance of the Dixie Pig between potato chips, I had a second. Lucille Grimes was halfway across the floor heading toward my booth.

Her hands were empty. Her bag dangled loosely from the strap on her arm.
That much I took in in the first split second. Then she was standing beside
the booth. "Sit down, if you can," I greeted her. "What color welts are you
wearing these days?"

She attempted a smile, but her eyes were murderous. She sat down. I
watched carefully until she laid her bag aside. I had no intention of playing
clay pigeon for this dolly. From the second she started talking it was plain she
had herself under a tight rein. "I came by to ask you to dinner tomorrow
night."

Now here was a switch, "Yeah? Where?"

"At my house."

Come into my parlor, said the spider to the fly. "At your house? What's
the occasion?"

"I want to talk to you." Even she seemed to realize that was a little weak.
"I might have a proposition for you."

"What about?"

She manufactured a smile. "Why don't you come and see? Possibly I can
use someone as foresighted as you appear to be."

"In the post office?"

She stood up. "Call me in the morning and let me know." She picked up her
bag and walked to the door. Her movements weren't as fluid as I remembered
them.

I moved out of the corner of the booth away from the window when she
went out the door. This was no campfire girl. The dinner invitation had to
mean one of two things. Either Franklin was so crazy mad to get at me he was
willing to drop a ton on me right in her house, or Franklin had given her such
a hard way to go the blonde was looking for reinforcements to get her out from
under Franklin. I couldn't see much nourishment for me in either setup.

Of course if it was Franklin and the blonde who actually had short-circuited
Bunny—

I decided I'd have to give the invitation more thought.

Out at the cabin I walked from the bathroom into the bedroom and looked down at Hazel tastefully attired in one thirty-second of a sheet. "Come on and let's take a shower, big stuff," I said.

She yawned, and stretched mightily. The effect was spectacular. "You must have otter blood in you, man," she complained drowsily. "The last two nights with you I been in an' out of that shower till my corns are waterlogged. Why don't you just tumble on down here an' relax your—"

As close as we'd been recently it had remained no secret that Hazel was touchy. I leaned down and goosed her, and she bounded from the bed to the middle of the room with a strangled yelp. I aimed my thumb at her again, and she flew into the bathroom. I herded her into the glassed-in compartment and turned on the fine needle-spray. I adjusted it to warm, and stepped in with her. We each took soap and in silence began to lather each other.

The water hissed softly, the single off-center fluorescent light glistened dimly upon sleek flesh, and warm hands glided gently over slippery body contours. It was a moment out of a lifetime. We stayed in the shower a long time.

The place was just about afloat when I stepped out and gabbed a towel. I picked up another one and handed it to Hazel, still in the shower. She turned the water off and buried her wet red head in the towel. I reached in behind her and flipped the handle over to full cold.

"Ooooooh-h-h!" I never heard such a catamount yowl in my life. Hazel boomed out of that shower like a fullback. She ran right over me. I was laughing so hard that when she turned and came after me, I couldn't defend myself. She got me down and enthusiastically banged my head on the tile. I couldn't get her off till I got into her ribs and tickled. She squealed, and rolled away.

Several wet towels and a couple of cigarettes later we were stretched out on the bed, the firefly glow of cigarettes the bedroom's only light. Beside me I could hear Hazel's deep, even breathing. She reached up over me to stub out her cigarette in the ashtray on the table beside the bed, and trailed her hand lightly along my body as she dropped back with a sigh. "You don't happen to think you're pretty far out sometimes reaching for sensations, horseman?" she asked in her rich voice.

"You can tell your grandchildren someday you did it under water," I told her.

She laughed, then sobered. "That parlay breaks down with the first dog out of the box. Children come before grandchildren, unless they've repealed a law of nature."

I didn't like what I heard in her voice. I changed the subject. "I didn't get a chance to tell you before, but I'm invited out to dinner tomorrow night."

Hazel came up on an elbow. "The blonde?"

"In the solid flesh."

In the increased glow of my cigarette as I took a final drag I could see the outline of her features, but not her expression. "Chet," she began, and hesitated. She seemed to be wondering whether to continue. "I don't want to know your business, Chet, and I'm not jealous of Lucille Grimes, but there's something I think you ought to know." She stopped again. I could have made it easier for her, but I didn't. I didn't because jealous was exactly what I thought she was. She made me sorry right away. "Blaze Franklin is asking questions about you all over town, Chet."

Instinct is a wonderful thing. I didn't have a stitch on, but my hand was up reaching for the butt of the Smith & Wesson in the shoulder holster with my clothes in the next room. "Like what kind of questions is he asking?"

"Where you came from. What you're doing here. Where you lived before. How much talking you do about yourself." Hazel's tone was quiet. "I don't want you to think I'm prying, Chet. I just thought you ought to know."

"Don't think I don't appreciate it." I thought about Blaze Franklin. It looked as though I had indeed underestimated the gentleman. He wasn't asking those particular questions because of anything that had happened between Lucille and me. I had no damn business lying here bed-bouncing with the wash out on the line and a storm coming up. "Any reaction from the questioned?" I asked Hazel.

"Even Jed was saying it was odd how little we really knew about you." There was no emphasis in the remark. She was reporting a fact. Her hand came up and settled on my arm. "I'm going to say one more thing, and then I'm going to shut up. If you think of anything I can do to help, let me know." She rolled over and sat up on the edge of the bed. "Let's get dressed," she said briskly. "I'm a workin' gal, and I've got to open up in the morning."

It was a fact the life had gone out of the party. We dressed and locked up and went out to the Ford. On the way back to town I had time to think about Hazel's last remark. "'If you think of anything I can do to help, let me know.'" That was just short of putting it in writing that she was on the team. More than that, she didn't care what the name on the uniform was. In my life I've run into few blanket endorsements. The big woman was all gold and a yard wide.

I appreciated it, as I'd told her, but I was damn well going to put a stop to it. She could get nothing but hurt.

It was two thirty when I turned into the Dixie Pig's crushed stone driveway and let her out beside her car. The routine good nights were an anticlimax.

I drove to the motel. There was only one reason Franklin could be asking those questions about me. He was interested in my interest in the saw-grass swamps and savanna intermingled with pine-land, salt meadows, and mangrove thickets on the east side of town. Franklin had stamped the brand on himself. Franklin was the reason I had come to Hudson.

Granting the fact, it left unanswered questions. How had a mulehead like Franklin outmaneuvered Bunny? Bunny could break him up with his bare hands. And why was Franklin nosing around me when by all rights he should have been lying doggo hoping nobody was looking in his direction?

I didn't know.

I didn't know, but I knew I was going to start finding out at dinner with Lucille Grimes.

There was no question now about my accepting that unwilling invitation.

For two thirds of its length the dinner was an eighteen-karat flop. We sat at opposite ends of a six foot table, and were served by a kid in a maid's uniform. Lucille sat at her end with an expression like an aristocrat among the peasantry. All I could think of was Lady Bountiful among the poor.

It was obvious that with the lady at the head of the table I was a stink in the nostrils. It was interesting that feeling as she did about me, Franklin had been able to force her into issuing this dinner invitation. It made Hazel a hundred per cent right about who was wearing the pants in the corporation.

Franklin was pushing her to set up the deadfall again. He didn't know what had happened to her that night. She wouldn't tell him. Franklin would naturally assume that after this expression of her majesty's gracious favor I would press hard for another date. Lucille knew better, but she had to go along with the idea.

It gave me an idea of my own.

"Glad to see you finally wised up to Franklin," I said to her when the little maid disappeared after serving the dessert.

Lucille's mind had been a long way off. Probably gloating over a mental image of me staked out over an anthill. She came back to earth in a hurry. "Wised up?"

"Sure. What the hell you ever saw in a jerk like that I'll never know. A big bag of wind." It was no trouble to make that sound convincing. "Having me to dinner like this shows you're a smart girl. You should have cut him loose a long time ago. You and I, now—we could really play chopsticks together on the same piano."

She didn't swallow it hook, line and sinker. Not at first. Her eyes were suspicious as I oiled up both sides of my tongue and greased her liberally. She couldn't believe at first I was so stupid as not to know her reaction to me, but the suspicion gradually died. She was used to such a response, for one thing. By the end of the meal she'd come as alive as though someone had just reported my painful demise. She was tossing them back to me as fast as I batted them at her.

Lucille was no fool. I was giving her an out on a problem on which she hadn't been able to see daylight. As far as Franklin was concerned, this was the way it was supposed to go. If she could report progress to him, that was a load off her back. If she could report progress that turned out to be fact, and that put my neck under the knife, why how lovely. She had nothing to lose.

She didn't overplay her hand a bit, either. "I was very angry with you the other evening," she said gravely. "I thought you were a gentleman."

Even the boob that I was supposed to be couldn't let her get away with that one. "You'd just set me up to get cut off at the knees, sweetheart. You're lucky I didn't really get mad at you."

"But you know I wasn't going to do anything—I wasn't—"

"You were just going to sit there and cheer. You got what was coming to you. Just like Franklin's going to one of these days." I threw that in as an afterthought. If she were really getting restless under the Franklin thumb—

She didn't appear to notice the opening. Honest curiosity shone for an instant through the genteel facade. "I admire clever men. Whatever led you to take rooms in two different names?"

"Self-preservation. I was at the head of the line when it was passed around. Look, maybe I was too rough with you, but admit it, you had it coming. I don't see why that means we can't get along. You're a smart girl. You and I make a much better team than you and Franklin. Just don't you try any more cute tricks and we'll be all right. I don't like bossy women. Do as you're told and we'll have no trouble."

I almost expected to hear her grinding her teeth after that little speech, but she smiled sweetly. She was a cinch to bring along a sawed-off baseball bat herself to our next motel room assignation. It oozed out of every ounce of her without her realizing it that she just couldn't wait to drag down into the dust the nose of this loud-mouthed braggart who had abused her. "I'll admit I'm not used to such a—such a forceful man," she said. "Shall we have our coffee on the patio?"

We had our coffee In the patio. I buttered her up some more. She buttered me up some more. Instead of the silver fingerbowls that were placed on our trays twin showerbaths would have been more appropriate.

She finally cut across the radius of the circle to the hub of the wheel. "What are you really doing in this area?" she asked me directly. "I never have believed that black maple story."

"A man can make a quick dollar if he stumbles onto the right patch of second growth out in that timber," I argued.

She wasn't ready now to let me get away with it. "You don't seem to me like the type of man interested in making a few dollars at a time."

I drained off the rest of my coffee and set my cup down with a gesture of finality. I rose to my feet. She rose, too, surprised. "You talk too much, sweetheart," I told her. I walked around the little marble table and took her by the arms, just below the edges of her short-sleeved dress, harder than I needed to. "You're going to have to break that habit." I shook her gently to and fro, not hard, but her face whitened at the pressure on her arms. "I'll give you a chance starting tomorrow night at dinner. Pick you up at five?"

"I'll—all right. Five," she said breathlessly.

"Okay." I let her go. Her hands came up instinctively to caress her arms. My handprints stood out on them lividly. "Thanks for the dinner. See you at five tomorrow. Good night."

"Good night," she echoed numbly.

I went down the outside walk to the street without going back through the house. I would have given a dollar bill to know what she was thinking as she stood there and watched me go. But on second thought I realized it would have been a dollar wasted.

She'd see to it that Franklin took me tomorrow night.

So she thought.

I'd see to it I took the pair of them.

I was positive now. Tomorrow night I'd wind up the whole ball of yarn.

I drove back to the motel and parked in the yard. It was still early, but I didn't feel like going out to the Dixie Pig. I opened the motel unit door carefully because Kaiser had a habit of sleeping against it. He wasn't against it this time. He was sprawled in the lefthand corner with his head at an awkward angle.

"Close the door," a voice said from behind it. Manny Sebastian's fat figure stepped into view. His hands were empty. The hands of the sandy-haired, bucktoothed man who moved out beside him weren't empty. A blued-steel revolver was trained steadily on my chest.

I stepped inside and closed the door.

IO

Bucktooth moved to my right, the gun steady. "Don't get careless," he said. His eyes were red-rimmed and wild-looking. I could see him only from the corner of my eye as his free hand snaked under my jacket and delicately removed the Smith & Wesson from its holster. He tossed it to Manny.

"He carries a Colt, too," Manny said. His round, swarthy face was shiny with perspiration.

From behind me Bucktooth gave me the shoulders-to-knees handpatting treatment. He discovered the Woodsman in my pants pocket. He didn't make the mistake of trying to take it out himself. "Throw it on the bed," he ordered me. "And be goddam careful how you do it."

I fished the .22 out with thumb and forefinger, and tossed it at the bed. I could see Manny relax. I wondered how the bastards would feel if they knew I still had the little three-shot .17 caliber puff adder on my shin.

"Let's get out of here," Bucktooth said from behind me.

"We're going to take a little ride," Manny informed me. He was mopping at his streaming features with a soggy handkerchief. My Smith & Wesson was in his other hand.

I went over and knelt down beside Kaiser. He was still, breathing. There was a ragged, bleeding furrow on his head between his ears, right alongside the still half-healed one from his trip into the ditch. I stood up and turned around. Bucktooth had moved in only six feet away from me, his gun reversed in his hand, the butt exposed. "Did you hit the dog, you sonofabitch?" I asked him.

"Just like I'll belt you if you make one more move like that without being told," he snarled.

I walked into him, swinging.

"Don't shoot! Don't shoot!" Manny bleated from behind me. "He's got to talk first!"

Bucktooth stepped back far enough so I missed him with my first swing. He stepped right back in again and clubbed at me with the gun. I got my head out of the way, but he landed on my left shoulder the same instant I smashed my right hand into his belly. I was staggering sideways when he doubled up. Before I could catch my balance Manny clocked me on the back of the neck with my own gun. I was on my knees all of a sudden without realizing how I'd got there. The room whirled sickeningly.

"Cut it out!" Manny said sharply to Bucktooth, who was lunging at me with upraised gun. Manny stepped in between us. "You can have your fun later." Bucktooth hesitated, his red eyes slitted. Reluctantly he backed away. "Get up," Manny said to me. I got to my feet, wobbly. "Where's the stuff?"

"Fifteen, eighteen miles out in the swamp," I mumbled.

"Didn't I tell you he'd say that?" Bucktooth growled.

"And didn't I tell you it didn't matter what he said?" Manny rebutted. "If it isn't wherever he takes us to, then you exercise that gun butt." He waved the Smith & Wesson at me. "Let's get going."

"Can't find th' tree—at night," I said.

"I don't expect to. We'll go in the morning. Right now we'll go to our place. Less chance of an interruption."

"The dog goes with us," I told him.

"Now here's one practicin' to be a character," Bucktooth said in a wondering tone. He shoved his face into mine. "The dog goes nowhere, jerk!"

"I'll show you where to leave him," I said.

Bucktooth made a sound deep in his throat. Manny caught his arm as he started to swing it. "We can't leave the dog here looking like that in an empty room," he said. He looked at me. "What's your play?"

"I know someone who'll take care of him," I answered. "Open the door. I'll carry him."

"No!" Bucktooth said violently.

"Pick him up," Manny said to me. "The dog will make a good excuse if we run onto anyone," he shut off his angry partner. "Shut up, will you? Rudy Hernandez told me years ago the guy was like this about animals."

I picked up Kaiser. In the shape I was in it was a hell of a lift. Bucktooth was right beside me. "Pretty soon I'm gonna ask you what happened to Red, pal," he said softly. "Right now you make one wrong move or one bit of noise an' you've had it. I won't kill you, but you'll wish I had. I'll break every bone in your stupid face."

"Open the door," I said.

Instead he leveled the gun at me again. "I'll cover you from the doorway till you get him in the car," he told Manny.

Manny opened the door. It was black night outside. I carried Kaiser out. Manny pointed to a big station wagon parked on the rim of the driveway. He opened the front door on the passenger's side. There wasn't a soul around. I climbed into the front seat with Kaiser on my lap. Manny got under the wheel. In seconds I could hear Bucktooth crawling into the seat behind me. I don't know if I could feel or sense his gun three-quarters of an inch from the short hairs at the back of my neck.

Manny took the wagon out of there. I'd intended to take Kaiser to the Dixie Pig, but rolling through town I saw a light on in Jed Raymond's second floor office. "Pull in anywhere here," I said. Bucktooth's gun came up level with my head as the car swung into the curb.

"What's the play?" Manny said to me again.

"See that light up there? I'll carry the dog up one flight of stairs and leave him outside the door of the real estate office."

"And I suppose you'll okay that, too," Bucktooth rasped at Manny.

"I'd just as soon humor him till we get our hands on the stuff," Manny said defensively. "This is one stubborn sonofabitch."

"I'll unstubborn him or anyone else in three an' a half minutes, guaranteed," Bucktooth snapped, but he opened his door and got out. He opened my door. "Come on, you. Sometimes I think the whole damn world's crazy."

I lugged Kaiser up the stairs and laid him down gently outside Jed's door. Bucktooth stayed a yard behind me all the way. I knew that if Kaiser came to before Jed found him, the big dog would smell Jed inside and wouldn't leave.

We were back in the wagon in two minutes. I felt a lot better. Jed would take care of Kaiser. I knew Kaiser liked him. Now I could concentrate on getting rid of these mongolian idiots.

Manny headed north on U.S. 19. About two miles above town he turned into a second-rate motel. "No noise," Bucktooth warned me as we got out of the wagon. By way of emphasis he banged me viciously in the ribs with his gun butt when Manny's back was turned. I nearly went down. Stumbling inside the motel room, I began to make plans for Bucktooth.

With the door closed, Manny turned to me, "How do we get to the stuff?"

"Airboat," I said.

Manny nodded.

"Air what?" Bucktooth wanted to know.

"Airboat," Manny told him. "They use them in swamps. An airplane engine on a plank, practically. No draught. They say they'll float on a heavy dew. I've seen movies of them."

"What's the arrangement when we get there, Manny?" I asked him. I didn't want him thinking I was going too easily. I wanted him unsuspicious.

If I'd ever been in doubt about their plans for me, the glance they exchanged removed it. "A three-way split," Manny said finally. "If it's all there," he amended it. "There's enough for us all." Bucktooth turned his head but not before I saw his ugly grin.

There was only one bed in the room. Bucktooth motioned me to a chair. "Squat, pal," he said to me. He produced a length of manila and efficiently roped me to the chair, my arms to the arms, a leg to each front leg. Manny tested the job, then stretched out on the bed, taking off only his shoes. Bucktooth soon joined him. They left the light on.

The room grew quiet. My head hurt. My ribs hurt. My legs went to sleep. I was uncomfortable, but I wasn't too upset. My time was coming. Daylight would signal the beginning of the end of the line for the two men on the bed.

When I got these two city types out in the swamp, I'd leave them there, permanently.

I must have dozed off eventually, because their stirring around woke me.

The light was still on, but at the edges of the curtains I could see early morning sunshine.

"Where do we get the airboat?" Manny asked me while Bucktooth was unwinding the rope from around me.

"We rent it. There's a place about seven miles east on Main Street." My arms weren't in bad shape after the night in the chair, but I couldn't stand up. I massaged my legs. It was ten minutes before I could walk. Bucktooth glowered impatiently while I hobbled around.

As soon as we got outside I could tell from the sun and the haze it was going to be a hot, humid day, a real stinger. So much the better. East of the traffic light in town we stopped for breakfast. They took turns going in while one stayed in the station wagon with me. Manny brought me out coffee and a sweet roll.

Out beyond the edge of town I didn't have to say a word. Manny saw the shack with the hand-painted sign "Airboat For Hire" I'd noticed my first day in Hudson. He pulled the wagon in under a tree. "Bring him on down when I signal you," he said to Bucktooth, and walked down to a little dock. We could see him talking to a slatternly looking woman, and in a couple of minutes a boy hand-poled an airboat up to the dock from around behind the shack. Manny raised his arm.

"We won't need any conversation," Bucktooth said, nudging me. We went down the path. I could see Bucktooth looking distrustfully at the wide-planked, battered hull with its high, platform seats, and the big propeller encased in wire mesh. Three or four of the planks were fresh where someone had ripped out the bottom on a snag.

I stepped up onto the boat and started the engine. It was an old type with a hand throttle and a rudimentary tiller. I revved it a few times, listening, then slowed it down and tested the plugs and the battery. I checked the gas gauge and the compass. I had no intention of being left high and wet in the swamp myself.

When the kid who'd brought the boat around saw I knew what I was doing, he wandered off back to the shack. The woman had already disappeared. "Can't you run this thing?" Bucktooth demanded of Manny when the kid left. "I don't like him runnin' it."

"I can run it," Manny said. I knew he couldn't from the way he said it. "He's the one who's got to find the right spot, though. Just keep an eye on him."

He climbed up into one of the front platform seats. Bucktooth settled himself in the dishpan cockpit, facing me, his back braced against a platform strut. He could watch every move I made in the navigator's bucket seat. "You'll get wet down there," I said.

"Just you see to it I don't get wet, pal," he answered me. I would have preferred them in reversed positions. Manny had the keys to the wagon, and my

Smith & Wesson. "How long's this going to take us?"

I shrugged. "Hour and a half each way." It wasn't going to take a third of that if I had my way.

I eased away from the dock. Bucktooth stared nervously at the brackish water lapping the boat's low sides. Up on the platform I could see Manny flinch the first few times I rammed the boat over deceptively solid-looking areas of saw-grass.

The sun beat down on us. In no time there were black patches of perspiration on Manny's back and under his arms. Bucktooth was sweating freely, too. Under the gnarled cypress trees with their trailing moss there was shade but no coolness. The swamp was a miasma of sticky heat. I turned right and left through wide channels, enough to get them thoroughly confused. I kept an eye on the compass, and an eye out for mangrove roots that might have tipped us over or stove in a plank. Beneath the thick, green jungle growth overhead the engine didn't sound as noisy. Mosquitoes and gnats hummed around us. Manny and Bucktooth swatted busily. My hide is tougher. Once or twice Manny turned to look back at me. I could see that for the first time he was beginning to have doubts about the expedition.

I gave them enough time to get relaxed, then began watching for a wide-enough space between the trees off the channel accompanied by a low-lying branch of the right height. I passed up a couple that didn't look exactly like what I wanted.

When I saw one that did, I didn't wait any longer.

The tree-opening was on the left, more than wide enough to slip the boat into. "Alligator!" I yelled, and pointed to the right.

"Where?" They bellowed it together. Bucktooth turned in the direction I pointed. Manny stood up to look. I slammed the throttle wide open and aimed hard left. The boat stood up on its port gunwale as it darted between the trees. The low-lying branch caught Manny in the chest. He went off the platform like an ice cube from a spilled cocktail glass. He slingshotted into the tree on the right. Even above the engine roar I could hear the splash he made as he hit the mud below.

With the tiller hard right and two thirds of the way around the first tree I shut the engine off. Bucktooth had grabbed with both hands to save himself from sliding overboard, and I reached down and slipped the little .17 caliber out of its shin holster. As we drifted back out into the main channel, Bucktooth started to turn to check on the shut-off engine. "Don't turn a thing but your head, man," I told him, my voice loud in the sudden quiet. Looking over his shoulder, he turned white when he saw what I had in my hand.

Desperately he looked up at the platform for Manny. His gaze sped then to the space between the trees, and his eyes bugged out at the sight of Manny in the mud, only his legs visible above the greenish water. The legs were kicking feebly.

"Drop your gun in the water," I directed him. I didn't even blink while he did it. I needn't have worried. His nerve was gone. He was ashen, and his hands were shaking. He was a long way removed from the gun-toting bully who'd taken so much pleasure in pushing me around last night. "You don't deserve it, but I'll give you a choice," I said. "I was going to leave you out here, with the heat and the mosquitoes and the bugs and the snakes and the alligators. You'll never make it in. I doubt if I could myself." His whole face was wet as he stared at me. "You won't go easy if you stay, so I'll give you the choice. Stay, or take one dead center from this," I waved the little hand-gun.

He couldn't speak at all for a second. "You'd—you'd shoot me?"

I laughed. "What the hell were you planning to do to me? Come on, make up your mind. Which is it going to be?" His eyes darted wildly in all directions. "Take the bullet," I said. "You'll go out of your mind out here in twelve hours." His chest was heaving as he tried to pump air through his constricted throat. "Take the bullet."

"No!" It was wrenched from him forcibly.

"Okay." I ruddered the boat over to a little saw-grass island with one half-grown scotch pine slanting up out of it. "Jump."

"Listen, you wouldn't—"

"Jump, you bastard. Or catch the bullet."

I moved my arm. He jumped. He shrieked as he went in up to his knees in the gelid ooze. He grabbed at the tree, and yelled again as something slithered away under his hands. He kept trying to pull his legs up out of the muck.

I started the engine and turned the boat around. The last I saw of him he was halfway up into the tree that was doubling over under his weight. If he was making any noise I couldn't hear him over the engine.

I went back to Manny Sebastian. His legs were under water now, too. I had a hell of a time pulling him far enough up out of the mud to get my Smith & Wesson out of his pants. I didn't bother with the keys to the wagon. I dropped him back in. If it was any consolation to him, I don't think he drowned. His neck was broken.

I rode the compass back to the shack. I poled in the last half mile and beached the airboat three hundred yards beyond the dock, behind a point. As long as the station wagon stayed there for security, the crackers weren't going to worry too much about their boat. By the time they started to I'd be long gone from Hudson.

I walked a mile, then hitched a ride into town. I made and remade plans all the way. I had a date with Lucille for five o'clock. I was through fooling around. Five o'clock was going to be the payoff, but I had a few things to do first.

In town it must have been ninety, but it felt almost chilly compared to the swamp. I went into the truck-stop diner south of the traffic light in the square and had a meal. I could hardly believe it when I looked at my watch and saw it was still only ten thirty in the morning.

I borrowed a sheet of paper, an envelope, and a pencil from the girl cashier. I took a couple of napkins and practiced composing telegraph messages. I finally hit on one I thought would do the trick. ARRIVING SOON MEET ME LAZY SUSAN URGENT YOU NOT FAIL ME. I addressed it to Dick Pierce, General Delivery, Hudson, Florida, and I signed it Roy.

I copied it out on the sheet of paper and sealed it up in the envelope along with two one-dollar bills. On the outside of the envelope I printed "Western Union." I sat there in the diner by the window watching the northbound, over-the-road, diesel-rigged, big vans pull into the yard, and I watched the drivers as they came in and sat down at the counter.

When a likely-looking middle-aged man came in off a furniture rig, I gave him a five-dollar bill and the envelope and asked him to drop it off at the Western Union office wherever he was at noontime. He said he'd be sure to do it. I sat there till he pulled out of the yard and up the road.

When that message hit the deck in the Hudson Western Union office it would be sent around to the post office and delivered to Lucille Grimes. When it was I should get a little action for my seven dollars. The telegram with that signature should give Lucille Grimes and Blaze Franklin something to think about besides Chet Arnold.

I walked from the diner to the motel. Inside I took the phone off the hook. If Jed was trying to call me about Kaiser, better he should think the line was busy than that he couldn't reach me. I took out the Smith & Wesson and I spent thirty minutes cleaning, oiling, and completely refurbishing it. Then I got into the shower and did the same for me.

At noon I was back uptown and parked across the street from the post office. Through the big front window I had a good view of the General Delivery window. The alphabetized slots were right behind the window. I'd specified noon for the sending of the telegram because from twelve to two Lucille was in the post office with just one clerk, and almost always handled the front herself.

I spread a newspaper over the steering wheel, and settled down to wait. I could feel the pressure building up. I don't have nerves, but I get keyed up. Everything around me is magnified a couple of dozen times, including the tick of a watch and the color of the sky.

It was hot in the car, even with the windows down, but not as hot as where I'd just come from. Not as hot as plowing up and down half-grown-over back roads on the east side of Main, either. I was through with that stuff. This little deal was going to pop the weasel right out of the box.

It was one twenty-five when the Western Union kid rode up on his bike. He kicked it up on its stand and went on inside. I saw him lay the telegram down on the counter, and in a minute Lucille appeared at the window and picked it up and looked at it. She looked at it a long time. I could see the kid reminding her she hadn't signed for it.

She scribbled her name, and the kid went out. She never even looked at the General Delivery slots behind her. Telegram in hand, she made a beeline for the back. Telephone call, I told myself. I folded up my newspaper and laid it on the seat beside me. In three minutes Lucille was at the front door. I could see her explaining something over her shoulder to the clerk she'd moved up to the front window.

She came out and walked hurriedly to a red MG parked three doors down the street. A double-parked delivery van had kept me from noticing it before. She climbed in, backed up, and ripped up the street. I was facing the wrong way. I swung in a wide U and took out after her.

She hightailed it through town, straight north on 19. I dogged her at a distance. I didn't need to stay too close. I knew where she was going. No farther than it took to meet Blaze Franklin, deputy sheriff, in some kind of privacy.

Actually they didn't bother too much about the privacy. From a quarter-mile behind her I watched her pull off onto the shoulder of the road. She tucked the red MG right in on the tail of a two-tone country cruiser. Blaze Franklin's thick-bodied figure was out of the cruiser and on the way over to the MG before its wheels had stopped rolling.

From a curve away I had no trouble at all in seeing his red face and the yellow flash of the telegram as he snatched it away from her and tore it open. She'd been afraid to open it herself, evidently.

Franklin climbed into the MG beside her. Their heads stayed close together for what seemed like fifteen minutes. I'd have given a quarter to be a fly on the windshield during that conversation. When Franklin jumped out of the MG and headed for the cruiser, I was ready. I swung around and headed back to town. At the first intersection I turned off and parked. In less than a minute the cruiser came flying down the highway, its siren rrr'ing. Franklin was hunched over the wheel, his tomato face like a bulldog's.

Three minutes later the MG came by. Lucille's face was white and strained-looking.

I followed along behind.

Curtain going up.

When I walked into the office of the Lazy Susan two hours later, Blaze Franklin was cocked up against the wall in a straightbacked chair, big as life and twice as nasty. If it had been me that's where I'd have been, too, but I still had to grade him A for nerve.

After the first quick look when I came in the door he paid no attention. Mr. Franklin had other things on his mind now than Chet Arnold. They had to figure now they'd had me in the wrong picture. I asked at the desk for mail, not that there ever was any. The young clerk behind the desk tried to engage Blaze in conversation after he'd finished with me. Franklin bit his head off neatly in about eight well-chosen words. The kid turned a dull red, and subsided.

I went out and walked down to my unit. From it I could see the office, and I could see Franklin. Twice in the first few minutes he got up and picked up the phone on the desk without a by-your-leave and made a call. It suited me fine. The longer he sat there the more things he could think of to go wrong. I wanted him shook. I hoped the phone calls were to Lucille. I wanted her shook.

Most of all I wanted Franklin right where he was. His uniform made it hard for me to move openly against him. I could kill them both, but that wouldn't get me the bundle. As long as Franklin was nailed down here, I could be sure of getting to Lucille with no interruptions. And if she gave me a hard time about where the bundle was, I'd shake her till she atomized.

I watched him off and on for another hour. He made a couple of more phone calls. He was a busy boy. At four fifteen I shaved and started to change for my date with Lucille. Buttoning my shirt, I went back to the window. I couldn't see Franklin. I could see the chair he'd been in, but he wasn't in it. I waited a couple of minutes. Wherever he was, he didn't come back.

I finished dressing in a hurry. I shoved the .38 in its holster, slipped into my jacket, and crossed over to the office. In the first quick look around I could see Franklin wasn't anywhere inside. I looked at the clerk. "The bird-dog gone?"

He didn't spit, but he almost did. "Good riddance."

"He say where he could be reached?"

"He said nothin'."

"He get a call from anyone?"

The kid shook his head. "He made enough of 'em, though. The last one he swore an' banged up the receiver an' took off."

I went outside and sat in the Ford. What in the hell had happened? Nothing on earth should have moved Blaze Franklin out of that chair. That telegram from Roy Martin should have made him afraid to move. He should have sat there, getting madder and shakier by the minute. That telegram should have immobilized him.

He must have seen that his only chance of keeping the lid on—once he read the telegram—was to intercept Roy Martin, and dispose of him quietly. Nothing should have been able to move Franklin away from that motel office.

I went back over it step by step. Gradually the only logical answer forced itself on me. I'd underrated the sonofabitch. Suppose he'd been smart enough to call the point of origin of the telegram and ask for a description of the sender? Once he knew the circumstances under which it had been sent he was right back in the saddle. With the telegram exposed as a phony, how much brains did he need to figure out who'd sent it up the road to have it bounce back here off his noggin?

So why hadn't he rushed into my motel unit and shot me up, down, and sideways and triumphantly hauled in the riddled corpse? It was exactly what he should have done. If he had the sense to short-circuit the booby-trap I'd set up for him, how could he have missed the obvious follow-up?

There was something I didn't understand.

Something I didn't know.

It was time I learned it.

I started up the Ford. Nothing was changed, really, except that I had to keep an eye peeled for Franklin. I drove up to the post office to collect Lucille.

11

She was standing out on the sidewalk when I pulled up in front. I opened the door and she got in. "Let's stop for a drink at the Dixie Pig first, shall we?" she said without any preliminary greeting at all.

My first impulse was to refuse. In the first place I didn't want to wave this long-legged blonde under Hazel's nose. I sneaked a glance at Lucille as she sat beside me, eyes straight ahead. She looked and sounded as brittle as glass. She might as well have worn a sign; whatever had pulled Franklin away from the motel, she knew about. The Dixie Pig was now just another gambit in the game.

Okay. We'd go to the Dixie Pig.

But not together. I drew up in front, reached across her and opened the door again. "You go on in. I just remembered I'm supposed to pick up a few dollars a guy owes me. I'll be back in ten minutes."

She didn't like it, but what could she do? She climbed out reluctantly and closed the door. "Hurry back," she said with an attempt at a smile. The shark's teeth were polished to a high gloss.

I circled the Dixie Pig driveway, and saw right away the hunch had paid off. Snuggled in among the six or eight parked cars was Franklin's cruiser. It had to be Franklin's. That's why she'd brought me here, so that he could without difficulty take up the trail for what they both felt would be the final act of the drama.

I pulled out on the highway again and in half a mile found a shiftless-looking country grocery. I stopped in and bought two pounds of brown sugar. Back in the Ford I opened it and set it down carefully on the seat beside me. I drove back to the Dixie Pig and around to the back parking lot. There was a hole two parking spaces away from the cruiser. I nosed into it.

I sat there, watching the two windows that looked out on the back parking lot. I couldn't see anyone in either booth. I picked up the sugar, got out of the Ford, walked around the rear of the car between it and the cruiser, removed the cruiser's gas cap, dumped in the brown sugar, slapped the cap back on, and crushed the bag and stuffed it in my pocket. It might have taken me six seconds. The sugar I spilled was indistinguishable on the crushed stone.

I brushed off my hands and walked in the Dixie Pig's back door. If they'd seen me drive in, I was right on schedule.

Franklin sat at the bar, his back elaborately to the door through which I'd entered. Lucille bounced up from a booth, so quickly she had to have seen me drive in. She met me in the center of the floor. "I don't think I feel like a drink right now, after all, Chet. Couldn't we wait till we eat?"

"Anything you say," I told her. We turned to the door. It was a rush act of superb proportions. I hadn't been in the place thirty seconds, but Franklin was already gone from the bar, ready to take up the pursuit in the cruiser. Behind the bar Hazel all but stood on her head trying to attract my attention. I avoided looking at her as we went out.

The cruiser was gone. Franklin would pick us up on the highway. How would he know whether to go north or south? I found out how he knew, "There's a new restaurant south on the highway, Chet. If you're feeling experimental, I understand it's quite good."

"Anything you say," I repeated. Full twilight wasn't many minutes away when I ran back down the driveway and out onto the highway. "How far is this place?"

"Oh, a dozen to fifteen miles. It's supposed to be quite attractive." Her voice was as cool as a mountain brook. Only the hands clenched in her lap betrayed her inner tension.

Fifteen miles was the superlative of fine. Franklin shouldn't be able to fetch half that before the sugar in his gas line froze his engine down tight. It was a bonus that he'd be decommissioned outside of town.

South of the square I switched on my lights. I watched the shoulder of the road. About a mile beyond we passed a car pulled off on the right, almost indistinguishable in the gathering darkness. If I hadn't been looking for it, I never would have seen it. In the rear-view mirror I watched its parking lights come on as it rolled out on the highway behind us. The wolf was in the sheepfold. We played follow-the-leader down U.S. 19 in the deepening twilight.

He dogged me from so far back I couldn't be sure where I'd lost him, or if I actually had. He hadn't needed to stay too close because he knew where we were going. After a few miles there were no lights of any kind behind me. I didn't think even Franklin would be running that letter-S stretch without them.

It was a silent ride. Each of us was busy with private thoughts. Lucille roused herself when we'd been on the road about twenty minutes. "You'll have to watch for the turnoff," she said, leaning forward in the seat. "There's a big white sign, and then it's off to the left about a mile."

Naturally they wanted a place not on the main highway. We both saw the sign at the same time. I was already slowing down when Lucille pointed. I turned into a graveled side road at eight miles an hour. No lights of any kind turned in behind us.

A half mile in a wagon-road branched off in the headlights. I turned up it. "Not that way!" Lucille said sharply. I paid no attention. I went up it about fifty yards, pulled up the brake, and cut the motor and lights. Insurance in case a raging Franklin again proved himself shrewder than I'd anticipated and succeeded in commandeering another car.

"Plenty of time for food," I said to Lucille, and slipped an arm around her. My purpose was to keep her from fleeing if she suspected anything. She didn't. She humored me to the extent of lowering her head on my shoulder. She was content to await the arrival of the rear guard. It was full dark under the trees.

I wished I could see her face. It would have interested me to be able to read her expression. As far as I was concerned, Lucille Grimes was already dead. It was just a question of when, and how. In a way it was too bad. This was a really talented bitch.

Right that second she gave me a demonstration of it. She grabbed the horn ring on the steering wheel. The horn blatted twice. She was reaching for the lights when I caught her arm. She sat there tensely with her arm in my grip, waiting for Blaze Franklin to come up out of the darkness and kill me.

I could sense the shriveling of her self-confidence when nothing happened. "You beginning to get the idea he's not coming?" I asked her. "He's not split-ting with you, Lucille. He's splitting with me. Your boyfriend's sold you out. I'm supposed to bury you twenty yards off this side road."

It shook her to her heels, but she was too smart to go for it completely. "He'll kill you," she croaked. She tried to look over her shoulder.

"Where is he, then?" I needled her. "Get smart, woman. It's lucky for you I like you. Now get on the ball and steer me to the money. I'll take care of Franklin for you."

There was only one thing she could think. Even if Franklin hadn't sold her out, if he'd flubbed his end of the deal she had to protect herself. She knew who I was, and she knew there was no reason on earth I shouldn't leave her body in the bushes beside the car. Her steel-trap mind should have been telling her she was in perfect position to play it cool right down to the finish line, and then choose up sides with the winner.

I couldn't understand why she hesitated so long.

"We—we never found the money," she said at last. Her voice was husky. "Only the thousand in the envelope and a few thousand on—on him." She drew a quivering breath. "If only I'd never mentioned to Blaze the big, odd-looking man who mailed such queer—" Her voice died away.

So that was why Franklin wanted me alive. He hoped I knew where the bundle was. The funny part of it was, I did. Now.

I tightened the grip on her arm. "Franklin killed him before he found out where the money was?"

"He—yes," she whispered.

So Franklin hadn't been able to crack Bunny. I started up the Ford. "Tell me where he was staying, Lucille." She was silent. I turned my head to look at her. Her face was just an indistinct pale oval. "Tell me," I warned her. "Franklin might not have been able to find it, but I'll find it."

She told me. She had trouble getting it out. The directions would have put Bunny's place north of town.

I pulled on the dash light. She was watching me, and she backed off as far as she could go. I crossed my hand over my chest and drew the Smith & Wesson. Her face crumpled with fear. I took hold of her and pulled her toward me, reversed the gun, and slashed her across her soft inner arm with the front gunsight. She cried out in pain and shock as the blood welled. "I'm giving you a chance to change that story," I told her. "Because if we get where you send me and there's nothing there, that's what happens to your face till my arm gets tired."

She changed the story.

The new one put Bunny's place east of town, which sounded a lot better to me.

I got out of there. Lucille sat huddled in the seat beside me. I hadn't expected her to go to pieces so completely. The way I'd sized her up she should have had no trouble at all riding with a foot on each saddle till either Franklin or I got dumped. She must be scared to death of Franklin.

We were on the right side of town but it still took us nearly an hour to get there. I had a funny feeling riding east on Main past the shack with the sign out in front, "Airboat For Hire." The side road Lucille reluctantly directed me up couldn't have been more than a couple of miles beyond the point where I'd been so painfully slogging over brambled trails. No wonder Franklin had been getting itchy.

It was a small cabin way out in the middle of nowhere. I got out of the Ford and ran a flashlight around the building. No telephone wires. Fine. I circled it cautiously. In the rear a mound of cut branches loomed up in the light. I pulled off a couple. There sat the blue Dodge, up on blocks.

So Lucille hadn't lied to me. I returned to the Ford. She still sat in it, motionless. I had to take her by the arm again to get her out. She didn't want to come with me.

I got a chisel and maul out of the trunk of the Ford, herded Lucille up to the door ahead of me, and broke the lock. A wave of dry heat rolled out at me as it opened, a musty, long-closed smell. I wondered if this was the right place, after all. I kept a good hold on Lucille's arm.

Inside I closed the door and stationed her away from it. I walked through the place. A skillet was still on the two-burner stove. Bunny's clothes hung neatly on hangers. There were two more locked doors. A couple of swings of the maul disposed of both. There was nothing at all in the first room. I beamed the flash rapidly around the interior of the second one, and then it hung there, motionless.

I'd found Bunny.

He was face down on the rough pine flooring. His wrists were handcuffed to ringbolts in the floor at right angles to his head. The ringbolts were new. Fresh pine sawdust was still visible where the holes had been drilled for them.

Dry as the air in the place was there was another odor. Bunny had been in the cuffs a long time. With his chest flat on the floor and his arms spreadeagled, not even his great strength could achieve leverage. In a final contortion he had thrown himself onto his right side. The bone of his left knee glistened at me out of raw-looking meat, the trousers and flesh long since abraded away in his ceaseless struggle with the flooring. His upper left arm was mincemeat where he'd gnawed at himself.

He'd lain in the cuffs till he died.

Which kills first, hunger or thirst? I couldn't remember. I couldn't think.

The game had dealt Bunny a tough hand. Looking into Franklin's gun, he must have temporized, thinking he'd find a spot to turn it around. He hadn't counted on the cuffs. He'd gone into them, but he hadn't cracked. How do you break a stubborn man? You starve him. When he's out of his mind with hunger and thirst, he'll lead you to anything he has.

If he's not too far out of his mind. With the hunger, the thirst, and the maddening heat, Franklin had returned to the cabin one day and found a mindless animal that could never lead him to anything.

I stooped and examined the head, cruelly battered from endless, raving contact with the floor. There had been no merciful bullet.

Franklin had left him to die.

Franklin and Lucille Grimes had left him to die.

I knew now why she'd been so afraid to come in here with me. She'd known exactly what I was going to find.

I straightened up and drew the Smith & Wesson. I walked out into the other room.

"Blaze did it!" she screamed when she saw my face. "Blaze did it! I wanted to let him—"

I shot her in the throat, three times.

"Tell your story in hell, if you can get anyone to listen," I told her. She thrashed on the floor, blood pulsing between the fingers of the hands clasped to her neck. "If they can patch up your lying voice."

I stepped over her. I had work to do.

I went outside, into the clean darkness. I looked up at the stars to orient myself. I knew where the sack would be. For a cache out in the country, Bunny and I had always followed a pattern. From the front door of the cabin I stepped out due north as accurately as I could figure it. I knew it wouldn't be more than thirty or forty feet from the cabin.

In the daylight it would have been a cinch, and even in the dark it wasn't hard. My feet told me as soon as I hit softer earth. Bunny had planted something green over it. I ripped it up, pulled the chisel out of my pocket that was the only tool I had, and tore into the loose ground. A foot below the surface I ran into the sack.

I hauled it up and by the light of the flash made certain that the bulk of the swag was still in it. Then I reburied it, stamping down the earth. No sense lugging it around with me. I'd be back for it. I'd be back for it when I brought

Blaze Franklin out here and roped him down to Bunny's body and left him to die in the same way he'd left Bunny.

I went back inside for a look around. Lucille was unconscious. Bubbles of blood pulsed gently now instead of jetting with each ragged breath. She wouldn't last long. She was lucky. If I hadn't been so mad that I hadn't stopped to think, I could have figured a different end for her. She was just as guilty as Franklin.

Death I'm used to, but Bunny's infuriated me. Where would Franklin be now? Back at the Lazy Susan, probably, chewing up the rug. He had to hope I came back there. He'd get his wish in a way he never expected.

I went back out to the Ford and got out of there.

I drove straight to the Dixie Pig. I wanted Franklin so bad I could taste it, but I had another errand first. I scouted the back parking lot carefully. No two-tone cruiser. I parked beside Hazel's car and went on in.

Hazel was behind the bar that had a half-dozen customers. Her face lighted up when she saw me. She made a circling motion with her hand that beckoned me behind the bar, and held up the hinged flap at the far end. I walked on in and out through the hanging curtain in the center of the back-bar. I'd never been out there before. It was set up as a lounging room, with a couch and a couple of chairs, a Primus stove and a coffeepot.

"Get a bag packed," I said to her when she came through the curtain behind me. "I'll be back for you in an hour."

Her big hand caught mine and squeezed it, hard. "Listen to me, Chet. Please." Her voice was low and intense. "Franklin has everyone out looking for you. There's half a dozen of them waiting for you down in the motel yard. They never dreamed you'd come back here."

So. End of the line in Hudson, Florida. And I couldn't get Franklin. I couldn't? The hell I couldn't. I held out my hand to Hazel. "Forget what I said about a bag. Give me your car keys."

She turned to her handbag on a chair. "Chet, please let me come—"

"Tell them I took the keys away from you," I cut her off. I couldn't take her with me now. I was something less than even money to make it. "Forget what I said about packing a bag." She handed me the keys. "Tell them I took—" I shut myself off. I was starting to repeat myself. I punched Hazel in the eye. Big as she was she went over backward and landed on the couch. The eye would be her alibi. "So long, baby," I said from the curtained opening. I didn't look back. I didn't want to see the expression on her face.

I drove down to the motel in her car. They should have been looking for my Ford, It turned out they were looking for anything. I'd no more than rolled into the yard and opened the car door when some eager beaver tapped his headlights. Instantly three more sets came on. I was semi-circled by cruisers. The motel yard looked bright as day.

Blaze Franklin came roaring out of the nearest cruiser, waving a gun. He had to be first. He couldn't let me talk. At ten yards I put five in a row into him a playing card could have covered. He went down, bellowing like a wounded bull. He was a wounded bull. A dark red stain spread over the front of his uniform trousers. He'd live. He wouldn't enjoy it. I put the last one into his jaw as he flopped on the ground, to keep him quiet if I made the getaway good.

Firecrackers were going off all around me. They couldn't shoot worth a damn. I dived back in under the wheel and aimed the car straight ahead through the largest gap in the encircling headlights. Gravel spurted. Someone shot out the windshield. I ducked flying glass, bumped over the lawn, through the flower bed, around the swimming pool, and over a white picket fence. I jounced down onto the highway and floored the accelerator. For the first five-hundred yards part of the fence kept banging against the front wheels of Hazel's car. Then it fell off.

Behind me were lights and sirens. No shortage of either. I busted right through the square and set sail for the Dixie Pig. In the souped-up Ford I at least had a chance of outrunning them. Right now I could just about smell the overheated engines behind me.

A thousand yards from the Dixie Pig I cut the lights, got over on the shoulder, and drove in darkness. If there had been anything parked out there it would have been Katy-Bar-the-door. I whirled the wheel hard when I saw the lighter outline of the crushed stone driveway. I took a section of hedge with me, but I made the turn. I belted it around to the back. Outside on the highway the cruisers screamed on by.

I yanked up the emergency and lit running. The door on the driver's side of the Ford stood open. I didn't remember leaving it open. I came to a sliding stop beside it, my hand on the butt of my .38 when I saw a dark figure on the other side of the front seat. I came within a tick of blasting it before I recognized Hazel. "Get the hell out of there!" I ordered her, trying to listen for sounds on the highway.

"Take me with you, Chet," she pleaded. "Give me a gun."

"Don't make me do it, baby," I warned her. "Get out of the car."

She got out. I could see she was crying. "Chet—"

"Stop making these losing bets, will you?" I got in under the wheel. "Get back inside and keep your mouth shut." I backed up, swung around, and rammed the Ford down the driveway. The last I saw of Hazel was the glitter of the silver conches on her cowboy boots in the big swing of the headlights.

I doubled back toward town. There were bound to be road blocks north and south on 19. I'd head east, on Main. The added power of the Ford felt good under my foot. I blasted the road. Approaching the traffic light I slowed down. I'd just started to make the left-hand turn when there was the snarl of a siren practically in my ear. Somebody in the posse had had the brains to leave a trailer. He was headed the wrong way, but I saw the shine of his lights as he swung around after me. My forty-five-mile-an-hour turn carried me up onto the sidewalk before I got straightened out on Main.

I really rolled it away from there. I was doing eighty-five on a road built for forty. The Ford was all over the road. I watched the dark ribbon of macadam unroll in the headlights. Behind me the wailing shriek of the siren pierced the night, but I was outrunning him. Then I burst out of a curve into a long straight-away, and far up the road winked the red lights of trouble.

Road block.

Instinctively I lifted my foot off the gas, but I still rolled up on it fast. A spotlight came on when they saw me. A tiny figure stood out in the road, waving me down with flapping arms. I sized it up. Two cruisers across the road, their snouts extending way out onto the shoulders. Three quarters of a car's width between them in the center. Ditch on the right. Open field on the left. And in the rear-view mirror the lights of the trailing cruiser rapidly gaining.

A road block you do or you don't. I mashed down on the gas and headed for the center opening between the end-to-end cruisers. I just might rip my way through. The fool with the flapping arms stood right in the center of the gap. The headlights picked him up solidly. Roaring down on him, I was suddenly looking through the windshield into the white, strained face of Jed Raymond.

I hoped he'd jump. Jed was a nice kid. If he didn't, though, he'd have to take his chances, as I was taking mine. I couldn't have been twenty yards from him—and he hadn't made a move—when Kaiser pranced out in front of him from behind a cruiser, head cocked, tongue lolling, tail waving.

My brain sent me straight on through, over the dog and Jed, to try the odds with the cruisers. But hands spun the wheel, hard left. Somebody else will have to explain it to you. I missed them both, caromed broadside off the left-hand cruiser in a whining, ear-splitting shriek of tortured metal, and hurtled a hundred fifty yards down into the field. The front wheels dropped suddenly into a ditch. There was a loud whump, and the Ford stood up on its nose. The doors flew open. I flew out. I hit hard, and rolled.

I didn't lose consciousness. I still had the gun. The Ford was down on its knees in front, its ass-end up in the air, the wheels still spinning. I started to crawl over to it, and knew in the first second my right leg was broken.

Up on the road the spotlight pivoted and crept down through the field. It caught me, passed on, hesitated, and came back. There was a sharp crack, and a bullet plowed up the ground beside me. Rifle. Sounded like a .30-.30. I crawled over the uneven ground to the Ford, underneath the back wheels where I could see up to the road. I reloaded in a hurry, and got the spotlight with my third shot.

They turned the other cruiser around—the one I hadn't hit—and its spotlight started down through the field. I popped it out before it reached me. Not that it made any difference. More red lights, sirens, and spotlights were whirling up to the roadblock every second now.

I reloaded the Smith & Wesson again. Nothing for it now but the hard sell. Nothing for it but to see to it a few of them shook hands with the devil at the same time I did.

To get me in a hurry they had to come through the field. By now they knew enough not to be in a hurry. The .30-.30 went off again, and a large charge of angry metal whanged through the body of the car over my head. The rifle would keep me pinned down while they circled around behind me.

The spotlights were crisscrossing each other in an eerie pattern in the open field, but one of them had the Ford pinned down steadily. A hump in the ground kept me in shadow. I couldn't see anyone coming through the field.

I heard the rifle's sharp crack again. Above my head there was a loud ping! Suddenly I was drenched to the waist in gasoline. The .30-.30 slug had ripped out the belly of the gas tank. I swiped at my stinging eyes and shook my dripping head. I looked up just as gas from my hair splashed onto the hot exhaust.

Whoom!

I saw a bright flare, and then I didn't see anything. The explosion knocked me backward under the car. I rolled out from beneath it. I didn't even feel the broken leg I was dragging. I couldn't see at all. My eyes were gone. I could hear the crackle of flames. Part was the Ford. Part was me. I was afire all over.

I tried to smother the flames on the ground. It didn't help. I still had the gun. I hoped they could see me and were coming at me. I knelt up on my good leg and faced the noise up on the road, bracing the Smith & Wesson in both hands. I squeezed off the whole load, waist-high, in a semicircle. I think the last shot exploded in the chamber from the heat of my burning hands. I threw the empty gun as far as I could in the direction of the road.

There was a dull roaring sound in my ears. I tried to put out the fire in my hair. I rolled on the ground. I could smell my own burning flesh.

The last thing I heard was myself, screaming.

12

I was in black darkness for six months. I may have gone a little crazy, too. I gave them a hard time. I went the whole route: baths, wet packs, elbow cuffs, straight-jackets, isolation. I stopped fighting them a little while ago. They don't pay much attention to me now.

Even before I could see again, I knew what I looked like. I could feel the reaction, when a new patient was admitted, or a new attendant came on duty. Hazel came to see me four or five times. I refused permission for her to be allowed in.

They don't know that I can see again, that I'm not crazy. They think I'm a robot. A vegetable.

I'll show them.

I have a hermetically sealed quart jar buried in the ground up in Hillsboro, New Hampshire, and another in Grosmont, Colorado, up above timber line. There's nothing but money in both. I don't need it. All I need is a gun. Some one of these days I'll find the right attendant, and I'll start talking to him. It will take a while to convince him, but I've got plenty of time.

If I can get back to the sack buried beside Bunny's cabin, plastic surgery will take care of most of what I look like. With a gun, I'll get back to it.

That's all I need—a gun.

I'm not staying here.

I'll be leaving one of these days, and the day I do they'll never forget it.

THE END

One Endless Hour
By Dan J. Marlowe

PROLOGUE

A narrow wagon road branched off in the headlights a half mile in on the dirt road heading east from Florida's west coast. I turned the Ford into the weed-overgrown trail. "Not that way!" Lucille Grimes said sharply.

I paid no attention. After a hundred yards I stopped, pulled up the brakes, and cut the motor and lights. Then I slipped an arm around the blonde. She wriggled impatiently, thinking I had romance on my mind. I'd done it to keep her from fleeing if she suspected anything.

She was sure that her boyfriend, Deputy Sheriff Blaze Franklin, was so close behind us that he'd arrive any moment and kill me. She didn't know that I'd disabled Franklin's police cruiser and left him miles back on U.S. 19.

After a moment she lowered her head onto my shoulder, awaiting the appearance of the rear guard. Under the trees it was full dark. Much too dark to see her expression. I wished I could. It would have been interesting. Lucille Grimes, the blonde postmistress of Hudson, Florida, was as good as dead as far as I was concerned. It was just a question of when and how. In a way it was too bad. She was a really talented bitch.

Right that second she gave me another demonstration of it. The silence in the woods must have got to her, because she grabbed for the horn ring on the steering wheel. The horn blatted twice. She was reaching for the light switch when I caught her arm. She sat there all tensed up, waiting for Blaze Franklin to appear out of the darkness and finish me off.

I could sense the shriveling of her self-confidence when nothing happened. "You beginning to get the idea he's not coming?" I needled her. "Blaze isn't splitting with you, Lucille. He's splitting with me. Your boyfriend's sold you out. I'm supposed to bury you twenty yards off this dirt road."

It shook her to her round heels, but she was too smart to swallow it whole. "He'll come," she said huskily, trying to look over her shoulder.

"Where is he, then? Get smart, woman. It's lucky for you I like you. Get on the ball now and steer me to the money. I'll take care of Franklin for you."

She was silent. There was only one thing she could think. Even if Franklin hadn't sold her out, he'd flubbed his end of the deal. She had to protect herself. Her steel-trap mind should have been telling her she was in a perfect position to play it cool down to the finish line. Then she could choose up sides with the winner.

I couldn't understand why she hesitated.

"We—Blaze never found the money," she said at last. Her voice quavered. "Only a few hundred on—on the man." She drew a long breath. "If only I'd never mentioned to Blaze the big, odd-looking man who mailed such queer...." Her voice died away.

So that was why Franklin wanted me alive. For a while. He hoped I knew where the cache was. The funny thing was that I did. Now.

I tightened my grip on the blonde's arm. "Franklin killed my partner before he found out where the money was?"

"He—yes," she whispered.

I started up the Ford. "Tell me where Bunny was staying, Lucille." She didn't say anything. I turned my head to look at her. Her face was an indistinct pale oval. "Tell me," I warned.

She told me. She had trouble getting out the words. I didn't like the sound of her voice or her directions. I took hold of her again and jerked her toward me. While she tried to pull away, I crossed my hand over my chest and drew my holstered Smith and Wesson .38 special. The blonde's features crumpled in fear.

I took her wrist, reversed the gun, and slashed her soft inner arm with the gunsight. She cried out in pain and shock as the blood welled. "Better change your story," I told her. "Because if there's nothing where you're sending me, that's what happens to your face until my arm gets tired."

She changed her story.

I backed onto the road and drove along it to another that bisected it. Following Lucille's new directions, I turned right. We seemed to be heading into the middle of nowhere. I was on the point of asking her to change her story again when she motioned at a small cabin off to one side. I'd have missed it if I'd been alone. I pulled into the brush and got out of the Ford. I took the car keys so she couldn't zoom off and leave me stranded.

I reached back in and took a flashlight from the glove compartment. I circled the cabin cautiously, .38 in one hand, flashlight in the other. There were no phone wires. In the rear, a mound of cut branches loomed up in the light. I pulled off a few. Beneath the tangled brush sat Bunny's blue Dodge. This time Lucille hadn't lied to me.

I went back to the car. I had to take hold of Lucille's arm to get her out of it. I took a chisel and maul from the trunk, herded the foot-dragging blonde up to the cabin door ahead of me, and smashed the lock. Dry heat rolled over me as the door opened. It had a musty, long-closed odor. Lucille was still hanging back, and I kept a good hold on her arm. I couldn't understand her reluctance to enter the cabin.

Inside, I closed and bolted the door. The bolt was rusty and I had to manhandle it. I lit a match and peered about the place. A skillet was on the two-burner stove, and Bunny's clothes hung neatly on hangers in an alcove. There was a candle in a bottle on a small table, and I touched the burning match to the wick. Soft light filled the room.

There were two more doors, both locked. Two swings of the maul disposed of the first lock. There was nothing inside the room at all. I demolished the second lock, then beamed the flash around the room's shadowy interior. Part-way around, the light hung, motionless.

I'd found Bunny.

He was face down on the rough pine flooring. His wrists were handcuffed to shiny new ringbolts in the floor. The ringbolts were at right angles to his head. Fresh pine sawdust was visible where the holes had been drilled.

Dry as the air in the place was, there was a persistent smell. Bunny had been in the cuffs for a long time. With his chest flat on the floor and his arms spread-eagled, not even his great strength could achieve leverage. He had thrown himself onto his right side in a final contortion. The bone of his left kneecap glistened at me out of raw-looking meat, trousers and flesh long since abraded away in his ceaseless struggle with the splintered flooring. His upper left arm was mincemeat where he'd gnawed at himself.

Bunny had lain in the cuffs until he died.

Which kills first, hunger or thirst?

I couldn't remember.

I couldn't think.

The game had dealt my partner a rough hand. Looking into Franklin's gun, Bunny had temporized, feeling he'd find a spot to turn it around. He hadn't counted on the cuffs. He'd gone into them, but he hadn't cracked. He'd told Franklin nothing. Right up to the end he must have hoped I'd get there in time. A hell of a lot of good I'd been to him, two thousand miles away getting a cop's bullet out of my shoulder so I could travel.

How do you break the will of a stubborn man? You starve him. You starve him until he's out of his mind with hunger, heat, and thirst, when he'll lead you to anything he has.

If he's not too far out of his mind.

With the hunger, the thirst, and the maddening heat, Blaze Franklin had returned to the cabin one day and found a mindless animal in the ringbolts. An animal who would never lead him to anything.

I stooped to examine the head, cruelly battered from endless, raving contact with the floor. There had been no merciful bullet.

Blaze Franklin had left him to die.

Blaze Franklin and Lucille Grimes had left him to die.

I knew now why the blonde had been so afraid to come into the cabin. She'd known exactly what I was going to find. I straightened up, drew the .38 again, and walked into the other room. Lucille was struggling with the rusty bolt in the front door, trying frantically to withdraw it. I peeled her away from the door and slammed her against the wall.

"Blaze did it!" she screamed when she saw my face. "Blaze did it! I wanted to let him go—"

I shot her in the throat, three times.

"Tell your story in hell, if you can get anyone to listen," I rasped. She collapsed in a heap and thrashed on the floor, blood pulsing between the fingers

of both hands clasped to her neck. "If they can patch up your lying voice."
I stepped over her.
I had work to do.
I went outside into the clean darkness. First I looked up at the stars to orient myself. I knew where the cache would be. For a hideout in the country,
Bunny and I always followed a pattern. From the front door of the cabin I
stepped out due north as accurately as I could reckon it. I knew the sack
wouldn't be more than thirty or forty feet from the cabin wall.
In daylight it would have been a cinch. Even in the dark and in the thick
brush it wasn't too hard. My feet told me when I hit softer earth. Bunny had
planted something green over the sack. I ripped up the bush, pulled the chisel
that was the only tool I had from my pocket, and tore into the loose ground.
A foot below the surface I ran into the sack.
By the light of the flash I made certain that the bulk of the Phoenix swag
was still in the canvas container. Then I reburied it, stamping down the earth
around the replaced bush. There was no sense in lugging the sack around with
me. I'd be back for it after I brought Blaze Franklin out here and roped him
to Bunny's body to die the same way Bunny had.
I went back inside for a last look around. Lucille was unconscious, bubbles
of blood oozing instead of jetting with each shallow, ragged breath. She would-
n't last long. Not long enough, actually. She was lucky. If I hadn't been so
angry that I hadn't stopped to think, I could have figured a different end for
her. A slower end. She was just as guilty as Franklin.
And where would Deputy Sheriff Blaze Franklin be now? After the motor froze up in his police cruiser from the sugar I'd dumped into his gas tank,
he'd have to make his way back to my motel, the Lazy Susan, and hope that
I returned there. That's where Blaze Franklin would be, and he'd get his wish
about my return in a way he never expected.
I went down the path to the Ford and got out of there.
I drove straight to the Dixie Pig, Hazel's place. I wanted Franklin, but I had
another errand first. En route, I shook a box of bullets loose in my jacket
pocket. I drove with my left hand and reloaded with my right. I've spent a
lot of hours practicing reloading one-handed.
At the Dixie Pig, I scouted the back parking lot in case Franklin had out-
guessed me. There was no two-tone police cruiser on the parking lot. I
parked alongside Hazel's car and went in the back door. She was behind the
bar, her six-foot figure towering above the half-dozen seated customers.
Her face lighted up when she saw me, but I thought her expression looked
strained. She held up the hinged flap at the far end of the bar. She was wearing her usual Levi's, cowboy boots, and short vest that emphasized her big
breasts and the smooth skin of her bare arms. She was far and away the most
woman I'd ever had. And the best.
I followed her along the duckboards and out through the hanging curtain

in the center of the backbar. The room behind the curtain was set up as a
lounge, with a couch and a couple of chairs, a Primus stove, and a coffeepot.
"Get a bag packed," I said to her. "I'll be back for you in half an hour."
Her large hand caught mine and squeezed it hard. "Listen to me, Chet.
Please." Her voice was low. "Franklin has everyone in the county looking for
you. There's half a dozen of them waiting in the motel yard. They never
dreamed you'd come back here."

So. End of the line for Chet Arnold in Hudson, Florida. And I couldn't get
to Blaze Franklin. I couldn't? The hell I couldn't. I held out my hand to Hazel.
"Forget what I said about a bag. Give me your car keys."

She turned to her handbag on a chair. "Chet, please let me come with—"
"Tell them I took the keys away from you," I cut her off. I knew I could-
n't take her with me now. I was less than even money to make it. Hazel
handed me the keys, and I punched her in the eye. Big as she was, she still
went over backward, landing on the couch. The eye would be her alibi when
the sheriff came asking questions. "So long, baby," I said from the curtained
opening. I didn't look back. I didn't want to see the expression on her face.

I drove down to the Lazy Susan in her car. I thought they'd be watching
for my souped-up Ford. It turned out they were watching for anything. I'd
no more than rolled into the motel yard and opened the car door when some
eager beaver tapped his headlights. Three more sets came on instantly. I was
semicircled by cruisers. The yard looked bright as day.

Blaze Franklin came roaring out of the nearest cruiser, waving his gun. He
had to get me fast, since he couldn't afford to let me talk about some of his
recent activities. At ten yards I put five in a row from the .38 into his groin.
A playing card would have covered them all. He went down in the dust, bellowing like a castrated bull. He was a castrated bull. He'd live, but he would-
n't enjoy it as much.

I put the last bullet into his jaw as he flopped on the ground. If I made good
on the getaway, I didn't want him talking until I'd gone back for the sack.
Firecrackers were going off all around me, but they couldn't shoot worth a
damn. I dived back under the wheel and aimed Hazel's car through the largest
gap in the encircling headlights. Gravel spurted beneath my wheels.

Someone shot out my windshield as I got moving. Prickling splinters of glass
laced into my face. I bumped across the lawn, through the flower bed, around
the swimming pool, and over a white picket fence. I jounced out onto the highway and floored the accelerator. For the first five hundred yards part of the
fence kept banging against the front wheels of the car. Then it fell away.

I reloaded. Practice almost makes perfect. I dropped only one oil-slick bullet while making ready the warm-barreled .38. Behind me were lights and
sirens. No shortage of either. I busted right through the town's square and
set sail for the Dixie Pig. In Hazel's car, I could just about smell the overheated
engines behind me. With the Ford's high-powered mill, I at least had a

chance of outrunning them.

A thousand yards from the Dixie Pig I cut the headlights, moved over onto the shoulder, and drove in darkness. If anything had been parked on the edge of the highway, it would have been all she wrote. I whirled the steering wheel when I saw the lighter surface of the Dixie Pig's crushed-stone driveway. I took out a section of hedge, but I made the turn. Out on the highway the cruisers screamed by.

I yanked up the emergency and lit running. The door on the driver's side of the Ford stood open. I didn't remember leaving it open. I slid to a stop with my hand on the butt of the .38. I came within a tick of blasting the dark figure on the passenger side of the Ford's front seat before I recognized Hazel. "Get the hell out!" I ordered, trying to listen for sounds on the highway.

"Take me with you, Chet," she pleaded. "Give me a gun."

"Don't make me do it, baby," I said. "Get out of the car."

She climbed out. I could see that she was crying. "Please, Chet, I don't care what—"

"Get yourself a winning horse, woman." I got in under the wheel and slammed the door. "Get back inside and keep your mouth shut." I backed up, swung around, and rammed the Ford down the driveway. The last glimpse I had of Hazel was the glitter of the silver conches on her cowboy boots in the swing of the headlights.

I doubled back toward town. On Route 19 there'd be road blocks north and south. I'd head east from the square. The added power of the Ford felt good under my foot. I blasted it down the road, then slowed approaching the traffic light. I'd just started my left-hand turn when a siren went off practically in my ear. Somebody in the posse had had the brains to leave a trailer.

He was headed the wrong way, but I saw the shine of his lights as he corkscrewed around after me. My 45-mph turn carried me onto the sidewalk before I straightened out, headed east. I really rolled it away from there. I was doing eighty-five on a road built for forty. The Ford was all over the highway. I watched the thin, dark ribbon of macadam unroll in the headlights while behind me the wailing shriek of the siren pierced the night. I was outrunning him, but then I burst out of a curve onto a long straightaway, and far up the road were the blinking red lights of trouble.

Roadblock.

I lifted my foot from the gas pedal, but I still rolled up on it fast. A spotlight came on when they saw me. A tiny figure stood out on the road, waving me down with flapping arms. I sized it up. Two cruisers across the road, their snouts extending onto the shoulders. Three-quarters of a car's width between them in the center. Ditch on the right. Open field on the left. And in the rearview mirror the lights of the trailing cruiser gaining fast.

A roadblock you do or you don't. I mashed down on the gas and headed for the center opening between the cruisers. I just might spin one and rip my way through. The fool with the flapping arms stood right in the center of the gap. The lights picked him up solidly. Roaring down on him, I was suddenly staring through the windshield at the white, strained face of part-time deputy Jed Raymond, my only male friend in Hudson.

I hoped he'd jump. Jed was a nice kid. If he didn't, though, he'd have to take his chances, like I was taking mine. I couldn't have been more than twenty yards from him when Kaiser, my big police dog that I'd left with Jed for safekeeping, pranced out in front of Jed, head cocked and tail waving.

My brain sent me straight through, over the dog, over Jed, to try the odds with the cruisers. Instead, my hands spun the wheel, hard left. Somebody else will have to explain it to you. I missed them both, caromed broadside off the left-hand cruiser in a whining, ear-splitting wail of tortured metal, then hurtled a hundred and fifty yards down into the open field.

The front wheels dropped into a ditch and the Ford stood up on its nose. There was a loud Whump! The door flew open. I flew out, hit hard, and rolled. I didn't lose consciousness, and I still had the gun.

I started to crawl toward the Ford, and knew in the first second that my right leg was broken. Up on the highway the spotlight pivoted and crept down through the field. It caught me, passed on, hesitated, and came back. There was a sharp crack, and a bullet plowed up the ground beside me. The rifle sounded like a .30-.06.

I dragged myself over the uneven ground to the Ford and crouched beneath its elevated back wheels. I could see the road and the spotlight, and I got it with my third shot. They turned the other cruiser around—the one I hadn't smashed into—and its spotlight started down through the field. I popped it before its light reached the Ford. Not that it made much difference. More red lights, spotlights, and sirens were whirling up to the roadblock every second now.

I reloaded the Smith and Wesson again. Nothing for it now but the hard sell. Nothing but to see that a few of them shook hands with the devil at the same time I did. To get to me in a hurry they had to come through the field. By now they knew better than to be in a hurry. The .30-.06 went off again, and a large charge of angry metal whinged through the body of the Ford, just above my head. The rifle would keep me pinned down while they circled around behind me.

The spotlights were crisscrossing the field in an eerie pattern. A hump in the ground ahead of the Ford kept its underside in shadow. I couldn't see anyone coming through the field. I heard the rifle's sharp sound again, and above me there was another loud ping! Suddenly I was drenched to the waist in gasoline. The .30-.06 slug had ripped out the belly of the gas tank. I swiped at my stinging eyes and shook my dripping head. I looked up toward the road again just as gas from my hair splashed onto the hot exhaust.

Whoom!

I saw a bright flare, and then I didn't see anything. The explosion knocked me backward, out from under the car. I dragged myself away. I didn't feel the broken leg. I could hear the crackle of flames. Part was the Ford. Part was me. I was afire all over.

I rolled on the ground, trying to smother the flames. It didn't help. I still had the gun. I hoped they could see me and were coming at me. I knelt on the good leg and faced the noise up on the road. I braced the Smith and Wesson in both hands and squeezed off the whole load, blindly, waist-high in a semi-circle. Then I threw the empty gun as far as I could in the direction of the road.

There was a dull roaring sound in my ears.

I tried to put out the fire in my hair.

I rolled on the ground again.

I could smell my own burning flesh.

The last thing I heard was myself, screaming.

The leg healed in six weeks.

I was in darkness a lot longer than that.

I gave them a hard time in the prison wing of the state hospital. I went the whole route: whirlpool baths, wet packs, elbow cuffs, wrist restraints, strait-jackets, isolation. Then I stopped fighting them. They don't pay much at-tention to me now.

I didn't talk to anyone, and my hands were burned so badly they couldn't take my prints. It bugged both the state and federal lawmen that they could-n't run a tracer on Chet Arnold. During their visits I listened to a lot of ques-tions, but I didn't supply any answers.

Even before I could see I knew how I looked. Hair gone. Eyebrows gone. Nose bulbous. Face scarred. Only my chin and throat had escaped fairly lightly. I could sense the reaction to my appearance when a new patient was admitted, or a new attendant came on duty. There was an almost tangible shrinking.

I refused permission for Hazel to visit me. She came to the hospital four or five times, and then she stopped coming and went back to her hometown in Nevada. There was no point in letting her drag herself down with me.

Because I don't talk, the attendants and the doctors think I'm crazy.

They think I'm a robot.

I'll show them.

There's a hermetically sealed jar buried in Hillsboro, New Hampshire, and another in Grosmont, Colorado. There's money in both. There's a stripped-down gun in both. I don't need the money, but I do need a gun. One of these days I'll find the right attendant, and I'll start talking to him. It will take time to convince him, but time I've got.

If I can get back to the sack buried beside Bunny's cabin, plastic surgery will take care of most of what I look like now. With a gun, I'll get back to the cabin.

That's all I need—a gun.

I'm not staying here.

I'm getting out, and the day I do they'll never forget it.

I

Spider Kern and Rafe James entered the prison wing of the state hospital together. Kern was a little man with big shoulders and hard-knuckled hands. He worked a spittle-soaked toothpick continually between his uneven teeth. His face was red and his thinning hair sandy. His key ring swung loosely at his hip where he dropped it after unlocking the heavy ward door with its wire mesh embedded in the glass. When my sight returned, one of the first things I noticed was that Kern's key ring was fastened to his studded belt by a metal clamp as well as a leather loop.

Rafe James went to the desk in the niche in the corridor that served as a ward office. James was thin, dark, and had a long face with a lantern jaw. He had mean-looking eyes and a beard so heavy he always looked unshaven. A foul-smelling pipe that never seemed to go out was as much a part of him as Spider Kern's toothpick was of the senior attendant.

James removed the inmates' folders from the old-fashioned wooden file behind the desk. Kern strutted down the ward in his short-man's swagger. He stopped in front of old Woody Adams, still a flaming queen despite his years. "Cigarette me," Kern ordered. The white-haired Woody simpered as he took a pack from his pajama pocket. Kern helped himself to half a dozen.

I had overheard muttering among the inmates about Kern's mooching practices. Old Woody would never become the leader in attempting to do anything about it, though. Not that I ever entered into inmate conversations. I never spoke to anyone except in monosyllables.

Cigarette going, Kern glanced around the ward. I was sitting in an armless rocker near a window overlooking the hospital grounds and part of the parking lot. The early-morning sun was still evaporating the night mist, which had sprinkled rose bushes and bougainvillea with a million drops of water that glittered like tiny pearls of light. I often sat by the window at night, too, after the lights went out on the visitors' side of the parking lot and only a single arc lamp was visible above the employees' cars.

Nearby chairs contained half a dozen dozing men, but the majority of the inmates were at the other end of the big ward near the games table. We all wore the loose, white cotton pajamas, drab gray flannel bathrobes, and pressed-paper slippers, that were the twenty-four-hour-a-day patient uniform.

"Everybody up!" Kern snapped at the sound of a key in the lock of the ward door. I didn't move, but there was a general shuffling of feet as the other men rose. I saw Rafe James's pipe disappear into a pocket of his white attendant's jacket. Dr. Willard Mobley, the hospital's chief psychiatrist, entered the ward followed by his usual entourage of doctors and nurses. With his bushy, snow-white hair and high coloring, Dr. Mobley had the look of a hard-boiled Santa Claus. He had a deep bass voice that lent authority to everything he said.

Rafe James fell in behind the group with his armful of file folders for the ritual twice-a-week walk-through of the ward. Mobley began a rapid circuit of the large room, talking steadily. He paused briefly in front of a few of the men, asking questions but not listening to the answers. The hatchet-faced head nurse, an elderly blonde known on the ward as Gravel Gertie, took notes.

Mobley took a file folder from James occasionally, and scribbled a line into the case history of the favored individual. The psychiatrist rarely spent more than two minutes with anyone. The group of doctors and nurses following him murmured chorused acquiescence to Mobley's drum-fire pronounce- ments like a flock of twittering parakeets. The nurses were old, the doctors young. Every one a has-been or a never-was in his profession.

Spider Kern posted himself a careful five yards in advance of the procession. A silence enveloped each group of men he approached. Except to respond to a direct question, no one spoke again until Dr. Mobley and his troupe passed. This was Spider Kern's Law, ruthlessly enforced. The protruding knuckles on Kern's hands slashed like knives. Rumor on the ward had it that Kern soaked his hands in brine to toughen them.

"Here's a case for you one of these days, Dr. Afzul," Mobley said briskly, halting in front of my chair. I stared straight ahead. "Been here—oh, five months. Burns resultant from the explosion of a car's gas tank while he was attempting to escape from the sheriff's department. A murder charge against him is being held in abeyance while we try to penetrate his catatonia."

I had already noticed a new face in the group, a spindly little man with dark mahogany features, slick black hair, big brown eyes, and a pencil-line mous- tache. He looked dapper even in his semishapeless hospital whites. "An in- teresting case," he agreed after looking me over. His Oxford-accented sibilants hissed like snakes.

He picked up one of my burned hands from my lap and turned it over to examine the back of it. He stared down at three obviously recent bright red marks in the previously burned flesh. The little knot of doctors and nurses stared at them, too. No one said anything. Dr. Afzul released my hand, and I let it drop limply into my lap.

The dark-faced little doctor put two fingers under my chin and tilted my head back to study my face. I had long since stopped looking into the mirror mornings at the lumpy scar tissue and disfiguring discoloration that extended down almost to my mouth. "A strong conssstitution," the doctor com- mented. "Shock alone from extensssive burns like these would have killed many." He removed his hand from under my chin and started to step back. I held my head in the position in which he had placed it. Dr. Afzul reached out again and tipped my head down into its former position.

"You can see that passivity is the motif in his case," Dr. Mobley said.

The group moved down the ward. I could see them out of the corner of my eye while I stared straight ahead through the window at the rose garden. The next stop was in front of Willie Turnbull, an undersized eighteen-year-old with a purplish birthmark covering the right side of his face.

Dr. Mobley gestured and Dr. Afzul moved forward again. His delicate-looking slim brown fingers probed lightly at the disfiguring growth. "It has always been of this dimensssion?" he asked.

"Sure has, Doc," Willie replied in his high, piping voice.

"And he says he steals automobiles because of it," Mobley interjected.

Willie grinned self-consciously. "How else is a guy looks like me gonna get a gal into the back seat?"

Mobley chuckled. One of the nurses snickered. The slender doctor dropped his hand from his palpating examination. "You would like it removed?"

"You can't fix it, Doc," Willie said. "Ma took me to all the relief doctors. They wouldn't touch it."

Dr. Afzul crooked a slim eyebrow. "Believe me when I say I can 'fix' it, as you put it. That is my business. Come along to my office."

Willie looked at Dr. Mobley, who nodded. The skinny kid fell in behind the procession as it moved along. When the circuit of the ward was completed, Spider Kern unlocked the see-through ward door. "Oh, Kern," Dr. Mobley said, "I want you to meet our newest staff member, Dr. Sher Afzul. Kern is our man in charge of law and order on the ward, Doctor. Dr. Afzul is from Pakistan, Spider."

"Pleasssed to meet you," Dr. Afzul said, extending his hand.

Spider Kern ignored the hand. He mumbled something unintelligible while he appeared to study the key ring in his hand. After an awkward pause, Dr. Afzul pulled back his hand. The group filed out of the ward with Willie Turnbull in their wake. Spider Kern tested the door behind them to make sure the automatic lock had caught. "Thinkin' I'm gonna shake hands with the likes of him," he grumbled to Rafe James, whose pipe once again was in his mouth. "Can't they hire no white men anymore?"

When I was first promoted from isolation to the ward, I couldn't understand why Spider Kern devoted so much attention to me. Personal attention. Physical attention. Sudden muscle punches on my arms and thighs. Long-armed feints at my face to try to make me duck. Cigarette burns on my hands and arms. I'd stopped taking showers during Kern's shift when he began following me into the shower stall with his fixed grin and goddamned cigarette. It wasn't only me, of course, Kern spread his sadistic business around, but I couldn't help thinking I received more than my share.

Even Rafe James noticed it. "You really work out on the loony, don't you, Spider?" he asked one day when Kern was making me flinch in my chair by applying the end of his lighted cigarette to my forearm. I'd steeled myself to wait for a count of five before removing the arm. "You'd think he was your mother-in-law."

"He shot up my buddy," Kern replied.

"Your buddy?"

"Deppity Sheriff Blaze Franklin. You must've read about it. Blaze 'n' me was on the force together awhile. This bastard like to blew his balls off with a thirty-eight. I'm gonna fix his clock. I think he's fakin' it anyway."

"He's a hell of a good faker if he can take what you been dishin' out without showin' nothin'," James observed.

"I've seen his eyes a couple times," Kern said. "He's fakin' it, even if I can't convince ol' Mobley."

I gave thought to Spider Kern after that. Not very productive thought. There was nothing loose in the ward that could be used as a weapon. All the furniture was tubular aluminum. Even a leg wrenched from a chair would be too light for my purpose. I'd get only one chance if I went after Kern. I couldn't afford a mistake.

So day after day I sat in my rocker and stared out over the hospital grounds. Not even rocking. Just waiting. I never doubted that I'd find a way. I'd been in tougher places. I waited, and meantime I toughed it out each time Spider Kern came down the ward to my chair.

Nothing lasts forever, I kept reminding myself.

Least of all Spider Kern.

Willie Turnbull was back on the ward in three weeks. His head was wrapped like a mummy's, and his right arm was elevated above his head with the flesh of his inner arm pressed against his cheek. For three-quarters of each hour he had to lie down on his bed to keep the blood circulating in his arm. The other fifteen minutes he would prowl the ward restlessly until the up-stretched arm started getting numb again. His meals were liquids taken through a tube. The only way he could sleep was under sedation.

Dr. Afzul came to see him every day. Twice a week he worked on Willie's arm and face without ever fully removing the facial bandages. "It isss coming," he said each time to Willie. "Don't get dissscouraged." Willie had become very discouraged. "You will find that it will all be worth it."

Once a week the slender little doctor would knock Willie out with a needle, loosen the bandages, and treat him for half an hour with a thin-looking liquid in an aerosol spray can. Then Dr. Afzul would wait for another half hour before he rebandaged Willie. During the interval Dr. Afzul would roam the ward, talking to the other inmates, "How do you feel today, sssir?" he would ask me, stopping in front of my chair. I would wait for a count of five; then nod my head slowly.

At first Spider Kern accompanied Dr. Afzul as he toured the ward, but as time went on even Kern became adjusted to the little doctor's continued presence in what Kern considered to be his own private domain. Occasionally the doctor would sit down with a magazine while he was waiting. He never looked at anything except the advertisements for cars, footwear, and men's clothing and jewelry.

He came into the ward one day with two young doctors. The three of them set up a portable tent around Willie Turnbull's bed, and they all disappeared inside it. Most of the men on the ward drifted in that direction for what they sensed was to be the unveiling. "What does it look like, Doc?" we heard Willie ask impatiently several times.

"Soon you will see for yourssself," Dr. Afzul assured him each time.

It must have been two hours before the doctors emerged from the tent. All three were smiling. Willie Turnbull followed them. His head was no longer mummified and his arm was at his side again although still bandaged. The lumpy, purplish growth on the right side of Willie's face was gone. In its place was a shiny, reddish, taut-looking sheath of flesh that didn't look too much like skin.

"The color will fade," Dr. Afzul said calmly, correctly interpreting the doubtful expressions on the faces of his audience.

"And it will blend," one of the young doctors confirmed.

"It will never match exactly the other ssside of your face, Willie," Dr. Afzul said. "But we will show you how to use cosssmetics so that few can tell the difference."

The third doctor shook hands ceremoniously with Dr. Afzul. "As fine a job as I've ever seen, Doctor."

Willie didn't sound nearly as certain when he voiced his own thanks.

From the time Willie walked out of the ward until the unveiling, the process had taken about twelve weeks. In another month the lobster-red coloring had faded to a dull pink and the shininess had begun to disappear. Every third day Dr. Afzul would come onto the ward and cover the new side of Willie's face with his liquid spray, wait for an hour, then do it again.

I had watched the program with more than an academic interest. What I had just seen accomplished was what I most needed myself. I waited until Dr. Afzul sat down near me with a magazine one day while his liquid concoction "set" on Willie's face. "How long would it take you to fix me a new face, Doc?" I said in a normal tone but without looking at Dr. Afzul.

"That isss hard to—" he began, then turned from his magazine to look at me. I was staring straight ahead as usual. The doctor glanced about the ward. Spider Kern was at its far end, out of earshot. Dr. Afzul lowered his voice before he spoke again. "I have not heard you ssspeak before."

"I want to talk to you, but not here."

He was looking at his magazine again. "I have my share of curiosssity. I will have you brought to my office tomorrow."

"Fine."

Neither of us said anything more.

After Dr. Afzul left the ward that afternoon, I experienced another break in my usual monotonous routine. Colonel Sam Glencoe of the state police came to see me. He'd come three times before, and each time I'd let him see a slight improvement in my supposed catatonic condition. Another man was with him this time, not in uniform. He looked like F.B.I.

They drew up chairs and sat down, one on either side of me. The first time Glencoe showed up, Spider Kern had tried to horn in on the interview. Glencoe sent him packing with a single hard look.

I knew it was still bugging Glencoe that he couldn't get a line on Chet Arnold. It probably bugged him almost a much that after talking to Hudsonites like Jed Raymond and Hazel Andrews, he didn't hear much that was wrong with Chet Arnold. Chet had arrived in Hudson as a stranger with a tool kit and a trade. A year in a lumber camp had made me a tree surgeon when I wanted to be. That and a crack shot.

I came to Hudson to try to find out what had happened to my partner, Bunny, who had gone there with the loot from a bank job in Phoenix. While looking for him, I did a little tree work and blended with the local citizenry. As I gradually uncovered the slimy trail of Blaze Franklin and his girl friend, Lucille Grimes, I developed an affair with Hazel that was the finest man-woman relationship I'd ever had. Then the roof had fallen in.

The unexplained explosion had baffled the sheriff's department, too, but they'd given up a lot more easily. Colonel Sam Glencoe wasn't naive enough to believe that a man of Chet Arnold's locally demonstrated dimensions had sprung full-blown from the earth, though. With no fingerprints possible, and me out to lunch mentally, as Glencoe thought, the colonel was frustrated.

"How are you feeling today?" he began.

I waited for a count of three instead of five. "Good."

His hard blue eyes inspected me. "What day is it?"

I waited again. "Tuesday."

"What month?"

"March."

"What date?"

I shook my head negatively.

Glencoe smiled, although it wasn't much of a smile. His frosty-looking features merely rearranged themselves in a different pattern. "If you'd known the answer to that, I'd have accused you of seeing me coming and boning up. There's plenty of days I don't know the date myself."

It was a surprise to me that he would even attempt a smile. He certainly hadn't on his previous trips. He'd sat and fired hard-voiced questions to which I'd supplied no answers while staring straight ahead. This time Glencoe was apparently ready to try sugar instead of vinegar. It suited me fine. Up to a point, I was ready to show progress.

"You've never told us anything about yourself, Arnold," Glencoe continued. "Now that you're communicating better, I want to ask again about your background. Where you're from originally, what you do for a living, how you happened to be in Hudson, what triggered the events there. . . quite a few questions. Where would you like to begin?"

I waited, then slowly lifted a burned hand to my scarred, ridged face. "I'd... feel... more... like... talking... if... I... didn't... know... what... I... looked... like."

"I'm sure the hospital staff is making plans to correct it," the state police chief said smoothly. I didn't reply, and he tried again. "There must be *some* loose ends in your background that it would be advantageous to you to pick up. Why don't you let us help?"

I wasn't going to reply, but even before I could have, the FBI man—if he was an FBI man—reached out suddenly and took hold of my hand still resting against my face. He bent down to look at the fresh cigarette burns on the back of the hand, and Glencoe leaned closer to look, too. Glencoe started to look down the ward in Spider Kern's direction, then caught himself and stared up at the ceiling instead.

When the man with Glencoe let go of my hand, dropped it into my lap. Glencoe cleared his throat and started over again. "Where's your hometown, Arnold?"

I sat there.

"Where were you living before you came to Hudson?"'

I sat there.

It went on for ten minutes. Questions with no answers They tired of it finally and got up to leave. "We'll be back," Glencoe promised. The usual threat was back his voice.

Before they left the ward, they stopped just inside the locked ward door and appeared to be arguing about something.

I didn't doubt that Glencoe would be back.

But just wait long enough, Colonel, I thought.

Wait long enough and I might not be here.

For the first time in months I'd begun to see a little daylight at the end of the tunnel.

Dr. Sher Afzul—as proclaimed by a nameplate on his desk—sat almost knee-to-knee with me in his office. The partitioned-off, windowless space couldn't have been more than twelve by fourteen. There was the desk, two chairs, a wall cabinet, and a four-drawer file. That was it.

He was smoking the thin tube of an aromatic-smelling cigarette as he leaned back in his chair to study me. Several more of the elongated tubes lay on the desk in front him. The tobacco in them looked black. "How is it that you so suddenly are no longer a vegetable in conversssation with me?" he inquired.

"I've never been a vegetable, Doc. Not since I came out of the very first bandages."

"You are a conssumately clever actor, then?"

"How clever does a man have to be to play idiot?"

His dark brown features creased in a quick smile. "And why am I favored now with the bright side of your sparkling persssonality?"

"You know why. You can give me a new face."

He nodded. "Yes, I can."

"I'll pay for it."

A slender eyebrow arched. "You will pay me for doing that for which the hospital already pays me?"

"I'll pay you additionally, Doc. They'll pay you for a quick-hurry-up job that would still leave me as the leading candidate for a role in a horror movie. I want a first-class job." I kept on talking when he would have interrupted me. "I overheard members of the staff saying it would have cost thousands in any private hospital in the country for the job you did on Willie Turnbull. If anyone in the private hospitals were skilled enough to do it. How come you're buried in a place like this?"

He smiled again. "Because I find that a prophet is without honor in countries other than his own, too. I was not without reputation in Pakistan. In Karachi. There I was of the upper-middle class. Here"—he spread his slender hands—"I qualify for—for—what is the name of your poor mountain region?"

"Appalachia."

"Appalachia," he agreed. "I knew that it would be difficult to establish myself here before I came, but not this difficult. It's not easy for a foreign doctor to be accepted in your country. Before the state examination can be taken, there must be both an accepted length of residence and demonssstrated hospital training. The red tape is ressstrictive."

I glanced around the shabby office. "They're not exactly overwhelming you with facilities here, Doc."

He held up both hands, then tapped himself on the forehead. "Here are my facilities. I need no other. When I first came to this country, I was in Grace Hospital in New Orleans, one of the largest and with the finest in facilities. I found, though, that someone was always watching over my shoulder. Checking on me and suggesting or ordering changes in my techniques. I decided this would be better. Here no one cares what I do."

"I care, Doc. You heard me say I'll pay well for a good job?"

"You will pay?" He looked skeptical. "I have examined the circumsssstances of your presence here. You are indigent."

"Only while I'm still inside the walls."

"So? The file shows that you have no assets or even a record of regular employment." The brown eyes were probing me. "The record, in fact, is more remarkable for what it doesn't show than for what it does. Did you know that you represent a problem to Colonel Glencoe, the chief of the state police?"

"Not a problem. A puzzle."

"If you like. Colonel Glencoe does not favor puzzles. Or loose ends. With the purpose in mind of gathering up same, he has already recommended to Dr. Mobley that plastic surgery be performed upon you to make you more communicative."

That must have been what Glencoe and the FBI man were talking about at the door of the ward before they left yesterday afternoon, I thought. "I don't want the kind of job they're talking about," I said. "I want the best job you can give me. For cash."

His head was cocked to one side like a bright-eyed bird's. "This cash," he said. "How much did you have in mind?"

"Twenty thousand. Half in advance."

His face closed up like a furled umbrella. "Your delusions of grandeur had previously essscaped me."

"Half in advance, cash," I repeated.

"But all this is just talk. There isss nothing—"

"When you're ready to take me seriously," I interrupted him, "I'll tell you where to go to put your hand on the first ten thousand. In untraceable cash. You keep that and bring me back whatever's hidden with it."

He still looked doubtful. "This hiding place—it is near here?"

"No."

"Then I would have to invest my time and money in this venture?"

"You gambled when you left Karachi, Doc. And twenty thousand would go a long way toward setting you up nicely in private practice." I tried to think how to get through to him. "When you first saw me on the ward, what were the odds against us ever having a conversation like this?"

"Astronomical," he admitted.

"You're still thinking of me like that. It's a mistake."

"You have a point." He said it slowly.

"Think it over." I rose to my feet. "The cash will be there anytime you give me the word you'd like to try for it."

"I sssuppose this is illegal money?"

I didn't answer his question. I opened his office door.

"Don't expect me to turn verbal handsprings the next time you see me on the ward."

His smile was unwilling and a bit sour. "That I will not expect." The smile turned to a frown. "But this proposssal—"

"Think it over, Doc."

I shuffled out into the corridor in my role of slow-moving dimwit. Dr. Afzul followed me and used his key to let me back through the heavy glass door into the ward.

I didn't feel that the conversation had been a waste of time.
I'd given Dr. Sher Afzul quite a bit to think about.

Three weeks later I heard one of the nurses saying that Dr. Afzul was going to New York to attend a convention of plastic surgeons. When I felt that
no one was looking at us the next time he came on the ward, I pointed a finger at myself and then at him. He nodded.

I was summoned to his office the same afternoon. "This is supposed to be
a preliminary examination of your condition prior to assessment on my part,"
he said, "but you have something to say to me?"

"A man can have a good time in New York, Doc, if he's properly fi-
nanced."

"So we're back on that sssubject?"

"We are. In New York you'll be close to the money."

It reached him. "How close?"

"About two hundred and twenty-five miles."

He tapped thoughtfully on his desk top with a pencil. "Tell me exactly what
it is you would have me do."

"Hire a car in New York and drive to the spot I'll tell you. It will take you
about five hours. Dig up a sealed jar eighteen inches below the surface of the
ground, remove ten thousand dollars and bring me whatever else is in it. And
remember that the ten thousand is only the down payment." He was silent.
"Does it make sense that I'd send you after nothing when I'll still be here
when you get back?"

"No," he acknowledged. He hitched his chair forward in sudden determi-
nation. "All right. Where isss this place?"

"In Guardian Angel Cemetery in Hillsboro, New Hampshire." He wrote
it down. "It's an abandoned cemetery. Drive in the front gate and follow the
circular gravel driveway to the right. Turn left at the first intersection. The
third headstone on the right will have the name Mallory on it. Twelve feet
behind the stone you'll find the jar."

"Suppose the gate is locked?" Dr. Afzul asked when he finished writing.

"There's no gate as such. Just an arched entranceway. The township has a
newer cemetery but still maintains the old one after a fashion. How long will
you be in New York?"

"Ten days." He said it absently. He was thinking of something else. "Dr.
Mobley has approved your facial reconsssstruction."

"Then we're in business."

"I have proposed to Dr. Mobley that in the interest of furthering my technique I do a full-scale rebuilding job. He is consssidering it." He hesitated for
a moment. "Even if he agrees, it will be tedious and painful," he warned. "It
will take a long time."

I refrained from stating the obvious. "Have a nice visit in the big city, Doc." I rose and went to the door of his office. I turned there and looked back at him. "Send a carton of cigarettes onto the ward for me with one of the nurses," I said casually. "Pall Malls."

I moved out into the corridor.

The cigarettes were a test.

I didn't know if I'd sold Dr. Afzul. If he dug into his pocket for the cigarettes, he was at least partially sold. If he didn't, it was time I began looking for another boy.

I'm not the worst judge of human nature, though, and on the way back to the ward I couldn't help feeling that for the first time in a long time I was once again in at least partial control of events.

2

Two days later one of the nurses in Dr. Mobley's group lingered near my chair during the usual walk-through of the ward. She waited until the group was huddled around Willie Turnbull and Dr. Mobley was taking bows for the change in Willie's attitude and personality, then hurriedly slipped me a carton of Pall Malls before she rejoined the staff.

I concealed the cigarettes by shoving the carton up the loose sleeve of my robe. I waited until routine had returned to normal in the ward before I left my chair and hid the carton under the pillow on my bed. Cigarettes weren't taboo on the ward, but Spider Kern controlled their appearance. I wanted a carton that Kern hadn't obtained for me.

At night I kept the carton between the coil springs in the bed, removing it each morning after ward inspection and replacing it under the pillow. It was Spider Kern's weekend off—each attendant had one weekend off in three—and I needed his presence for the next move in my chess game.

Kern was back on Monday, and so was Dr. Mobley. The psychiatrist stopped in front of my chair during his tour of the ward. He was flanked by the usual tight semicircle of doctors and nurses. Mobley seldom got closer than ten feet to the inmate to whom he was speaking. The technique made sense in that it was a preventive against sudden assault by a man roweled by the up-tight monotony of long days in the prison wing of the hospital. There could have been another reason, too. Four days out of five that we saw him, Mobley's nose was cherry-red. I had almost decided that Mobley's standoffish tactics were employed to keep from calling undue attention to his bourbon breath.

"Glad to hear you're finally responding to treatment, Arnold!" the chief psychiatrist boomed at me.

Responding to treatment was a joke, but I had a reason for showing response. "I'm... feeling... better... thank... you," I said.

There was a murmur from the group around Mobley. The majority of them had never heard me speak before. I could see Spider Kern eyeing me speculatively from his position five yards away. Spider hadn't known I was "responding," either. I spoke because I felt I had to demonstrate to Mobley that he wouldn't be wasting the institution's money by okaying plastic surgery for me. From the way he beamed I felt I'd made my point.

Dr. Afzul wasn't with the staff. I hoped it meant he was already en route to New York for the surgeons' convention. Now that matters had started to show progress, I was anxious to accelerate the process.

Spider Kern came back to my chair after Mobley and his entourage had left the ward. I'd been expecting him, and I spoke before he could. "Something...

for... you... under... my... pillow," I told him. He stared suspiciously, but he went away without saying anything. He was too cagey to go directly to my bed. I never did see him go to it, but the next time I looked the cigarettes were no longer under the pillow. In the next couple of days Kern's attitude became markedly more friendly.

I knew he hadn't really changed. He still had it in for me because of what I'd done to his buddy, Blaze Franklin. Nor had my attitude toward Kern changed. The cigarettes for him were intended to make a point. Since Kern controlled the normal channels for introducing merchandise onto the ward, a man who could flash a carton of cigarettes without Kern's assistance could-n't be entirely without friends beyond the locked doors. And if that were true, then the man shouldn't be an open target for the lighted-end of Spider's malice. I could do without Kern's lighted-end cigarette treatments while I was healing from Dr. Afzul's surgery, if and when.

There was Kern's well-known greed, too. He'd figure that if cigarettes appeared mysteriously, perhaps there would be something else for him. If Dr. Afzul didn't fail me, there would definitely be something else for Kern. The broad-shouldered, swaggering little man was an integral part of my escape plan.

Ten days passed, more slowly than usual even, before Dr. Afzul reappeared on the ward. He didn't look in my direction during Mobley's morning tour, but that afternoon I was called to Afzul's office. The first thing I noticed when I sat down was that he was wearing an expensive pair of English brogues, shoes that must have cost eighty dollars. I nodded at them. "I see you had no trouble finding the jar, Doc," I said.

"No." His expression was sober.

"Then I'll take what you brought for me." The little man seemed ill-at-ease. He reached into a jacket pocket of his hospital whites and removed a folded-over wad of bills, which he handed me. I riffled it quickly. There was twenty-two hundred in hundred-dollar bills. I put it in a pocket of my robe. "That's not all that was in the jar, Doc."

He shook his head. "I cannot give you the gun."

"We made a bargain." I pressed him, although I had never really expected that he would turn over the weapon.

"When I left here, I doubted the exissstence of the money, even," he said. "Finding the gun with it raised quessstions. Serious quessstions. I am now con-cerned to what end you would put a new face. It's not that I care what you do to yourself in the pursuit of your goal, whatever it may be, but there will be innocent bysssstanders."

"I don't understand your morality, Doc. You took my money, but you don't deliver."

"My morality isss my own affair," he retorted, unruffled. "On the new face, I will deliver. On the gun, no."

"What can I say to change your mind?"

"Nothing," he said flatly. "There is self-pressservation to be considered, you see. You will be gone, but I will remain. And you might not get clear away, in which case there would surely be an exhaustive invessstigation." He was silent for a moment. "You will have to make up your mind that the new face I will consstruct for you will be worth your invessstment in me."

"All right." I shrugged it off. The gun would have helped, but the cash was next best. "What's the program now?"

"We will begin on your face next week. A few quessstions now, please. You are a good healer? Or perhaps a cut heals slowly?"

"It heals quickly."

He nodded. "I will take blood sssamples. You should know there is a choice in the type of skin graft possible. With the dermatome, a skin-slicing machine, we are able to cut extremely thin slices of skin from a wide area. The choice comes in the thickness of the skin removed. We can take the top two layers, known as the epithelium and the deeper corium, which would conssstitute what is known as a full-thickness graft. Or we can take a thinner slice including only half the corium, a partial-thickness graft."

"What's the difference, Doc?"

"All transsssplants contract and change color after healing. The thicker the transsssplant, the less change, which is important in connection with the face. Conversssely, though, the thicker the transsssplant the more difficulty in getting it to take permanently. A partial-thickness graft is sometimes more efficient though less esssthetic."

I held out my stiffened hands to him, showing him the encrusted burn scars. "The hands are more important than the face, Doc. I've got to get good usage from them again. Couldn't you do these first? That way we'd know more about how I heal before you get into the tough part of things." I had a better reason than the one I was using. I wanted all the healing time possible to my hand to restore suppleness.

"Your point has merit," Dr. Afzul acknowledged. "Except that in the case of the hands the procedure is different. I will cut loose flaps of skin in your chest, known as pedicules, and insert your hands inside until the skin of your chest grows to the backs of your hands. Then a series of incisssions will detach your hand from your chest while new skin is growing underneath. One hand at a time in this process, of course."

"What about the face?"

"Two different techniques will be involved. For the forehead and the nose, I will probably peel flaps of skin down from scalp, since you will have to wear a hairpiece anyway. For the rest, mobile transplants from arms, back and thighs. Not everything we attempt will be successful." He pursed his lips. "One thing I will tell you now. Do not get burned again, at least not in the same areas. What I do this time, no one can do a second time."

I was only half listening. "How long will all this take?"

"With trial and error, ten months. Perhaps longer."

I'd hoped for something quicker, but he was the doctor. Literally. "Okay. Blow the starting whistle anytime."

He took the blood samples before I left the office.

That night I slipped out of bed after everyone in the ward was asleep and Kern and James were having coffee in the galley. I walked to the john and opened the closet door where they kept the brooms, mops, and disinfectants. There was a case of toilet tissue in one corner of the closet. I had looked it over good a week before. The case contained ninety-six rolls of tissue, packed eight across and twelve deep. Only about a third of the rolls were gone from the case.

I dug down into the case, removing a roll from each layer until I reached the bottom. I took the bottom roll out entirely. From the pocket of my robe I removed twelve hundred-dollar bills, which I rolled loosely and stuffed into the cardboard core of the toilet tissue roll. I put it back in the bottom of the case, covered it up with the rolls I had lifted out and set aside, and went back to bed. The remaining thousand dollars was still in the pocket of my robe. When the next-to-last layer of toilet tissue was reached, I'd slip into the john again at night and transfer the hidden money elsewhere.

It was late the next afternoon when I was able to manage a confrontation with Spider Kern when no one else was present. I was sitting in my usual place, looking out over the hospital grounds, when Kern came into the alcove to close the Venetian blinds. I beckoned to him when he turned to leave.

He paused, staring at me as if unsure his eyes weren't playing tricks on him. I beckoned again. He approached me warily. "What the hell d'ya want, Arnold?" he rasped.

I took the thousand dollars in bills from my pocket and handed it to him. "For... you," I said. His hard-looking mouth was already open to snap something at me when the feel of the crisp bills in his hand sank into his consciousness. His mean-looking little eyes bulged as he saw the denomination on the outside bill. He thumbed the wad rapidly, then jammed it into his pocket. "Where'd you get—" he started to bluster.

"More... later," I cut him off. "We'll... talk."

"Yeah," he agreed avidly. "Okay, okay. We'll talk." I could see that curiosity was consuming him.

"No... hurry," I said.

"Okay," he said again. He glanced around the alcove to reassure himself that no one had witnessed the transfer before he left me.

I was under no illusion about what I'd bought from Spider Kern. A little time, that was all. A little healing time during Dr. Afzul's remaking of my face. Leopards like Spider Kern didn't change their spots overnight. He'd still plan his revenge for what I'd done to his buddy, Blaze Franklin, but first he'd wait to see if there were any more hundred-dollar bills around.

As I expected, during the night the thought came to Kern that he might not have to wait. While we were at breakfast, Spider staged one of his periodic ward shakedowns, searching for "contraband." I could tell that my bed and the area around it had received special attention, but it hadn't done Kern any good.

That brought him back to me. "What's on your mind?" He came directly to the point when he had maneuvered us into a private tête-à-tête. A saliva-saturated toothpick danced in one corner of his mouth with each word.

I almost smiled. A week previously Spider Kern wouldn't have admitted that I had a mind. "I... want... a... gun," I said.

He blinked. He hadn't expected anything that blunt "Well, now, you know that's—" he began to bluster.

"For... five thousand dollars," I cut him off.

His lips pursed in a soundless whistle as he stared at me.

I didn't have five thousand, but then I wasn't going to get a gun from Spider Kern, either. Not while he knew anything about it, anyway. With visions of a possible five thousand filling his mind, though, my healing period should remain uninterrupted. Kern wouldn't get me a gun, but with his eye on the money he would pretend to get it.

"When do you want it?" he asked me.

I was pleased to see that the train of thought he'd been pursuing for himself was just what I'd programmed for him. I touched my face. "When... finished."

He nodded. "Time enough. Okay, for five thousand." He paused as though considering all aspects. "C.O.D."

"C... O... D.," I repeated.

That concluded our conversation.

It also concluded the first step in setting up Spider Kern's pratfall.

The next ten and a half months I'd just as soon forget. Not that there was anything excruciatingly painful about Dr. Sher Afzul's sophisticated techniques. It was nothing like having a .38 slug rip through an arm, for instance. Mostly it was the awkwardness and inconvenience of the flesh-to-flesh transfers. Plus the accompanying boring monotony. I spent a lot of time in bed because it was too much trouble to do anything else.

Twice I thought we were finished, but little Dr. Afzul would have none of it. "I can increase the degree of naturalness," he said both times, and patiently began another complicated transplant. My own patience was just about gone.

He didn't let me see the result of any of his efforts except those upon my hands, which had healed nicely. "It would upset you too much," he insisted while he was still working on my face. "Better that you should see it all at once. Luckily you have most of your eyelashes. A hairpiece you can buy, and eyebrows I can give you, after a fashion, but eyelashes gone are gone forever."

He talked continuously all the time he was working on me, explaining in detail what he was doing. If I'd paid attention, I could probably have done a fair job of plastic surgery on someone else's face. I had the full course. I was so damned impatient to have the job finished though, that at the end I wasn't listening at all.

"When will the bandages come off for good?" I asked him on the day he assured me the final transplant had taken and we were in the last healing stage.

"Ten days to two weeks," he answered.

That was sooner than I had expected.

It was time I got back to Spider Kern.

I wanted to blow the joint after the surgery was completed but before the bandages were removed. That way no one would know what my new face looked like. Neither would I, for that matter, but I could wait.

I couldn't make up my mind if Dr. Afzul recognized my intention or not. I'd already swiped from his office two cans of the liquefied spray he used after bandages were removed so I could use it on myself. If he missed them, he didn't say anything.

Kern was ready for me when I approached him. "Gettin' close?" he asked, eyeing my facial bandages, which were much less elaborate than in the initial stages.

"Right. How are we coming?"

"I've been thinkin' about it," he said. "I'll be back after lights out when we can talk."

For the balance of the evening I sat immobile in my chair in the alcove. I ignored Spider Kern, but I watched Rafe James. Twice as he moved about the ward James turned his mean-looking eyes in my direction. The expression upon his long, mournful-looking features could only be called speculative. It was the indicator as far as I was concerned. Whatever Spider Kern was setting up for me, Rafe James was to play a part in it.

It was just after midnight when Kern came to my bedside. Officially he had just gone off duty. "Let's go out to the sun deck," he muttered. I got out of bed and followed him to the silent solarium. He sat down and lit a cigarette before speaking again. I could have predicted his first words. "You've got the cash?" he asked.

"I'll have it." I didn't want him thinking he could shake me down close to the deadline and find it on me.

"No mistakes," he warned.

"There'll be none."

He took a long drag on his cigarette. "You're talkin' pretty good now, huh? Been puttin' us on all this time?"

"Would you be getting five grand if I hadn't?"

He grinned. "Guess not. When you plannin' on handin' over the packet?"

"When you deliver me to the main highway."

He nodded. "I been thinkin' the same way. I want you off the grounds when the blowoff comes."

"I'll need clothes, shoes, and a hat. And the gun."

"Okay." He frowned, considering. "It works out," he decided. "When we're set, I'll bring you the stuff and you can dress in the john. We'll walk out the ward door here together. I'll take you down the corridor to the side door that'll let us out onto the parkin' lot. From there I'll drive you to the highway in my car."

"It sounds fine," I pretended to agree. "I'll be picking up the cash alongside the driveway between the hospital and the highway." I stopped as though I'd said more than I intended.

I could see him changing gears while he thought that one over. The critical moment for me would be when Spider Kern thought I had the cash in my hands. I was sure that it was his intention to gun me down as an escapee at that moment. "All right," he said after a moment. "When's it gonna be?"

"How about a week from tonight?"

"That soon? No reason why not, though." He was studying me. "You're pretty sure of yourself, ain't you? Pretty cool?"

"I'm just leaving everything up to you."

"Yeah, that's the way. Okay, anything else we need to know or do?"

"Make sure the hat's a broad-brimmed one."

"Right. I'll pick up a straw sombrero. We'd better make the move around eleven P.M. so I can get back on the ward before the shift changes at midnight. I want your disappearance discovered on the owl shift, not on mine. Okay, let's pack it in."

I went back to bed but not to sleep.

Despite Spider Kern's question about my coolness, I felt far from cool after the months of inactivity.

All during the final week I paid close attention to the manner in which Dr. Afzul rebandaged my head after each session with the aerosol spray can in his office. There was less bandaging necessary each time. Mornings in his office I would unbandage myself while he was making his preparations. At night in bed I practiced unbandaging and rebandaging myself following Afzul's patterns until I was sure I could do it alone.

I still hadn't seen myself. There was no mirror in the doctor's office, and all my practicing was done in the dark. If Dr. Afzul ever noticed anything different in the arrangement of the bandages when I walked into his office mornings, he never said anything.

"You'll be getting a package in the mail one of these days with no return address on it," I told him on the morning of what I hoped would be my next-to-last day in the institution. "Don't open it until you're alone."

He knew what I meant. It would be the balance of the twenty thousand I'd promised him for the face job. I said it casually, as though it were still something a long way in the future. There were ways he could have helped my getaway, but I didn't ask. During the hours he'd worked over me I'd probed him sufficiently to be sure in my own mind that he wasn't flexible enough to help actively in my escape. I had no intention of jeopardizing the half loaf I had for a potential whole one.

Then something happened that made me wonder if I hadn't bought more of Dr. Afzul than I'd realized. For the first time in our association, he went out of his office and left me alone in it. I didn't waste time worrying about whether he suspected that my leave-taking was imminent. I hurried to his cabinet and removed a flat packet of gauze and a roll of tape, which I shoved into a pocket of my robe.

There were a stack of makeup kits in the cabinet, and I moved the top layer aside and opened the bottom kit. I took from it two tubes of a facial cream that Afzul had explained to me some time before would improve my appearance during the healing process. I put everything back so that no one could tell there had been tampering until the bottom kit was opened. I passed up the chance to take the entire kit. It was too bulky.

I would have liked to say goodbye to little Dr. Afzul when he returned to his office, but I didn't trust him that much. He had carried his share of the load, and I didn't want to rock the boat. Back on the ward I put gauze, tape, and makeup under my mattress. The aerosol cans were already there.

I had had to move my twelve hundred dollars several times during the months of plastic surgery. Each time the case of toilet tissue got down to the next-to-last layer, I removed my cash and stashed it temporarily until a new case went into the closet and I could hide the bills in the bottom layer again. I didn't think Kern was going to do anything to derail the situation now that he undoubtedly had a plan for taking care of me, but it didn't hurt to be careful.

It was a long day. I had made all my preparations, and there was nothing to do but wait. I didn't have a foolproof plan by any means. A major weakness in it was the timing, but I'd been unable to find a way around it. Kern and James went off duty at midnight, which meant my escape had to be made before then.

This timing meant that I'd have only a short period from the moment I reached the outside until the midnight change of shift. If anything happened to Kern and James during my escape, and there was almost no way as I saw it that nothing could happen, they would be missed at midnight. There would be an immediate bed-check, I'd be found missing, and the alarm would sound.

Aside from the short lead time, the advantage was with me. The options of Kern and James were limited by the fact they had to coddle me until they had the cash. When they did, I was expendable. They would never intend for me to return to the ward alive. A dead escaping prisoner told no stories.

My own options were flexible. My first plan was to kill Kern on the ward, take his keys, and let myself out of the place and take his car in the parking lot. A drawback was that although I knew which key on his key ring opened the ward door, I didn't know which one opened the side door to the parking lot. Even near midnight I could hardly stand at the door trying a succession of keys without risking observation and questioning by someone.

There was another factor. An overriding factor, the more I considered it. From his conversations with me, Kern planned to take me to his car and drive me to the point between the hospital and highway at which I would presumably hand over the money. Almost surely Spider would want Rafe James along on the expedition so that when the moment came no mistakes would be made in disposing of me.

James could hardly be waiting in Kern's car, though, since even a supposed dimwit like me might reasonably be expected to balk at two-to-one odds at such a critical moment. That meant Rafe James in another car, following us. The more I thought about it the more sure I was that was the way it had to be.

And the more I thought about it, the better I liked the idea.

Properly handled, it would give me the chance I needed to add to my lead time following my escape.

3

The final hour of waiting was the worst.

I was ready mentally long before "lights out" arrived at 9:45 P.M. I waited another half hour for the ward to quiet down, then slipped out of bed and removed aerosol cans, gauze, tape, and cosmetics from under the mattress. I wrapped them loosely in my robe.

I lifted the hospital bed, worked free the steel caster in its leg, and pulled it out. I walked around the bed and did the same thing on the other side. I stretched out on the bed again with fists balled around a caster in each hand, a precaution against Spider Kern's accelerating his intended double cross.

It was forty minutes later when a shadow flitted by the end of the bed and tapped lightly on the metal. It was Kern's signal that everything was ready. I waited five minutes longer before I got out of bed and walked in darkness to the ward washroom, bundled robe under my arm, steel caster in each hand. There was only a night light on inside the long room with its familiar odor. The only sound was the water running in the urinals. I opened the door of the last cubicle. Piled on a stool were shirt, trousers, sport coat, socks, shoes, and a broad-brimmed straw hat.

I added robe and casters to the pile, then closed the door. Kern was supposed to be standing guard outside to keep anyone from entering until I was ready. It still didn't leave much time. I went to the closet with its cleaning materials and pulled the case of toilet tissue toward the front. With no need for finesse, I pitched rolls of tissue until the back of the closet was waist deep before I reached the bottom layer in the case and once again retrieved my twelve hundred dollars.

I retreated to the cubicle and dressed quickly. The clothing was cheap and ill-fitting. The jacket was too tight and the trousers much too loose. I managed. I distributed all my contraband in various pockets except the right-hand pocket of the jacket. That one I kept empty.

I left the hospital clothing on the floor where I'd dropped it except for one white institutional sock. I put the two steel casters into the sock, then carried it to the nearest washbasin where I added a jumbo-sized bar of soap to it. I put the loaded sock into the empty right-hand jacket pocket.

I stood in front of the washbasin mirror and tried on the plantation-style straw hat. It fitted snugly over my head bandages, but it fitted. The bandages extended downward only as far as my nose. Under the high-crowned, broad-brimmed hat, they were even more inconspicuous than I had hoped.

When I left the washroom, Spider Kern was standing just outside the door, where he was supposed to be. There was no sign of Rafe James. "All set?" Kern asked me. He made no comment on my appearance. I could hear tension in his voice. The action was getting to him, I decided.

"All set," I said.

"Let's go, then."

He led the way down the ward in the dim light. He glanced through the heavy glass door before unlocking it. No one was in sight in the outside corridor. We passed through the door. I heard it click behind me for what I had made up my mind was the last time. I wasn't coming back.

Kern glanced across at me once as we walked side by side the twenty-five yards to the side door leading to the parking lot. I kept my right hand on the weighted sock in my jacket pocket. There was always the chance that Kern's sadistic tendency would outweigh his greed for money. He might lead me right up to the outside door, then shout the alarm and "capture" me. If he tried it, the steel casters in the sock were going to see to it that Spider Kern needed plastic surgery worse than I had.

In the better light in the corridor I tried to locate a suspicious bulge on Kern that would pinpoint a weapon. Even in his thin hospital whites, I couldn't see anything. It had to mean that Rafe James was carrying the armament.

I was keyed up so high for what I felt was the crucial moment at the side door that Kern had it unlocked and we were outside almost before I realized it. The night air felt warm and moist. It was my first breath untainted by the odor of hospital antiseptics in almost two years.

"My car's around the corner," Kern whispered. He started alongside the building, walking on the grass. I knew where his car was. I fell in a half step behind him. The almost total darkness on the visitors' side of the huge parking lot was relieved only by a faint refraction of light around the corner where a single arc-light on its standard illuminated the employees' cars. I couldn't hear a sound except the soft pad-pad of our feet on the grass and the occasional distant cheeping of a brook frog.

I took the loaded sock from my jacket pocket before we reached the corner of the building. I gripped it by the ankle elastic with the heavy soap and casters dangling in the toe, swung it twice around my head in a tight circle, and smashed it as hard as I could behind Spider Kern's right ear. He gave a kind of coughing grunt, stumbled, then pitched forward on his face in the grass.

I knelt beside him quickly, sock upraised, but he was unconscious. I would have liked to finish him off, but I had a use for him alive. I went through his pockets rapidly. I took his car keys and his wallet. He had seven hundred of the thousand I'd given him, and seven or eight dollars in loose bills. I was glad to see them. I'd need them when I had to get gas later. My own money was in hundred-dollar bills.

Amidst the clutter in Kern's pockets was a penknife. I used it to cut his metal-studded belt in two places and then I removed his key ring. The penknife saved removing his belt altogether. Without his keys, it would take Kern quite a while to get back inside the hospital. I listened for a moment to the sound of his stertorous breathing before I rose to my feet. He wouldn't be moving at all for a while. Long enough for me to handle Rafe James.

I shook a caster out of the sock and placed it in my hand with the long steel pin protruding between my fingers. I left the side of the building and walked out into the darkness of the main parking lot. I made a deep circle and came up behind the little cluster of employee's automobiles around the corner. I moved along the row in a crouch until I saw a head silhouetted against the night sky.

I approached the open window on the driver's side noiselessly. The outline of Rafe James's horse-like features was dimly visible. He was watching the corner of the building around which Kern and I were supposed to appear. Something bulky rested on James's lap.

I took a step closer, reached inside the window with my left hand, and jabbed the steel pin of the caster into the back of James's neck, hard. "Don't move!" I barked. "Or I'll shoot!"

He stiffened, then froze.

I reached down with my hand and took the bulky object from his lap. It was a sawed-off double-barreled shotgun. The stock had been cut down, too. It wasn't any longer and not much heavier than an old-time dueling pistol, but probably fifty times as lethal. "Out of the car," I ordered James. He complied numbly. He was in a state of shock. I handed him the keys to Spider Kern's automobile. He looked down at them blankly. "Get into Kern's car," I said.

He led the way to it. It was parked four cars away. If Kern and I had entered it and started through the hospital grounds, Rafe James would have been right behind us, shotgun at the ready. When I handed over the supposed thousand to Kern for aiding my escape, my life would have run its useful course as far as the two attendants were concerned. James would have stepped in with the shotgun.

I had the shotgun now. I held it on James while he got under the wheel of Kern's car, then slid into the passenger's seat myself. "Drive to the farthest corner of the dark side of the lot and park it again," I said. "Then we'll walk back to your car." James did as he was told. There was a sheen of perspiration on his face. Walking back to his car he held his arms stiffly at his sides as though he didn't know what to do with them. "Now out to the highway," I directed.

I knew that it was a mile to the highway. "Stop here," I said when I judged we were halfway. The headlights showed thick bushes on either side of the road and a ditch on the left. "Get out," I said when James hit the brakes. He started to whimper. "Out," I repeated.

I nudged him with the shotgun. He started out slowly, bolted and started to run. His lank frame zigzagged as he picked up speed. "Stop running!" I yelled at him. I had intended to knock him out, tie him up, and leave him in the ditch. I scrambled out after him. I couldn't wait. I didn't know the load in the shotgun. At twenty yards I touched off the front trigger. *Ker-blamm-m-m!* Whatever the charge was, it picked up Rafe James's running figure bodily and rolled him down into the ditch.

I looked up and down the road for advancing headlights. There were none. I climbed down into the ditch to check on James. From the look of him, the shotgun had to be loaded with buckshot. Even with the unchoked, sawed-off barrel, he must have caught half the charge. Rafe James was no longer a part of the problem.

I left Spider Kern's hospital keys and car keys beside the body. It might help to confuse the issue when James was found. I thought I knew how Kern would think when he regained consciousness. He would look first for his keys, then for his car. When he couldn't find either, and couldn't find James, Kern would assume I'd somehow got the drop on James and forced him to drive me away in Kern's car. Spider's self-preserving account of the situation should have the police looking for two men, one with head bandages, in Kern's car.

Instead, I'd be alone, without head bandages, in Rafe James's car. Kern's car wouldn't be noticed until daylight disclosed it in the morning. It gave me a few hours incognito. I rolled away from there.

When the gateway leading out to the highway loomed up in the headlights, I pulled off onto the shoulder of the road again. I removed my bandages and took one of the tubes of facial makeup, squeezed some onto my palm, and worked it into my scalp and face. In the hospital I had seen in the case of Willie Turnbull how the makeup dulled the pink gloss of new skin.

I put the hat back on. Without the bandages, it fitted more loosely. I opened the glove compartment when I was ready to take off. There were half a dozen loose shotgun shells in it. I examined one in the dash light. All were number 0 buckshot. Each pellet was the equivalent in size of a .32-caliber bullet. No wonder a single barrel had cut James down. At twenty yards a quarter of the load must have gone right through him.

It was ironic that the attendant I would have preferred to see dead, Kern, I had had to leave alive, while the one I didn't care about either way, James, had copped it because he expected me to blast him as he had intended to blast me.

With luck, by the time Kern's car was noticed in the morning and a corrected all-points went out on the police radio, I'd be close to where I wanted to be. Bunny's cabin where the Phoenix loot was buried.

I started up the car again, turned on the radio, and moved out onto the highway.

4

Rafe James's car wasn't much automobile.

In the first mile I noticed a shimmy in the front wheels; in the second, a lack of acceleration indicating fouled plugs or pistons. I hadn't looked at the tires, but there wasn't much point in stopping to inspect them now. They were all the tires I had. I hoped they'd hold up. A lot of things depended upon my reaching Hudson before daylight.

I found that the turn signals didn't work when I turned off the main highway at the first intersection. Staying on the heavily traveled main route was a risk I couldn't afford. Secondary roads were a risk in a different way. The gas tank was only half full, and I had only a slim chance of finding an all-night filling station open on a byroad. Getting off the central highway would probably stretch my driving time to five hours or more too, but it was still a lot safer.

The car radio squawked country music and drawled an occasional weather bulletin. My head began to feel hot under the plantation-style straw hat. It didn't seem as though I was perspiring. It seemed more as if the new flesh were drawing. The makeup on my face had dried rapidly but now began to feel moist again.

I encountered only two other cars in the first twenty miles away from the main highway. With the front-wheel shimmy, I had to concentrate on my driving. I passed two blacked-out gas stations at darkened crossroads. When I came up on a station with lighted pumps, I was afraid to pass it. I pulled in.

For a moment nothing happened. I thought the owner might have gone home, forgetting to turn off his lights. Then a shaggy-haired, sleepy-eyed kid stumbled out the door of the shacky-looking building and approached the car. "Fill it up," I told him.

The kid went to the pump with the regular gas and lifted down its hose. I leaned out the window to tell him to put in premium gas, then closed my mouth. James's car had probably never run on anything but regular gas. Premium might give it mechanical dyspepsia.

The zombie-like teenager reappeared beside the front window. "Three forty," he yawned.

I gave him four one-dollar bills. "Bring me a state road map with the change."

When he did, I lost no time in moving out. In the rearview mirror I could see the kid already shuffling his way back to the shack. There shouldn't have been anything memorable about our encounter that would cause him to remember me. Even without the shadowing hat, the feeble light from the gas pumps had hardly turned the service area into Times Square on New Year's Eve.

Forty-five minutes down the road, the singing voice of Eddy Arnold was cut off in mid-bar. "We interrupt this program for a special bulletin," the radio said. "A prison-ward patient from the state hospital has escaped and is presumed to be heading north in a stolen automobile. The car is a late model, green and white Dodge sedan with Florida plates two four four dash three five six. The occupant is considered armed and dangerous. Do not attempt to apprehend this fugitive. Any person seeing an automobile fitting this description please notify the nearest State Highway Patrol post immediately."

There followed an accurate description of the clothes I was wearing, and then the entire bulletin was repeated. There was no description of me as an individual. It amused me to think of the dispatcher's frustration. "Where's the guy's description? What the hell do you mean you don't know what he looks like?"

The police had probably had the flash thirty minutes before it went out over the commercial station. Spider Kern's car was a late model green and white Dodge with Florida plates 244-356. I was in fairly good shape as long as the police kept looking for that car. I had to get out of the clothes Kern had provided, though. Just as soon as I had my hands on the sack with the Phoenix loot buried in the ground near Bunny's cabin, getting rid of that clothing assumed top priority.

I pulled over to the side of the road, opened up the map, and studied it in the light from the dash. I saw that if I back-tracked five miles I could get off the black-topped secondary road I was on and complete the remainder of my drive to Hudson on little-traveled dirt roads. It would add to my driving time, but country roads were less likely to have troopers in prowl cars on the lookout for me. I dropped the map to the floorboards, covering up the sawed-off shotgun, and started up again.

I swung around and headed back along the macadamed road toward the dirt road turnoff I'd seen on the map. When I swung onto it, I almost chickened out in the first hundred yards. It was narrow, no more than eighteen feet wide, with a high crown and a deep drainage ditch on either side. The road was covered with a fine powdery layer of reddish dust. In the rearview mirror I could see it streaming behind in the taillights like a granular fog.

The map had showed it as a usable road, though, and the weather had been dry for days, so I kept on. The headlights bored a bright path in the darkness through a green tunnel of huge trees meeting over the road. I saw the trunks of jackpine, cypress, chinaberry, and shagbark hickory fringing the edges of the ditches.

I had no watch, so I could only estimate the time. I knew that sunrise came about six thirty at this time of the year. I hunched over the wheel, apprehensive about the sideways drift of the rear wheels in the loose dust every few hundred yards. My doubts increased with each passing moment. If someone took the notion, one man alone could roadblock an army on a road like this.

But the miles fell away behind me with no sign of life except an occasional rabbit darting through the headlight beams, kicking up puffs of dust from the road. I changed course twice as I had plotted it from the map when inter- secting dirt roads loomed up in the headlights. Sooner than I would have be- lieved possible, I found myself approaching the outskirts of Hudson.

I had planned my approach so there was no need for me to drive through the town. If anyone had the cabin staked out, they should be looking for me to drive in from U.S. 19. Instead, I took a seven-mile detour around three sides of a square. When I ended up on the road that led past Bunny's cabin, I was moving in on it from the side away from town.

I drove until I estimated I was within a mile of the cabin, and then I pulled Rafe James's car as far off the road as I could manage. The brush was so thick I couldn't penetrate it deeply, but at least the car wasn't out in plain sight. I picked up the shotgun and started down the road on foot. The air was clammy, moisture-laden from the nearby swamps. Wisps of fog were begin- ning to curl up from the damp ground. My head felt hot and uncomfortable.

I had only an occasional glimpse of the stars through the thick foliage of trees meeting far above my head. It was so dark I was beginning to wonder if I'd passed the cabin without seeing it when I heard a metallic ping from some- where ahead of me. I stopped and listened. The faint ping was repeated. I moved over to the side of the road and advanced a cautious step at a time. Even at that, I almost ran into the automobile before I saw it.

It was pulled off to the side as I had pulled James's car off. I eased up to it silently. No one was in it. I couldn't make out its color, but I could see the domed silhouette of the flasher on its roof. The car was a police cruiser. I was going to have unwelcome company at Bunny's cabin.

I placed my hand on the car's radiator. It was warm, almost hot. The metal- lic plinking sounds I'd heard had been the metal of the radiator cooling and contracting. I opened the cruiser's door boldly, knowing that interior lights don't come on in a police car. I was hoping to find a spare handgun, but the only thing in the front seat was a riot gun locked into its boot. Even if I could have worked it free, it was no improvement over the shotgun I already had. A dark blur on the left side of the back seat turned out to be a trooper's uni- form on a wire hanger. It was enclosed in a thin plastic bag. On the back seat lay a wide-brimmed trooper's campaign hat.

I started up the road again, leaving the car door open. Two hundred yards ahead there was a break in the trees, and I knew I was at the cabin. I started to take off my shoes, then stopped. All I needed was to put my foot down on a cottonmouth. I edged in from the roadside a careful step at a time. A chill dawn breeze rustled the bushes on either side of me, reminding me that time was running out. I wanted to move faster, but I held myself down.

The blacker outline of the cabin came into view. I studied it for a moment before moving in. At my first step there was the sound of a slap from inside the cabin. "Damn mosquitoes!" a hoarse voice muttered.

"Shut up!" Blaze Franklin's voice replied instantly.

"Don't get narky," the first speaker replied in an injured tone. "We'll see his headlights comin'. How 'bout a cigarette, Blaze?"

"I told you no cigarettes, Moody! This bastard is smart and dangerous!"

"At least you could tell me who this dangerous bastard is," Moody returned sulkily. "An' why you dragged me out here to wait for him at this God-forsaken place."

"Because a friend put through a telephone call," Franklin replied. "You just stick with me an' you'll wear diamonds."

"Like yours?" Moody said. His voice turned sly. "The boys been wonderin' where you're gettin' your money since you resigned from the force."

"We should be listenin' instead of talkin', Moody."

Moody grunted but subsided. I moved stealthily away from the cabin. I didn't like what I'd overheard. If Franklin were living high as a nonworking civilian, it almost had to be on the Phoenix money. He'd had plenty of time to look for it. The thought that he might find it had somehow never occurred to me.

I looked up at the star-dotted sky and moved straight north from the cabin's front door, exactly as I had that other night that seemed so long ago. Even in the dark I noticed that there was a lack of brush. Someone had cleaned it out. The ground was soft and shifting underfoot. Someone had patiently dug up the area foot by foot. Franklin had dug up the area. Franklin had found the money.

Dry paper rustled under my feet as I turned around and looked toward the cabin. I bent down and reached for as much of it as I could find without moving my feet. It felt like newspaper. I twisted it into a tight spill, put it under my arm, and crept back to the cabin. Franklin was going to tell me where the money was.

When I was a few yards away from the front door, I could hear them talking again. I couldn't make out what they were saying because this time the solid cabin wall was between me and them instead of the side containing an open window. Had Franklin bolted the front door? I doubted it. It would restrict mobility they might need. If the door was bolted, we were in for a prolonged shootout. If it wasn't, and I could burst inside with the element of surprise in my favor....

I moved within a yard of the door. I took the tightly rolled newspapers, found my matches, and lighted the paper. When I was sure it was going well, I positioned myself, shotgun in left hand, burning newspaper in right. I took a step backward, then slammed my heel into the cabin door with all the force in my leg muscles.

The door flew open. I tossed the flaming newspaper ahead of me into the center of the room. Startled exclamations greeted me as I darted inside and knelt down, out of line with the door. The newspaper sputtered, almost went out, then flared brightly. I recognized Blaze Franklin in a turtleneck sweater and slacks. Alongside him stood a trooper in uniform. Both were rigid in grotesque attitudes of surprise.

"Freeze!" I demanded, leveling the shotgun halfway between them. Moody reacted first—and fast. His right hand dipped toward the gun on his hip. I shifted my aim slightly and touched off the forward trigger. In the confined space the shotgun's roar shook the cabin. Moody was still upright while half his head and all his brains were plastered on the wall behind him. Then he spun in a half turn and fell forward on what was left of his face.

"Hold it!" I ordered Franklin, swinging the sawed-off toward him. I wanted him alive, but his gun was already halfway out of his shoulder holster. There was no time for further conversation. I squeezed the second trigger and gut-shot him. He went backward in a stutter step until he smashed into the stove, rebounded, doubled up, and hit the deck. The blast had almost cut him in two, but he was still alive. He crawled in circles on the floor like a huge wingless beetle.

He was still alive, but the first look was indication enough he was never going to tell me where the money was. I crossed the cabin and put a foot on him to stop the crawling. I went through his clothes rapidly. I took his wallet, keys, and .38, wiped the blood off my hands on his trouser legs, then backed toward the door. The crawling started up again, but more slowly.

Outside, I thought of putting a match to the cabin. It didn't seem necessary. If Moody didn't know why they were there, Franklin hadn't told anyone. It would be a long time before they were found, if ever. I still had one chance left at recovering the money and no time to waste.

I walked rapidly from the cabin to the road.

Dawn was painting the eastern sky flame-red when I reached the police cruiser. I stripped off the clothing that Spider Kern had provided, took Moody's uniform from its hanger in the back of the cruiser, and tried it on. It was too big, but that was much better than having it too small. I took reefs and tucks in it to make it look as presentable as I could. The trooper's hat was far too large. I padded its sweat band with the necktie that was also on the hanger. That helped considerably.

There was less than half an hour until full sunrise. I wadded up the discarded clothing and placed it on the front seat beside me as I got under the wheel. I backed the cruiser out onto the road and headed away from town. It was the wrong direction for what I eventually had in mind, but first I had to get back to Rafe James's car.

I parked the cruiser and scrambled through the brush to James's car. I started up the engine, backed out to the road to get traction and a short run, then rammed it straight ahead with the accelerator floored. Metal scraped and brush crashed. The front end reared up as the axle scaled a low stump. For a moment I thought that was it. Then the car slithered off the obstruction and lurched ahead again. The rear end bucked as the same stump caught the housing. That did it. The rear wheels whined as they spun without traction. I got out and made my way back to the road.

I looked back toward the car from the roadway. I couldn't see anything. I threw the keys into the woods on the other side of the road. It would take the combination of an accident for someone to find it and a major effort on the part of the finder if that automobile were ever returned to civilization.

I climbed into the cruiser again. There was a flashlight in the glove compartment, and by its light I read the address on Franklin's license. Three twenty-seven Riverside, Hudson, Florida. It was the same boarding house where he had lived when he and Lucille Grimes had been shaping nooses for my neck. I rolled the cruiser down the road until I found a spot where I could turn around without dropping a wheel into the ditch, then headed toward town.

The powerful motor made the cruiser feel as though it had wings compared to James's car. I switched on the police radio when I swung onto U.S. 19 and turned toward downtown Hudson. If the cruiser were labeled missing, I needed to know it. I didn't think it would be, though. Everything overheard at the cabin indicated that Franklin had enlisted Moody during the deputy's off-duty time. Since it was a fact of life in Hudson that deputies drove home in their cruisers, this one shouldn't be missed for a while.

I drove to Franklin's address and parked in front of his boarding house. Both boarders and neighbors were used to seeing cruisers parked there. I took Franklin's keys and his flashlight and ran up the front steps. The streetlights were still on, but a dirty gray daylight was infiltrating the area.

The front door had a Yale lock. That made it easy; there was only one Yale key on Franklin's key ring. Inside, I put the flash on the mailboxes in the hallway. The beam picked up the card with its faded typing in the name slot: Franklin, 2-C. I climbed the stairs, making no effort to move quietly. The boarders were used to all-hours comings and goings.

In the dark second-floor hallway I shone the light on doors until I found 2-C. I had to try three keys before the door opened. I went right to work inside. There was no point in being subtle. I opened drawers and dumped their contents. I stripped the bed and dragged the mattress onto the floor. I opened the closet and threw the clothing item by item into the center of the room. I checked the baseboards, the pictures on the walls, the lighting fixtures, the radiant heat unit. I checked every possible place where Franklin might have hidden the money.

I found ten fifty-dollar bills lying openly in a bureau drawer, and that was all. Franklin had cached the bulk of the money elsewhere, and he was never going to tell me where. I hadn't realized how much I had geared all my planning to the recovery of the Phoenix loot. Counting the money in Franklin's wallet and what I'd found in the room with what I'd brought with me, I had less than four thousand dollars. Hiding out was expensive, and four thousand dollars wouldn't last long enough for me to lay low until my appearance became more normal. I would have to drive on to Colorado to dig up the other jar, or pull a job a lot sooner than I would have liked.

The sun was above the horizon when I closed the boarding house front door and walked down the steps to the cruiser. I headed north on U.S. 19. The cruiser was the least likely car on the road to attract official attention as long as it wasn't reported missing. The fact that I wore a uniform wouldn't hurt either.

I passed out of range of the Hudson sheriff department's radio after forty minutes. New voices took up the routine police calls on the same wave band. I knew that all law enforcement agencies except the state police and the largest cities used a common wavelength. Nothing appeared to be disrupting the even tenor of police routine that morning. I put plenty of highway behind me for four hours at ten mph above the speed limit, then turned west at Capps on Route 90-A.

I stopped at a large carwash on the outskirts of Tallahassee and got a sandwich from a vending machine, then set out again. When I came to the city limits of DeFuniak Springs, I slowed down and took the river road. A few miles along it I saw what I was looking for: a freshly painted sign that said: TOM WALKER'S CABINS. I was happy to see the fresh paint because it meant that Walker, a blind Negro, was still operating his seedy cabin camp as an underworld underground railway.

I drove past the sign and stopped at a roadside stand down the road. I bought two washable, sport shirts and two pairs of washable slacks from an elderly colored woman. She eyed my trooper's uniform but didn't say anything. The second turn beyond her stand I found a dirt road and turned into it. Within a few yards semitropical foliage hemmed in the cruiser on both sides. I parked in deep shade where the car was almost engulfed in big trees.

The sound of the engine died out to be replaced by the sound of insects. I relaxed my hands on the steering wheel and drew a deep breath. It was still only eleven thirty A.M. I had reached this point with a minimum of difficulty, and if I connected with Blind Tom as I was sure I could, I had it made.

I stripped off the uniform, climbed into the back of the cruiser, and went to sleep. When I woke, the car was in even deeper shadow. It was nearly sundown. I was in a lather of perspiration from the buildup of heat in the car, but rather than expose my new skin to mosquitoes I kept the windows closed. I knew what I had to do, but I needed darkness to do it.

When the thick blackness of the Florida night suddenly enveloped the area, I wriggled into sport shirt and slacks. With the aid of backup lights I inched my way out to the highway. I headed toward Tom Walker's Cabins, but a quarter mile away I turned into a sandy lane.

There was no road. The headlights picked out a baseball diamond, a horse-shoe court, and a tennis backstop in the nighttime-quiet of the county park. I drove on dead pine needles through widely spaced trees to the riverbank. I stopped on a slight downgrade, cut the headlights, pulled up the emergency, and got out of the car, leaving the motor running.

I checked everything twice. Cash in my pocket and extra slacks and sport shirt on my arm. Everything else in the cruiser including the trooper's uniform, Franklin's keys, the sawed-off shotgun, and the clothing Spider Kern had supplied, which I'd brought with me in case I needed to get out of the uniform suddenly. It was too dark to see the swift-running current below me but I could hear it. I leaned through the front window, put the cruiser in gear, then released the emergency brake.

The car crept toward the bank. The front wheels went over, and then it hung. I thought I was going to have to push, but the bank crumpled under its weight and the cruiser lunged forward. It dropped off into the darkness with a splash I could hardly hear. I knew the river was deep enough at that point so it was unlikely the cruiser would ever be found.

I walked out to the highway and on to Blind Tom's. All the known artifacts of Chet Arnold had disappeared with the cruiser. If I could stay out of sight for a while, the break would be clean. The big advantage I had now was that no one knew what the ex-Chet Arnold looked like in his new incarnation.

I turned in from the highway at the cabin-camp entrance. The same crazily tilted, hand-lettered sign I remembered hung on the wall of the building that served as a gatehouse. The sign said OFFIS. The gate was chained, barring traffic unapproved by the "offis." Tom paid off to avoid surveillance. It was this factor that brought him steady customers.

The only light in the gatehouse came from the dial of a desktop radio. I knocked once and entered. A white-haired, elderly Negro sat at the shabby desk. "Hello, Tom," I said. "Can you take care of me for a while?"

His blind walleyes stared in my direction while his wrinkled features screwed up in concentration. Blind Tom Walker had a fantastic memory for voices. "Mought be," he said cautiously at last. "Dependin'."

"I'd like to have the riverbank cabin with the full-size bed on the north branch of the Y, Tom."

"Flood got that one three—four years ago," he observed. "But I rebuilt." He was silent again, evaluating.

I remembered something. "How's Cordelia, Tom?" Cordelia was a five-foot female alligator Tom kept penned at the river's edge.

"Cordelia in love," Tom informed me solemnly.

"In love? Who with?"

"With love." Tom chuckled unexpectedly, a high-pitched cackle. "You take that cabin on the Y, the bulls courtin' Cordelia every night gonna keep you awake with their roarin'." He leaned back in his chair. "Drake," he said. "That's who you be. Drake. You fixed a thirty-two for me."

Seven years ago I had passed as Earl Drake, itinerant gunsmith, during my stay with Tom. Earl Drake had never been in trouble with police anywhere. It was as good a name as any. "That's right, Tom. Earl Drake. And this time I'd like to buy a thirty-two from you."

"They come high," he cautioned me.

"Like the cabin?"

He grinned toothlessly. "Hundred a week."

"Only if you fix me a mess of catfish Sunday evenings."

He cackled again, then sobered. "Fixin' to stay awhile?"

"Yes."

"Then mought be we could shave a mite off the rate."

"What about the thirty-two?"

He fished a key from a ragged pocket of his tattered white pants and unlocked a drawer in the desk. "How 'bout this one?" he inquired, pulling out an automatic and handing it to me.

It was a German-made Sauer, the 1930 model with three-inch barrel and duralumin slide and receiver, which reduced its weight to fifteen ounces. I turned the knurled block at the rear of the slide and eased slide and assembly forward from the barrel. It was reasonably clean. The standard thumb safety was on the left side of the receiver and the magazine release catch was in the butt. Magazine capacity was seven cartridges, and it was fully loaded. Although hardly a modern gun, the Sauer was a well-made weapon.

"You've sold a thirty-two, Tom," I told him. "How much?"

He rose to his feet. "We'll settle up t'morra," he said. "C'mon."

He led the way from the office and struck out surefootedly in the darkness along a dim path. No flashlight was ever necessary for Blind Tom. I stayed close behind the sheen of his once-white pants. We took the north fork of the branch of the Y in the path that I remembered, and I could hear the river again. Tom was unlocking the door of a cabin high on the riverbank before I could even see it in the blackness. He handed me the key. "If Cordelia's beaus get noisy, throw a saucepan down," he advised me.

"I'll do that," I promised.

He went back down the path. I opened the cabin door, went in, and turned on the light. The flood that had taken the old cabin had been a blessing in disguise, I decided. Tom had rebuilt it completely and the furnishings, while not new, looked much more comfortable.

I made a quick, approving tour of the facilities, then started shedding clothes. My day had begun at eleven P.M. the previous night when Spider Kern had given me the all-clear signal to go into the hospital washroom and change into my escape clothing.

By any standards, it had been a full day.

I slid into bed and relaxed fully for the first time in nearly twenty-four hours. Not Cordelia's beaus nor anything else woke me until morning sunlight streaming in the cabin window hit me in the face.

5

Even as a kid I was a loner.

I never knew why, since I was the youngest in a family of eight. I had five sisters who tended to tell me what to do. Long before I was in my teens I ran them off the reservation on that point. They got the idea eventually that I'd manage my own life. They pouted, but they got the idea.

What clinched it was an incident that happened when I was twelve. I had a Persian kitten named Fatima. I never played with the other kids the way my family kept urging me to do. I played with Fatima. She was a ball of fluff with bronze eyes.

Some women in the town put on a pet show. I entered Fatima, and in the finals of the judging I was in the ring with her. So was a fat boy who went to the same school that I did. He had a big boxer dog. Fatima didn't like dogs, and I asked the fat boy to keep the boxer away. He laughed and let the dog come closer. The boxer sniffed curiously and Fatima raked his nose. The dog snapped once and Fatima died in an instant of a broken neck.

I really climbed the fat boy. The women running the pet show pulled me off him finally. I went home and didn't say anything to anyone. The next day I caught the fat boy on his way home from school and I climbed him again.

The fat boy's father came to my house that night. My father was surprised to hear about Fatima. The fat boy's father said he'd get me another kitten. I told him I didn't want another kitten. My father took me upstairs and talked to me. I told him I didn't want the kitten.

The next day after school I had to chase the fat boy to within two blocks of his house before I caught him. It didn't help him when I did. My father gave me a licking when he got home. The minister came to our house that night. When he left, I don't think he felt his talking had accomplished much.

After two more go-rounds with the fat boy, I was kicked out of school. I waited for the fat boy on his way home and gave it to him again. By now he screamed like a girl at the sight of me. I got another licking at home that night. It didn't change anything.

The fat boy started leaving school by different doors at different times. When I had trouble catching him, I slipped out of the house mornings and caught him on his way to school. Each time his father called my father I got another licking. My mother argued with my father about his handling of me. I was sorry to hear it. I didn't feel like a martyr. I felt like someone doing what he had to do.

It went on for three weeks. Then one of my sisters ran into the house one day and said there was a big moving van in front of the fat boy's house. The fat boy's family was moving away.

They let me back into school in two months. Around the house the subject was never mentioned. In a year I think everyone had honestly forgotten.
Except me.

Then during my senior year in high school I got crossways with a bullying
local police sergeant. It started out as an honest misunderstanding. He was
hardheaded, though, and so was I. We locked horns. I ended up at the police
station. By that time he knew he was wrong, but he wouldn't back down.
Neither would I. He roughed me up in a cell. I hit him in the face with the
heel of my shoe. Afterward they took me to the hospital.

My father in his anger talked about suing the city. I wouldn't cooperate. I
knew what I was going to do. It wasn't too difficult when I got out of the
hospital. Three men had been in the cell with me. I watched them. I got the
first two a couple of months apart, each in situations where his age and
strength didn't help him.

Each time the chief of police came to our house afterward and all but accused
me of it. I smiled at him and said nothing. I couldn't understand why my father grew more nervous-looking every day. The police hadn't a scrap of evidence.

The sergeant took longer. He was on his guard. No snotty kid was going
to make a laughingstock of him. He came up his slippery front steps one night
during a sleet storm, and I got him with a piece of pipe. Someone found him
at the foot of his steps before he froze to death.

The chief of police was at my house before daylight the next morning. He
was raging. Leave town, he told my father. You're harboring a wild animal.
Cage him, or leave town. I couldn't believe it when a "For Sale" sign went
up on our front lawn. The police couldn't prove a thing.

I didn't intend to inconvenience the family, though.

My father might not be able to cope, but I could.

I left home, and I never went back.

I drifted a few hundred miles north and got a job in a gas station. It was
night-shift work, and I slept days in a cheap rooming house. Working the hours
I did, I met few people, but one odd duck took to turning up at the filling station during my midnight-to-eight shift.

He was older, perhaps thirty. He was educated, and he brought me books
to read. I could see that he was lonely. At first I thought he was a homo, but
he never made a move. He was interesting in the things he could tell a kid who
had never been anywhere.

Then one night the police came and scooped him. The charge was molest-
ing a small girl. It turned out he'd done time for the same thing twice before.
That should have been that, except that I learned the hour he was supposed
to have committed the molestation. I knew he'd been picking up some of his
books at my rooming house at that time.

I went to the police. They wouldn't listen to me. They'd decided that he'd done it. I insisted that whatever he had done before, he hadn't done this. I made no impression. I did my talking to a lieutenant who could have been die cast from the same mold as my hometown police sergeant.

The lieutenant ran me off. I tried to go over his head. All of a sudden I had no job, and the next day I had no room. I walked the street lugging my bag all one wintry night until the bus station opened in the morning.

I left town because it wasn't possible to get another job. The police saw to that. I ended up a hundred miles away working as a stock boy in a super-market. The job was so low-paying I couldn't accumulate any money. I lived from day to day. Nights in my room I had plenty of time to think over my two encounters with police. Then one noon at lunch I picked up a discarded news-paper and saw a paragraph that said that my acquaintance from the filling sta-tion had been convicted and sentenced to fifteen years.

I knew he hadn't done it, but there it was—fifteen years. If that was the way the system worked, I'd had enough of the system. I never went back to the supermarket. I couldn't accumulate there the money I needed for what I had to do.

I began robbing filling stations at night, on foot at first, until I'd heisted enough for a car. I faked a gun at first until I was able to buy one. The week I had it and the car, too, I drove the hundred miles back to the town where the police lieutenant lived. When he opened his front door, I killed him. I couldn't do anything about the fifteen-year bum rap, but I was damned if I was going to let the bastard responsible for it get away with it.

For the next couple of years I knocked around from place to place. I grad-uated from filling stations to theater box offices to liquor stores. Then I met a guy who introduced me to a group setting up a bank job. There were five of us, and we worked on it for four months. Nothing went right. Two were burned down during the getaway. The rest of us holed up in a barn where we were found the next day. Another one was killed there and two of us were captured.

As a kid with no record, I drew three-to-five. If I could have shown a means of support, it might have been probation. It taught me something. My cellmate taught me a lot more. He was an embittered old dynamiter whose lungs were eroding. Forget the elaborate, complicated jobs, the old lag urged me. Smash-and-grab. Hit-and-run. In, out, and away in four minutes. I listened, and was convinced.

I didn't apply for parole. I did the bit and came out with no strings on me. When I hit the street, I had to shake the FBI tails waiting for me to go back for the unrecovered bank loot. I went up into the Pacific Northwest to get away from them. I took a job in a lumber camp. I became handy with an axe, and I practiced with a handgun until I was the equal of any circus trick-shot artist.

I came out of the woods when I figured I had the prison smell off me. In-

side, I'd made plenty of contacts. I could pick and choose. I'd made up my
mind I was going to do things my way. I contacted a man and laid down a few
rules. They included scouting the job in advance to make sure it was worthwhile, thus holding the action down to a job or two a year. He was agreeable,
and we went to work.

The time spent in the lumber camp had given me a legitimate occupation.
Everywhere we went I passed as a tree surgeon. I could do the work, and I
kept a name clean to work under. I always worked a couple of months a year.
They were never going to get me again with that no-visible-means-of-support
gag.

My partner and I had a two-year run that was peaches and cream. We took
five banks for the equivalent of a comfortable living. Then a suspicious husband came home early one night and my partner wound up on a slab in the
morgue.

I found another partner. All told, I ran through five of them in thirteen
years. None of them cashed in on a job with me. They all insisted in branch-
ing out for themselves. They'd have been better off if I'd kept them busier,
but how much money can a man spend? I've never been a high liver.

Bunny was my last partner, and the best. We'd needed a driver for the
Phoenix job, and we imported a kid from Juarez who panicked during the
show. I took a slug in the arm trying to hold things together during the getaway. Bunny went on to Florida while I was hiding out, healing. He sent me
a thousand a week in hundreds, registered mail. I didn't want my share of the
swag around until I was a hundred percent mobile again.

The cash was mailed to me from Hudson, Florida, where Bunny holed up.
The regularity of the registered letters to me attracted the curiosity of the
Hudson postmistress, Lucille Grimes. She mentioned it to her boyfriend, a local deputy, Blaze Franklin. He steamed open an envelope, found the cash, decided on a shakedown, and went after Bunny.

He didn't get the bulk of the loot. Not then. I knew something had happened to Bunny when the mail stopped coming. I drove to Florida when I
could travel. It took me a while, but I ran down Lucille Grimes and Franklin,
and what was left of Bunny. I evened the score for my partner, but I ended
up in the prison wing of the state hospital for a long healing period.

I was out now, and I intended to stay out.

6

A knock at the cabin door woke me in the morning. When I opened it, no one was there, but a bag of groceries was propped up against the wall. I carried it inside. After I unloaded it, the kitchen table was covered with coffee, tea, salt, sugar, butter, bread, milk, cereal, hamburger, and two TV dinners. That was one thing about Blind Tom's: the price was high, but service came with it. Anyone staying at one of Tom's cabins never had to leave it unless he chose. A shopping list Scotch-taped to the outside of the door each night would provide the supplies delivered in the morning.

I put the perishables in the refrigerator. I wasn't looking forward to eating my own mediocre cooking during the interval it took me to heal properly. I'm a fair subsistence cook and that's about all. Taking my meals in the cabin guaranteed privacy, though, and for that I was prepared to put up with my own culinary shortcomings.

Thinking about the necessary healing period sent me into the bathroom. I wanted to see my new face. The day before, I had had fleeting glimpses of myself in the cruiser's rearview mirror, but never so that I could see the overall effect. Then last night when I reached the cabin and tried to see myself in the dim light of the low-wattage bulb illuminating the water-spotted mirror, most of my new face was in shadow. All that showed up was my clean, bare skull with its spider web of perforations from sutures. Now in the bright morning light I could see myself clearly.

The scarred, crimson, rough-looking features that confronted me in the mirror were no surprise. Neither was the upper body with its patchwork effect where missing healthy skin had been transferred to other areas. There was one surprise, though. Dr. Afzul had given me the features of a man ten years younger. Not a handsome man, but then it had never been a handsome face. It was certainly a different face. I made a mental note that I still owed the little plastic surgeon ten thousand dollars. He had certainly earned it.

I left the bathroom and rummaged in a closet until I found a pair of faded swimming trunks and sneakers. I pulled them on, left the cabin, and descended the steeply winding, rutted path to the river's edge. Each spring after the high water receded, Tom had truckloads of sand dumped in front of each of the riverbank cabins. The result was instant beaches. All the cabins were strategically placed along the winding channel so that none commanded a view of any of the others.

I waded out into the cool water and splashed around for a moment. Then I swam the seventy or eighty feet to the opposite bank, rested a bit, and swam back. Each morning I intended to add another lap to my morning swim to restore muscle tone lost during the months in the hospital.

I stayed only ten minutes in the early-morning sun. Dr. Afzul had warned me that my tender new skin would have to be treated to sunshine only in brief, gradually increased doses. When I left the water and started to climb up the path to the cabin, a grunting sound to the left caused me to detour. Twenty yards along the riverbank I came upon an arrangement of telephone poles and steel cable interlaced with barbed wire. This was Cordelia's dwelling place. She lay there sunning herself on a mud-bank.

If I had changed since Cordelia last saw me, the same was true of her. She had been a svelte five-foot maiden 'gator. Now she was a barrel-bodied ten-footer, and if Blind Tom were to be believed, complacently steeped in 'gator sin. At the sound of my approach she opened her eyes, fixed me with a cold stare, and closed them again.

I returned to the cabin and breakfasted on cereal, milk, and a cup of coffee. I waited half an hour and did a few of the RAF exercise series, then took out the .32 Sauer I had acquired from Blind Tom and cleaned it carefully with tools and gun oil I found in a drawer. In a couple of days I'd take it out into the woods to sight it in and learn its shooting characteristics.

I skipped lunch in favor of the river again. The spring-fed coolness of the swift current was wonderfully refreshing, and I prudently made myself return to the cabin to avoid the sun's rays before I was actually ready. I took a nap in the afternoon, and in the early evening I broiled a part of Blind Tom's hamburger. Afterward I took a chair outside the cabin and cocked it up against the wall. I sat in the swift-gathering twilight and listened to the increased volume of woods noises. The river breeze swept the majority of mosquitoes inland, leaving me comparatively unmolested.

By the time darkness fell and the river disappeared from sight if not from sound, the day-long combination of sunshine and exercise resulted in stifled yawns. I fought off sleep while I did some mental arithmetic. In the very near future, money was going to be a problem. In order to move on I needed a car, which Tom would have to purchase for me. It needn't be much car, but any kind of transportation worthy of the name wouldn't return much change from a thousand dollars.

I also needed a hairpiece. I didn't want Tom to know my need for one, so it would have to be one of the first orders of personal business when I left the cabin. I didn't see how I could stretch my stay at the cabin much longer than three months without leaving my bankroll dangerously low before I had made a connection. I hoped that three months would be long enough to restore a normal color so that I wouldn't be the conspicuous beneficiary of plastic surgery, but regardless, I'd have to be moving on.

I knew my next stop. I planned to drive to Mobile and look over the Golden Peacock, a nightclub. When it had been run by Manny Sebastian, the place also had functioned as a meeting spot and armament center for a hard-core underworld elite, those who operated on a major scale behind a gun. Manny Sebastian was buried under a mangrove root in a Florida swamp, but no one knew it except me. Sebastian had been one of the preliminary hurdles in my abortive effort to recover the Phoenix bank loot.

Regardless of the identity of the new proprietor, it was unlikely that the high-profit end of the Golden Peacock operation had changed. I even felt I knew who the new man would be. Sebastian's second-in-command at the nightclub was a slim, dark man named Rudy Hernandez. More than likely he had taken over. Hernandez had known me slightly, but he wouldn't know me at all with my new face. Sebastian had known me well, but not well enough to stay clear of me when his quick, greedy mind connected me with the Phoenix job.

Assuming that nothing else had changed, I could find out more quickly at the Golden Peacock than anywhere else what I needed to know: who was in circulation, who was not, and why.

I climbed out of my chair, entered the cabin, and went to bed.

For sixty seconds I heard the crisp night breeze whispering through the window screens, and then I didn't hear anything.

I sunned myself every day that it was possible, and I swam every day in the river whether it was sunny or not. Each time I came out of the water I applied some of the healing liquefied spray in Dr. Afzul's aerosol cans to my face. The first week I examined myself in the bathroom mirror each morning. I stopped when I could see no apparent progress. Every fourth day I permitted myself a quick look. Change was more noticeable that way, although it still came slowly.

The raw look of the transplants faded in the same proportion that the fish-white hospital pallor of normal skin gave way to a subtle tan. Even when I felt able to increase the sun dosage, the surgical scars were another story. They would be with me for a long time. During the time I could stay at the cabin the healing wouldn't be far enough advanced to conceal the fact that plastic surgery had taken place, but it would be far less evident.

Nobody came near the cabin except Blind Tom, who brought late-night sacks of groceries in a child's little red wagon. Sometimes I waited up for him. By the time he reached my cabin there was only one other sack left in the wagon. I didn't even know how many cabins were occupied. I didn't want to know. I saw no one during my daily swims and my forays into the woods to practice with the Sauer. Privacy was what a man's money bought for him at Blind Tom Walker's, and privacy was exactly what I wanted.

Six weeks after my arrival I stopped the old man one night on his rounds. "Keep an ear out for a thousand dollars worth of automobile," I told him. "Nothing fancy. Just transportation."

He nodded sagely. "Big?" he inquired. "Small? Sedan? Station wagon?"

"A small sedan," I decided.

"Volkswagen okay?"

I hesitated. I was used to thinking in terms of horsepower that could out-run pursuit, but horsepower cost money. And at the moment it wasn't es-sential. "Sounds all right, Tom."

"I'll listen," he said, and shuffled away.

A week later he lingered while I was unpacking the sack of food. "Got you a Volks to look over," he informed me.

"In good shape?"

"One owner. Ol' whore who on'y used the back seat," he said without cracking a smile.

"How about a license and registration for Earl Drake?"

"It cost a bit."

"I expected it would. Where's the car?"

"Behind the office."

"Leave the keys in it. I'll come down in the morning and try it."

I made the trek along the rutted path at sunrise. I drove the VW down the road a couple of miles. It was clean, and it handled all right. When Tom stopped at the cabin that night, I counted out ten hundred-dollar bills. Tom held each up to his ear and crackled it slowly. "Come on, Tom," I said. "You know you can't tell the amount on a bill from the sound."

"I c'n tell if'n it's good or bad paper," he said dryly. "I'll check on the de-nom'nation later."

"Let me know when you have the license, title, and registration."

He nodded and started to shuffle away.

"Oh, Tom!" I called after him. He turned and came back. I disliked putting the direct question, but I knew no way to maneuver around it. "What do you hear about the Golden Peacock these days?"

"It in business," he said, and waited.

"Sebastian still running it?"

"Last I heard he in Europe."

"Europe?"

"Vacation," Blind Tom explained.

It figured when I thought about it. Sebastian had disappeared, and who-ever was running the club wouldn't know for sure from day to day when he might reappear. Some sort of story would have to be put out. "Thanks, Tom," I said, and the old man went surefootedly down the path.

I was beginning to have second thoughts about the Golden Peacock. Through a combination of circumstances, some fortunate and some not, I had acquired a new face that no one could connect with the old one. If I went to Mobile, the task I'd be setting for myself would be to move in as a total stranger and convince someone that I was one of the regulars without giving away my past identity. But if it wasn't the Golden Peacock, then what was my next move?

What put me in a real squeeze was my short bankroll. I hadn't been so low on cash in years. By the time I felt it was reasonably safe to leave Blind Tom's, I wasn't going to have money enough left to lallygag around the Golden Peacock while I did a selling job on the new operator. Either I made a quick sale and acquired some helpful information, or I made a move for myself.

I'm not a worrier ordinarily, but nights in the tree-rustling darkness I found myself staring up at the dim outline of the cabin's rough plank ceiling, thinking myself into the dead ends of blind corners.

When my cash shrank to eighteen hundred dollars, I told Tom I'd be moving on. I took a final swim in the river, stopped to pay my respects to Cordelia, who intimated that she couldn't care less, walked down to the office with my extra slacks and sport shirt over my arms, and headed the VW west on the highway.

Clothing was another problem, I decided as I drove. I'd always been fussy about my clothes, without being fancy, but right now I was outfitted for a backwoods camp and nothing else. I didn't want to spend any money on clothes until I took care of something else first. I had one more expenditure coming up, and I turned south to drop down into Pensacola to take care of it.

Under "Wigs," the Yellow Pages listed five places of business. The first was in a run-down neighborhood, and I kept on going. The second looked better, and I pulled around the corner from it and parked. In the windows of the shop I approached there were wigs of all kinds, but only women's. There were no customers inside. A single clerk, a big blonde with a high-piled hairdo in the twisting curlicue Mae West style, stood near the door. A second look disclosed that it wasn't only the hairdo that made the blonde resemble Mae West.

Shrewd blue eyes examined me in detail while I fumbled for an opening line. "You need a hairpiece," the blonde informed me.

I was relieved to have her take the bull by the horns. "I didn't see any men's—you take care of men, too?"

"We'll take care of a rhesus monkey if he's got the price," she declared cheerfully.

"Yes, but—" I reached up and removed my broad-brimmed hat, then touched the top of my skull. "This is kind of total."

She raised her arms, put her hands over her ears, and lifted. What looked like about forty-five pounds of hair rose straight up in the air, disclosing a nude, polished skull. Oddly enough, the revelation didn't materially damage her sexy look. "Rheumatic fever got mine," she said, lowering the wig into position again.

"Mine was a chemical explosion."

She winked at me. "We guarantee that our hairpieces will restore your sex life to its former level."

Her voice was low and throaty. With the wink, it made me suspect the whole thing was a put-on. I started to reply that on the basis of restoring my sex life to its former level several million red-blooded American men would feel themselves shortchanged, and then I stopped. "Did anyone ever tell you that you look like Mae West?"

She nodded. "Thousands." She gave me a bright smile. "I did right by them all."

"It's your shop?" I asked for lack of something better to say.

"Yes, it is. You've already seen that I'm acquainted with the problem. Oh, sure, half the wigs I sell are to dizzy dames interested in seeing if a color change will add an inch to their boyfriends' muscle, but it's a challenge like yours that I try to do right by." She strolled over to me and studied my features. She had a rolling gait like a sailor's. "What people who need prosthetic hairpieces don't realize is that makeup is just as important as the hair," she went on.

"Makeup?"

"Exactly. I teach you how to use television makeup so that you can blend your face with your new hair so that only a makeup expert can tell it's not your own."

I had used up the supply of healing cream I had smuggled from the hospital during my first month at Blind Tom's. The healing had been well along by then, but I was still conscious of the visibility of the scars. "How long would it take you to teach me?"

"Half an hour. The practice necessary to do it correctly takes longer, of course." She moved away from me, behind the counter, and began rummaging in drawers. "Was your hair brown?"

"Before it turned gray."

She looked up at me. "You want gray again?" There was a definite twinkle in her saucy-looking eyes. "You don't need it."

"Thanks. I'll leave it up to you."

"That's the boy," she approved. "I'm glad you're not the type who comes in here sniveling because his face was burned. 'Why, man you've got it made,' I always tell them. 'Your face isn't going to change. You'll look exactly the same twenty years from now when every woman you know is envying the hell out of you.'" She removed a hairpiece from a drawer. "Come sit over here."

I moved behind the counter and sat down on a three-legged stool placed before a mirror with angled wings that showed the sides of the head as well as the front. The well-endowed proprietress sat on another stool slightly behind mine after enveloping me in a barber's apron.

"'Course most men who come in here are afraid they're never going to make it with a woman again," she continued in her free-wheeling fashion. "And I can understand that. When I lost my hair, the first thing I thought was that I'd never get to do the split on my back again." In the mirror I could see her bright smile over my shoulder. "It didn't work that way. I even experimented. A few times I took the wig off just to see what would happen. Some guys just shriveled, but it turned on a few johns like you wouldn't believe."

While talking, she had arranged a makeup tray beside me. Stubby tubes numbered from one to eleven rested in troughs along with three different kinds of powder in jars. "First the clippers on the back of the neck to blend the hairline," she said. I flinched at the cold touch of the steel, but she clip-clipped away, unheeding. "I recommend not wearing a hat," she went on. "Ninety percent of the trouble in wig wearing comes from hats and the complications they cause."

Finished with the clipping, her cool fingers trailed lightly across the back of my neck several times. I knew she was doing it on purpose, but I couldn't restrain the shiver that rippled through me. "Suppose it rains?" I addressed myself to her last remark.

"Unless you're with a gal you're trying to impress, take the hairpiece off and put it in your pocket. Otherwise, carry an umbrella. She'll think you're British and very gallant." I said nothing. "You see the numbers on the tubes? The range of color in them will take care of most facial gradations. The lower numbers are from light pastel pink to beige. The higher numbers are tan, brown, and dark brown. From the skin on your arms, you look as though you should be number six or number seven."

She picked up the number six tube, squirted a gob of the creamy material onto her palm, then worked it onto her fingertips. "Now watch this," she said, and began rubbing it into her cheeks with a rapid, circular motion of her fingers. Her white skin darkened: "This foundation not only supplies the basic color you need but it also covers the scars." She picked up a tissue and wiped off her face. "You try it."

I directed the tube at my palm and squeezed it awkwardly. "Too much," she said at once, leaning over my shoulder and halving the dose. I could smell her heady perfume. "There, try that."

I began spreading it lightly on my face, watching the mirror to make sure there were no gaps in the coverage. It was almost miraculous the way the seams and craters disappeared. In the midst of my efforts, she reached up casually and placed the hairpiece on my head. She attached two tabs in the lace-like foundation just above my ears but underneath the netting. I couldn't believe the difference it made. "How about that?" she crooned over my shoulder.

"I think well of it," I said fervently.

"I knew you would. It's not cheap, but it's the most natural-looking hairpiece I have in the shop." She reached around me for a jar on the tray, opened it, studied my face in the mirror for a moment, then closed the jar and opened another. "These different shades of powder permit natural blending

with your own skin at the jawline and throatline," she explained, showing me
how to use it.

I examined the completed job in the mirror. The hair looked natural, but the
face didn't. It still looked stiff, but it was a huge improvement over the shiny
gloss that had called attention to itself before. "Each application is good for
twenty-four hours unless you run into a cloudburst or something," she advised
me. "Even then it won't run, but it might spot."

"How much for the works plus an extra makeup kit?" I asked.

She reached into a partly opened drawer and took out a wig identical to the
one on my head except that its color was a deep coppery red. "Wouldn't you
like a change-off?" she asked. "Six eighty would cover everything."

More than most men I could use a change-off. I stared at the burnished
bronze of the second hairpiece.

"You haven't asked me the question usually asked by my men customers,"
the proprietress said.

"No? What's the question?"

"Whether everything will stay put while they're enjoying a roll in the hay."

"I can see how it would be embarrassing if it didn't. What do you tell
them?"

She smiled sweetly. "I tell them that if they're worried about it we'll lock
the front door and go into the back room and try it out."

"I'll bet you sell more wigs that way."

"Hairpieces," she corrected me with another smile. "Well? I'll bet you
haven't had a piece since the explosion."

"You're right, but it's that fact that makes me gun-shy about the back
room."

"Nonsense," she said briskly. "You've come to the right place for retrain-
ing." She rose from her stool, went to the front of the shop, inserted an "Out
to lunch" sign in the window, and locked the door. She came back and took
me by the hand. "Come on. You need a little hairpiece therapy."

"Just a minute." I freed my hand from hers and counted out six hundred and
eighty dollars. "You've made a sale regardless."

She put it in the pocket of her uniform, then took my hand again. She led
the way into a back room, which was comfortably fitted out as a bed-sitting
room. I was curious, but I was also apprehensive. "This could be a disaster,"
I warned her as she disappeared behind a screen.

"Hang your clothes in the closet and relax," her voice floated out to me.
"Just leave everything to me."

I was startled by a full-length view of myself in a pier-glass mirror attached
to the closet door. Almost literally, I didn't recognize a single thing about myself. I was still staring when another figure moved into view beside me in the
mirror. She wore a single sheer garment, which for lack of a better term might
be labeled a short shirt. It half contained the jutting thrust of milky white

breasts above while it flirted at mid-thigh with hinted-at shadowy depths be-neath. I felt a long-dormant stirring.

"Relax," she repeated, and took charge of my undressing. She led me to the bed. She was self-assured, bold, eager, and skillful. I had never been physically seduced before. My response was as gratifying to me as I hoped it was to her. For a moment, with what seemed acres of sleek female flesh in my hands, my mind drifted to Hazel Andrews and her cabin just outside Hudson. But only for a moment.

"It didn't hurt a bit, did it?" my companion inquired when I rolled, ex-hausted, to one side of the bed. She patted my shoulder. I got up finally and went to the mirror. The hairpiece was firmly in place. When I turned, she was smiling at me from the bed. "If you're not completely satisfied, come back any-time for an additional adjustment," she said. With her sexy voice, it was the epitome of a Mae West double entendre.

I dressed and prepared to leave. Back in uniform, she preceded me to the door and unlocked it. "No need to worry about a thing," she assured me breezily. "You proved that to both of us."

"Thanks," I said as I departed, and I meant it.

I was a dozen miles along the road toward Mobile when I realized that I did-n't even know her name.

7

I spent a week in Mobile and accomplished nothing.

Or almost nothing.

I had underestimated the difficulty in making meaningful contact on my own terms. With my new face, I came as a total stranger. Still, I had expected to arrive at the Golden Peacock as Earl Drake, establish myself as a member of the breed, acquire some necessary information, and move on.

It didn't work that way. It wasn't only that no one at the Peacock would have known me as either Chet Arnold or Earl Drake. In my business, names were meaningless anyway. In thirteen years I'd used a lot of names. The major cause of my difficulty was that affairs at the Golden Peacock were in a complete state of flux.

As I had expected, Rudy Hernandez was in charge. Still, I had to go slow. It was only natural that I begin by asking for Manny Sebastian, even though I was the only one who knew positively that Manny was never going to return to the Golden Peacock. Not surprisingly, my questions about Sebastian's absence were parried by Hernandez' evasive answers. For all Rudy knew, Manny might show up that very night after his unexplained vacation. There was an increasingly proprietary air about Hernandez when I talked to him nights at the bar, though. Each day he was obviously more confident that in some inexplicable manner he had fallen heir to the establishment.

But he was cautious. I could have come out flatfooted and identified myself. I couldn't see doing it, though. What was the point in so painfully acquiring a new face if the old identity were to be tied to it for everyone to know? I would be giving away a priceless break with the past that I had literally gone through hell to achieve.

I had expected that in the give-and-take of bar conversations I could establish to Hernandez' satisfaction that I had been in the game for years. If I had had sufficient time, I could have done it eventually, but with motel and restaurant draining my meager resources daily, I had no time.

It came down to a point where I could either identify myself to Hernandez, or I could forego the information for which I'd come to Mobile. Once or twice I came close to capitulating. I was strongly tempted, but each time I held off. Our little talks went round and round in circles. "Jim Griglun?" Hernandez said one night in response to a query of mine. "I haven't heard his name in years. He's out of the game entirely. Nerve's gone. I don't know what he's doing now."

"He had nerve enough when he and Slater Holmes and Gig Rosen and Duke Naylor pulled off the Oklahoma City job," I said. "They got over a hundred thousand that day."

"You don't look old enough to be going back that far," Hernandez replied. "I remember that Rosen and Naylor were burned down on a job the very next year."

"In Massillon, Ohio," I contributed. "And Clem Powers was killed two days later when the rest of the gang holed up in a barn."

"Yeah," Rudy agreed. "That was a bad one. Ol' Barney Pope and some punk kid were rounded up in the barn an' sent over the road. I remember that was one of the few jobs set up by the Schemer that went all wrong."

I had been the punk kid on that job, but did I want to say so? While I was trying to make up my mind, Hernandez kept on talking. "Hadn't thought of Clem Powers in years. That boy was really a stud. Reminds me of Dick 'Ladykiller' Dahl nowadays."

A glass rapped sharply on the bar, and Hernandez moved away to serve the customer. His remark about the Schemer turned my thoughts in a new direction. Robert "The Schemer" Frenz was a professional who set up bank jobs for a fee or a percentage of the gross. Frenz would case the entire job, supplying escape routes, local police procedures, and the most detailed information on the bank premises and the bank personnel. He never took part in the actual operation, but he could really lay one out. I'd used the Schemer's prepackaged deals twice, when Big Ed Morris was my partner, before he was killed in a drunken argument in a bucket of blood in Santa Fe. I usually preferred to set up my own jobs, but I knew good workmen who relied upon the Schemer completely.

It nettled me that I had so badly underestimated how difficult it would be to get through to Hernandez. I could hardly blame him, though. Local cops, the state, and the Feds were always snooping around places like the Peacock hoping to pick up useful information. If I were an FBI plant, I could have been briefed on jobs and names, so I made it a point during the four or five nights I stopped in at the bar to touch upon subjects that couldn't have been known by the law. I named hangouts and hideouts, mistresses' names and wives' names.

Hernandez was impressed, but he wouldn't open up. His own talk referred to the past, never to the present. I decided I was paying the penalty for Hernandez's insecurity in regard to Manny Sebastian's status.

Once I began to think in terms of Robert "The Schemer" Frenz, though, the prospect opened up. I had been using the name Carl Kessler when I used him before. My changed face would be no problem, because the Schemer had a peculiarity. He met no one face to face. He did all his business by telephone and mail.

I eased a hundred-dollar bill out of my wallet and laid it on the bar top. When Hernandez returned to where I was sitting alone, I pushed the bill toward him. "I've been out of touch with the Schemer lately," I said. "What's his business phone now?"

Hernandez supplied it promptly. That's how the nightclub made its real money, acting as a message drop. Rudy was guaranteeing nothing by giving me the number. It would be up to me to satisfy Frenz that I was legitimate. It was a Washington, D.C., number as it had always been before. It changed about once a month, though. I sat at the bar for another hour, said goodnight, and left. On the way to my motel I stopped off at a lighted highway phone booth and called the number. I had forgotten how late it was. "Schemer, this is Carl Kessler," I said when his familiar high-pitched voice came on the line. "I got your number in Mobile at the Golden Peacock."

"Kessler," the voice said tentatively, then continued more alertly. "Oh, yes, you came to me through—"

"Ed Morris," I supplied when Frenz waited for me to supply the key information. "What have you got on the shelf ready to go?"

I could all but hear the wheels clicking in the Schemer's computer-like brain. "You've been keeping a low silhouette recently," he countered.

"It happens," I said. "Sometimes a man's talking when he should have been listening." Let him think I'd taken a fall and been on ice for a while. "Listen, when you call Mobile to verify where I got your number, you might find that Rudy Hernandez doesn't know my name. He stayed so buttoned up with me that I returned the compliment."

Frenz chuckled. "I'm not unhappy to learn that you both stayed buttoned up. There's too much loose talk in this business." He cleared his throat. "I do have a package I've been saving for a first-class man."

"The usual ten percent afterward?"

"You have been out of circulation. It's twelve and a half percent these days. Inflation, you know."

"It had better be worth it, Schemer."

"It will be." He sounded confident. "Where shall I mail the kit?"

"To Earl Drake. General Delivery at—" I stopped to think.

"Washington, D.C?" Frenz asked.

I knew the General Delivery window in the main post office in Washington, D.C. It certainly wasn't my first choice. It could be staked out for a look at a man picking up an envelope. I didn't know that the Schemer was that curious, but I didn't know that he wasn't, either.

"Make it Richmond, Virginia," I decided. The General Delivery office there was a cubbyhole no one could hang around without making himself conspicuous. "And this is only for a look, Schemer. If I decide to take on the job, I'll call you again."

"Right," Frenz said briskly. "The plans will be in Richmond tomorrow afternoon."

And I won't be far behind, dear boy, I thought, but I didn't say it. "I'll be in touch," I said before hanging up. It had worked out well.

If anyone should become curious about Carl Kessler, former partner of Ed Morris, any backtracking would lead only to Morris's grave in a potter's field in Santa Fe.

I drove on to the motel and went to bed.

I started early in the morning.

I slept well, something I had been doing infrequently recently. I used to think I didn't have a nerve in my body, but recent events made me aware that even at a subconscious level, I knew I was in a tighter financial box than I had been in years.

My money was running out. I still had the jar buried in the Colorado mountains, but if I retrieved that and got into a jam afterward, I had absolutely nothing else to fall back on. Without a reserve such as the Colorado jar represented, a situation like the one I'd found myself in at the prison hospital in Florida could well have been the end of the line.

It was a relief to be in action again, however tenuously. I wouldn't really know if it was action or not until I saw the contents of the Schemer's kit, of course. The week of making no progress with Rudy Hernandez hadn't been wasted, though. I had time to practice with the contents of the makeup kit the blonde in Pensacola had sold me, and I was satisfied that now only a professional eye would be able to discern the plastic-surgery scars beneath the makeup. It was a bonus that with further practice I could become adept at making subtle changes in my appearance. I could sufficiently alter skin tone and shadows before going on a job so that descriptions would be confusing. All I really needed was to knock over a quick one and remove the hot breath of financial insecurity from the back of my neck.

I reached Richmond at noon the second day. I used the driver's license supplied by Blind Tom Walker when I asked for mail at the General Delivery window. The clerk handed me a large manila envelope that had seventy-two cents worth of stamps on it to cover the indicated first-class postage.

The bulk of the envelope disturbed me. It suggested an extremely detailed plan, which in turn pointed to a complicated job. I hadn't time for such a caper. I went back to the VW and drove to the Holiday Inn on Route 301. After checking in, I stopped off in the coffee shop for a chicken sandwich and a glass of iced tea, then went to my room. I locked and chainlatched the door, sat down in an armchair, and opened the envelope.

The bulkiness of its contents was explained immediately. It was made up of sheet after sheet of stiff-paper line drawings, which in effect were blueprints of the floor plan of a bank. In addition, there were page after page of biography on the habits of the bank employees, both at work and at home.

There were an additional two pages in single-spaced elite type describing the police routines for the area. The bank was in a suburb where official jurisdiction overlapped, and the typewritten sheets gave chapter and verse on the schedules of both the city police force and the sheriff's department of the county. On a separate sheet was plotted possible escape routes, with traffic lights indicated in red and one-way streets in blue. Robert "The Schemer" Frenz was nothing if not thorough.

Clipped to the top sheet, which was labeled "Summary," was a typewritten note. Its message was brief. "Three-man job," it said. "Known available workmen: Sandy Bascombe, Dick Dahl, Thirsty Huddleston, Preacher Harris, Bob Wolfe, Jess Burkett. Call me."

I pushed everything else aside while I scanned the summary sheet. The bank was in Thornton, a suburb of Philadelphia. I knew the area, which helped. It was apparent at once that the pivotal point of the proposed job was that the suburban bank received cash by armored car after closing each Wednesday afternoon. On Thursday mornings the cash was separated among the tellers for making up factory payrolls and cashing checks. If the bank were entered before business hours on a Thursday morning, it should be possible to pick up the armored car delivery still in bulk before the usual distribution.

A complication was that the vault combination was shared by the bank manager and his assistant. Each had only half the combination. This meant that both had to be separated from their families early in the morning on the day the job was to be pulled. They would have to be herded to the bank together. The other employees would have to be immobilized as they entered the bank until the time lock on the vault went off and permitted it to be opened by the manager and assistant. Otherwise it appeared that the job called for standard operating procedure.

I set the summary aside and stared at the blank gray face of the room's television set. I didn't like the plan. There were so many variables in the Schemer's proposal that I hesitated on the brink of instant rejection. The plan called for too many people to be managed, in too many different places, by the unknown quantities in the way of partners I'd be forced to employ.

But what choice did I have? I could ask Frenz for a one-man package, but if he didn't have one on the shelf, what then? Walk in off the street cold with a brown paper bag and show a teller a gun? I'd seen too many men panicked by circumstances who'd gone that route when squeezed. It kept the jails full.

I picked up the summary sheet again with its attached note and reread the names. Sandy Bascombe, Dick Dahl, Thirsty Huddleston, Preacher Harris, Bob Wolfe, Jess Burkett. Huddleston I knew. He had nerve, but he wasn't called Thirsty for nothing. I drew a line through his name.

Dahl rang a bell. I sat there thinking about it. Finally it came to me. Hernandez had mentioned Dahl's name at the Golden Peacock. Rudy's remarks had coupled Dahl with the memory of Clem Powers, a fantastic cocksman. "Ladykiller," Hernandez had called Dahl. It was hardly a recommendation. I drew a line through Dahl's name.

Wolfe I didn't know. Burkett I didn't know. Two more drawn lines. Harris I knew. Preacher Harris, although I'd never worked with him, had the reputation of being a cool and steady operator everywhere except at the card and dice tables. Harris was a compulsive gambler, but when he was broke enough he was all business. I put a circle around his name. Bascombe I didn't know. Another line drawn.

So I had one possible from the list. Could two men do the job? I spread the floor plan of the bank in front of me and went over it carefully, then referred to the summary again. Fifteen minutes later I reached a conclusion. Two men couldn't swing it. Too much maneuvering would be needed to get the right people to the right place at the right time.

I put everything back into the envelope again, put the envelope under my arm, and left the room. I called Frenz from the pay phone in the lobby, a few feet away from the registration desk. When he came on the line, I gave him the number of the pay phone. "I'll call you back in ten minutes," he promised.

I sat in the phone booth waiting for his call. When it came, I heard the ding-ding-ding of coins, indicating that Frenz had moved to a pay phone, too. I went right to the point. "You've handed me a three-man package, Schemer, and I'm alone. What do you have in the way of a solo shot?"

"Nothing that isn't too risky," he replied. "I'd really like to see you take this job on. I've been saving it for someone who's an organizer. You saw the list of names?"

"I saw them. Harris is the only one I know favorably. What the hell are you doing recommending a drunk like Thirsty Huddleston?"

"I'm not recommending anyone." A touch of acid crept into the Schemer's smooth delivery. "I gave you a list of the men available. If you don't want to work with them, that's your business."

"Why didn't you give one of them the package?"

"Because they're followers, not leaders. I have to hitch them onto the tail of someone else's kite." There was exasperation in Frenz's tone. "Listen, I haven't all day. If you don't like the look of the job, I'll give you a post office box number to return the envelope."

The trouble was I had to like the look of it. "Don't jump the rails, man. Where's Harris now?"

"Vegas."

That figured, all right. "Can you reach him?"

"Sure."

I crossed the Rubicon with a rush. "Have him meet Earl Drake at the Marriott Motel across Key Bridge from Washington, D.C., day after tomorrow."

"Fine. Who else do you want?"

I ran through the list of names again in my mind. Eenie, meenie, minie, moe. "What about Dahl? Is it true he's a womanizer?"

"Professionally, perhaps."

"Professionally?"

"He makes nudie movies, which he distributes through a chain of art theaters. It takes him a long time to get his money back from his releases, if he ever does. He finances his films by jobs like this."

A gambler and a maker of nudie movies. It hardly sounded like a winning team. The Schemer sensed my hesitation. "Dahl has nerve and can pass anywhere," he said.

In the end it always comes back to nerve, I thought. There were a lot of good workmen on the street who had lost theirs and were out of the business. If a man had nerve, he had a chance in the racket. Without it, nothing else could do him much good.

I made up my mind. "Send him to the Marriott, too."

"Will do." Frenz said it in the manner of a businessman who has just seen the prospect sign the contract. "And good luck."

Once I'd thought I didn't need luck. I was younger then. I'd take all I could get now. "Where do you want your end sent, Schemer?"

He gave me a post office box number, said goodbye, and hung up.

I had a day and a half to study thoroughly the Schemer's plan before I met Harris and Dahl.

I went back to my room.

8

People tend to think that a bank robber does nothing else for three hundred and sixty-five days a year. Nothing could be further from the truth.

I've known professionals who ran legitimate businesses in their home-towns and left them only for the quick trips necessary to bring off a job. One of the best I ever had contact with was a middle-aged funeral director in a small town.

I probably came closer than most to being full-time, but even I always took a legitimate job a couple of months each year, usually as a tree surgeon. The one infallible way to be sure of taking a bumpy ride was to be picked up on suspicion and have no visible means of support.

Except at the highest level, bank robbery is far more of an avocation than it is a vocation. As is the case with most hobbies, not enough time is given to it. I'd always avoided that pitfall. I made it my business never to make a move until I was sure I had eliminated as much of the risk in a job as possible.

By the time I left the Holiday Inn in Richmond, I knew more about the operation of the Manufacturers Trust branch bank in Thornton, Pa., than the majority of its employees did.

Dahl reached the Marriott first on Monday afternoon. My first ten minutes with him nearly put me off the whole deal.

He was good-looking, with a big, toothy smile. He was also brash, extro-verted, and noisy. I didn't appreciate any of it. He walked into the motel room wearing a sixteen-millimeter movie camera of the hand-held type slung by a cord about his neck. I was to find out he never went anywhere without the thing, unless it was into the shower. Later I was able to convince myself that it wasn't wholly a bad idea. A camera-carrying bankrobber? Hardly. But at first sight it set my teeth on edge.

"What's the deal, cousin?" he demanded breezily after we'd shaken hands. "I'm a busy man. I'm shooting a movie in New York City right now. If any-one except the Schemer had called me, I wouldn't have dropped everything to come down here."

"Let's wait until Harris gets here and I won't have to go through it twice," I said to put him off.

He shrugged and sat down on the bed. His glance as he examined me was speculative. "Why the makeup, cousin?"

"I'm actually a lesbian in drag." I tried to say it lightly, but it nettled me that he had spotted the makeup so easily. ·

"It's not that obvious, but makeup's my business," he said. He studied me

intently. "Do I know you, cousin?" he continued. "What's your passport?"
"Schemer's my passport," I retorted. "And you know me right now as well
as you ever will."

His eyes narrowed. "The bossy type, huh? How'd I get on your list?"
"It was the Schemer's list. He said you had nerve."
"That's me." He said it complacently. The compliment appeared to mollify
him. "Okay. Just don't try putting a ring in my nose, see?"

I didn't answer him. I picked up the telephone and ordered sandwiches and
beer from room service. When the knock came at the door and I opened it to
admit the boy with the tray, Dahl disappeared into the bathroom without my
having to say anything. He had passed a test, and I began to feel a little better about him.

In the next two minutes he lost the ground he had gained. He paced the
floor while gulping down a sandwich. Then he flicked aside the draperies
pulled across the window. He seemed charged with nervous energy. "Good-
lookin' head in a bikini by the pool," he announced. "Be right back."

He was out the door by the time I reached the window. He strode across
the intervening courtyard, unlimbering his camera as he went. He took a slow,
sweeping panoramic shot of the pool area, then the camera lingered lovingly
on the mini-bikinied girl, who eventually reached self-consciously for a towel.
Dahl gave her a white-toothed grin and a wave of his hand as he started back
toward my room. En route he paused to take a shot of two schoolteacherish-
looking women who were unlocking the door to their room.

"Suppose the girl's boyfriend or husband had arrived and objected to your
making free that way?" I said to Dahl when he was inside again.

"The chick would slow him down," he asserted cheerfully. "They love bein'
on film, with or without clothes. Ninety-eight percent of 'em, anyway."

"What about the two older women?"

"Never know when you can blend alfresco shots like that. Cut to a pair of
lesbians frolickin' on a bed an' you've saved some footage."

"You mean you'd show innocent people in the kind of stuff you film?"

"Don't get shook, cousin. There's two hundred million people in this
country, an' a lot of them look like other people. I never been sued yet." He
sank down into a chair. "What time's Harris gonna get here? I got to get back
to New York."

"If that's the case, what are you doing here at all with a job in prospect?"
"I'm here to do a quick job, cousin, an' then cut out."

"It's not that kind of a job," I began, and stopped at the sound of a knock
at the motel door. Dahl did his disappearing act again while I opened it. None
of us wanted to be seen together by anyone who could identify us as a pair
or a group afterward.

The man at the door was tall, slim, and dapper. He had deep-set eyes, and
there was a touch of gray in his brown hair. He wore a dark suit and carried

a Panama with a conservative band in one hand. "I'm Harris," he said.

"Drake," I returned, letting him inside. Dahl emerged from the bathroom when I closed and chain-latched the door.

"Hiya, cousin," he greeted Harris, who nodded. "How've the dominoes an' celluloids been treatin' ya?"

"Not too well," Harris said with a faint smile. His voice was as low-keyed as his personality.

"I could use a touch, too," Dahl said promptly. He looked at me. "So how about gettin' down to business?"

"A sandwich?" I suggested to Harris.

He shook his head. "I had lunch on the plane."

Dahl was energetically shoving chairs together in the center of the room. "Let's go, cousins," he urged, plunking himself down into the easy chair and leaving straight-backed chairs for Harris and me. "Time's money an' all that silt."

Harris and I seated ourselves, and I talked for ten minutes. I told them everything except the name and location of the bank. I went over in detail the Schemer's dossiers on the bank operation and the personal lives of the bank's chief officers.

"The bank manager has three children, the assistant manager none," I concluded. "If we go to the assistant manager's home at three A.M. and take him and his wife to the manager's home, we'll have the two key employees—the ones with the bank vault combination—under our thumb, plus a ready-made group of hostages in the persons of the wives and children, who will assure the two men's good behavior. We'll take the men to the bank before daylight on Thursday morning, and after that it will be—"

"Hold it," Dahl interrupted me. "Thursday morning? And today's Monday? I can't hang around here that long."

"I'm not talking about this Thursday. Or even next Thursday. It might take a month to set the job up properly."

Dahl rose to his feet. "Count me out, cousin. I've got other perch to fry."

The mild-looking Harris was apologetic when I turned to him. "I can't hold off for a month, either. Financially, I mean."

I would be shaving it close to the bone myself, but I damn well wasn't going to put my head into the lion's mouth without pulling as many teeth as possible. "Why don't we relax and go over this again and work out what we have to do to make—"

"Listen, why the horsing around?" Dahl interrupted again. "What's the matter with setting something up right now and knocking it over in the next hour?" He said it challengingly.

"Not in the next hour," Harris said after a glance at his watch. "Banks close in the next fifteen minutes. But what about tomorrow morning?"

I might not have gulped, but I felt like it. Both men were looking at me.

"What about this job?" I temporized, indicating the Schemer's file folder.

"You set it up an' we'll be back in a month an' knock it over on its back, too," Dahl said confidently. Harris nodded. "We'll work out the split to cover your time," Dahl continued. His tone turned silky. "If you come in with us on a job in the mornin'."

I vibrated on the brink of flat refusal. I wanted nothing to do with a walk-in. They were always high-risk operations with uncertain returns. But there were my own empty pockets to consider. A walk-in with three men stood a better chance than a walk-in with one man. And if I said no, I lost these two prospects for the Thornton job and would have to start all over again.

"I'd want you both on the ground a week beforehand," I said at last. "For the big one, I mean."

"We're in, if you're in," Dahl said. "Right, Preacher?" The taciturn Harris nodded.

"So we each scout a location tonight, meet here in the mornin' at eight, take a vote, get the job done, an' be halfway home by noon," Dahl declared. His eyes were focused on me. "You aboard, cousin?"

"All right," I said reluctantly. "What about a car for the job? Pick up a rental?"

"Naaah," Dahl said disdainfully. "Not for a quickie like that. Leave the wheels to me." He tapped himself on the chest. "Dick Dahl, Boy Car Thief. I never saw a piece of iron I couldn't roll."

"Eight o'clock tomorrow morning, then," I said.

"Great!" he enthused, and went out the door like a brigantine under full sail.

In my own mind, eight o'clock committed me to nothing. If I didn't like the sound of what I heard in the morning, I'd cut out. Harris eyed me while he waited for an interval to elapse before he followed Dahl from the motel room.

"You don't like it," he said in his quiet voice.

"I won't like it if one of us doesn't come up with a likely-looking opportunity."

"I scouted a bank across the District line a year ago," he said. "Near Rockville. I'll take another look at it tonight. But we'll find something." He left the room.

One thing about Preacher Harris, I reflected as I walked to the window and parted the draperies to watch him cross the motel yard: in any crowd I'd ever seen he could blend as the Invisible Man. Nothing about him clashed with his surroundings.

I went back to the armchair that Dahl had preempted and ran through the situation again. Number one, although I didn't like it, I desperately needed the cash myself. And number two, if I cancelled out and went back to the Schemer for new partners there was no guarantee I'd do any better, and I'd have lost valuable time. I tried to convince myself that I was spoiled because I'd been so used to calling all the shots myself and picking my own partners.

I certainly didn't care for a job in Rockville, though. Rockville was in the jurisdiction of the Montgomery County Police who, although not numerous, tended to react quickly over a wide area. The District cops, in contrast, were more plentiful in their ten-square-mile enclave but often got in each other's way.

Harris's suggestion reminded me of something, though. A few years ago, when Bosco Sheerin had been my partner—before an irate husband returned home unexpectedly one evening and discovered Bosco in the intimate embrace of the husband's wife and sent both Bosco and the wife to join the angels— we had cased a job in the District of Columbia. It was a branch bank located near the intersection of Piney Branch Road and Georgia Avenue. This placed it only two miles from the northern border of the District, assuring a quick crossover into Maryland if it seemed convenient. Other escape routes abounded.

I sat there trying to remember why Bosco and I had finally decided against trying it. Police patrols? It seemed unlikely that the area was any more heavily patrolled than any other section of the nation's capital. I couldn't recall why we had abandoned the project. If not too much had changed in the interval, though, it was a bank I knew something about, which was a hell of a lot better than taking on one stone-cold. I rose from my chair and checked the Yellow Pages in the phone book to make sure the branch bank was still in the same location.

It was, and I went outside to my car and drove across Key Bridge to the District. I followed M Street and Rhode Island Avenue to Logan Circle, then traveled north on Thirteenth Street. I turned eastward on Decatur and moved over onto Georgia Avenue. The area seemed very much the same. Above Brightwood, it consisted principally of used-car lots, cleaning establishments, and aging restaurants.

I looked to my left at the Piney Branch Road intersection. A filling station took up the northwest corner. Just beyond it on Georgia Avenue was the bank, not a particularly prepossessing building. The same wide alley I remembered still served as part alley, part parking lot between the bank and the neighboring A&P store. At the present hour in the afternoon the alley was congested, but it was less likely to be so in the morning.

I drove past the bank in the flow of traffic. In the first mile beyond it the area turned from commercial to seedy residential. A mile from the Maryland line I made a U-turn at the east gate of Walter Reed Army Hospital and wheeled back to the bank. It still looked all right. Alternative exits and escape routes were plentiful. It was hard to imagine being cornered by patrol cars after pulling off the job.

I turned into the alley and drove along its length, re-verifying that a left turn at its upper end led out to Piney Branch, bypassing the traffic light at the Georgia Avenue intersection. There was a new warehouse-type building at the end

of the alley, but nothing else appeared changed. It was hard to escape the feeling that a quick run down the alley and out onto Piney Branch would be the
best way of losing pursuers in the teeming morning traffic. And if by some
chance the Piney Branch exit were blocked, it was just as easy to turn right
at the end of the alley, beyond the new warehouse, and double back onto
Georgia Avenue, there to head north or south as the situation dictated.

I was still sour on the idea of a hit-and-run job with so little advance prepa-
ration, but I had to admit that for the first time in a long time I had little
choice.

I drove back to Virginia and the motel room, made a couple of sketches of
escape routes from the bank, and went to bed although it was still daylight.

I was glad that Preacher Harris arrived at the motel in the morning before
Dick Dahl. "What about it?" I asked him bluntly. "Is this your usual style of
operation?"

"No, it isn't." Harris had on a fresh shirt and tie and looked even more conservative than he had the previous day, if that were possible. "But I need the
cash." It was his turn to become blunt. "You're afraid of it?"

"Not as much as I was last night. I went out and scouted one I'd looked over
some time ago."

"You liked it for today?"

I handed him my sketches and a large-scale map of the District. "Take a look
at this. It'll go like a player piano," I said, turning on the hard sell.

He sounded relieved. "Good. I took another look at the setup in Rockville
and didn't think as well of it."

So I hadn't needed the hard sell. Harris sat down in a chair and spread the
map and sketches on his knees. He was still studying them when Dahl arrived.
Dahl carried a briefcase, which he tossed onto the bed. "Everything set?" he
inquired breezily after I chain-latched the door. He opened the briefcase and
took out three Halloween masks. "Greatest little deceivers in the world, boys."
He looked at Harris in his chair. "What'cha got there?"

"Drake sized up a job after we left here yesterday," Harris said. "It looks
good."

"Fine with me," Dahl said. He looked and sounded completely indifferent
as to which job it was. "So long's I'm out of town by noon. With the kind
of operation I've got in New York, things tend to go to pieces if I'm not there
to keep my finger on the button. Where do we take our shot?"

I let Harris tell him as a means of checking Preacher's absorption of the details. Watching Dahl, I got the impression he wasn't even listening closely.
He kept nodding his head and glancing at his watch. "All right," he interrupted Harris's very sound explanation of the elements involved. "Let's put
it on the road."

"Do we split up right after the job?" Harris asked me.

"We sure as hell do," Dahl replied before I could say anything. Since his statement echoed my own sentiment, I kept my mouth shut. I picked up the map of the District and showed it to Dahl. "We'll park my car on Military Road, halfway between Georgia Avenue and Thirteenth Street so we can approach it from either direction if there's pursuit. We'll meet—"

"There won't be no pursuit," Dahl said confidently. "We'll be gone like big birds. I'll go into the bank first an' herd the customers away from the cages an' the tellers out of them. Either one of you can come in next an' stand by the entrance to control the action. The third man in cleans out the cages an' is first man out an' the getaway driver."

I looked at Harris, who shrugged as much as to say it was simple enough to work. "What about a weapon for the man at the entrance who's controlling the action?" I asked. "A handgun won't do it."

"There's a riot gun in the trunk of my car," Dahl said.

"Bring it along." I marked an "X" on the District map. "Harris will ride with me, and we'll park here on Military Road, a mile beyond the viaduct where it drops down off Georgia Avenue. Dahl, you park in Brightwood, steal a car and pick us up, and we'll return you to your car after the stolen car gets us from the bank to my car on Military Road."

"Nothin' to it," Dahl said. "Let's go, cousins. You bring the briefcase. I'll bring the riot gun in the stolen car."

"Pick us up at nine fifteen," I told Dahl. "You leave here first."

"Like I've already gone," he said. He walked to the door, took off the latch, opened the door a crack and peered out, gave us a wave of his hand behind his back without looking around, and went out.

"Well, the Schemer said he had nerve," I said.

Harris didn't reply. He went to the bed, stripped a pillowcase from a pillow, folded it neatly, and tucked it into the briefcase. "I'll take the cages," he said. "You take the entrance."

"Fine with me. Walk out to the highway now while I check out of the motel."

Harris looked like any businessman on his way to work, briefcase in hand, when I picked him up ten minutes later. We had plenty of time. I drove slowly. Harris sat quietly, eyes straight ahead. I had no idea whether he was thinking about the job or the next whirl of the roulette wheel.

We had eight minutes to spare when I parked on Military Road. There was no conversation. Tension pressed downward from the roof of the car like something tangible. Harris took a package of gum from his pocket, peeled off a wrapper, and crammed a stick into his mouth. He offered the package to me, but I shook my head. It was a long eight minutes.

In the rearview mirror I saw a sleek white Oldsmobile draw up behind us. Dahl waved from behind the wheel. Harris and I got out of the VW and

walked to the Olds. "Didn't even have to jump the switch," Dahl said cheerfully. "Found two in a row with the keys still in 'em. I took the one with the
most horses."

Harris was staring at a blanket-wrapped bundle on the front seat beside
Dahl. Alongside it was a bright-checked sport coat with one red sleeve and
one blue one. "What the hell is that thing?" Harris demanded, pointing at the
coat.

"Camouflage," Dahl grunted. "It gives the animals somethin' to look at besides my height, weight, an' peculiar arrangement of molecules." He picked
up the coat and began to struggle into it while still seated behind the wheel.

"You sit in back," I said to Harris. I got into the front seat with Dahl. The
blanket-wrapped bundle was the riot gun. A half dozen loose shells were in
the blanket, too. While I was loading the short-barreled, pump-type shotgun,
Harris leaned over the front seat and placed two Halloween masks between
us. I watched the road until no cars were coming toward us, then tried on the
mask to make sure I could breathe properly. It wasn't too bad. There were
sticky tabs at the temples—almost at the same place as my hairpiece tabs—
and one under the chin to hold the mask in place.

I removed the mask. When I looked toward Dahl, he was grinning broadly.
"What's the good word, cousin?" he asked. He was a bizarre-looking figure
in the outrageously flamboyant jacket and the ever-present movie camera once
again slung around his neck.

"Roll it," I told him. I gave him directions that would bring us into the bank
alley from the Piney Branch Road exit. It was a short run. We turned
smoothly into the exit when I pointed it out and headed up the alley the
wrong way. Without my saying anything, Dahl turned the Olds around and
headed it in the direction from which we'd come. There were only two cars
in the alley. No chance of getting hemmed in by a car pulling in too tightly.

We put on our masks. Dahl was first out of the car. With the psychedelic
jacket, the mask, and the camera, he looked like a freak pitchman for a carni-
val show. I carried the riot gun beneath the blanket draped over my left arm.
My watch said nine twenty-two A.M. as we walked single file toward the
bank's front entrance. There wasn't a soul in sight in the alley.

Dahl pushed on the revolving glass door and entered. Harris and I were right
behind him. I took up a station just inside where I could watch the entrance
and the bank's interior, including the offices on the mezzanine. I looked for
a guard but couldn't see one. I let the blanket drop to the floor, exposing the
riot gun.

There were half a dozen women tellers in the cages, plus three customers
on the bank floor, a man and two women. A single man was visible on the
mezzanine. Beyond the line of tellers' cages a low railing separated a row of
bookkeeping machines from the bank lobby. "Everybody inside the railing!"
Dahl's voice boomed out.

For an instant there was a hush, broken by two or three stifled shrieks as his role was recognized. "You, up there!" I called to the man on the mezzanine. "Don't move!" He didn't. There were gasps and another shriek as my voice called attention to me and to the riot gun. Dahl drove the three customers through a gate in the low railing, then herded them and the women tellers away from the cages, which were so high they hid him from my view.

Harris was already inside the railing. Steel clattered and banged as he opened, emptied, and slammed cash drawers. The man on the mezzanine remained wide-eyed and motionless. I had looked at the large wall clock at the back of the bank when we entered. Now I looked again. A minute and a half had gone by.

The revolving glass door pivoted and the bank guard walked in from the street. He was carrying a tray with eight or ten cups of coffee on it. He saw me and flinched. He tried to react so rapidly that the coffee cups sailed off the tray and spilled all over the floor. "Keep moving," I told the guard. "Inside the gate." He did as he was told.

A chorus of twittering feminine protests rose from behind the tellers' cages. Dahl's menacing voice drowned them out. Then it was quiet again. All of a sudden a soft bright light was glowing, its source invisible to me. I could see Harris looking in that direction, and I moved in a step from the door. Then Harris went back to rifling cash drawers. I relaxed and moved back to my former position. Outside, cars went by in a steady stream along Georgia Avenue.

I was sweating under the mask. I hoped my makeup was holding together. Harris ran for the railing, the laden pillowcase dangling from his left hand. He placed his right hand on the railing and started to vault over it. I could hear the squeak as his sweating palm slipped on the smooth surface. He turned over in the air and landed on his stomach in the longest slide since Pepper Martin stole third base in the World Series. Harris scrambled erect and ran past me to the door.

He was already out in the parking lot when Dahl appeared behind the railing, retracing Harris's route except that with his superior height Dahl stepped over the railing. A gun dangled loosely in his right hand. I picked up the blanket and re-covered the riot gun as Dahl's coat-of-many-colors went through the revolving door, the camera dangling from the cord around his neck. I swung the gun in a final semicircle to freeze all movement, then backed out the door.

I was halfway through the hundred-and-eighty-degree swing of the door to the parking lot when Dahl charged in on the other side, heading back into the bank. I froze. I couldn't imagine what he was up to. From my position with my back to the exit I could see the bank guard coming across the floor of the bank at a dead run. He shoved his foot into the protruding edge of the section of revolving door inside the lobby, and Dahl and I couldn't go anywhere. We were locked inside the revolving door.

I raised the riot gun, but before I could draw a bead Dahl fired three times from his compartment inside the door. Shattering glass crashed in massive quantities. The guard ducked to one side, unhurt but shaken. The sudden acceleration of the door as his foot was removed thrust me out into the alley. In a second Dahl came winging out as the door completed the circuit. "What the hell were you doing?" I panted as we ran for the car.

"Thought you might need help."

"When I need help I'll ask for it!"

Harris was under the wheel of the Olds with the motor running. Dahl and I piled into the back seat. We were moving down the alley by the time I got the door closed. Dahl jerked off his loose-fitting red-and-blue-sleeved jacket and threw it on the floor. "Masks off!" I rasped as Preacher made the turn at the end of the alley onto Piney Branch. The fresh air felt cold against the perspiration on my face when I pulled mine off.

Dahl reached over the back of the front seat and lifted the pillowcase into the back seat. I half turned on the seat so I could watch him and still keep an eye out the back window for possible pursuit. We were headed south in a traffic flow that seemed ordinary. Dahl dumped the contents of the pillowcase onto the floor and began sorting it into three piles. "Damn, damn, damn!" he swore softly. "Small stuff."

"I know," Harris said without turning around. There were no red lights behind us and no sirens. "What's the take look like?" His voice sounded husky.

"Less'n twenty thousand," Dahl grumbled. Harris's grunt was eloquent of disgust. I refrained from saying that a properly planned job would have guaranteed that the amount of cash available made the risk worthwhile. "Check it," Dahl said to me, pointing to the piles of money at his feet.

"Watch the rear," I said. I went through the cash quickly. I checked by packages of banded bills, not by counting. "It looks all right." Dahl reached down to the stack nearest him and began stuffing packages of bills into various pockets.

I did the same. We had reached Military Road by the time I looked around. Still no sign of police pursuit. Dahl picked up the third pile of money in both hands and dropped it on the front seat beside Preacher. "This'll hardly keep me goin' three weeks," he said gloomily.

"That's right," Harris chimed in. "Unless my system takes hold real quick this time." He looked belligerently at Dahl. "That was the most stupid thing I ever saw done on a job!"

Dahl started to laugh. "You're jealous, cousin. I—"

"What was this stupid thing?" I asked Harris, interrupting Dahl.

"This mongoloid had the women tellers bare-assed on the floor, taking movies of them."

"All but one who wouldn't pull her pants down even when my gun was an inch and a half from her twitch," Dahl affirmed in high good humor.

"Must've had the rag on. You never know when you can use a little good pussy footage, cousins."

I wondered how much of the bank area the camera had covered. "If I ever hear that you've used that film commercially, I'll find you and nail your ears to the nearest telephone pole," I threatened Dahl.

Harris pulled the Olds onto the shoulder of the road before Dahl could reply. "What do we want to take?" he asked.

"Nothin' but the gun," Dahl said sullenly. "Leave the masks."

Harris was scooping money into his pockets. "Let's keep moving," he urged. His voice was husky. He sounded as though the strain was beginning to catch up to him. We walked across the wide highway to my car and I slid into the driver's seat. Harris got in with me, Dahl in back.

I handed the blanketed gun to Dahl. "Wipe it clean."

He was already working on it when I swung the VW around in a U-turn and headed toward Brightwood and Dahl's parked car. The final look I took in the rearview mirror showed the white Olds glistening on the shoulder of the road. Harris broke the silence. "This touch wasn't much of a stake," he said.

"It's enough to get us together again for proper planning on the Schemer's job," I said. "And that time I think we should remember that we do just as long a bit for ten thousand as we'd do for Fort Knox. Let's make sure the cash is there."

Dahl spoke right up. "Suits me," he said. "When?"

"How about next week?"

"Make it two weeks," he said. "I've still got a movie to shoot. You in, Preacher?"

"I guess so," Harris said unenthusiastically.

"I'll drive to Philadelphia and get set up," I said. "I'll let the Schemer know where I am, and when we're ready to go you can call him to find out where to meet me."

"Let's make the meeting two weeks from today," Dahl said.

"Fine."

"All right," Preacher Harris said a tick later.

We were approaching Brightwood. "Where are you parked?" I asked Dahl.

"In the middle of the first block, across from the post office," he replied. "Pull in anywhere." He was carefully rewrapping the riot gun in the blanket. "So long, cousins," he said when I double-parked momentarily alongside a line of cars parked at the metered curb. "Don't spend it all in one place." He stepped out, slammed the door, waved, and jogged across the street.

"I don't ever want to work on a job with *him* again!" Harris burst forth as I pulled away.

I knew what he meant. I wasn't happy about the botched aspects of the job myself, but I didn't want Harris too unhappy with it. I knew how long it would take to recruit new partners. "Now that we know he's a kook, we'll keep our fingers closer to the button next time," I said soothingly. "And you have to admit that nothing fazes him."

"No brains, no feeling," Harris snorted, but he subsided. "Let me out at the next cab stand," he said a minute later. "I'll take a cab to the airport."

"Take one to Fourteenth Street and then another to the airport," I advised him. "The police are sure to check cab sheets from this area for riders to Union Station and National Airport."

"Yeah, good idea," he admitted.

"Here we are," I said, easing in behind a two-cab stand. We weren't more than five blocks from the bank we'd taken. "The next one will be a piece of cake too, and we'll all get well on the proceeds. Don't forget to call the Schemer."

Harris's smile was wan as he got out of my car. As I drove off I had the feeling that whether he called the Schemer or not depended very much upon how his luck ran at Vegas's dice and card tables for the next two weeks.

I headed over to Bladensburg Road in northeast Washington and had lunch. Then I went to a neighborhood movie where I watched the Redskins lose again. When I came out of the theater, the 4:30 P.M. homeward traffic was just starting to thicken up. I joined it, moved along to New York Avenue, and—eventually—to the Washington-Baltimore Expressway.

There were no roadblocks or car inspections barring exit from the District of Columbia.

If there had been earlier, the police had decided that the hit-and-run bank robbers were long gone.

I settled down for the drive to Philadelphia.

9

When I had a chance to count it, my end of the District bank job came to sixty-four hundred dollars.

It wasn't worth the risk, but it had been a long time since I needed sixty-four hundred so badly. I felt reprieved. It eased the money pressure, which had led me to take on the helter-skelter operation just completed. Professionally, I could hardly approve of the job, some elements of which had been almost farcical, but the important thing was that it had worked.

I fully intended that tapping the bank in Thornton, Pa. would be a far different story. With time enough to prepare properly, it should indeed be the piece of cake that I had promised Harris. A useful bonus from the hasty job just done was that I felt I knew Harris and Dahl now. Harris was colorless, Dahl flamboyant, but both had performed. With two weeks to work up a detailed plan, it shouldn't be too difficult to arrange Dahl's contribution so his kookiness didn't jeopardize the whole show. I had already selected a motel near Philadelphia where I had stayed before to serve as a base of operations. En route to it, I detoured slightly to the northwest to drive through the suburb of Thornton. It was a residential community, generally known in real estate jargon as a "bedroom" community. Row after row of well kept up, better-priced homes on neat-looking streets bespoke a maximum of financial security. No air of quiet desperation existed in Thornton. Male Thorntonites might commute to the city daily to scuffle for the elusive buck at their places of business, but when they returned home evenings it was to an oasis of tranquility.

Ordinarily I would have set myself up in the area as a tree surgeon, a gunsmith, or a locksmith, occupations in which I could cut the mustard. With only two weeks, there wasn't time. I had to have a cover story, though. Nothing is so conspicuous to local police as an unfamiliar face or automobile seen repeatedly, and I would have to spend some time in Thornton.

Before leaving town, I crisscrossed the town's business section twice. It looked prosperous. The absence of empty stores indicated few worms in the local economic apple. There was industry nearby, but not within the city limits. I drove south to Media, a few miles from Philadelphia, and put up at the Carousel, a middle-class motel.

After looking Thornton over, I decided to pass as a survey taker, an individual who walked into places of business and checked off answers to a list of prepared questions. It had worked for me a couple of times before.

I didn't plan on being just any ordinary survey taker, either. Over the years I'd learned that big names open doors wider. Names like U.S. Steel, General Electric, and IBM.

The name I chose this time was Bell Telephone. The only disadvantage in claiming to work for a large company was that one might occasionally run into a supposed fellow employee, but this could actually be turned into an advantage. A man working for a giant corporation, no matter how far up the ladder, could hardly be expected to know what all the other departments of his company were doing.

Back in my room after a late dinner, I picked up the telephone directory for the Philadelphia area and turned to the Yellow Pages section. I tore out the familiar Yellow Pages logotype from the first page, then trimmed it neatly with a penknife, leaving a half-inch margin all around it.

I read Bell Telephone's own plug for its Yellow Pages advertising in the back of the phone book, then armed myself with a sheet of motel stationery and a ballpoint pen. Rewriting as I went, I drew up a list of ten possible questions. I boiled this down to six, and finally to four. I didn't want to burden my "prospects" with more than two and a half or three minutes reading time.

I wound up with the following:

1. Are you listed in the Yellow Pages?
2. If not, do you realize that advertising placed in the Yellow Pages is never lost, misplaced, or forgotten?
3. If not, do you know that advertising campaigns in support of the Yellow Pages encompass all major media from television, newspaper, car cards, and radio through magazines, billboards, and direct mail, and that this advertising is your advertising if you are listed?
4. Would you like to have a space salesman call upon you with additional facts and figures?

When I was satisfied with the wording of the questionnaire, I slipped it into my jacket pocket and prepared for bed. The last thing I did before turning out the light was to phone the Schemer. "We had a little trouble getting our schedules together," I told him, making no mention of the District job, in which he had no part anyway. "But we're set for two weeks from now. When the boys call you, tell them I'm at the Carousel Motel in Media near Philadelphia."

"Will do," Frenz replied. "Have you looked over the layout yet yourself?"

"In a preliminary way."

"You'll find it's a winner."

"I can use a winner. Goodnight."

"Goodnight," he echoed.

I went to bed and dreamed repeatedly of bare-bottomed girl bank robbers sliding on their tummies across the slick tile floor of the Chase Manhattan Bank in New York City.

In the morning I drove to Philadelphia with my list of questions and my Yellow Pages logotype. I cruised back streets and side streets until I spotted a dingy-looking basement printing shop. I parked the VW and descended narrow iron steps until I found myself ankle-deep in discarded paper and cardboard in a dimly-lit interior that obviously hadn't been swept out in months. From the look of the place, if the payment were spot cash the proprietor would be unlikely to question my motive even if I wanted a five-dollar bill printed on one side of a 2 1/2 x 6 sized piece of paper with a verse from the Bible backed up on the other.

There was no one in sight, but I could hear an offset press rattling out in back. "Anyone home?" I called.

The press noise stopped, and a sour-faced man with a limp Pancho Villa moustache came out into the front of the shop. "Yeah?" he said ungraciously.

I showed him the logotype and questions. "I ran out of flyers," I explained. "How much for five hundred of these on fairly good six-by-nine stock?"

"I got no time to wait for you big companies to get around to payin' your bills," he whined. "I got to pay cash for my supplies."

"Cash it is if I can have them tomorrow."

He fingered the logotype. "It'll have to be offset."

"I don't care what it is."

"Eleven A.M., then," he said, and did some figuring with a pencil stub. "Sixteen eighty for five hundred." I handed him a twenty-dollar bill. He made no move to take it. "I got no change here this early in the mornin'."

I found I had seventeen dollars in fives and ones. "No sob story tomorrow," I warned him as I gave him the bills. "I've got to have this material right away."

He grunted something unintelligible as the bills disappeared beneath his ink-smudged apron. He was already on his way to the rear of the shop before I began to climb the iron steps.

I spent the afternoon at the Philadelphia Public Library. In the reading room I went through the past year's issues of the magazine *Banking: The Journal of the American Banking Association*. I hoped to find some reference to the Thornton Bank that would contain some indication of recent changes in floor plan or equipment. The Schemer had a detailed floor plan of the bank in his kit, but I had to be sure that it was up-to-date.

In the past I had acquired helpful information from a column "The Country Banker" in *Banking*. It was a chatty affair that mentioned bank remodeling, new vaults, new cashiers' cages, and the like. I found nothing on the Thornton bank, however. I'd still have to check it out, but there was a reasonable chance that nothing had changed there recently.

On my way back to Media I saw a theater marquee advertising "Around the World in 80 Days." In the ten years since it was made I'd seen it four times, but I stopped in to see it again. It says something about the economy of this country that the admission charge has been higher each time I saw it. It's a remarkable movie, though. A bench mark in the industry. I enjoy professionalism wherever I see it.

The next afternoon I picked up my Yellow Page flyers. They were ready, somewhat to my surprise. The general atmosphere of the print shop hadn't been such as to induce confidence in promised performance. The flyers looked fine. Sharp black print on good quality paper carries its own authority. I stopped at a drugstore and picked up a clipboard to add an official touch to my survey sham. It assured my professional status.

I arrived in Thornton again at eight thirty A.M. the following morning. My first stop was a lunchroom across the street from the bank. I gave the girl at the cash register one of my flyers at the same time I bought a morning paper from her. "I'll show it to the boss after his breakfast rush dies down," she said after a glance at it. "He's the chef."

"No hurry," I said. "I'm having breakfast myself, and I'll be around town for a few days."

I took a seat at a table for two near a window that commanded a view of the bank's side entrance, which was used only by employees—a fact made known to me by the Schemer's fact-gathering. I spread my paper out in a manner that would discourage anyone from taking the seat across the table from me even if the place became crowded, then hitched my chair around slightly so I could see the bank parking lot without turning my head. At this hour the cars pulling onto the lot would contain employees only. Right now I was interested in their arrival times.

I ordered hotcakes and coffee when the waitress arrived at my table. Mentally I reviewed the descriptions of the bank manager and assistant manager contained in the Schemer's voluminous dossiers. Thomas Barton, the manager, was forty, five feet ten and a soft two hundred pounds, dark-complexioned, and had a quick, nervous way of walking. The Schemer had him down as a Casper Milquetoast type with a pushy, clubwoman type wife whose kids tended to run loose.

George Mace, the assistant manager, was fifty. He was thin, balding, bespectacled, and invariably wore a cardigan sweater to work, changing to a linen duster inside the bank. The Schemer's file on Mace said that the man had worked in the bank for twenty-one years and had refused several offers of a branch bank managership for himself because he didn't want to leave town.

My interest in these two men was elementary: between them they had the combination to the bank vault. I was hoping that if they got to work early enough in the mornings, as bank men often did, that it might be possible to intercept them at the bank's rear entrance and force them to let us enter with them, risky though it might be. It would eliminate the aspect of the Schemer's plan that I liked least, the necessity for manipulating the families if we had to pick up the two men at their homes and take them to the bank with us.

The first morning I saw enough to convince me that the Schemer had the right of it and that my hope was in vain. When my watch showed 8:58 and I hadn't seen either Barton or Mace, I was beginning to think I had missed their arrival. Then a man who was unmistakably Barton from the Schemer's description hurried toward the bank's side entrance from a parked car.

But it was 9:17 before a man in a fuzzy gray sweater who was just as unmistakably Mace alighted from a mud-stained Rambler. He was thin, stooped, and ailing-looking, and he shuffled toward the entrance with a kind of patient weariness. I wondered if the tellers kept cash locked in drawers so they could operate for a few moments in the morning without the vault being opened. If they didn't, there must be some disgruntled bank customers standing around waiting for Mace to contribute his half of the vault combination to the opening of the vault so the day's banking business could get started.

The late arrival convinced me of something else. We were going to have to pick up Barton and Mace and take them to the bank with us. Even at 8:58, when Barton arrived, the majority of the employees were already inside the bank. That was no good as far as we were concerned. We had to be inside first to assure ourselves that we could herd the clerks, cashiers, janitors, and guards where we wanted them to go as fast as they entered. It looked as though the only way we could be sure that Barton and Mace would be there early enough for us to do the job right would be to take them there ourselves. I'd watch them further, of course, but this first viewing was hardly encouraging to my wishful thinking that we might not have to get involved with the families.

I made my hotcakes and coffee last another twenty minutes while I clocked additional customer arrivals at the bank's front entrance. I had already seen that in the five minutes nine people went inside. This was only slightly fewer than those who entered in the next twenty minutes. The heavy initial traffic gave me additional pause. We could hardly expect to force Barton and Mace to open the vault, clean it out, and make our getaway in less than eight to ten minutes. And in addition to the regular bank personnel, we couldn't hope to cope with the flow of bank customers I'd seen in the first few moments the front doors were open. We'd have to keep the customers out of the bank somehow. There were ways. It would come down to the question of selecting the best way.

"More coffee?" the waitress's voice said in my ear.

"Thanks." I held up my cup. Looking at the girl, my glance went beyond her, and I got a shock. Two uniformed young cops were seated at counter stools, looking in my direction. It took me an instant to realize that they were looking at the waitress, whose uniform nestled a bit snugly about her derriere. The cops laughed and said something to each other, then said something to the girl when she returned to the counter. She joined in the laughter, and I released a breath I'd been holding.

When the cops left, I left too. I spent the balance of the morning passing out a few more of my Yellow Pages flyers. I planned on making only half a dozen calls a day. I had to make the business section last until we pulled the job. None of the storekeepers wanted to take the time to talk to me. Two passed me on to their assistants, both of whom were women. The women wanted to talk about it, which was all right with me. I was in no hurry.

A couple of businessmen gave me a fast brushoff. "I'm already in the book," one said grumpily. "And with you in town coaxing my competition into it, you're cutting my throat." There wasn't much I could have said to that argument even if I'd been legitimate.

I toured the area on foot most of the morning, memorizing street patterns and traffic lights. There's nothing more anonymous than a salesman making a one-time call. In between stops I drank coffee to kill time until my kidneys were awash. By the time I made my last call the proprietor knew who I was supposed to be before I even began my pitch. That's a small town for you. It was why I'd gone to the trouble of setting up the gimmick to give me a reason for spending time in the area. My cover was established.

I drove back to the Carousel and checked my firsthand information acquired about the bank that morning against the Schemer's files. He was right on the button in every respect. That was his reputation, of course.

For the balance of the week I ate breakfast each morning in the lunchroom across the street from the bank. It helped my digestion when I discovered that the two young cops stopped in every morning because one of them was giving the waitress a big rush.

Barton and Mace never varied their pattern, unfortunately. They were consistently late in their arrival at the bank parking lot. I reluctantly came to the conclusion that once again the Schemer was right and we'd have to take them in their homes rather than in the bank itself. The third morning the bank had eleven customers who were either waiting for its doors to open or who arrived within the first two minutes. It confirmed my thinking that the customers somehow had to be excluded.

When I was back at the Carousel again, I looked up the section of the Schemer's report dealing with the bank's opening time. True to form, he had pinpointed the early influx of customers as a problem. Moreover, he proposed a solution. Have a card printed and place it in the bank door, his report suggested. Have the card say BANK EXAMINERS HERE, DOORS OPEN AT 10:00 A.M. TODAY.

It wasn't a bad idea. It might even work. That's why the Schemer was worth his ten percent. Twelve and a half percent, I reminded myself.

On Wednesday I made two trips to Thornton from my motel. I checked out the employees' arrival times in the morning as usual. In the afternoon I returned to watch the arrival of the armored truck making the delivery in which we were interested. The delivery was perfectly routine. On Thursday morning I made particular note that there was nothing unusual—at least nothing that was visible from across the street—in the bank's personnel or routine in dealing with the extra volume of cash.

So eventually it came down to the fact that there were no insuperable problems if we could find a way to control the families of Barton and Mace in their homes during the time we were taking the pair to the bank to open the vault. I stayed away from the homes. Time enough to check up on the Schemer's detailed reports on the home routines when three men paired up differently could operate less conspicuously than a single man. It could wait until Harris and Dahl arrived in town.

If they arrived.

It was time I heard from them.

Dahl called me at the Carousel on Friday night. "How's it look, cousin?" he asked in his usual breezy manner.

"We can do it," I told him. "Be here Sunday night and we'll go to work the following Thursday morning."

"Sounds great," he said heartily. "Sounds like you really been behind the plow, too. You know that all work an' no play makes Drake a dull boy. I'll be in around ten Sunday night, an' I'm gonna bring along with me a few feet of film that'll tickle the risability in your staff of life."

"We won't have time for anything like—"

"Relax," he urged me. "This'll do you good. See you Sunday."

And the connection was broken.

The phone call from Harris came at three A.M. Sunday morning. It roused me from sleep. I had been about to give up on him and call the Schemer for a replacement. "How about it, Drake?" he asked in his flat, Midwestern accent.

"We can do it." I repeated what I had said to Dahl. "I had this coming Thursday earmarked if you can make it here by tonight."

"It'll be late," he said. "Right now I've got to get some sleep. I've just come from twenty-two hours at the table." From the tone of his voice I didn't need to ask him which way it had gone. "I've looked up connections. There's a feeder plane that'll get me into Philly around midnight."

"One of us will pick you up at the airport."

"That means Dahl's still aboard?"

"He's still aboard."

There was a momentary silence. "I hope we can keep the damn fool under wraps this time," Harris said finally.

And the connection was broken.

I thought it over afterward.

I didn't need to go ahead with it. I didn't need to take on a job with two partners neither of whom I would have selected myself if the circumstances had been different.

There were at least two men in the country to whom I could have gone, identified myself, asked them to throw in with me, and had never a qualm about their performance.

But if I did that, I had to give away the secret of my new face and my totally new identity.

Was it worth it?

I finally decided that it wasn't. I'd stay with the program.

It's not only in the marriage contract that the phrase "for better or worse" occurs.

IO

Dick Dahl called me from the airport on Sunday night two hours earlier than I'd expected. He balked at first when I told him I'd meet him behind the first lane of cars in the parking lot. "Don't be so damn lazy," I said. "There's absolutely no point at all in our being seen together in the terminal." He gave in reluctantly.

He was waiting when I parked and walked to the rendezvous point. "Got away sooner'n I thought," he said, his good humor restored. "What about Preacher?"

"He won't be in until after midnight."

"No sense hangin' around," Dahl said. "We might as well go to your motel."

Since this agreed with my own thinking, I led the way to my car. Dahl had the ever-present movie camera slung around his neck. The man really traveled light. The first time I'd seen him he carried a briefcase. This time he had a suitcase, lightweight airplane luggage. From the way he leaned away from it, though, it was heavy.

The airport parking lot was well lighted. As we approached my car, a woman was getting out of another car in the next row. The man with her locked the car doors while the woman walked toward us, her high heels click-clicking on the macadam. She wasn't pretty, but she carried herself well. "Hurry up or we'll miss them," she called over her shoulder. When she passed us, the thin sheath of her dress made it readily apparent that her hips measured twelve inches more than her waist.

Dahl dropped his suitcase with a thump. He bent over it, snapped the catches, grabbed up a powerful-looking light, and clamped it onto his camera. The bright beam of the light shot out, enveloping the undulating tick-tock movement of the woman's haunches while the camera whirred. At the sudden glare of light, the woman looked back at us in surprise.

The man strode toward Dahl and seized him by the arm. "What the hell you think you're doin', Jack?" he growled belligerently. He was two inches shorter than Dahl, but broader. He had an inch-and-a-quarter cigar butt between his teeth and a two-day growth of beard.

Dahl shook off the hand and turned to me, ignoring the man. "The assistant district attorney is at the exit," he said to me.

"Assistant district attor—" The heavyset man paused. "What you talkin' about, mister?"

Dahl turned back to him. "Just tell the truth and everything will be all right." He removed the light from his camera and restored it to the suitcase.

The belligerence had departed from the stocky man's attitude. "Truth?" he said uneasily. "Truth about what?"

"You can call your lawyer later," Dahl said, bending over his suitcase again to snap its catches.

The man spun on his heel and hurried after the woman. He took her by the arm and hustled her along while she protested. They veered from the parking lot exit toward which the woman had been headed and went toward another some distance away. "Works every time," Dahl said to me with a broad grin as we got into my VW. "Sometimes I think everyone in the world has secrets, sexual and otherwise, that he doesn't want to talk to assistant district attorneys about."

"You'll pull that on a bishop someday and wind up in court for invasion of privacy," I said.

"Not a chance. A bishop would have run. You wouldn't believe their sex habits."

"You're an authority on the sex habits of bishops?"

"I'm an authority on sex habits, period," Dahl said calmly. "You got anything to drink at the motel?"

"Stop somewhere and I'll pick up a bottle of Scotch."

"This is Sunday, remember? In Philadelphia."

"Oh, yeah. Stop at a hotel, then, an' I'll scrounge a jug from a bellboy."

Twenty-five minutes later we arrived at the Carousel, the fifth of Scotch firmly in Dahl's hand. He splashed two liberal drinks into water tumblers and handed me one. Then he opened his suitcase on the bed—I could see only a spare shirt in it in addition to all his movie equipment—and removed a projector. "Got somethin' to show you, cousin." He sounded pleased with himself. He fitted a small reel of film into the maze of sprockets and gears on the projector, then aimed the lens at the expanse of white wall at the end of the room.

The last thing I wanted to do was view home movies. "We should be going over—"

"Only take a minute," Dahl said smoothly. He flicked a switch, and a blurred image appeared on the wall. Dahl adjusted the focus, and a brilliantly clear color shot showed a girl in a bikini sitting beside a swimming pool. The camera lingered on her until she glanced up and reached self-consciously for a towel to place between herself and the camera.

It was only when the scene cut suddenly to two women unlocking a motel room door that I remembered the movies Dahl had taken at the Marriott during the occasion of our first meeting. Before I could say anything, the scene changed again. Clearly in focus were a group of women in what appeared to be an institutionalized setting I didn't recognize. Backs to the camera, two of the women were in the process of lifting their dresses and slips up around their shoulders, and I realized with a sense of shock that these were the movies that Dahl had taken inside the Washington bank.

Three women were facing the camera, obviously arguing, but in seconds they turned and emulated the first pair, who now had a girdle in one case and panties in the other down to the backs of their knees. Up went more dresses and slips as the first bare-bottomed duo dropped to the floor and stretched out. Another variety of underwear dropped and two more bare behinds popped into view, and then as the camera drew back slightly, three more. All five plumped out attractively as their owners doubled up awkwardly and joined the first pair on the floor. The camera swept back and forth lingeringly over what appeared to be a field of nude buttocks of all shapes and sizes, the entire homogeneous fleshy expanse broken only by the intrusion of two garter belts and one angry-looking red pimple.

"You'll notice that although there's two good-lookin' young heads in the crowd the best-lookin' ass belongs to that woman on the left, who must be forty-five if she's a nickel," Dahl said. "You'd be surprised how often it turns out that way."

I had been so intent upon the image upon the wall that Dahl's voice irritated me. It was an intrusion upon my concentration. In another instant the picture flickered slightly and then the wall went dark. I forced myself back in my chair, in which I had been crouched forward tensely.

"First time I've seen it myself," Dahl said cheerfully, backing up the reel of film. "Just got it back from the processor. I'm gettin' better at those inside shots. Anyone can shoot an orgy in a woodland glade, cousin, but it takes practice to get those interiors. Let's look at it again."

I sat and watched the reappearance of the bare behinds upon the wall while I tried to analyze the effect the first viewing had had upon me. By nature I'm not the easiest individual to "turn on" sexually. Most men have some one sexual totem pole which invariably accomplishes erection. It had never been that way with me. All my life I was never sure what was going to bring it about. Sometimes at embarrassing moments nothing brought it about.

That was why it had been so great for me with Hazel Andrews. After an initial fiasco, the big woman and I had hit it off in bed together in a manner I'd never experienced before. Over the years I'd become so hesitant at making an effort with women for fear of something going wrong that Hazel had been an exhilarating experience.

Dahl was watching me as he disassembled the projector and put it back into his suitcase. "Kind've got to you, cousin?" he said, shrewdly. "Don't get shook. It gets to most."

I had forgotten my Scotch until Dahl picked up his glass and took a swallow. "These nudie movies," I said after emulating him. "Do they really have such an appeal to—"

"That's not a nudie," he broke in. "What you just saw, I mean. It's never a nudie till you see the broads' snatches. In the trade we call these 'sunsets.'

Don't ask me where the name came from. All you show is a few boobs and butts. They're as far as you can go in tight censorship areas. Then there's the nudies, which I don't bother with—after all, when you've seen a couple dozen bare asses you've seen 'em all—an' finally the ones I make, the exploitation movies."

"Exploitation?"

"Yeah. A movie that tells a story but with a couple of zippy sex scenes in it that can be exploited in the ads. A nudie is just an ol' swimmin' hole background or somethin' like that, and with a couple of recent Supreme Court decisions the market is openin' up. But hell, anyone can make a nudie." His tone was scornful. "A good exploitation movie is art, though. An' Dick Dahl makes the best."

"Then why do you need to keep on . . ." I hesitated.

There was nothing shy about the movie maker. "Why do I need to keep takin' banks to get up a fresh bankroll, you mean?" His grin was wry. "Because I get carried away. I've lost money on my films because I couldn't get my best sex scenes past the censors in the big-money markets."

"Then why not tone them down?"

He turned serious. "Listen, cousin, when you make a movie you make it right, don't you?"

"Even if it loses money?"

"Even if it loses money. 'Course, a couple more court decisions like we been gettin' lately an' I figure I can reissue all my back films. They'd go right now if they had a European stamp on 'em. It's a hell of a note when hard-workin' American film makers are discriminated against."

He sounded so injured I almost laughed. It wouldn't have helped our relationship, because he was in deadly earnest. "I don't understand where you get your actors," I said.

"No problem. I've got a notebook full of names. Two notebooks, actually. One with people workin' re'glar who moonlight in films, hopin' to make it big, an' one with volunteers for the blue stuff."

"Volunteers?"

"Sure. You wouldn't believe the exhibitionists in this world. I always got more than I need. An' I can whistle up five eager chicks for every guy on my list. Somethin' about everyone she knows seein' her ballin' it in livin' color really turns on a certain type of tomato." He took another swallow from his glass and changed the subject. "What's the job look like so far?"

"Everything in the Schemer's blueprints has been right on the nose. Around the bank, anyway. In the next couple of days the three of us will check out the homes of the manager and assistant manager for arrival and departure times of the families. Wait a second and I'll get the file. I want you to look over the escape routes."

Halfway across the room I remembered something and detoured to the telephone. One reason I had selected the Carousel was because it had direct phones in each room that didn't go through a switchboard. "There's one thing in the Schemer's notes I want more information on," I explained to Dahl as I dialed the Schemer's number in Washington, D.C. "Schemer? Earl Drake. Call me right back at the motel, will you?"

I hung up the phone, took the scale drawings of the bank and the access roads around it from my briefcase, and handed them to Dahl. He pointed to the phone. "What's with this call back business?"

"The Schemer's ultracautious. He never talks business over his own phone. He never meets anyone face to face, either."

"You mean you've never even seen the guy?"

"That's right."

"Then how'n'ell does he get paid?"

"Through the mail."

Dahl whistled. "He sure must wind up waitin' at the gate for the postman. Waitin' in vain, I mean."

"Not as often as you'd think. You only miss with him once. Then he puts you on his blacklist, and he's so well and so favorably known that once on his list you'll have trouble hooking up with the right kind of people for your next job."

Dahl still looked dubious. "I say it's no way to run a railroad. He must—"

The telephone rang. I picked it up. "Drake here."

"Why the call?" the Schemer's voice asked.

"One small point," I explained. "Your notes say the manager and assistant manager each has half the vault combination. What happens if either of them doesn't make it to work?"

"I didn't have that in there?" Irritation threaded the clipped syllables. "I'm slipping. If it's the manager, Barton, who doesn't show up, his half of the combo is in the hands of the retired chairman of the board. I don't remember his name, but it's in the list of bank officers. If it's the assistant manager who misses, the bank attorney, who is also a director, has his part of the combination. His name is Carlisle and his office is right across the street from the bank."

"No luck," I said ruefully. "I was hoping someone might have goofed and one man like the board chairman would have both halves. That way we could have bypassed the families."

"I didn't say it was going to be easy," the Schemer said. "Anything else?"

"Nothing. We're getting close."

"Fine. I kept that job on ice for quite a while waiting for the right workman."

The connection was gone. Dahl looked at me quizzically as I replaced the phone. "No shortcuts, huh?"

"It was worth a try. Now we follow the blueprint." I looked at my watch.

"Time to pick up Harris. There's no need for you to come. I'll drive you down the road where you can get a room."

Dahl stretched, yawned, and glanced at one of the large double beds. "What's the matter with sackin' out right here, cousin?"

"No," I said. "We're not going to be seen together any more than is absolutely necessary. You'll need to hire a car in the morning anyway."

Dahl grumbled a bit but finally put himself in motion. He carried his suitcase out to my car. It was only a three-minute drive to the other motel. "You sure we're gonna knock this one over next Thursday?" he said when I stopped on the shoulder of the road in front of the motel.

"Unless we get a bad break," I promised. "Goodnight."

" 'Night," he echoed. He walked up the driveway to the motel office, lugging his heavy suitcase. I watched from the car to make sure he got a room. I drove off when I saw the clerk swing the register in Dahl's direction for him to sign. It reminded me that I should have asked him what alias he intended to use.

At the airport I found I had a forty-five-minute wait for the arrival of Preacher Harris's plane. I left word at the airline counter for him to be paged upon arrival and I left a phone number for him to call. The phone was a pay phone at one end of the terminal. When it finally rang, I was sitting five yards away from it. "Harris," the voice at the other end of the line said when I picked up the receiver.

"Drake," I identified myself. "Let's meet behind the first row of cars in the parking lot."

"Be right there," he said.

He was obviously tired when I met him. "Bad flight," he said briefly. "I chucked twice. I need to sack in."

I suspected that at least part of the dark circles under his eyes and the strained expression around his mouth came from more than a bad flight. Long, losing hours at the tables in Las Vegas had evidently preceded the flight. "I'll take Dahl on a dry run in the morning," I said. "You can sleep till noon and we'll look it over together then."

The sound of Dahl's name seemed to rouse him. "Is he just as cocky as ever?"

"No ego shrinkage that I could see." I didn't tell him about Dahl's movie made inside the bank. If I knew Dahl, Harris would be seeing it for himself very soon. I drove to a third motel, this one ten miles from the Carousel, on U.S. 1 near Lima. "What name are you going to use if I want to reach you?"

"Harris James. James is my real first name."

"That's easy to remember."

I remembered an armored truck job years before in which a change of plan had come up at the last moment. The critical interval came and went with one partner hammering on door after door of a motel because he couldn't remember what alias his partner was using.

At the motel I waited again until I was sure that Harris had a room, then drove back to the Carousel.

We would be starting the last lap in the morning.

212 DAN J. MARLOWE

II

Dahl and I drove to Philadelphia at five A.M. the next morning. He picked up a rented car, and I parked the VW. We continued to Thornton with Dahl driving. A light rain was falling and the streets were slick. It was full dark, and would be for another hour of the late-August morning.

Dahl appeared to be in good humor during the thirty-five-minute drive. He hummed as he drove. When I directed him to the street in Thornton where George and Shirley Mace lived, he asked his first question. "Who we lookin' over this mornin', cousin?"

"The assistant bank manager and his wife. Slow down now." A block away from the Maces' I noticed a sign on a lawn that said TOURISTS—ROOMS. That would be a good spot to park one of the cars. The police wouldn't pay any attention to a strange automobile parked in front of such a building. "Turn here. Fourth house on the other side of the street. If a cruiser gets nosy, I'm being transferred out of the territory on my advertising job, and I'm breaking you in." I opened my briefcase and showed Dahl my Yellow Pages flyers.

He looked speculatively at the house, which was in a neighborhood that had seen better days. "What's to know about this pair that can do us any good?"

"Their habits, especially in the early mornings. Circle the block and park where we can watch the house."

"Are they gonna be a problem?"

"The Schemer doesn't think so. They never go out together, for one thing. They don't seem to have any social life at all. Even when he takes a vacation, Mace shows up at the bank almost every day."

"Sounds like a guy who's afraid someone's gonna find out he's been tiltin' the pinball machine."

"If he is, he's good at it. He's worked at this same bank for twenty-two years. He refused a couple of transfers with advancement. He and his wife have lived in this same house all those years, too."

"Refusin' a chance to move up sounds even more like a man who doesn't care to have anyone lookin' too close at his operation," Dahl said.

"I'm sure the bank took that into consideration."

"Just so there's somethin' left to grab when we make our move. Maybe he's just not makin' it with his war department. But imagine shackin' up with the same broad under the same roof for twenty-two years if you weren't cuttin' it with her?" He was silent for a moment. "Speakin' of there bein' somethin' for us to grab on a job," he resumed, "what we really need is a union, you know. Some outfit that could set up priorities. A good friend of mine is doin' twenty-to-life because he walked into a bank with his gun out when the FBI was standin' right there investigatin' another heist pulled in the same bank forty-five minutes before. It shouldn't happen to a dog."

I made no reply. We sat and watched the neighborhood come to life. Men of all shapes and sizes emerged from their homes, climbed into their cars, and drove to work. The teen-age generation was apparently taking advantage of the last few days of summer vacation to sleep in. There were none visible. A few small children appeared in front of their homes in increasing numbers until the neighborhood took on the appearance of a tricycle headquarters. The wives, like the teen-agers, remained invisible at that hour of the morning.

"What time we gonna hit the place?" Dahl wanted to know.

"This house? We'll have to work out a timetable. Early enough in the morning to have this home and the manager's under our thumbs so we can get the two men to the bank before daylight."

"Sounds like an all-night job." Dahl sighed. He fingered the camera suspended from the cord around his neck. "Good, clear shootin' day. Hate to waste it."

I was mentally running through the Schemer's notes again. Shirley and George Mace; no children; seldom any visitors; little social life. Side-door entrance hidden from the street by hedge along the driveway. It was hard to see a problem.

The other house could be a different story. Thomas Barton, the bank manager, had three children. If Dahl and I went to the bank with Barton and Mace—no, after Dahl's antics during the Washington job it had better be Harris and I escorting the bank officials. Dahl could remain behind to keep the families hostage. That meant consolidating the families, and the easiest way would be to shift Shirley and George Mace to the Barton home when the time came.

It could wait until we'd looked over the Barton home. Some circumstance there might make me want to change it. We wouldn't look it over today, though; we'd already spent enough time in the Mace neighborhood.

When George Mace came out his side door at 9:10 A.M. and backed down his hedge-bordered driveway in his fender-dented Rambler station wagon, I nudged Dahl. "Back to the motel," I said.

"We're not gonna case the manager's house?"

"Harris and I will do that tomorrow."

"You mean I'm gonna waste the whole day tomorrow?"

"You won't be wasting it. You'll be out buying enough cord to make adequate slip-noose tie-cords for the hands and feet of two wives and three children."

He grunted acquiescence. "What about gags?"

I considered it. Who could tell what might happen? "You'd better have gags ready." I thought of the children again. "Yes, you'd better have them ready."

"Okay."

We left the city limits of Thornton behind us at 9:15 A.M.

If all went well, on Thursday morning we would also leave the city limits of Thornton behind us at 9:15 A.M.

The next morning at six A.M. Preacher Harris and I were sitting in Harris's rented car diagonally across the street from the Thomas Barton residence. The streetlights were still on. In contrast to his Sunday night tenseness, Harris seemed much more relaxed.

I felt reasonably secure about the surveillance. The Schemer's notes had made it clear that the city police had developed a pattern of returning the cruisers to the station at five A.M. while reports were made out. The state police cars never left the state highways unless called. In many communities there is a gap in police coverage during the early morning hours.

At 6:15 a half-ton enclosed van rumbled down the street and parked in front of the Bartons' house. A man ran up the walk with a bundle in his arms, tossed it onto the porch where it landed with a thump, and ran back to the truck, which pulled away.

"Newspapers," Harris deduced although there were no markings on the truck. "Did the Schemer's file say the Barton boy had a paper route?"

"No."

"If he does, I don't like it," Harris said. "People are used to getting their papers at the same time every morning."

I didn't like it myself. It was a complication, but the only thing to do was work around it. The Barton front porch light came on and a boy in T-shirt and shorts came out the front door and bent down over the bundle. He was followed by a girl three or four years older. She had on a shortie nightgown, and even in the weak porch light she was something to see. "Dahl should be here," Harris said dryly. Dahl had insisted upon showing Harris his bank movies the previous afternoon. "That's a good-looking girl."

The boy cut the rope binding the papers and handed one to his sister. He put the papers in a wire basket on a bicycle parked on the porch, wheeled the bike down to the street, and rode away. The girl yawned, looked the neighborhood over, stretched casually, and reentered the house. The porch light went out.

I opened the car door. "Follow the boy," I told Harris. "I'll stay here."

"Follow him? For what?"

"There can't be more than thirty papers in his bundle. If we know his route to make sure he can't make a wrong stop, one of us can go with him Thursday morning." I stepped out onto the sidewalk. "I'll walk up to the next corner where I can still watch the house."

Harris drove off after the fast-pedaling boy. Daylight came shortly after 6:45. It would be a tight fit to wait for the boy to return from his paper delivery and still get his father to the bank while it was dark. No newspapers delivered probably would bring phone calls from subscribers, though, and an unanswered phone call might trigger someone's unhealthy curiosity.

Harris returned in twenty-five minutes, during which there had been no further activity visible at the Barton home. "Not too bad," he reported. "He never gets out of a four-block area. He leaves a paper at almost every house."

"But where is he now?"

Harris shrugged. "He rode off somewhere. I only stayed with him till he got rid of the last paper. I thought I'd better get back to you."

It was all right if his absence didn't mean he was picking up more papers for additional delivery, I thought. I didn't say anything. Harris was staring reflectively at the Barton home. Although not very far in distance from the Mace home, it was a world apart in milieu. "What about that shortie-nightgowned job?" Harris asked.

"What do you mean, what about her?"

"What did the Schemer have to say about her?"

"According to him, she's a swinger. Pretty wild by high-school standards. Why?"

"That girl is still in high school?" Harris answered a question with a question. "She sure as hell doesn't look it."

"Why the question?" I asked again.

Harris grinned. "I just kind of had a picture of Dahl and his camera in the car with you here this morning instead of me. He'd have been right up on the porch asking her to pose."

"The hell he would," I said grimly. "I've had enough of that camera foolishness."

"I guess you're not turned on by the dollies any faster I am," Harris said. "With me, the main line has always been two dice or fifty-two cards on a green felt table."

We watched the house in silence for a moment. "How'd you happen to go the gambling route, Preacher?" I asked.

"Only thing I ever really wanted to do," he said softly.

"It's not everyone's game."

"Yours, for instance?"

"I might have bet fifty bucks on a horse three times in my life."

"I never got around to horses," Harris said. "Dice and cards gave me all I could handle."

"And banks," I said.

"Just another gamble."

We fell silent again. The neighborhood grew lighter. The Barton front door opened and a blonde, pig-tailed pixie in a preteen version of a miniskirt bounded down the front walk. She was carrying a violin case. "That must be Margie, their eleven-year-old," I said.

"I sure hope she doesn't take a violin lesson on Thursday morning, too," Harris said.

"We'll check it against the Schemer's blueprint on everyone's whereabouts at the critical time."

Harris lit a cigarette. "How much does he have the jug figured for if we get it all?"

"Two-hundred twenty-five thousand."

"A third of that'll buy the croupier a few drinks," Harris said dreamily. He savored the idea for an instant. "Although it doesn't seem possible in a town this size."

"There's industry on the outskirts," I said. "The armored car delivery on Wednesday is to make up factory payrolls."

"It's a wonder anyone pays by cash any longer. Sure would put us out of business if they quit, though."

"It's changing," I said. "I can remember when I started in the business. A delivery like this one would usually consist of two-thirds cash and coin and one-third paper. Checks, bank money orders, bonds, that sort of thing. Now it's about reversed. That's why it pays to buy a job from someone like the Schemer. You know the cash is there and that you're not going to have your work for nothing."

Harris turned in the front seat to look at me. "Who's going into the bank on Thursday morning?"

"You and I."

"That's good," he said earnestly. "I don't mind telling you I get nervous thinking about Dahl roaming loose inside a bank for the length of time we'll have to be there. He may be long on nerve but he's short on brains."

"We'll supply the brains." I tried to soothe him.

He wasn't listening. "How are we going to handle it when we get there with the manager and assistant manager?"

"I've been thinking of the old Willie Sutton routine. You know, staking one of them out in plain sight with a dog chain around his ankle and a heavy piece of furniture to anchor him in place so the employees entering the bank will think that everything is all right. Then as they come in we'll intercept them and take them to an out-of-the-way area so they can't get to any alarms. I want to look at the Schemer's diagram again before we decide just where. When the time lock goes off, we make Barton and Mace open the vault. Then we grab the cash and go."

"Do we take Barton and Mace with us?"

"My thinking now is that we'll lock them in the vault. If it has air vents.

Most of them do these days for that reason."

Harris considered it. "What happens when the bank doesn't open up at nine A.M. and the customers start pounding on the door?"

"The Schemer thought of that, too. This afternoon I want you to drive into Philly and locate a sign painter. Have him letter a sign that says 'Examiners present—Open at 10:00 A.M.'"

"Banks don't do that, though, do they?"

"Who knows that they don't? It's better than the two of us trying to manhandle a bunch of customers in addition to bank personnel while we're getting Barton and Mace to open the vault."

"Yeah, I guess so." Harris still sounded doubtful though. "And Dahl will be watching the women and children all this time?"

"To make doubly sure Barton and Mace don't get balky about opening the vault," I confirmed.

"It sounds all right," Harris agreed. "If nothing—"

The Barton front door opened. Thomas Barton emerged, trotted down his front steps, and walked around to his side yard. I looked at my watch: 8:44 A.M.

Barton's car backed out into the street, then pulled away.

"Back to the motel," I said to Preacher Harris.

That afternoon Harris picked up the hand-lettered sign for the bank door, plus the dog chain. On Wednesday morning I sent Dahl to check again on the Maces while Harris and I did the same with the Bartons. No significant differences in the family patterns emerged from this surveillance.

Wednesday afternoon I sent Harris and Dahl to Thornton in my VW to check on the arrival of the armored car at the bank. When they came back to the motel, they reported that everything had happened just as the Schemer's schedule had predicted.

At ten thirty P.M. Wednesday evening I telephoned both Barton and Mace to verify that neither had been called out of town unexpectedly. As an excuse I inquired if either wished to buy the new edition of the Britannica. Both were polite in saying no.

H-hour was set for three A.M. on Thursday morning. We would meet at the Carousel and drive to Thornton in the two rented cars and my Volkswagen.

At three thirty A.M. we would force the lock on George Mace's side door. We were as ready as we were ever going to be.

12

Thursday morning at three A.M. it was warm and muggy with a hint of rain in the air.

I wore my coppery-red hairpiece. Harris and Dahl both carried their Halloween masks, but I didn't bother. I knew I couldn't keep a mask on for six hours without perspiration ruining my makeup and revealing scar ravages beneath.

Each of us drove to Thornton. Although I intended us to eventually drive to the bank and later leave it in Barton's car, I had Harris park his rental near the bank in case anything went wrong and we needed a spare during the getaway. Harris then got into Dahl's car and they followed my VW.

I parked in front of the house I had previously selected, the one with the sign that said "Tourists—Rooms." The VW shouldn't be noticed in front of that house. Harris and Dahl picked me up, and at 3:34 A.M. we sat in Dahl's car where he and I had watched the Mace house the first morning. Harris and I left the car with Dahl still sitting at the wheel. We walked up the Mace driveway to the back door.

"Look at that!" Harris muttered hoarsely.

There was a light on in the kitchen.

The rest of the homes in the neighborhood were as dark and as silent as an abandoned silver mine, but the house that we intended to enter was brightly lighted. I knew we couldn't afford to be held up at the very outset of the operation. There would almost surely be unavoidable delays later on. "Someone probably forgot to turn it off," I said. "Don't get spooked."

I went up the three steps to the back door. I had a celluloid pick in my hand and a steel pry-bar in my pocket. When I pulled on the handle, the unlatched screen door swung open. The back door itself was locked. I inserted the pick. I wasn't afraid of noise even if someone was in the kitchen. The Schemer's diagrammatic drawing of the house had showed a long passageway between the back door and the kitchen. The intervening space was used for storage.

There was a faint click as the celluloid slid back the tongue of the lock. I opened the door a crack. The passageway was dark. I couldn't hear a sound from inside the house. "Let's go," I whispered to Harris, who was standing on the step behind me. There was a blur of movement I knew was caused by his putting on his mask. I lined myself up with the doorway and moved straight down the black passageway to avoid bumping into anything.

My outstretched left hand made contact with the wood of the inner door. I groped for the knob, found it, and turned it. The door inched open. It wasn't locked. I reached across my chest with my right hand and drew the Sauer from its holster. I opened the door wide and walked into the lighted kitchen with the automatic showing my hand.

A woman in pajamas with her hair up in curlers was standing at the stove. She was stirring a steaming pot with a long-handled ladle. She appeared middle-aged although her complexion was unlined. Her mouth opened but no sound emerged as she stared at me. The ladle hung in midair where her arm movement had frozen. Liquid dripped from it to expire with a hiss on the burner. On the kitchen table beside the woman there was a green wooden tray with deep troughs containing wooden dishes and bowls and wooden utensils.

The woman's eyes passed fearfully from the gun in my hand to the masked Harris, who appeared beside me. "What—what do you want?" she whispered.

"Call your husband," I said in a normal tone. "But carefully. No panic. No one's going to get hurt."

She moistened dry lips. "He—he can't hear me if I call him from here."

"Then let's go where he can hear you. Carefully," I said again. She dropped the ladle into the pot. I followed her from the kitchen in gradually diminishing light through a dining room to a flight of stairs at the front of the house. I could hear her clear her throat. "George!" she called huskily. There was no response. "George!" There was an edge of panic in her tone until a muffled voice answered from upstairs. "Please bring my robe down to the kitchen."

She led the way back into the lighted area of the house. I heard footsteps on the front stair treads, and Harris moved to one side to widen the distance between us. Slippered feet shuffled through the dining room. "You know it's your turn to get the meal, Shirley," George Mace was complaining as he entered the kitchen with his wife's robe over his arm. "Why did you—"

His plaintive query choked off as he focused on Harris and me. His startled glance took in Harris's mask and my automatic. "What's going on h-here?" he said in a tone he tried to make forceful but which quavered in spite of him.

His wife held out her hand for the robe. He handed it to her automatically. She slipped it on as Harris spoke for the first time. "Do what you're told and nothing will happen, Mace."

"You know my name?" Bewilderment took over from fear.

"You and your boss are going to take us down to the bank in a couple of hours," Harris informed him. "In the meantime, just behave yourself."

"Whatever it is you're planning, you'll never get away with it!" Mace said sharply.

I was looking at the tray on the kitchen table with its wooden bowls and spoons. "Who's the meal for?" I asked Shirley Mace.

She swallowed. "M-me."

"You wouldn't need a tray. Who else is in the house?"

"N-nobody."

"She was bringing the tray up to me," George Mace said quickly. "I haven't been feeling—"

"Shut your mouth," I told him. I looked at the woman. "Tell me. Right now."

"It's for my—our daughter," she got out painfully.

"You haven't any kids!" Harris said at once. His tone was brittle. A stubby-barreled Colt appeared in his right hand. He took two long strides toward Mace and placed the gun against his head. "Who else is in this house?"

"It's the truth!" Shirley Mace burst out. "It's—it's the truth, that's all!"

I gestured for Harris to step away from the ashen-faced assistant bank manager. "Then take the meal to her," I said to the woman. Shirley Mace stared at me blankly. "I said take the tray to your daughter."

She looked at her husband. I had never seen such an expression on a grown man's face. George Mace looked as if he were going to cry. "Do—do what they say, Shirley," he said. His voice broke.

"And no tricks," Harris added, his tone hard.

Shirley Mace turned back to the stove. She ladled the bowls on the tray full of a rich-looking stew. Considering the hour of the morning and the soggy temperature outside, it was a heavy meal. Mrs. Mace went to the refrigerator and removed a large plastic glass of milk. She placed this in a slot on the tray, added half a dozen cookies, and picked up the tray. "Open the door, George," she said in a dull tone.

Her husband stepped forward and opened a door I had thought led to a pantry. Steps were visible leading down to a basement. Mace leaned forward and snapped on a light. Mrs. Mace started down the stairs. I moved in behind her. "You go, too," Harris said from behind me to George Mace. I could hear their footsteps coming down the stairs behind me.

The basement was well lighted. At first glance I thought it was small. Then I realized that what appeared be a foundation wall was actually a high wooden fence. The area inside the fence took up most of the space in that basement. Mrs. Mace went to a door in the fence, balanced the tray on one arm, and pulled a wooden pin that latched the door.

The opening of the door disclosed that the interior was actually a stockade. It, too, was brightly lighted. Floor and walls were padded with mattresses. A tubular-steel jungle gym like the type seen in playgrounds stood in one corner. Seated on the floor mattress was a naked girl. She was stocky, with wide shoulders and good, clear skin. She had long black hair streaming down her back, and she was smiling at us with the childlike smile of a five-year-old welcoming visitors to a pretend tea party. Physically, she could have been twenty-five.

Mrs. Mace approached to within a couple of yards of the seated girl and stooped to place the tray in front of her. "Here's your dinner, Rachel," she said in a stifled voice. I noticed that she didn't get too close to the girl.

onds

I looked at Preacher Harris. He was staring in horror at the mentally retarded Rachel, who had picked up one of the bowls of stew and was slurping down its contents without bothering with a spoon. Some of the greasy stew spilled over and ran down between her full breasts. She paid no attention.

I moved over to George Mace, who was standing in the open doorway with a wounded look on his face. "Twenty-two years in the same house and the same job," I said. "No vacations, no social life together. One of you stayed with her all the time?"

"Exactly," Shirley Mace said bitterly. For the first time she sounded as though she were coming out of the shock induced by our appearance in her kitchen. "He wouldn't have her put away."

"That's enough, Shirley," her husband said with the air of a man who has been over the same tired ground innumerable times. "She's ours."

I looked at the interior walls of the wooden stockade, which showed signs of reinforcement in several places. "She's dangerous?" I asked Mace.

"She's very strong," he replied. "Can we go upstairs now?"

Preacher Harris was tugging at my arm. When I turned to him, he drew me to one side. "Let's pack it in here,'' he said urgently. "Altogether." He was looking at Rachel stuffing whole cookies into her mouth and dribbling as much milk into her lap as into her mouth. "This—this—I can't—" Harris drew a deep breath. "We could never move her to the Barton house, anyway."

"Just take it easy," I said. "We'll work it out."

Shirley Mace reapproached her daughter when the girl set down the empty glass and beamed vacantly at us again. "Over to the shower now, Rachel," she said in a coaxing tone. The girl rose and shambled toward the corner where an open shower stall stood. En route she had to pass the jungle gym, and she reached upward and hand-walked the length of the overhead bars effortlessly.

The girl had a good figure although not a particularly feminine one. Her shoulders were extraordinarily broad, almost like a husky boy's. Her hips were boyishly small, too. With long hours of nothing to do except exercise on the jungle gym, it was no wonder she had developed the shoulders and upper arm musculature of a man.

Shirley Mace took a small hose and sluiced her daughter down from head to foot. Water splashed everywhere as the girl pirouetted, squealing happily. It was the first sound I had heard her make. When her mother turned off the hose, Rachel slapped herself on her bare stomach invitingly. "No more now, dear," Mrs. Mace said. She returned to us at the doorway. We went outside, and George Mace fastened the pin in the latch.

We filed up the stairs. "We'll turn it around," I said to Harris when we were in the kitchen again. "We'll bring the Bartons over here. Where is there a better place to keep everyone than in that basement stockade? We'll—"

"No!" Shirley Mace exclaimed violently. She said it so loudly that her husband jumped. "I won't have the Bartons here to see—to see—"

"Quiet, you," Harris said to her. He appeared glad of the chance to sound off his frustration on someone. "Will it work?" he asked me.

"Better than we planned," I assured him. "You stay here while Dick and I round up the Bartons and bring them here."

"Right," Harris said. Removed from the disturbing presence downstairs, he was beginning to function again. He motioned with his gun at the Maces. "Sit down, you two."

"We'll be right back," I said, and left the kitchen. After the bright lights in the basement, the night seemed triply dark outside. I went down the side walk and diagonally across the street to Dahl's car.

"Where's Harris? Where's the Maces?" he demanded.

"Change in the blueprint," I said as I opened the car door. "We're bring-ing the Bartons over here."

"No kidding? What the hell for?"

"Because it's a better setup. Drive slowly," I said to shut him up.

"But what—"

"Let's get ready to do the job we have to do."

I could tell he was sulking, but he drove to the Barton home, which was dark. We left the car and walked up the driveway to the rear of the house. When the first pass of the celluloid produced no result, I didn't feel I could wait. I took the pry-bar, inserted it between the sill and the edge of the door, and jacked the door away from the lock. The door sprang open with only a rasping squeak. Inside, I took Dahl's arm and pointed him toward the dining room. "The phone wires come in beneath the end window. Cut them."

I stood at the foot of the stairs leading up to the second floor until he re-turned from the mission. "Do we go up after 'em?" he wanted to know.

"Yes. The kids first. You have the tie-cords and gags?"

"Sure."

We climbed the stairs. They were well padded and well carpeted. We made no sound. The Schemer's diagram showed that the first bedroom at the top of the stairs was Tommy's, the fourteen-year-old son. His door was open. We could see him, face down, clad only in the bottoms of his pajamas, sleeping soundly.

"Let me handle this," Dahl muttered. He handed me two slip-knotted tie-cords. Approaching the bed, he flipped the boy onto his back, pinning him down at the same time as he clamped a hand over his mouth. "Ankles first," Dahl said. I noosed them before Tommy had sufficiently roused from sleep to struggle. "Hands behind his back," Dahl continued, rolling the boy over while maintaining his hand gag. That was more difficult, but I managed.

"Reach in my right-hand pocket," Dahl went on. I found gauze pads and adhesive. It took only a moment to fashion a gag and apply it as Dahl removed his hand. Dahl then took the loose ends of the tie-cords and knotted them to-gether, fastening wrists to ankles on a short tether. It prohibited much movement. The boy's flashing eyes glittered at us above the gag. He appeared more angry than afraid.

"That'll do for this one," Dahl assured me. He led the way to the bedroom of the eleven-year-old across the hall. The mechanics of the operation went exactly the same except that Dahl wasn't quite as rough. "Lie still, honey. Nobody's gonna hurt you," he whispered before we departed.

Ellen's room was next. I was afraid of this one. It was unlikely that the seventeen-year-old would be as heavy a sleeper as the younger children. The door to her room was closed. Dahl eased it open an inch at a time.

I was standing right behind him. I couldn't imagine why he kept opening the door wider and wider, far more than was necessary to slip inside. I put my lips to his ear. "What's the matter?" I murmured.

He opened the door all the way and moved to one side to let me see for myself.

Ellen Barton's bed was neatly turned down, but it hadn't been slept in.

And of Ellen Barton herself there was no trace.

13

"D'you think she's sleepin' at a girl friend's?" Dahl muttered.

"More likely a boyfriend's," I replied, thinking of the Schemer's report on the elder Barton daughter. "Let's make sure of the Bartons."

Ellen Barton's disappearance from her room was just one more thing gone wrong in a night notably full of same. We backed out of her bedroom and moved down the hall. The door to the master bedroom was closed, too. I could hear snoring.

There was no need for finesse now. There was no one left to be wakened by a scream. I opened the bedroom door and walked in. Behind me, Dahl flicked on the light switch. Dahl and I were standing on either side of the bed by the time Thomas Barton struggled from the depths of sleep to a sitting position. Thelma Barton snored on.

The bank manager blinked at Dahl's mask. "What—what—" he stammered.

"Quiet," Dahl ordered. His eyes on the sleeping Thelma Barton, he picked up the husband's pillow.

At the sound of Dahl's voice, the snoring stopped. Thelma Barton spoke with her eyes closed. "Put out that light, Tom," she said. "You shouldn't have had that last bottle of beer."

"Dear," her husband began.

I don't know what it was she thought she heard in his voice, but her eyes snapped open. I could see the scream starting from her toes. Dahl saw it, too. He dropped the pillow onto her face. The scream dissipated itself in a hissing sound. Dahl held the pillow in place till she stopped fighting it. "Quiet," he warned again, and removed the pillow.

Thelma Barton sat up. She was the picture of indignation. Her hair was in curlers and her nightgown had slipped off one shoulder, disclosing an undersized breast. "You two will go to the electric chair for this," she proclaimed, jerking the gown back into place. She had a jaw-line like a grenadier guard. "Where are my children?" she demanded, glaring at Dahl.

"In their beds," Dahl replied. I could tell from his voice he was enjoying himself. "Except Ellen."

"Except Ellen?" Mrs. Barton's voice rose an octave. "What do you mean 'except Ellen'?"

"Her bed hasn't been slept in."

"Hasn't been—" Thelma Barton's bare feet hit the floor with a splat. Beneath her gown, her long, thin legs scissored toward the doorway. Dahl followed her. I could sense his smirk at the woman's semitransparent dishabille.

When they disappeared down the hallway, I looked at the man in the bed.

"We're going to the bank shortly," I said.

"The bank!" he exclaimed, his eyes bulging. "I thought—"

"It's not a house burglary."

"But you can't possibly hope to accomplish—"

I was listening to Thelma Barton's audible return from her daughter's room. "Imagine!" she was saying as she burst into the master bedroom. "That vixen has gone out over the roof again! After all our lectures, Tom! I'll—"

"Get dressed, Mrs. Barton," I said.

"Dressed? What for?"

"We're all going to the Mace home."

She got the picture. Her tone lost some of its incisiveness. "What about Margie and Tommy?"

"They'll come when Tommy delivers his paper route."

"How did you know—"

"Evidently they have it all planned, dear," Thomas Barton said quietly. "For the children's sake, we must do what they say." He slid out of bed. He was a short, paunchy man. Both Bartons began to dress.

I moved over to Dahl, who was lounging in the doorway. "Sure wish I'd brought my camera inside with me," he said wistfully. He was eyeing Thelma Barton's struggle to dress under cover of her nightgown.

"You stay here and wait for Ellen," I said to Dahl in an undertone. "I'll take this pair to the Mace's, then come back and go with the kids on the boy's paper route when it's time. Margie's presence should assure Tommy's cooperation. When I'm ready to take them to the other house, hopefully you'll have corralled Ellen and added her to the collection. Give me your car keys and"— mentally I counted heads —"five pairs of your tie-cords."

Dahl handed them over. Five minutes later I ushered Mr. and Mrs. Thomas Barton out the back door of their home. I had no fear of antics on their part. They knew that Dahl was remaining with the children.

I drove Dahl's rental to the Mace house and delivered the Bartons to Preacher Harris in the basement. I had time only for a glimpse of the startled looks on four faces as the Maces and the Bartons met under other-than-ordinary circumstances. Rachel was as beamingly nude as before although there was a shredded sheet beside her on the mattress floor. "I tried to cover her up but she tears everything," Harris explained.

"So I see." I handed him the tie-cords. "You've got enough here now so they might be tempted to jump you. Tie them up. The girl first." I explained the hangup with Ellen and the fact that Dahl was waiting for her. "I'll be back with the kids," I concluded.

I left the house and started down the driveway to the car. A police cruiser was moving slowly through the block, one of the occasional "irregulars" that the Schemer had warned the police put on to avoid being typed by people like us. I stopped in the shadows. The cruiser's spotlight flicked on and lingered on the rental license plate, but the cruiser kept on going.

The danger would come on the cruiser's next swing through the area, if there was a next swing. Nine nights out of ten all the cops would have been back at the station, drinking coffee and writing up their reports, but this was the tenth night. One more look at those rental plates and the cop in the cruiser was liable to stop and try to find out the reason for its presence.

I went back into the house and called down to Harris in the basement. He came halfway up the stairs, looking angry. "I'm going to gag that goddam Barton woman," he declared.

"What's the matter?"

"She's getting everyone upset, running her mouth about the criminal irresponsibility involved in keeping the idiot girl a prisoner all these years. Mrs. Mace is almost in tears, and the two men are sitting there trying not to listen. We don't want Mace upset before he gets to the bank, do we?"

"Suit yourself about the gag, but find out from Mace where he keeps his car keys." I explained about the police cruiser. "I'm going to drive the Mace car and put the rental job in his driveway."

"Good deal." Harris went down the steps. "They're in a mixing bowl inside the first wall cabinet as you come in the back door," he called up to me in a moment.

"Right." I closed the basement door. I found the car keys and went outside again. I switched cars, although the sound of the Mace Rambler station wagon's engine made me uneasy. The car was unlikely to be dependable for anything but short hauls.

Dahl was waiting for me at the head of the stairs when I climbed to the second floor of the Barton home. He was grinning widely. "Ellen came in the window ten minutes ago," he said. "And would you believe she's stoned on Mary Jane? How do you like these small-town kids?"

"Let's take a look at her," I said.

Dahl led the way to her bedroom. "She'd never have made it if a couple of her pals hadn't boosted her up onto the porch roof. You never heard such giggling," he said. He turned on a bedside lamp. A tall, black-haired, beautiful girl was sprawled on her side in the bed, clad only in a pair of transparent panties. She was breathing raggedly but deeply. I could detect the sweetish odor of marijuana. A trail of feminine clothing extended from the open window to the bed. "She shed her clothes like they were on fire," Dahl continued. "How we gonna move her to the other house?"

"Mummified in a blanket, if we have to."

Dahl was staring down at the girl on the bed. "Great pair of teats. Nothin' wrong with the ass, either, even if she has been workin' it overtime tonight."

"Working it overtime?"

He smiled knowingly. "You don't have the eye for these things that I have, cousin. That isn't goose grease smeared all over her pussy hair."

I turned away from the bed. "Tie her up in case she comes around. Then we'll wait downstairs for Tommy's papers."

Dahl rejoined me in a few moments in the downstairs sitting room. "I just checked the younger kids," he said. "They're okay. The little girl is mad, though. When I took her gag off for a second, she told me I was a bad man." Dahl chuckled.

We sat in darkness, waiting. I was trying to think of so many things at once that my nerves were fluttering. Had we overlooked anything? What exactly remained to be done, and in what order? I made mental lists, adding and subtracting.

A whistling noise brought me halfway up out of my chair. I stared through the window at the darkened porch. The noise was repeated, and I realized that it was behind me. The whistle ended in a snort. Dahl had fallen asleep and was snoring. I reached out a foot and kicked him in the ankle. "What the hell, Dahl! Do your sleeping later!"

"Restin' my eyes," he grunted. "The papers here?"

"Not yet. Stay awake and listen for them. I'm going upstairs and get the kids ready."

I climbed the staircase and went into Tommy's darkened room. I sat down on the edge of the bed beside him before speaking. "You and Margie and I are going to deliver your papers this morning, Tommy," I said. "I know the number of your deliveries and where you make them. If you're tempted to give an alarm, Margie will still be in the car with me. Do you understand?" He nodded, and I removed his gag and his wrist and ankle cords. "Get dressed," I told him.

I went across the hall to Margie's bedroom. Despite her uncomfortable tied-up position, she had fallen asleep. The healthy nerves of children. "You and I are going with Tommy when he delivers his papers, Margie," I said to her when I shook her awake. "If you try to give an alarm, it won't go well with Tommy." I removed her bonds. "Now get dressed."

I was on my way across the hall again when Dahl's whistle floated up the front stairs. "The papers just came," he informed me when I went to the head of the stairs.

"We'll be right down."

I went back into Margie's room. She was dressed in blouse and shorts, and her face was damp from a quick washing. I motioned toward her socks and sneakers on the floor. "Bring those along and we'll go to Tommy's room."

She led the way, her pigtails bouncing on her slender shoulders. There was a light on in Tommy's room. The boy was seated on the edge of his bed, dressed. I was getting my first good look at him. He was a handsome kid with wavy dark hair and a clear complexion but with a sullen expression. He grinned at his sister but said nothing.

I moved to turn out the light. "Better leave it on," he said casually. "Peo-

ple are used to seein' lights upstairs here at this time of the morning." He had
a point. I removed my hand from the switch. "Where's Ellen?" he continued.
"In her room."

"Flaked out as usual?"

I glanced at Margie, who had seated herself on the bed and was drawing on
socks and sneakers. "She's asleep."

"Asleep!" he said derisively. "Stupid broad!"

I studied him. "You feel that way about Margie, too?"

"Not yet." He grinned. "She still thinks it's to sit on. She'll be givin' it away
one of these days, though."

"I do too know what it's for!" Margie said indignantly.

"That Ellen, though," Tommy went on. He shook his head. "A commercial
setup I could at least understand. She—"

"That's enough of that," I cut him off, looking at the pigtailed Margie.

"Oh, I know all about Ellen!" the younger girl said scornfully. "She hasn't
got brains enough to sell it."

Eleven years old, I thought to myself. Eleven years old.

"Stop showing off, Margie," Tommy frowned. He was looking at me.
"This is about the bank, isn't it?"

I saw no point in lying. "Yes."

"I hope you take 'em for plenty," he said. His tone was serious. "I hope you
shake up this whole crummy town."

"Why?"

"Because you'd be hittin' 'em where it hurts. All the parents I know spend
their time tryin' to figure out how to swindle someone. At least you've got
the guts to go take it."

I remembered something. "How many mornings a week do you take a violin lesson?" I asked the girl.

"Only on Mondays."

"You really cased this job, huh?" Tommy said. He was looking at me with
respect. "If I was a couple years older, I'd go with you." He scuffed at the
carpeting with a sneakered foot. "I'm at a hell of an age," he concluded
gloomily.

"You certainly are," Margie said smugly. "Standing in front of your mirror
nights and admiring—"

He reached out and slapped her. She jumped up from the bed and kicked
him in the shins. I grabbed a shoulder of each and pulled them apart. This was
a demonstration of the familial love I'd been depending upon to make the pair
solicitous of each other's welfare? I felt gloomy myself.

I marched them down the stairs. Margie slid behind me as Dahl approached
us. Evidently his size impressed her, if anything impressed her generation. I
took the wrapped and tied bundle of papers that Dahl handed me, then herded
my charges out the front door and onto the porch.

"Hey, that's ol' Mace's car!" Tommy exclaimed at first glimpse of the Rambler across the street. "Is that where the folks are?" He followed up that question immediately with another. "Can I drive the car?"

"You can deliver the papers," I told him. The sky was still dark but beginning to lighten. "You have twenty minutes."

"I don't like the Maces," Margie announced. "They don't give parties."

Once under way, the paper delivery went swimmingly. Tommy folded papers while Margie gave me driving directions in a superior tone of voice. She knew the route as well as her brother did. At each stop he opened the door on the passenger's side and with a flick of his wrist scaled folded papers toward doorways. His percentage of hits was high.

There was only one untoward incident during the short run, but it was a heart stopper. In the middle of the second block of deliveries, I saw the same police cruiser heading toward us. Tommy was out of the car, firing a paper up onto a second-floor balcony. I placed a hand on Margie's arm. The cruiser stopped opposite us. Tommy turned in its direction and sailed the folded paper in his hand across the street and through the cruiser's open window. The cruiser blinked its lights and moved away. I breathed again. "Stupid cops," Tommy said contemptuously when he returned to the car for another paper. "They graft a free one from me every morning that they're out."

"Stupid cops," Margie echoed.

We completed the route and returned to the Barton home. Dahl was waiting inside the front door when I brought the kids in. "Get Ellen," I told him. "We're ready to go."

He went upstairs. When he came down, he was half leading, half carrying the good-looking girl, whom he had swathed in a blanket. She looked the gathering over fuzzily. The pupils of her eyes were pinpoints, but I judged that the depth of her involvement was lessening. "How's the easiest lay in town this morning?" Tommy inquired with brotherly affection.

"Shut up, you little wart." The girl's voice was blurry but functional. "What's—you're not cops. What's this all about?"

"Shut up yourself and walk," Dahl ordered.

She tried to kick him. His return kick was more accurate. I broke that one up and we went out to the Rambler. I drove. Ellen had drifted off into the land of hashish dreams again. When we reached the Mace house, Dahl carried her inside. Harris heard us coming and met us at the top of the basement steps. He and Dahl muscled the tall girl's dead weight downstairs.

The younger kids blinked at the transition from shadowy darkness outside to the stockade's bright illumination. Tommy's fascinated gaze fastened upon the slavering nude Rachel, who was chewing at the bonds on her wrists. Margie favored her brother with a superior sisterly smile.

Harris had gagged Thelma Barton. Dahl dumped Ellen to the floor where she sprawled three-quarters out of the blanket, then marched over in front of

Ellen's mother. "What the hell kind of a parent are you?" Dahl demanded. "Don't you know where your kids are nights? Don't you care?"

Thelma Barton's features turned purple from the intensity of the abortive effort she made to reply. Dahl turned away. Harris drew me to one side. "Mrs. Mace wants to talk to you privately," he said. "She says it's important."

"Bring her outside, then. And get the tie-cords off Barton and Mace and onto the kids."

I went out into the basement proper. Harris led out Shirley Mace and then went back inside. The woman wasted no words. "There's a burglar alarm at the bank in the writing desk just inside the side door," she said. "You'll have to keep everyone away from it."

I couldn't help thinking that never in my life had I had more cooperation from such unlikely sources. First the bank manager's kids, now the assistant bank manager's wife. "You have a reason for telling me this, of course."

Her eyes met mine levelly. "I do. You're a ruthless man. I want you to kill Rachel before you leave. You can make it look like an accident."

"Well, now—"

"You'll be doing everyone concerned a favor," she insisted. Her tone turned acid. "I've spent twenty-two years in slavery because of George's truckling to his conscience. I don't propose to do it any longer. I've given you information which might easily make the difference in your getting away or not. You owe me a favor."

"We'll see," I said in the manner of a parent speaking to a petulant child, avoiding the outright "no" because of fear of the resultant emotional explosion. "Get back inside." She hesitated as if there were something more she was about to say, then led the way.

Barton and Mace were on their feet, rubbing their wrists. Everyone else except Shirley Mace was on the mattress floor, bound wrist and ankle. Harris speedily added her to the lineup. Ellen had thrown off her blanket and was staring defiantly at her family. Sometime since I had seen her on the bed in her room, either she or Dahl had removed her panties. The girl was as naked as Rachel.

"More bare pelt on the loose around here tonight," Dahl commented, seeing my expression. I kept a grip on myself. This was no time for a discourse on adult juvenile delinquency. For an instant I debated the wisdom of leaving Dahl with the group. I had committed myself to Harris, though. The gambler would be disturbed by a last-minute reversal of roles. "Harris and I are leaving now with these two," I told Dahl, nodding at the men. "Hold the lid on here till we get back. We'll take Mace's Rambler and leave your rental job in the driveway. If we're not back by nine twenty, go for yourself."

"I read you loud an' clear, cousin," he declared.

We climbed the basement steps with me in the lead, Barton and Mace in the middle, and Harris bringing up the rear. "Do you have your key to the bank's side entrance?" I asked Mace.

"It's on the Rambler key ring," he answered.

"Make sure of it," Harris warned. "You wouldn't like what happens to the people downstairs if it isn't."

Neither Mace nor Barton said anything. I wasn't sure that they caught the bloodthirsty reference to the hostages. We went out to the street. It was getting light. I put the two men in the back after Mace made sure that the bank key was on the key ring. Harris sat in front, watching them, although I think both he and I were convinced by that time there was no fight in either.

"I did the right thing!" George Mace burst out as I pulled away from the house. "She was mine! She is mine! She's my responsibility! How can your wife say we should have put her in a home, Tom!"

Barton said nothing. He looked like a man who had his own troubles. I drove through the quiet streets to the downtown area and parked Mace's car in its usual slot on the bank parking lot.

"We know there's no burglar alarm on the side door because the cleaning people have to get in at odd hours," Harris told Barton and Mace. "But the first man who makes an unexplained move inside has had it."

It was still dark enough so that I doubted anyone on the street could see us as we approached the bank. I handed Mace the Rambler key ring and motioned to him to open the bank door. Harris had his hand inside his jacket on the butt of his gun.

Mace unlocked the door. We all filed inside, our footsteps echoing cavernously in the stillness. I watched closely, but neither man made a move toward the alarm switch in the desk just inside the entrance about which Shirley Mace had warned me. "Take them into their offices and tie them up again," I said to Harris. "Each in his own office."

When he led them away, I stationed myself where I could watch the parking lot and the approach to the side door. Nothing moved in the steadily increasing light. "There's a coffee percolator all loaded and ready to go in Barton's secretary's office," Harris reported when he returned. "Should I make coffee?"

"If you like. Don't forget the sign for the front door."

"I'll get it up in time." Harris glanced at his watch. "I wish we didn't have this long a wait."

I wished it, too, but there was nothing we could do about it. I explained to Harris the necessity for keeping incoming bank personnel away from the desk near the entrance. I didn't tell him how I knew about the alarm. We checked the space available, and decided to place the bank employees in a lounge just off the rest rooms as fast as they appeared for work. The lounge had only one entrance and a door that could be locked from the outside.

Then there was nothing to do but wait.

We divided up into thirty-minute shifts the task of keeping an eye on the side entrance approach to prevent surprise. During my off periods I sat in one of the smaller offices. The sight of a roll of Scotch tape on the desk reminded me of something I had intended to do previously.

I rummaged around in the desk until I found an empty box of medium-stiff cardboard of the type in which new checkbooks are mailed out, and a sheet of wrapping paper. I folded the paper several times and slipped it into my jacket pocket. In that desk and the one in the adjoining office I found address labels, a pen that wrote with India ink, loose stamps, and the roll of tape. I tore the top label from the pad and printed an address on it: DR. SHER AFZUL, STATE HOSPITAL, RAIFORD, FLORIDA. In one corner I added FIRST CLASS MAIL. I put label, stamps, and tape in the box, then put the box in my jacket pocket along with the wrapping paper.

I settled down to wait again.

At eight thirty A.M. I released Barton from the chair into which he was tied and took him into the lobby. Using Harris's dog chain, I fastened Barton by one ankle to the leg of a heavy customers' desk. All employees entering the bank would see Barton standing there and assume that everything was all right until the instant that either Harris or I intercepted them and put them into the lounge.

At 8:35 Harris took up a position just inside the door, behind it so that he would be invisible each time it opened. At 8:41 there was the sound of a key in the lock. The uniformed bank guard whose duty it was to unlock the side door each morning entered. With him was a white-haired woman carrying an umbrella. "Good morning, Mr. Barton," she called across the lobby as the door closed behind them. "Nice to see—" Her voice deteriorated to a choked gasp as Harris stepped out with his gun leveled.

He took them to the lounge. The guard put up no opposition. I took Harris's place just inside the door. Three more people arrived at 8:44. I took them to the lounge while Harris took my place at the door. After that it was a shuttle service. We took them in groups as fast as we could make the round trip. I took time out only to send Harris to the front entrance to tape up his sign: BANK EXAMINERS HERE. OPEN AT 10:00 A.M. TODAY.

At 8:58 the rush was over. "You take it here," I told Harris. "I'll take Barton and Mace to the vault. Lock this door each time you have to leave it. Latecomers will think someone forgot the latch. They'll rattle the door, which will give you time to get back to it. Now give me your knife."

He handed it over. I released Barton from the leg of the table and took him with me while I cut Mace free from his bonds. "No mistakes," I said as I walked them to the door of the vault. "You both have more riding on this than I do."

Mace rubbed his hands together nervously. Neither man said anything. There was a red light on above the vault door. I watched it. At eight seconds after nine by my watch the red light went out and a white light came on. I didn't need to say anything to Barton. He stepped up to the vault door with its huge combination dial. He spun the dial once right and once left with his body shielding his movements, then backed away. Mace moved in and did the same, then took hold of the door handle and tugged. The massive door slid open silently on its oiled tracks.

"Inside," I said to them. I followed them into the steel-lined room. A metal cart with seven canvas sacks on it was just inside the door. It was the cart we had seen used for unloading the armored car two weeks in a row. I dug my toe into the sacks. Three were heavy, obviously filled with coin. I pushed them off the cart onto the vault floor. The others I slit with the knife near the wax-impressed seal on the locked cord around the necks of the sacks, just enough to get my hand inside. Two sacks contained bundles of canceled checks, two contained neatly wrapped packages of greenbacks. I shoved the sacks with the canceled checks onto the floor. "Is this vault vented?" I asked.

"Yes, it is," Barton replied. It was the only thing I'd heard him say since we left the Barton home.

"Then relax until they come and get you here."

I pushed the cart outside, swung the monstrous door closed, and spun the dial. I rolled the cart through the lobby to where Harris was still waiting just inside the side door. "One latecomer still due or else there'll be an absentee today," he reported. He eyed the cart. "That's it?"

"That's it. Skip out and drive Mace's station wagon alongside this door."

It took him only a moment. I pitched the two sacks into the station wagon. It was a critical moment if anyone walked around from the front of the bank, but nothing happened. I kicked the cart back inside, set the latch so no one could get in without a key, and slammed the door. Harris drove us out of the bank parking lot. My watch said 9:08.

I fumbled around inside a sack until I found two packages of fifty-dollar bills, each wrapped a hundred bills to the package. I showed them to Harris before taking my prepared box and wrapping paper from my jacket pocket. "Paying off a bill," I explained. He nodded, his eyes swiveling back to the roadway. It wasn't until later that I realized he thought I meant the Schemer.

I crammed the bills inside the box, wrapped it in the paper, sealed it, applied the address label and the stamps, which covered one whole side, and Scotch taped the whole thing again. I dropped the parcel in my pocket. When I looked up, we were within a block of the Mace house. "I'll get Dahl," I said. "You switch the sacks into the rental car and leave Mace's car in the driveway."

"Right," Harris said. He parked in front of the house, leaving the driveway unobstructed.

I walked up the driveway and went in the back door. I knew something was wrong the instant I entered the kitchen. The basement door stood open, and I could hear a feminine voice talking in the front of the house.

I drew my gun and crept through the dining room and living room. In the front hallway, Ellen Barton, nude, was gabbling into the telephone. "—Barton's daughter," she was saying. "They must be at the bank. Bank, do you understand? Stop telling me to speak more slowly! There were three of them." She hadn't heard my approach. I reached her in two jumps and sapped the back of her pretty neck with the butt of the gun. A corner of my mind wondered if I would recognize this girl with clothes on. The telephone receiver clattered and banged to the floor as she fell forward in a loose-limbed sprawl over the telephone table, then slid to the carpeting, unconscious.

I sprinted toward the basement stairway. At the foot of the stairs the stockade door stood wide open. I slid to a stop in the entrance. Thelma Barton, Shirley Mace, Tommy Barton, and Margie Barton were still lined up in a row against a wall, tied wrist and ankle.

Rachel Mace was not.

The four against the wall stared bug-eyed at the naked idiot girl crouched above Dick Dahl's prostrate figure, her hands at his throat. She was crooning softly to herself. Dahl's face was blue-black. To one side a tilted camera tripod and a smashed movie camera indicated how he had been spending his time.

Rachel looked up at my entrance. She drooled at me as I charged her. She fastened a hand like a steel claw on my ankle. With fantastic strength she began to pull me down onto the mattress. I swung the gun at her head. It crashed against her temple and she crumpled. The steel claw fell away. I took a closer look at Dahl and changed my mind about trying for a pulse indication. Dick Dahl was gone.

I couldn't remember if there was anything incriminating on his film aside from what he'd been shooting here. With Dahl one never knew. I grabbed up the smashed camera, jerked out the film cartridge, jammed it into my pocket, and threw the camera down. "Don't leave us here with her!" Shirley Mace screamed at me as I started for the door. "She'll kill us all!"

I kept on going. I knew the police would be there before the idiot regained consciousness. And after the police saw what had happened, Rachel Mace would be someone else's responsibility from that day forward, not the Maces'.

The early-morning rain had renewed itself in a steady drizzle as I ran down the driveway to the rental car Harris had parked at the curb. "Dahl won't be coming," I said as I slid into the front seat. "It just became a two-way split." Harris paled. "The police!" he guessed.

"No, but they'll be right along. Drive to my VW in front of the tourist home." Harris started up the car like a sleepwalker. I looked into the back seat. There were no sacks. "Where's the money?"

"In the trunk," Harris said. He appeared to be having difficulty in swallowing. He turned two corners and pulled in behind my car. "What do we do now?"

"Get onto the highway leading into Philadelphia. You know the route. I'll follow you. If we become separated, take a room in the Bellevue-Stratford Hotel and wait for me. Leave the car in the hotel garage." I punched him on the arm. "We'll lick this thing yet."

"Yeah," he said, but his attempted smile was wan.

I opened the door of the rental car. "Stay within the speed limit," I warned him and ran for the VW. Harris moved away as I started it up. I followed him, but not too closely. At the first traffic light I inched into the curb and dropped my package addressed to Dr. Afzul into the gaping maw of the curbside mailbox. When the light changed, I slid in behind Harris again.

One loose end bothered me. Harris was now driving Dahl's rental. His own was parked downtown near the bank. If things had gone properly, we'd have gone back for it. Now the police would find it eventually, with the risk that the rental clerk might be able to identify Harris. We couldn't venture downtown again, though.

The homes in the residential area thinned out. As we approached open country, I pulled off my red wig. I reached into the glove compartment, took out the black one, put it on one-handed, and fastened the tabs. I threw the red wig into the glove compartment. I'd take care of a makeup change during my first gas stop.

When the trees began flying by too rapidly, I looked down at the speedometer. Harris was driving too fast. I backed off my accelerator, and he drew away from me at once. It was panic scraping at his nerves. I could see the rental swaying from side to side on the rain-slick road as he forced it. In minutes he was out of sight, a curve or two ahead of me.

I felt no sense of shock when I saw fresh heavy black skidmarks in the middle of a sharp curve. I came out of the turn myself to find the rental across the road with its driver's side wedged solidly against a big tree. A puff of smoke or a cloud of dust still was poised above the crumpled hood. The car had hit so hard parts of it had exploded from the frame. Pieces of metal were still rolling in the street. As I braked the VW, a tongue of flame licked up over the back of the rental, and burning gasoline trickled down the rain-washed gutter.

I pulled off onto the shoulder and ran across the street. I could hear the ominous sound of crackling flames. The whole car was catching fire, the back end the worst. One look into the driver's side was enough to show that it made no difference to Preacher Harris whether anyone got him out or not. His neck was broken, wrenched completely around on his left shoulder. Blood was running from a corner of his mouth.

I reached in through the smoke, wincing, and snatched the car keys. The money was locked up in the trunk. I dashed to the rear of the car and tried to force the key into the burning trunk. The heat drove me away. I tried it again, but as I did I heard the words of Dr. Afzul in the hospital as though on a tape recorder: "Do not get burned again, at least not in the same areas. What I do this time, no one can do a second time."

But the money was in the trunk.

I tried it again.

The flames were roaring viciously, and they drove me away.

I gave up.

I stood there for what seemed minutes, just a few yards away, watching the bank loot burn up. Then another car pulled around the same curve and brakes screeched as the driver saw the burning wreck. I threw the rental's car keys back into the front seat and ran across the wet street to the newcomer. "Call an ambulance!" I yelled at him to get him away from the scene. He nodded and gunned his car ahead down the road.

I got into the VW, made a U-turn to reverse direction, took the first left to angle back onto the Philadelphia highway, and was at the Bellevue-Stratford in half an hour.

It hadn't really sunk in that no one was going to meet me there.

14

It was six months before I found out what actually happened at the Mace house that night.

I stayed in a motel for three days after checking out of the hotel the next morning. When I felt sure the initial heat was off, I drove to Texas. I worked for three months as boss in a sawmill in Sweetwater. Then for a change of pace I went up to Hugo, Oklahoma, and worked a couple more months as assistant on a survey crew. One reason I stayed with it so long was that I needed the money. Another was that I needed a breather to assess what the bungled job had done to my nerve.

Then I moved on to the west coast. In Los Angeles I found a back-street film processor who agreed to develop the cartridge of color film I'd scavenged from Dick Dahl's movie camera. The processor almost backed out when I insisted upon going into the darkroom with him. He finally went through with it. I was taking no chances on him making a duplicate negative on spec since he knew I would hardly come to him with anything legitimate.

So almost six months to the day after the fiasco I rented a projector and sat down in my motel room one night. There were no surprises at the opening of the film. It started with views of the wide-hipped woman in the airport parking lot. Then it shifted abruptly to a vacantly staring Rachel Mace, who somehow managed to appear more naked than any female without clothing I had ever seen.

Then suddenly a pinpoint-eyed Ellen Barton was doing a dance of the seven veils in front of the lens, without any veils. Dahl hadn't been able to resist the chance to film the two nude girls. The camera, which had been handheld previously, suddenly shifted to a new, higher perspective. It was now on the tripod I had seen, I decided.

And I found that I had seriously underestimated Dick Dahl. He walked into focus in front of his own camera without a stitch on. He coupled with the willing Ellen for some time, then turned his attention to Rachel. I could see the idiot's pleased reaction at the attention turn to doubt and then to anger. I saw the unbelieving look on Dahl's face when those terrible hands clamped down on him. And I watched Rachel Mace strangle Dick Dahl to death while Ellen Barton stood by, laughing.

When the film ran out, I didn't rewind it. I stripped it from the reel, took it into the bathroom, and burned it. It stunk like hell. I flushed the residue down the toilet.

Dahl would probably never forgive me for not burying the reel of film in a pot of flowers and taking it east and putting it on his grave.

Too bad I'm not the sentimental type.

So I'm at a loose end right now.

I'm trying to make up my mind what comes next. There's the Schemer, for one thing. I owe him money. Not 12 1/2 percent of $225,000, since I wound up with nothing, but on the other hand he can't sell the Thornton, Pa., job again. I owe him something, and I don't have it. I could go to Colorado and dig up the jar at timberline and set myself up so that I could pick and choose on the next job. But I still consider that jar mistake money. Right this minute I can't seem to make up my mind. Once in a while I even think I might run up to Ely, Nevada, for a few days and look up Hazel Andrews. I'll shake my-self out of it one of these days, though, and then everything will be back to normal.

THE END

Dan Marlowe Remembered

by Gary Brandner

I first met Dan Marlowe when I was a neophyte attending my first Mystery Writers of America Edgar Awards dinner. I must have looked like I just fell off the turnip truck as I wandered around wide-eyed at seeing that all those names from magazines and book covers were real people. Lawrence Treat, Ed Hoch, Stanley Ellin, Dorothy Davis, John Lutz, Bill Pronzini, Ellery Queen (2 real people). A sturdy, smiling man introduced himself. "Hi, I'm Dan Marlowe."

As if I didn't know who he was. Dan was a top-of-the-line writer of the hardboiled school. His series character, Earl Drake, safecracker and bank robber, was the model for many tough guy heroes to follow. I mumbled a few words about admiring his novels, he pretended to be impressed by my handful of short stories in Hitchcock and Ellery Queen magazines. Best of all, he invited me to his party that evening. Never mind that it was open to all the MWA members, I felt like I'd just won the Edgar.

Dan's parties were famous at the Edgar affairs. He took over one of the hotel ballrooms and presided as generous host to a rollicking group of a hundred or so scribblers—famous, beginner, mid-list, it made no difference. You were a Mystery Writer and you were welcome. Dan managed to get around and greet just about everyone, and damned if he didn't remember the title of one of my stories. By any measure, it was the high point of my weekend in New York.

Back at my home base in Los Angeles I returned to work, and to a fabled writing group called, for unknown reasons, The Pink Tea. It included Clayton Matthews, our de facto leader, who wrote in any genre, his wife Patricia who did historical romance, Arthur Moore, writer of Westerns, Charles Fritch, the funniest man I've ever known, playwright Jack Matcha, Robert Colby with several mystery novels to his credit, and Warner Law, who impressed us by selling to *Playboy*. Also in the group was Al Nussbaum, who did hard time for bank robbery, during which he tried his hand at writing. For tips of the trade he wrote to Dan Marlowe. Dan was generous with advice to help along Al's career. Al's case was adopted by Dan Marlowe, who worked tirelessly for his parole.

It took a couple of years, then ironically as Al Nussbaum was freed, Dan Marlowe was stricken with medical problems that limited him physically and mentally. With no hesitation Al provided any help he could give to his friend on the outside.

My next meeting with Dan was the night Al Nussbaum brought him to a Pink Tea. He was shy and subdued, far from the bluff and hearty Dan Marlowe of the MWA parties. He was pounds lighter and looked much older than we remembered him. He continued to come with Al to our weekly sessions. He sat quietly and said little as the rest of us read and critiqued our work. We treated him gently, unsure of exactly where he was in his recovery, and little by little he gained strength.

The day finally came when Dan brought a story of his own. It was a slight tale, but there were touches of the old tough Marlowe. We offered honest comments, which Dan noted. Week by week his work grew stronger until we could recognize the old chronicler of beautiful babes and hardboiled guys, mystery and mayhem. Someone noted that his heroines were often big, lusty redheads. We asked if Dan in real life had known such a babe. He threw back his head and laughed as he admitted he had indeed known such a babe. It was our sign that the Old Dan Marlowe was coming back.

He was a good friend and a hell of a writer. I will not forget Dan Marlowe.

NOVEMBER 2012